SWEET LITTLE LIES

CARRIE ELKS

Aiden Black steered his Audi RS onto the grassy cliff overlooking the beach, and climbed out of the car. He wanted to breathe in the sea air, see if it tasted as good as he remembered. His mom had always said the ocean was a little sweeter in Angel Sands. But everything had been a little sweeter in those days.

Until it wasn't.

He didn't want to think about that now. He walked toward the cliff edge, his hair lifting in the breeze. The sun was shining brightly, reflecting off the foam-topped waves as they crashed into the shore. He scanned the long stretch of sand, trying to ignore the memories attempting to creep into his brain. Those long youthful days of surfing. The even longer teenage nights around the makeshift bonfire. It all seemed so long ago.

A sudden movement caught his eye. He turned to see a woman in the distance, running along the water line. As she darted in and out of the ocean, her long blonde hair rippled in waves behind her. For the shortest of moments he let himself believe it was *her*. Pretended he could hear her laughter lifting in the wind. Pretended he could see her running toward him, her smile brightening her face the way she always brightened his day.

On the beach below, the woman turned and called out. Somebody else appeared. A child? Not her, then. The boy was young, but not *that* young. Maybe seven or eight. He ran toward her, his arms held up in front of him. As soon as he reached her, she lifted him up, swinging him around.

Aiden felt as though he was an intruder, seeing something he shouldn't. The scene playing out before him made his chest ache. Shaking his head, he pulled his sunglasses down over his eyes and turned back to the Audi, climbing in and cranking the music loud.

He wasn't here for the beach. He wasn't here for the girl, either. Not even if she was still living around here. He was here for business, not to reminisce about old times, let alone old flames.

It was important to remember that.

"Mom, can we watch a movie tonight? And have some popcorn too?"

"Sure we can. What movie were you thinking about, Nick?"

Brooke Newton kept her eyes on the road as she swung into the long driveway leading up to the house, her lips curling into a smile at the thought of a night with her son. Between his school and her college work, not to mention the volunteer work she did at the local animal shelter, having a free Friday evening was almost unheard of.

"Can we watch 'The Greatest Showman' again? I like the songs."

Brooke opened her window and pressed in the keycode to

the gates, waiting as they slowly swung open. With her foot on the break, she glanced back at her eight-year-old son who was smiling and swinging his legs – still covered in sand from their impromptu visit to the cove on their way home from school. Yes, she'd be working on her assignment late into the night thanks to their detour, but it had been worth it.

Every moment with her son was worth it.

The gates had fully opened, revealing a sprawling white stucco mansion set on the clifftop, sun rays bouncing off the sparkling windows. But rather than head toward the circular fountain with angels and cherubs adorning the front driveway, Brooke steered her Nissan toward the service road to her bungalow at the back.

It was a pool house, really, built for guests of her parents when they first had the house designed back in the early 1990s. But for the past eight years it had been their home.

Compared to the main house it was sparse. Though it was finished with the same white stucco as her parents' home, the low red-tiled building consisted of two small bedrooms, a bathroom, and a main living area – big enough for Brooke and her son. And every time she pulled up outside she felt grateful for having this safe haven, even if the cost was sometimes more than the meager rent she paid to her parents.

As she put the car into park, Brooke finally responded to her son. "Let's put some dinner on and change into our pajamas while it's cooking. That way we can watch the movie as soon as we've finished up dinner." She turned again, watching as Nick unfastened his seatbelt and tugged at the door knob. "And tomorrow, we both have to do our homework."

"Ugh, I hate homework." He jumped onto the graveled driveway as Brooke climbed out to join him. "Hey look, there's Grandma." He started to wave. "Grandma, we went to the beach," he shouted. "Mom chased me into the ocean and I got my legs wet."

Lillian Newton smiled at her grandson as she walked toward them from the main house. As always, she was immaculate. Her hair was perfectly styled, and her make-up beautifully applied on her unwrinkled face. Her pale grey skirt and pink blouse were modest and still emphasized her slim figure – something Brooke had inherited from her.

Glancing down at her own attire – a pair of cut-off jeans and a tank – Brooke took a deep breath and arranged her face into a smile.

"Hello, darling," her mom said to Nick, leaning down to press her lips against his cheek. Her body was angled to make sure the sand which clung to his legs and shorts had no possibility of touching her clothes. "How was school?"

"Good." Nick shrugged. "We're having a movie night. Mom promised we can watch 'The Greatest Showman' again." His eyes sparkled. "In our pajamas."

Lillian brought her cool gaze up to Brooke, her nose wrinkling as she took in her daughter's attire. "Remind me to call my personal shopper. It looks like your closet needs an overhaul."

Brooke took another deep breath. She should be used to this by now. "I was at the animal shelter, and then I went to the beach," she said, keeping her voice as even as she could. "That's why I'm wearing some old clothes. There's no point in wearing anything else. They'd get ruined."

"I don't know why you spend so much time at the shelter." Lillian wrinkled her nose. "All the things you could do, all the contacts we have, and you prefer clearing up animal muck."

"It's animal poo," Nick said helpfully. "And it stinks."

Lillian smiled indulgently at him, and Brooke felt the stiffness in her spine relax. She and her mom might have their differences, but they both loved Nick with a passion.

"Anyway, there's a reason for my visit. I've been calling you for the past hour."

Brooke thought of her phone casually thrown into her purse. The only time she checked it regularly was when she wasn't with Nick. When they were together – and she knew he was okay – she preferred to spend time with him rather than staring at a screen.

"I'm sorry. I haven't checked it for a while." She passed her keys to Nick. "Why don't you go open up the door for me?" she asked her son. "And remember to go wash your legs."

"If you let us buy you a new car you could connect your phone to Bluetooth. That way you'd actually answer when I call." She looked over her shoulder at Brooke's old Nissan. "I hate having this pile of junk parked behind our house. I'm sure everyone must think it belongs to the maid."

"You do enough for us already." Brooke shot her mom a conciliatory smile. She could feel this conversation slipping and sliding into their familiar refrain. "And anyway, I like to pay my own way as much as I can. Maybe I'll upgrade once I finish my degree."

"I hadn't thought of that. Maybe we can buy you a car as a graduation present."

Brooke shook her head. "Mom, no..."

"Oh you're infuriating." Lillian shook her head. "We'll talk about it later. I'm sure Daddy could find you a lovely little run-around. Anyway, that's not what I wanted to talk to you about. Since I couldn't get ahold of you, I called Cora. She'll be here at eight."

"You called my babysitter?" Brooke frowned. "Why?"

"That's why I was trying to get ahold of you. Daddy wants you to come to dinner tonight."

"But I promised Nick a movie night. You heard him. He's excited."

Lillian paused for a moment, and Brooke wondered if she'd found her weak spot. But then she remembered her mom didn't have a weak spot. You didn't get to be the uncrowned queen of Angel Sands without having a skin made of armor. "I'm sure Cora will watch a movie with him. And there's always tomorrow if you want to reschedule."

"I have an assignment to do tomorrow. I don't want to fall behind."

"Stop making things so difficult. Your father specifically asked me to invite you. It's important to him. He wants his daughter with him tonight while he entertains some important guests." Her voice was clipped.

Brooke's thoughts turned to the low rent her parents charged her. The rest she paid in ways like this. They'd been having this conversation in one form or another for the past nine years – ever since she'd brought shame on them by admitting she was pregnant at the age of eighteen. It felt as though she'd been paying for it ever since.

As though she sensed a softening, her mother pounced for the kill. "And anyway, Daddy wanted to talk to you about Nick's hospital statement. The latest bill came in yesterday. Why didn't you tell us you took Nick to the ER last week?"

"It was the middle of the night." Brooke rubbed her face with the palm of her hands. "He was at a sleepover and had a reaction. I met the ambulance at the hospital." Maybe she should have told them, especially as they were the ones who paid for his insurance and medical bills. And thank God they did. Nick's peanut allergy was manageable, but the older he got, the more freedom he wanted. It was frightening knowing he could stop breathing if he had the smallest mouthful of peanuts.

And those damn things were everywhere. At home,

Brooke was like the nut police, constantly scanning their surroundings for danger. But when she wasn't with him, she had to rely upon the vigilance of others – teachers, sports coaches, and of course, the parents of his friends. It was inevitable something would go wrong.

"He's fine now," she told her mother. "He thought it was an adventure. And they're so good at the hospital. They took good care of him."

"So they should. They're charging enough for it. Daddy said he could have bought a new golf set for the amount it cost."

Brooke swallowed. "I'm sorry about that."

"Maybe you can tell your father about it when you come over tonight. You know we don't mind helping you out, you're our family. We like to take care of you."

Brooke knew defeat when she saw it. All thoughts of her soft pajamas and curling up on the sofa with Nick disappeared from her mind. She started to calculate how long it would take her to get ready. And that meant *Newton* ready. Hair washed, a cocktail dress on, legs free of any hairs daring to peek out of her skin. An hour? Two? Why hadn't she washed her hair this morning? Oh yeah, she'd been dragging Nick out of bed at some ungodly hour to get him to breakfast club so she could make it to her classes on time.

"I might be a bit late," she said, a sense of resignation washing over her. "I need to feed Nick and take a shower."

A satisfied smile lifted Lillian's cheeks. She uncrossed her arms, and turned back toward the bigger house, her court shoes crunching on the gravel. "I'm sure it won't take you very long. We'll see you at eight."

"How did it go?" the old man asked him.

Aiden loosened his tie and unbuttoned his collar, rolling his thick neck to relieve the tension. "It was fine. I met with the project manager and discussed the plans. We're looking at eighteen months until the work on the resort is finished."

"That's not what I'm asking about and you know it." Robert Carter raised an eyebrow and tipped his head to the side, his thick helmet of silver hair glinting in the sunlight. "Did you do what you needed to?"

Aiden nodded. His hands curled into fists, his biceps bulging beneath the white cotton sleeves of his shirt. He paid handsomely for them to be tailored to fit him – his broad shoulders and muscled arms had caused more than one shop-bought shirt to come apart at the seams. One of his ex-girlfriends had once described Aiden as a wrestler in a designer suit, thanks to the physique he'd inherited from his father.

"Yeah, I scattered her ashes on the clifftop like she'd instructed." His voice was thick. He closed his eyes, remembering the moment when he'd opened the urn and said goodbye to his mom for one final time. Releasing her into the wind at the place she'd always loved the most. She hadn't been back to Angel Sands in almost a decade, yet her one request was that she be scattered there in death, back in the town where she'd been born.

"How about your brother? Did he turn up?"

"The prison wouldn't let him out for a second time. They allowed one day for the funeral and that was all." Aiden shrugged. He wasn't phased by Jamie's absence. In fact, he welcomed it. Though there was little more than a year between the two brothers, everything else about them was completely different.

Where Jamie had spent most of his teenage years and early twenties drugged and waist deep in crime, Aiden had worked his way up from nothing. Putting himself through college and business school, before joining Robert Carter's hotel chain as an intern.

"Was it strange being back there?" Robert poured them both a glass of whiskey. "Because you know, it's not too late if you want to pull out. I can send Francis down to oversee the development instead. There's plenty of work for you here." He smiled warmly at Aiden. "You know that."

Aiden wasn't sure how to answer that one. The three of them – Aiden, his mom, and Jamie – had left Angel Sands under the blackest of clouds, heading to LA to try to find somewhere to settle down. That had been almost a decade ago, when Aiden was a freshman in college and Jamie was a high school dropout. Yesterday had been the first time since they'd left that he'd made the two-hour journey back.

"I don't want to pull out," Aiden told him firmly. "I want this job. I know the town and I know the people. I can make this work for you."

Carter Leisure had bought the dilapidated Silver Sands Resort earlier that year. The once-elegant cove to the east of

Angel Sands, full of art-deco hotel buildings and Spanish style bungalows, had fallen into disrepair since its heyday in the middle of the last century. But Robert Carter had seen something special in the resort – and had managed to knock it down to a bargain price.

"I know you can do it. I'm wondering why you'd want to." Robert leaned back in his black leather chair and took a sip of the whiskey. "Do you have something to prove?"

Aiden caught the old man's eye. "Yeah. Maybe I do have something to prove. That town treated us all like crap. My mom, me... even Jamie. I want to go back and show them exactly who I've become." His eyes flashed. "They expected me to become a criminal like Jamie and my dad. I want them to know how wrong they were about me."

Robert nodded slowly. "Okay," he said, approvingly. "That's exactly what I wanted to hear." He leaned forward, resting his hands on the polished wooden desk. "So how was your meeting with the project manager?"

Aiden took a slow breath in. "It was fine. The timing's going to be tight, and the budget is already looking low, but Miller Construction knows that's what they have to work with. They're experienced; they've worked on a lot of hotel projects."

"And you think the zoning committee will pass our plans?"

"It will if we speak to the right people. That resort's been an eyesore for years. Redeveloping it and bringing money into the town should make everybody happy."

Robert smiled broadly. "It'll make me happy if you bring it in on budget."

Aiden raised an eyebrow. "Yes, sir."

"And you're all set to move down this week?"

"Yep. I've found a house to rent, and the movers are packing my things up as we speak." Not that he had a whole lot. A lifetime of poverty had taught him to only buy what he needed. Even now, when he had more money than he knew what to do with he was still careful with it. And there were his mother's hospital bills to pay.

"Alice wants you to come to dinner tomorrow. Call it a farewell party if you like. She won't take no for an answer," Robert warned.

"I would never say no to Alice." Robert's wife was as close to a mother as Aiden had left. "I'll call her to let her know I'll be there."

"Cheers." Robert lifted his tumbler of whiskey. "Oh, and Aiden?"

"Yeah?"

"Good luck in Angel Sands." He raised his glass in the air, as if giving a toast. Aiden did the same, until his tumbler came in contact with Robert's, their crystal glasses singing at the touch.

"Thanks," Aiden told him. The truth was, he'd need it.

***

Brooke stifled a yawn with the palm of her hand as she walked into the animal shelter. Weren't weekends supposed to be relaxing? So why was it on Monday morning she found herself more exhausted than ever?

Maybe it was a combination of her parents' Friday night soiree, and spending Saturday having fun with Nick before pulling an all-nighter to get her college assignment in on time. Whatever the reason, she rolled her shoulders and painted a smile on her lips – one that became real as soon as she saw Max Jenkins, their volunteer vet, crouched down in front of a giant dog, the mutt's paw on his shoulder as he patiently let himself be examined.

"Is he new?" Brooke asked, pulling her long wavy hair into a pony tail as she walked toward the giant dog. "What's your name, big guy?" She crouched down beside Max. The dog immediately moved his paw from Max's shoulder to hers, placing it firmly down on the green cotton of her scrubs.

"He hasn't got one yet. He was brought in yesterday, somebody found him wandering along the beach. I'm hoping his owner comes forward."

"Does he have a chip?" Brooke asked, running her hand along the dog's shoulder where an implant was usually placed.

"Not one that's working. And no collar either. Maisie's putting him up on our Facebook page and sending out the word. Hopefully we'll get him home soon."

The dog leaned in to nuzzle Brooke, his furry face tickling hers. "Hey bud," she whispered to him, scratching behind his ears. "Try to think of this as a little vacation before we get you home."

"I've got to head off to surgery," Max told her, standing up and stretching his arms, as though he was as tired as she felt. It was no wonder – on top of volunteering at the animal shelter, Max ran the Angel Sands Veterinary Practice, taking care of all the town's pets. An older man in his fifties, he had taken Brooke under his wing as she completed her studies to become a veterinary technician. When her college studies completed in June, he'd promised her a position at his practice. She couldn't wait to make a start there.

"Oh, and we've had a call from the Silver Sands Resort. They want us to send somebody out there," Max said, tipping his head to the side and giving her a wink. "They've found a dog and she's not playing ball. Asked if we could send out our local mutt whisperer."

"I'm not a mutt whisperer," Brooke said, rolling her eyes at him.

Max grinned back. "You're the closest we've got. Plus, I don't know how long the dog's been there and you're the best person to check out her health. If she's having any problems bring her straight to the practice, okay?"

"You know, if they weren't bulldozering that place they wouldn't be upsetting all the animals who've made it their home," Brooke pointed out. "I can't imagine how many of them are going to have to find somewhere else to live. Those hotel buildings have been standing empty for decades and suddenly they're all getting turfed out."

"That's the price of progress," Max said, shrugging his shoulders. "And at least they called us to come and help. Better than the alternative."

She shivered. The alternative generally meant the animals being euthanized before they had a chance to save them. Max was right, at least they were giving them a chance first.

"By the way, how did your assignment go?" Max asked her as he lead the big dog into a pen, making sure he was settled before closing the door.

"It was tough, but I managed to get it in before the deadline." She raised her eyebrows. "Just."

"Only a few more to go and you'll be finished."

"Plus all those exams." Brooke wrinkled her nose. "If I get through the next few months alive I'll be amazed. Nick's already told me he doesn't want to go to college when he's older. He says it looks too hard."

Max laughed. "When it's over we'll have to throw you a big party. Ellie's been asking for weeks when you're coming around for dinner. I keep telling her you're busy."

"I'll call her later." Brooke felt bad. Ellie Jenkins had been as much a friend to her as Max had been, taking her under their wing as she studied for the past few years. "We miss her, too. Nick keeps asking when we can go and see Shadow." He'd fallen in love with the Jenkins' horse as soon as he'd first met him, the gentle giant leaning down to allow Nick to feed him some oats. "I wish there were more than twenty-four hours in a day."

"I don't. We both work enough of them as it is. Speaking of which," he glanced at his watch, "I'd better go. My first surgery starts in half an hour." He checked the big dog one more time before he lifted his hand to wave at Clara who was sitting in the office surrounded by paper. If there was anybody who worked harder than Max, it was the director of the animal shelter. Between running this place and raising the funds for it, she spent most of her life in that office.

Clara looked up and waved back with her free hand, the other holding a phone to her ear as she shouted down the mouthpiece.

"Good luck at the hotel," Max told Brooke as he grabbed his black leather case and headed toward the door. "And don't forget to have a good look around. Ellie will want to know all about it."

"Oh I will." Brooke was as intrigued as the rest of them about what was happening at the Silver Sands Resort. Grabbing some supplies and a blanket, Brooke waved at Clara – who was still on the phone – and headed out to her car, putting the bag into the trunk and sliding into the driver's seat.

Glancing in the mirror, she allowed herself one last yawn before she turned the ignition key and the engine rumbled to life.

It was time to go and save a dog.

※ 3 ※

For as long as Brooke could remember, the Silver Sands Resort had been derelict. Thanks to the tall tales her friends would tell each other, she'd been afraid of it as a child. Stories about angry ghost clowns and headless chamber maids, all determined to wreak their revenge on small children.

As a teenager she'd seen the resort a little differently. A blush stole its way up her neck as she remembered the things she'd done here. The way she'd been kissed, touched, held...

She'd become an expert at compartmentalizing in the past ten years, pushing down the memories that caused her pain. And she wasn't ready to think about them now, either. Not when she had a job to do. Breathing in a sharp mouthful of air, she pulled her car into the construction lot outside the ten-foot fence, and grabbed her bag and the blanket. Though she couldn't see a thing through the thick wooden boards, she could hear the hum of machinery and the occasional shout as workers called to each other.

At the gate she pressed the buzzer, adjusting her ponytail and tucking the stray hairs behind her ears. She was still wearing her green scrubs – her habitual clothing when she was working with animals. They were roomy enough for her to bend and lift an animal easily, but thick enough to withstand the kind of wear and tear which came from working closely with animals.

"Hello?" a voice echoed through the speaker.

"My name's Brooke Newton. I'm from the Angel Sands Animal Shelter. I've come to look at a dog."

The connection crackled.

"Please wait there. Somebody will come let you in."

"Thank you." Brooke stepped back and looked around. To her right were the golden sands of Silver Cove, leading down to the sparkling Pacific Ocean. The waves lapped gently against the shore as though they were in no rush to arrive or leave, and a gentle draft rustled through the palm trees lining the edge of the beach. The same breeze caressed her skin. For a second she closed her eyes and let the warm Californian sun invigorate her, a smile pulling at the corner of her lips as she inclined her head to the sky.

"Miss Newton?"

She opened her eyes quickly and saw a tall man standing in front of her. In jeans and a thick shirt, his brown hair was mostly covered by a yellow hard hat, another in his hand.

"Yes, that's me."

"My name's Brecken Miller, I'm the project manager here. Before we go in I need to give you a little safety briefing. Let's start with the hat. You need to wear it at all times." He held it out to her and Brooke took it, pulling it down on her head. It almost swamped her, making the man grin. "I see you're wearing sneakers. That's fine for where we'll be going. You'd be surprised how many people turn up wearing sandals, expecting me to let them step foot in this place."

Brooke nodded at him. He looked to be around her age – maybe a little older. His skin was paler than most local people, and she wondered where he was from. "I work with animals all day. Wearing sandals would be asking for trouble."

For the next five minutes he told her about safe areas and keeping within yellow lines, how to avoid machinery, and that she'd need to be accompanied when on site. She listened intently, maintaining eye contact to let him know she understood, and from the expression on his face he appreciated it.

"Okay, let's head over to the other side of the site," Brecken suggested, holding the gate open so she could walk through. Once inside, he led her in the direction of the bungalows on the far side of the site, keeping up a steady stream of conversation as they walked.

"How long have you been a vet?" he asked her.

"I'm not a vet. I'm in my final year of training to be a veterinary technician. I guess it's kind of like being a nurse for animals."

"So you do all the work and get none of the glory?"

She laughed, liking this man. "Not quite. The training takes a lot less time than it does to become a vet. But it's a good job and I enjoy it." She looked up at him. "Have you been in Angel Sands long?" she asked him. "I haven't seen you around here before."

"I came over from Boston," he said, as they reached the cluster of bungalows leading down to the beach. "But I was originally from here. I moved away when I was seventeen." He shrugged. "A long time ago now."

A man was standing at the bungalow about ten yards ahead of them. In contrast to Brecken, this guy was wearing a pair of dark blue dress pants and a shirt, unbuttoned at the neck with the sleeves rolled up. His body looked almost too big for his clothes – his shoulders broad and arms rippled beneath the thin white cotton. But it wasn't his body that made Brooke's breath catch. It was his face.

His face.

She hadn't seen him in almost ten years, but she would have known who it was even if all she could do was breathe him in. All those memories she'd pushed down so deeply inside her rose up in a maelstrom of emotion.

The last time she'd seen Aiden Black he'd been wearing torn jeans and an overwashed shirt. It had felt so soft and warm against her cheeks. He'd been strong and broad, but he'd been a teenager. This Aiden Black was all man.

Time stood still as they stared at each other. Brooke wasn't sure if the sound rushing through her ears was her own blood or the steady rhythm of the waves. She took a ragged breath in, trying not to let her mouth drop open at the sight of him. And as for Aiden – he looked equally as shocked. His smooth brow pulling down until three lines furrowed through it, his full lips pressing together as he took her in.

"Aiden? I didn't know you were coming over this way today." Brecken stepped forward and shook his hand. "I guess they told you about the dog?" He turned back to look at Brooke. "This is Brooke Newton. The animal shelter sent her over. I'm hoping she's gonna solve all our problems. Brooke, this is Aiden Black, he's a director with Carter Leisure, the new owners of this resort." He was oblivious to the atmosphere growing between her and Aiden.

Somehow, Brooke managed to pull herself together. She let out a mouthful of air and nodded at the man in front of her. "We've met before," she said, her voice thin. "Hello, Aiden."

He said nothing for a moment, but she could feel those dark eyes taking every inch of her in. There was something unfamiliar about him. It wasn't quite foreboding but it was on the borderline. She got the impression nobody messed with Aiden Black.

A shiver snaked down her spine.

"Brooke," he finally said, holding his hand out for her to

shake as though they were mere acquaintances. "How are you?"

For a moment she considered giving him a honest answer. Shocked. Nauseous. Wondering where the hell he'd been for the past ten years. "I'm good, thank you," she replied, holding his hand firmly in hers. It was warm, strong, and sent the biggest jolt up her arm. In spite of the heat, her skin broke out in goose bumps.

"And your parents? Are they well?" The corner of his lip curled up. Was that a sneer?

"They're good, too." She nodded. "And you? How have you been?"

There was a twitch in the corner of his jaw. His face was as sculpted as she remembered. Though he was freshly shaven, she could remember the way it felt as she pressed her lips against his stubbled chin, kissing her way along his jawbone.

Stop it, Brooke. She didn't need to be thinking about this, not now, and not ever.

"I'm doing fine."

"And your family?" she asked. "How's your mom? I missed her after..." Her voice trailed off. How could she even begin to talk about that time? And from the way Aiden's eyes darkened at the mention of his mom, he clearly didn't want to talk about it either.

"She died last year."

"Oh." She covered her mouth with her hand, and tears sprang to her eyes unexpectedly. She blinked them back, lowering her hand to her neck, her fingers grasping at her skin there. "I'm so sorry. I had no idea." When she managed to uncurl her fingers from her neck, she reached for him without thinking, her hand stopping in mid air as she realized what she was doing. "If I'd known I would have sent flowers," she said, quickly pulling her arm back. "She was a good woman."

"Yes she was." Aiden's eyes looked darker than ever. "The best."

As if the atmosphere between them was making him uncomfortable, Brecken interjected. "So the dog is around this corner. We think she must have had a litter recently because there's some kind of nest there. But no sign of puppies."

"It might have been a phantom pregnancy. They happen sometimes." Brooke turned to him, thankful for the distraction.

Brecken led them inside the half-crumbled building, pointing to the corner of what must have once been a living room. Sure enough, there was a dog there – medium size with a dark brown coat. Brooke squinted, trying to work out the breed. A little bit of lab, maybe a dash of german shepherd, and at least four other pointers that made her realize the bitch was a mix of everything. As soon as the dog saw her space being invaded, she started snapping at them, barking loudly as she got into an attack position.

"Shit," Aiden said. "Brooke, you shouldn't be in here. That thing might be small but it could hurt you." His voice sounded tight.

She raised an eyebrow at him. "She's more likely to hurt *you*," she said to the huge man standing next to her. "I know what I'm doing." She glanced at Aiden and Brecken. "I want you to stay back as much as you can. You're both big men and dogs can be scared of that. Especially if they've been badly treated in the past." Grabbing a couple of things out of her bag, Brooke lay the blanket in front of her and knelt down, being careful not to make direct eye contact with the dog.

"What are you doing?" Aiden asked, as she lay herself down on the dirty floor. Her scrubs already covered in dust.

"I'm making myself as small as possible. Less of a threat to her. I want her to get comfortable with me before I try and call her over." She pulled a few treats out of the pouch she was holding. "Hey sweetie," she said softly, keeping her gaze to the right of the dog. "I bet you're hungry, aren't you? And scared, too. I don't blame you. But I promise we won't hurt you."

A shadow passed over, and she saw Aiden scoot down, mirroring her position as he laid down beside her. Brooke bit down a smile. Behind her she heard Brecken mutter something and he scrambled to the floor, too.

"Shouldn't you have a tranquilizer gun or something?" Aiden whispered.

"Do I look like I want to shoot a dog with a dart?" she replied, keeping her body still. "If I missed she'd go crazy. It's better to win her over." Slowly, she pushed a treat across the dusty floor, before she pulled her hand away quick. The dog stopped barking, eyeing her warily, but refused to approach the food.

"It's okay. We've got as much time as you like," she told her. "And there's more food where that came from if you want it." Brooke glanced at Aiden. He was staring at her intently, his brows pulled down as he watched her work.

"You want me to make it worth your while?" she asked the dog, keeping her voice light and high pitched. "Okay, here's another couple. Try them. I guarantee you'll like them."

As she pushed another two treats across the floor, the dog tipped her head to the side, her big black eyes following Brooke's movements. As Brooke let the treats go, the dog stepped forward, snapping at her. She quickly pulled back her arm, ignoring the adrenaline rushing through her.

Take it easy. There's no rush.

"It's okay. They're yours."

The dog snarled again, and beside her she heard Aiden's

breath catch. "Don't be scared," she crooned at the animal, her heart beating fast. "I'm not going to hurt you."

It was almost a minute before the dog took a step, this time not barking at all. She took another until she was only inches away from the food. The pup dipped her head and sniffed again, before looking up with a wary glance.

"Don't panic," Brooke reassured her. "I'm not going to touch you."

"You aren't?" Aiden whispered. "How are you going to remove her?"

"Don't worry. She's going to come to us."

With a final look at them, the dog dropped her mouth down to snaffle up a treat. Clearly liking what she tasted, she ate the other two in less than five seconds, her eyes widening as she hoovered them up.

"You like that, huh?" Brooke said, her lips curling into a smile. "I got plenty more where those came from." This time, she put the treats in the center of her palm, reaching out across the dusty floor until her arm was stretched right out. The dog hesitated, whimpering, before she padded over. Next to her, Brooke felt Aiden stiffen.

"You're going to let her get close?"

"I need her to trust me. It's okay, I've done this before." She looked at Aiden, his eyes catching hers. For a second she felt herself shiver all over again.

He smelled exactly the same as she remembered. Warm and woodsy, every inch of him enticing. How many times had she buried her face in that broad chest and felt safe in a way she never had before?

Concentrate, Brooke. You've got a job to do here.

The dog had reached her palm. Brooke felt the coarse hair of her muzzle tickle her palm and the warm lick of her tongue as she scooped up the treat. Even after it had gone, the dog was still licking her skin, and the sensation made her giggle with relief.

"What's she doing?"

"Tickling me." With caution, Brooke turned onto her side and reached her other arm out. She waited for a minute to check that the dog was okay, before Brooke touched behind her ears, where she knew the skin was sensitive. The dog closed her eyes as Brooke stroked her, still nuzzling against her palm. "There's a girl," Brooke whispered. "Such a good girl."

Still stroking her, she softly spoke to Aiden. "Can you pass me the collar?"

"Sure." Like Brooke, he rolled forward slightly, handing her the blue nylon collar. Still stroking the dog, she slipped it over her head, and curled the leash in her hand. "Good girl," she whispered again, pulling out another treat and feeding it to the dog. "Okay, sweetie, let's see if we can get you out of here."

Aiden lifted the trunk of Brooke's car open and unhooked the cage door inside, standing back as she loaded the dog into it. The animal was calm as Brooke leaned forward and fed her another treat, stroking her head as she whispered to her softly. "We're gonna take you to the vet," she told the dog. "Get you checked out. And after you'll get a nice big dinner."

It was weird seeing her again – this wasn't how he'd pictured it at all. He'd assumed she'd be married by now, wearing designer clothes and holding court at the Junior League the way her mom did. Not dressed in scrubs and covered in dust.

He felt his body react to her and he hated it. He'd wanted

to hate *her*, too, but it was almost impossible. Who could hate a woman who saved a dog the way she had?

Brooke closed the cage, and the trunk, turning to look at him. Her face was smudged with dirt, as was her hair, strands falling out of the pony tail she'd fixed behind her head. "I should head off," she said, her sparkling eyes meeting his. "I want the vet to look her over. After that, I'm pretty sure she needs a bath."

"You look like you need one too."

She laughed. "It's an occupational hazard." She looked down at her grubby clothes. "This is good compared to how I usually look." She bit her lip, her teeth digging into the plump flesh. "It was nice to see you again. And I'm really sorry about your mom. She was really special to me."

It was like she'd slapped him. All those soft feelings evaporated, replaced by the hard shell he'd been wearing for years. "I should go back to work," he said, his voice sharp.

Brooke frowned, confused by his sudden change. "Um. Okay." She reached down and laced her fingers together. "Thanks for your help back there."

"No problem." He willed her to get in the car and get the hell out of there. Since the moment she'd stepped on site she'd put him at a disadvantage. And wasn't that exactly like a Newton? So she was good with animals, but she always had been. That didn't change anything.

Nothing at all.

She reached up to wipe the dirt away from her cheek, but only succeeded in smudging more on. He had to curl his hands into fists to prevent him from reaching out to wipe it away. "Thanks for taking the dog. Goodbye, Brooke." His voice was firm, though he wasn't sure who it was for – himself or her. Either way, as she climbed inside the driver's seat of her car and pulled the door closed, he had to grit his teeth to ignore the emotions swirling inside of him.

She was staring at him through the windshield, hurt painted all over her expression. He took a deep breath in, telling himself it was okay. He wanted her to hate him, the way he hated every single Newton in Angel Sands.

Including the girl he'd once loved.

And if it felt as though his body was alive in a way he hadn't for a long time? Well, that was hormones and memories. Nothing more. She pulled her gaze from his and started up the engine, backing her car out of the lot and turning it around, before pulling away, dust dancing in her wake.

He continued to stare long after the dust had settled back down, and her car became a spot in the distance, his jaw twitching as he clenched his teeth tightly. Finally, he turned around and headed back inside the site, pulling the gate firmly shut behind him.

It was time to get back to work and forget about Brooke Newton.

Hah. As if it was that easy.

4

Aiden turned his car left at the intersection, making his way to the east side of town, passing the boarded up shops and overgrown front yards that signaled he wasn't in the good part of Angel Sands any more. He was in the streets he'd grown up in – the ones he'd fought to escape from. Yet, looking at the peeling townhouses, all huddled together as if to shelter from the wind, he felt a pang of nostalgia.

Glancing at the clock on his dash, he saw it was a few minutes after three. He'd spent all of Saturday morning in the office, replying to emails and writing reports he hadn't had time to do all week. He'd taken an hour to stare at the plans he'd already agreed with Miller Construction on, trying to work out if there was anywhere they could save some money.

In the end, he'd pushed the blueprints away and walked outside, feeling the hot sun beating down on his neck. He climbed into his car, determined to find some peace with his hands on the wheel, as the California air breezed past him, the soft top down.

And now he was pulling up outside a two bedroom house that had seen better days. Even when they'd lived here, it had been well past its prime. He could remember the hours spent repairing the creaking pipes, banging new planks into holes on the decaying deck. There was always *something* going wrong at 1733 Parkman Place.

Climbing out of his sedan, he slammed the door shut, leaning on it as he scrutinized the house. There was a child's bicycle chained to one of the fence posts, and a small kid's pool filled with an inch of dirty water. The grass was high – where it grew at all – and for some reason the sight made Aiden wince. His mother may have been dirt poor, but when she lived there she had rules and pride. The grass was cut every Saturday, the pathway swept on a Monday morning, and she would never have hung her wet underwear out on a line strung up along the front of the house.

"When you have nothing, you can't get away with anything," she would tell him. *"You have to try three times as hard and you still won't match up."* Maybe that's why he'd pushed himself until he scored a 4.0 in his GPA, and ran track until he managed to get a partial scholarship to the University of California. He'd pushed himself some more, determined to get himself and his family out of this place. To find something better than the life they'd had here.

Yes, they'd left this house. But their reasons for leaving had all been wrong. And as such, it took its toll on his mother. He'd seen her wither and waste until she was only a shadow of the woman who'd brought him up.

Christ, he missed her.

A loud bang to his left brought him out of his thoughts. For the first time he realized how out of place he must look here. With his expensive car and tailored shirt – no suit today, it was a Saturday after all – and the sunglasses that would have cost him half a summer's wages back when he toiled over at Paxton's Pier.

"You looking for someone?" An older man walked down

the stairs, a wife beater pulled tightly over his rounded belly. His hair was thick and curly, long enough for the ends to reach his shoulders. "You from the bank or something?"

The man reached the end of his yard, and pushed open the half-hanging front gate. There was something familiar in the way he walked. Aiden frowned for a moment, trying to place him. "No, I'm not from the bank."

The man looked him up and down. "So why are you here?"

"I used to live here." Aiden lifted his glasses from his eyes, trying to get a better look at the guy. He looked like he was in his late thirties, maybe early forties.

"No you didn't. I've lived here all my life, and I don't recognize you at all." The man crossed his arms over his chest, resting them on his gut. "If you're one of those loan sharks, you can get out of here now. We don't deal with people like you."

Finally the recognition set in. The guy in front of him wasn't in his late thirties at all. He may not have even reached his thirties yet. No wonder the walk was so familiar, Aiden had seen it every day of his childhood. "Paul?" he asked. "Paul Thurso?"

"Who wants to know?" The man shifted from side to side. His tone was suspicious.

"I used to live here," Aiden said again, pointing at the yard in front of him. "My mom rented that house for years."

Paul shook his head, his dark curls lifting as he turned. "You know Joan Black?"

"She was my mom. I'm Aiden. I used to catch the school bus with you."

Paul's mouth dropped open as he took a wide eyed look at Aiden. "No shitting, you're really Aiden Black? Jesus, I didn't recognize you. What are you doing driving around in that thing?" He pointed at Aiden's Audi. "Did you steal it or something?" The questions came out in a rush.

Aiden wanted to smile, but it felt wrong. He'd bought the car with cash. "No, I didn't steal it. It's mine."

"It's beautiful," Paul whispered, taking a step toward it. "Christ, a car like this must cost a fucking fortune." He looked back up at Aiden. "How've you been, man? I haven't seen you for years. I haven't seen any of you, not since that summer Jamie came back."

Aiden felt a chill wrap around his neck.

"After you all left so suddenly, we didn't think we'd see any of you again. Then Jamie came back the following summer, spent some time with the Grant brothers. The next thing I knew he was arrested for something and that was the last we saw of him." Paul looked up. "Is he doing okay?"

Aiden shrugged. "He's in jail." He swallowed, remembering the way his brother had looked at their mother's cremation. Wiry, muscled, eyes full of hate. "I don't keep in touch with him." He smiled, though it didn't reach his eyes. "And how about you?" he asked. "You doing okay?"

"Can't complain. I got a job at Newtons. And I've got two little girls – the light of my life." For the first time, Paul grinned. "They're with their mom this weekend. My ex-wife." He looked around again, nodding toward his house. "You want a beer or something?"

There was a squeal of brakes as a kid rode his bike down the center of the road, pulling up on his handlebars until he was balancing on the rear wheel. A little girl playing in the front yard of the house on the corner started laughing, clapping her hands together with glee.

In his mind's eye, Aiden could picture himself as a young boy, carrying his books in his hands because his mom couldn't afford to replace his bag until the following school year. His hair was cut short at the collar – courtesy of his mom's kitchen scissors – and his pants were flapping around his ankles, thanks to too many growth spurts, none of which they could afford. And yet, as he used to turn the corner into the road, and kick the front gate open with his sneakered foot, he always felt a sense of warmth suffuse him, warming him from the inside the same way the sun heated up his skin.

Looking at it now, the house he'd grown up in had been too small, too run-down, and too expensive for them to afford. And yet it had been full of love.

It was home, and that was somewhere he hadn't visited for a long time. Not for ten years.

Bringing his gaze back to Paul, he felt his mouth lift into an unexpected smile. "Yeah, sure. I'd like that a lot."

"There they are!" Nick pointed toward a blanket about ten yards ahead of them. He ran off, kicking the sand up beneath his bare feet, and breathlessly apologized to a woman who somehow got a faceful of grains. Brooke followed behind him, weaving her way through the maze of chairs and towels the sun lovers had placed on the beach, a backpack full of towels and toys on her back, the food and drink cooler in her hands.

It was a beautifully sunny day. The ocean was still, much to the disgust of the surfers who were gathered around the boardwalk, their boards leaning against the side of the surf shop. She looked out across the expanse of green-blue water, topped in the distance with barely-there white foam. Some-times, when the conditions were right, you could spot dolphins blowing water out of their spouts.

"You made it. Come here, you gorgeous boy." Ally stood up and ran over to them, lifting Nick in the air and swinging him around. The soles of his feet were covered in sand, the rest of him pale from a liberal application of sunscreen. "You wanna come get a soda and cake?" She pointed over at the coffee shop. "Nate's inside. I'm supposed to be working, too, but I wanted to see you first."

With her fiancé, Ally ran the coffee shop, along with overseeing the chain of Coastal Cafés Nate was slowly developing. The two of them, along with Nate's sixteen-year-old daughter, Riley, were disgustingly happy. It made Brooke so pleased to see.

"Can I, Mom?" Nick looked at her with puppy dog eyes.

"Sure. But make sure you keep your hat on if you sit outside." She threw him the LA Galaxy cap. "Are you sure you can keep an eye on him?" she asked Ally, who was pulling the cap down over Nick's dark hair. "I can come over too if it helps?"

"I'm sure. And if I get busy, Nate will be there. Now go and talk to Ember. She's stressing about what to get Lucas for his birthday. She's been driving me mad for my entire break."

Waving goodbye to them, Brooke closed the gap between herself and Ember, who was laying on a blue and yellow checked blanket, her hair twisted in a top knot. Two thin wires connected her to the phone she'd propped on the towel beside her. "Hey, sleeping beauty," Brooke said, flopping down beside her. "What are you listening to?"

Ember sat up, pulling her ear buds out. "Just some Spotify playlist. Where's Nick?" She looked around expectantly. "And you missed Ally. Her break ended five minutes ago."

"I saw her leaving. She took Nick with her to grab a soda." Brooke laid the cooler in the shade of Ember's umbrella, and grabbed two towels from her backpack. "How are you doing? Ally said something about Lucas's birthday gift."

Ember tipped her head to the side. "Ugh, I don't want to talk about that any more. I have no idea what to get him. I thought about a new surfboard, but he went and bought himself one. What do you buy the guy who has everything?" She sounded frustrated.

Brooke bit down a laugh. "Is he surfing right now?"

"Surprisingly not. He's out with Jackson and Griff on the boat. Afterward they're going shopping for tonight's cook out. You guys are coming, aren't you?"

"Of course. We wouldn't miss it. You know how Nick likes hanging around with the guys."

Ember caught her eye. "They like hanging with him, too."

It was funny how much of a thing Nick had for Ember's boyfriend, Lucas. Since he'd arrived in town last year, the two of them had a bromance going on. It warmed Brooke's heart. One of the worst things about being a single mom was the way she couldn't give her son the masculine influence all the psychology books said he needed. Lucas and Nate filled the role nicel, and it warmed her heart.

"Oh, and there's a new guy in town. Lucas's old friend is working on the Silver Sands Resort. He's coming tonight." Ember wiggled her eyebrows. "He's hot and he's single if you're interested."

The mention of the Silver Sands Resort was enough to make Brooke's chest feel tight. And of course her thoughts slid to Aiden Black – the way they had all week since their encounter on Monday. She hadn't mentioned it to her friends – what would she say? The guy she thought she'd never see again – the one who'd broken her so badly she'd never been the same – was back?

"What's his name?"

"Who?"

"The new guy. Lucas's friend?"

"Oh, Brecken Miller. He runs the construction company that's renovating the resort."

Brooke's stomach churned. She wasn't sure whether to be disappointed or relieved that it wasn't Aiden who would turn up at Ember's cook out. From the corner of her eye she saw Nick sitting opposite Ally, drinking a milkshake through a straw and relief coursed through her. She couldn't let Aiden see him – he'd know as soon as he did. And there were some secrets she never wanted to share.

"So are you interested?" Ember asked her, smiling. Brooke breathed out a mouthful of air. Her friend had no idea what she was going through. Maybe it was time to fill her in.

"No. He's a nice guy but not my type."

"Wait. You've met him?" Ember frowned. "Where? When?"

"I went to the resort on Monday to rescue a dog. He was the one who showed me around."

"I didn't know that. Why didn't you tell me? We've spoken at least three times since." There was an edge of hurt to her voice that Brooke could detect, even if her friend tried to hide it. They always told each other everything – Ember, Ally, and Brooke. They'd been friends ever since the first day of kindergarten and been together through thick and thin.

"I was afraid to talk about it," Brooke admitted. "Something happened there and I don't know what to think about it."

Ember leaned forward, her eyes wide. "What? Was it something to do with Brecken? Did he do something to you?"

"No. It wasn't Brecken Miller at all. It was Aiden."

Ember frowned. "Aiden?" It took a moment, but realization washed over her face. "*Aiden?*" she said again, this time her eyes wide. "Aiden Black? You saw him at Silver Sands?" She reached out for Brooke's hand, folding it between her own. "Oh my God, Brooke, I didn't know he's back."

"Nor did I before I came face to face with him at the resort."

"What's he doing here? Has he come back for you?"

Ember always had been a romantic. And it had worked for her, after all. She'd fallen for a guy who'd whisked her off her feet, and was the boyfriend of her dreams.

Brooke knew better. Fairytales belonged in the old tattered books she read to Nick at night time. She'd learned the hard way dreams didn't come true.

"He's in charge of the new resort," Brooke said, her voice thin.

"So he's back for good?" Ember leaned closer, as though Brooke was whispering. "Did he say anything to you? Did he ask about Nick?"

"I don't know how long he's here for," Brooke admitted. The fact was, she knew very little about him at all. "And he didn't mention Nick at all and nor did I. He didn't ask me anything."

"So maybe he doesn't know." Ember rubbed her chin. "He's going to find out though, isn't he? If he stays here long enough."

The two of them looked at each other for a moment, connected by a mutual fear. Right as Brooke was about to voice her concern, her phone started to buzz. She picked it up, seeing her mom's name on the screen.

"Ugh. I should take this. She's been trying to get ahold of me all morning. Hold that thought, okay?" She swiped her finger across the screen and lifted it to her ear. "Hi, Mom."

"Where are you? I tried knocking at your door but you weren't there."

"We're at the beach."

"You are? Why didn't you say anything? I would have come with you. I haven't been to the club for ages."

Brooke swallowed down a smile. "We're not at the club. We're at the public beach."

"Why would you go there?" Her mom's voice held a note of distaste. "It's full of... people. You should have used our pool instead. It's much cleaner."

"I'm with Ember," Brooke said. Luckily, her mom liked Ember. One less battle to fight.

"Well what time will you be home? Daddy's invited some friends over for supper this evening, and one of them is single."

"I'm busy this evening."

"Not that working thing again. It's only a couple of hours, Brooke. Your father does a lot for you. You really should show him some appreciation." Her mother cleared her throat. "And now that you're almost at the end of your degree, you should start thinking about your next steps in life. Isn't it time you thought about settling down? For Nick's sake at least."

She could feel her pulse drumming through her ears, drowning out the sound of children laughing, and the sea lapping gently on the sand. "I really am busy," Brooke said again, looking straight at Ember. "Nick and I are going to Ember's tonight. Otherwise I'd have loved to come over."

Ember shot her a sympathetic look.

"Can you cancel?" her mom asked.

"No, it would be rude." She decided to appeal to her mom's sense of propriety. "Maybe next time, okay?"

They said goodbye and hung up, then Brooke slid her phone back into her bag.

"I thought you were going to give in for a minute," Ember said. "I'm glad you didn't."

"Yeah, well I'm not afraid of my mom."

"You know, if you keep telling lies you're going to end up with a long nose."

"It's okay," Brooke said, catching Ember's eye. "If I do Mom'll insist I have a nose job."

This time Ember burst out laughing, and Brooke joined in, despite herself. Yes, things weren't as easy as they could be, and it felt like she had a hundred different things pulling her in every direction, but with friends like hers she could face anything.

Well, *almost* anything.

5

A lly and Ember appeared on the sidewalk as Brooke parked her car on the street behind Ember's cottage. She looked up, a frown creasing her face, as she opened the door.

Before Brooke could open her mouth, Ally beat her to it.

"Nick!" she said, her voice unusually high. "You wanna come with me? I need to walk down to the coffee shop to pick up some supplies." Ally pulled open the back door and helped him out. Whereas Ember hung around the driver's door, wringing her hands as though they were dripping wet.

"What's up?" Brooke asked as she climbed out of the car, grabbing her purse and the grocery bag full of soda and chips. "You two look as though you've seen a ghost.

Ally and Nick had already walked around the corner of the beach cottage, his hand safely in Ally's as she talked to him.

Ember's poker face was nowhere near as good as Ally's. Her eyes were wide and her chest was rising rapidly, as though she couldn't quite catch her breath. "Aiden's here," she said quietly.

"What?" A warm breeze gusted around the corner of the cottage, carrying the smell of salt water up from the ocean. "Aiden?" she repeated. "*Here?*"

Ember nodded rapidly. "Breck asked if he could bring a friend to the cookout." She bit the corner of her bottom lip. "Lucas had no idea who the friend was. Just said the more the merrier, the way he always does. I'm so sorry. He doesn't know about who he is to you, or Nick."

Brooke took in a mouthful of air, the saline coating her tongue. She could hear low voices carrying up from the beach. No doubt all the guys were clustered around the grill the way they always were, talking cooking time and heat levels the way they did when the cooking was happening outside. "He doesn't know about Nick," she whispered, trying to ignore the way her heart was pounding against her chest. "He has no idea at all."

"I know." Ember nodded, her eyes catching Brooke's. "That's why Ally's taken him down to the café for a while. I thought we should talk before..." her voice trailed off.

Before Aiden laid eyes on him.

"Damn it." Brooke shook her head. It felt as though her brain was full of mush. "What the hell should I do now?"

"Take a breath," Ember advised, though her own breathing was as ragged as Brooke's. "We can make a plan. We're good at those, remember? And he doesn't need to know a thing."

"What if somebody tells him?" Brooke whispered.

"Who would tell him? Only the three of us know the truth. You know Ally and I will guard it with our life. We'd never let Nick get hurt."

Brooke's mind flashed back to nine years ago. To the three of them – Ember, Ally, and Brooke – huddled in a tiny bathroom, their eyes fixed on a white stick as it slowly revealed her future.

She felt the same sense of panic she did then, when she'd discovered there was a tiny human growing inside her. As though her life was a runaway train, it was all she could do to cling on for dear life.

"Does Lucas know about Nick?" she asked Ember.

Her friend slowly shook her head. "He's never asked and I've never told. We made a promise, remember?"

Brooke closed her eyes, seeing three teenage girls behind them, all clustered around a plastic white stick. None of them had said a word until the two lines appeared clearly across it.

What a mess.

"Should I go home? Take Nick with me?" It was hard to think clearly. "But Aiden's going to see him eventually, right? And it will look suspicious as hell if we leave. People will notice I'm not here."

Ember took her free hand, the one that wasn't clutching onto the grocery bag. "Honey, you do whatever you need to do. But you're right. He's going to either see Nick or hear about him before too long. This town is way too small for him not to."

"Okay." Brooke took another deep breath in, letting the air fill her lungs as she paused for a moment, trying to get her head in the game. It was okay. She wasn't eighteen any more. She was a grown woman, a mother. She could do this. "Give me a minute and I'll follow you around."

Ember gave her the smallest of smiles. "You can take as long as you want. Ally's not going to bring Nick back until we message her that we're ready. He's probably drinking a giant milkshake."

He was safe. He was okay. Nothing else mattered. "Please don't tell anybody about him," Brooke said, even though she knew she didn't have to. She trusted Ember and Ally more than anybody in the world.

"Never. I promise." Ember squeezed her hand. "I'm going

to go back around before Lucas hunts me down, okay? Take a minute and get your breath back." She kissed Brooke's cheek. "You've got this, honey. You're an awesome person and a perfect mother. You do what you need to do." Taking the bag of groceries from Brooke, she disappeared around the corner, her dark hair swinging.

Locking the car, Brooke shoved the key into her purse, her fingers shaking as she pushed it into the inside pocket. It was okay. She could do this. Strange how even meeting Aiden again at the Silver Sands Resort hadn't freaked her out, not the way the thought of him meeting Nick was itching at her skin. They were two different parts of her life. Unconnected and yet so completely related. She was afraid the two of them coming into contact would light a fuse she had no control over.

The resulting explosion could decimate everything.

And yet what choice did she have? Aiden was here – maybe twenty yards away from where she was standing, talking to her friends, immersing himself in her world, even if he didn't realize it. There was nowhere to run, and hiding was impossible. She was going to have to face it.

Aiden took a sip of the beer Lucas had given him and smiled as Brecken Miller introduced him to all his friends, reaching out his hand to shake theirs as they greeted him one by one.

"So you've already met Lucas," Breck said, "And this is our old friend, Griff. He runs the whale boats out of Paxton's Pier."

Griff grinned at him from beneath his shaggy beard. "It's good to meet you."

"And this is Jackson, he's a wizard at technology." Breck

smiled. "I'm hoping he might be able to help us bring the resort into the twenty-first century."

"Always happy to help," Jackson said, nodding at Aiden. "Once you've scoped out what you're looking for, I'll come down and give you some suggestions."

"What did you say your last name was again?" Griff asked him. "You look kind of familiar."

"Black."

"Any relation to Jamie Black?"

"He's my brother." Aiden felt the smile die on his lips. He could see Jackson doing the rough calculations. The only reason any of them would know of Jamie was because of his notoriety. Even among the good kids in Angel Sands – and Aiden could tell from the way they were acting that Griff, Lucas, and Jackson had been *good kids* – Aiden's brother was well known.

"I haven't heard his name around in years. Where is he now?"

It was the second time that day he'd been asked that. It'd been easier to answer Paul – after all, they were all cut from the same cloth on that side of town. Which side of the law you ended up on was more a matter of luck than design. But in front of these guys – the ones who never knew poverty or envy or the way your stomach started eating itself when you hadn't eaten for days – it felt so much worse. As though he was being judged. "He's in jail."

Griff didn't look surprised at his answer. He didn't look judgemental either, much to Aiden's surprise. Instead he shrugged.

Maybe it wasn't going to be so bad after all. That gave him some relief.

"Another beer?" Griff asked, grabbing a handful of bottles from the cooler. He passed them over, and twisted his own bottle lid off. "Man, the surf is looking awesome right now."

It was as though he'd noticed Aiden's awkwardness about his brother, and decided to change the subject. Whatever the reason, Aiden felt himself relax as Lucas and his friends ribbed each other about missing out on surfing to cook food instead.

A petite brunette walked around the side of the house, a smile curving at her lips as Lucas slid his arm around her waist. "Hey, baby," he said, leaning down to kiss her cheek. "Aiden, this is my girlfriend, Ember."

Aiden shook Ember's hand. "I think we've met before," he said. He didn't need to look twice to know who she was. He'd heard her name enough times back when he was living here in Angel Sands.

Her smile faltered. "Um, yeah. I was thinking you look familiar."

"You were friends with Brooke Newton, weren't you? My mom used to be the housekeeper at her house when I was a kid."

"You know Brooke?" Lucas asked, smiling. "Damn, this really is a small town. She'll be here in a minute. You'll be able to catch up on old times. And you'll get to meet Nick, of course."

"Nick?" Aiden asked. He was immediately annoyed at himself. So Brooke had a boyfriend. What did he care? He took another sip of beer and ignored the way his stomach turned at the thought of another man in her life.

Coming back to his home town didn't seem like a good idea after all.

"Actually, we've already ran into Brooke," Breck said. "She came and saved a dog at the site last week."

Lucas laughed. "That sounds like Brooke."

"She seems like a really nice girl."

"And here she is," Lucas said, staring over Aiden's shoulder. He felt his skin prickle, knowing she was behind him.

Reaching back, he rubbed the back of his neck, refusing to turn around to look, even though every muscle in his body was poised to do so.

"Where's Nick?" Lucas asked. "Don't tell me you left him at home."

A small laugh. Aiden instantly recognized it as hers. "He's with Ally. They should be hear any minute," Brooke said. "In fact, there they are now."

"Nick, get over here. I need your help," Lucas shouted out, grinning. From the expression on all the guys' faces, they were delighted to see this man. Aiden felt another wave of something wash over him. It tasted acrid to his tongue. Whoever this Nick was, he was clearly popular.

And he was Brooke's boyfriend. No doubt, one her parents approved of.

Aiden turned his head slowly to see Brooke standing behind him, the strangest of expressions on her face. Her chest was high, as though she was holding her breath, her eyes wide as his gaze caught hers.

She looked scared. But why? Did she think he was going to say anything about their past to this Nick guy?

A young boy ran up to her. Fresh faced and with a dark mop of hair covering his brow. Aiden could tell from the way he leaned against Brooke, his hand curled into hers, that the child was bashful.

"Hello, Brooke." Aiden nodded. There wasn't a cell in his body that didn't feel awkward. Even his stance felt wrong, as though he was standing on a ship and could stumble to the side and fall into the ocean at any moment. He looked down at the kid again. He had her features, soft and expressive. Her hand fluttered up to her neck, and he noticed it was shaking.

"Aiden." She was breathless. "It's good to see you again." Her free hand tightened around the boy's palm. "This is Nick. Nick, this is Aiden, an old friend."

The boy let go of his mother's hand, and reached out for Aiden. "Hello, sir, it's good to meet you." His smile, when it appeared, was as expressive as Brooke's.

"He's your son?" he asked her.

Brooke nodded but said nothing.

"I didn't know you had a son. You didn't mention him at the resort."

"I was too busy trying to save the dog," she said, her voice low.

Aiden shook the little boy's proffered hand, and the kid's touch sent a shiver through him. "How old are you?" For one crazy moment, he imagined what he'd do if Nick was ten. The urge to laugh came over him. There was no possible way this kid could be his son.

But what if he was? *What if?*

"He's eight."

That was that. No possibility at all, even if his hair was as dark as Aiden's. He tried to swallow down the feeling of disappointment he knew shouldn't be there. It's not as though he needed more complications in his life. Brooke had clearly moved on since he'd left, and so had he. "Is your husband here too?" he asked her, looking behind her shoulder.

"I don't have a husband," she said quickly, her gaze dropping to look at Nick's head. Aiden got the message – don't ask questions.

"Well, it's good to see you both." He breathed in, feeling the rush of air force its way past his tight chest. It really was good to see her. She was wearing her hair down, the silver-gold waves hanging past her shoulders. Though she'd applied light makeup, he could still see the line of freckles dotted across the bridge of her nose. God, he remembered those freckles, remembered tracing them with his finger. Not just the ones on her face, either.

"Okay, I think it's time to put the steaks on the grill," Lucas said, as the flames in the grill died down, leaving a shimmering heat in their wake. "Babe, can you bring the meat out from the refrigerator?" he asked his girlfriend, his eyes soft as he looked at her.

"Sure." She glanced at Ally and Brooke. "You guys want to help me make the salads?" she asked them. "Nick, come in and grab a drink," she suggested. "I have some sodas in here too."

The three women headed into the house, closely followed by Brooke's son. As Aiden watched them disappear through a door on the far side of the home, he lifted his bottle and took a big mouthful of beer.

For the second time in his life, it felt as though he'd been hit by a hurricane, threatening to break up everything he'd ever worked for.

Like last time, it's name was Brooke Newton.

"Are you going to tell him about Nick?" Ember asked when the little boy had taken his soda and headed back outside to join the men. She was chopping up salad ingredients on the wooden counter in her small cottage kitchen, scraping them from the board into a huge glass bowl.

Ally reached into the refrigerator and grabbed a bottle of wine, pouring it into three glasses.

"Not for me," Brooke said when she tried to pass one over. "I'm driving, remember?"

"I thought you might need it." Ally's eyes met hers. Her sympathetic look twisted Brooke's gut.

"I do. But I can't." Brooke leaned on the counter, watching her friend work. "And yes, I guess I'll have to tell him some time. First I need to figure out what to say." She took a ragged breath in. "I'm scared," she told her friends. "About what he'll do if he knows the truth."

Ally reached out and wrapped her hand around Brooke's. "Of course you're scared. It's natural." She twisted her lips, thinking for a moment. "Are you sure he needs to know?"

"Yeah, I really think he does. Even if he walks away, at least I'll know I did the right thing. Part of me regrets never telling his mom when I had the chance. Did you know she died?"

"She did?" Ally was wide-eyed.

"Yeah. I didn't know either until Aiden told me the other day."

Ally squeezed her hand. "I'm sorry, I know you were close to her for a while."

"She was like a second mother." More of a mother than her real one, truth be told. When she'd left town with her sons, it had been devastating. "I wish she'd met Nick before she died." Brooke bit her lip. "I guess Aiden deserves to know."

"Okay, so when are you going to do it?" Ember asked, whisking up a salad dressing in a small jug. "You want to talk to him now?"

"No!" Brooke replied. "Not today. Not with Nick here." She swallowed hard, though her mouth was dry. "I'll do it next week."

"You're so brave."

"I don't feel it." Brooke took another sip of her coffee. "I feel scared and frightened. What if he freaks out at me?"

"You think he will?"

"I don't know. I haven't seen him for ten years, I don't know anything about him anymore."

"Aiden was always one of the good ones," Ally said softly. "It's going to be okay."

"Ember?" Lucas called into the cottage. "The steaks are ready. Can you bring out some plates."

Ember looked up at them both, her eyes soft. "We should go back outside," she said, "If you're ready for it."

"I'm ready," Brooke said, her voice more resolute than she felt. "You bring the salad and I'll bring the plates."

Ember smiled. "Okay."

6

Aiden raked his fingers through his hair, surveying the construction site. Dust danced through the air, a thin coating lining his jacket and hard hat, coloring everything the mellowest of yellows.

This was the slowest project he'd ever overseen. The site was a historical location – rather than a parcel of land they were building on from scratch – and it gave an added layer of complications. Well, more like six added layers, if he was honest. In trying to keep the renovations as close to the original resort as possible, they were having to source materials from locations they wouldn't normally use, and employ artisans who would usually have a long waitlist. Thank God money talked – and Carter Leisure had enough of it.

"Hey," Brecken Miller greeted him as soon as he walked into the trailers they'd shipped in and placed on the edge of the site. "Can I have a quick word?"

"Sure." Aiden took his hat off, shaking the dust from his body. He'd long since given up wearing the suits that were his normal uniform when he was working out of LA. Instead, he wore dark tailored pants and a white shirt – sleeves rolled to counteract the constant beating of the sun.

He'd forgotten how warm it was this far south. It was coming back, as well as a whole host of memories he'd hoped he'd forgotten.

"The Spanish rooftiles have arrived," Breck was telling him. "But half of them are cracked. They're sending another shipment, but they won't be arriving until late Friday night. Either we lay on some overtime for the weekend or the schedule will be put back a week. I'm sorry, man." Breck sighed. "I know it's not what you want to hear."

"How many men do you need?"

"I'm thinking twenty. Eight hours each day should work. I'll be on site to supervise them."

"Okay, do it. But see if we can charge the suppliers for some of it. It's their fuck up."

"I will." Breck slid his hard hat back over his dark hair. "I'll call them now." With a nod he was gone, and Aiden made his way across the main lobby of the office trailer to his office. His laptop was loaded with emails and messages he'd ignored while he'd been out on the site. He opened them up as he slid into his seat. It was already six o'clock – late enough that the rest of the office staff had left for the day. Even the construction vehicles were silent. As always, he would spend another hour or so here trying to play catch-up, replying to the accountants and marketing teams, and updating Old Man Carter on the progress they'd been making.

Avoiding going home where his mind would be too free to wander. Because there were some thoughts he'd been avoiding all week.

In the main lobby the buzzer vibrated, signaling some-body waiting at the site gate. Aiden frowned. They weren't expecting any deliveries this late in the day, and any visitors had long since left for the evening. Pushing himself off his chair, he made his way in, leaning over to press the intercom.

"Hello?"

"My name's Brooke Newton. I'm here to see Aiden Black."

Aiden's head snapped up as though she was standing in front of him. For a moment he considered telling her he wasn't here. She wouldn't know it was him, after all. But curiosity got the better of him. She hadn't been far from his thoughts all week – at least when he'd allowed himself to acknowledge them. At night when he'd closed his eyes he'd pictured her standing against the backdrop of the beach, her silken blonde hair contrasted against the deep blue of the ocean, her eyes soft as she watched her son play.

Her *son*.

That had been a shock he hadn't expected at all. In all his thoughts about returning home for the first time in a decade he'd imagined she might be married, but never that she'd have a kid. And yet a part of him had always known she'd make the perfect mother. She was always so caring, so protective, even as a child. The number of animals she'd saved from starving or nursed until they'd overcome an injury – they all added up to show her nurturing personality.

His mom had described her as steel wrapped in wool, and it was as good a description as any. She didn't like hurting people, but if somebody else hurt them – she'd go in fighting.

Aiden pressed the intercom again, moistening his dry lips with the tip of his tongue. "Wait there. I'll come and let you in."

"Thank you."

If she'd recognized his voice she didn't let on. Grabbing his hard hat plus an extra for his visitor, Aiden glanced at himself in the rusty mirror affixed beside the door. His shirt was covered in dust, his pants wrinkled from a day working hard on the construction site. He had a fighter's body, like his brother's. Strong bones and even stronger muscles, bred from generations of men who punched their way through life.

It was a short walk from the construction offices to the gate. Keying the number into the pad, Aiden released the lock, pulling it open to see her standing right in front of the gate. Like the first time she came to the construction site, she was wearing scrubs – the green shapeless ones which somehow made her look more attractive than ever. He held the yellow hat to her and she took it, pulling it down firmly on her head.

"Sorry if I'm disturbing you. I probably should have called." She shifted her feet and looked down. "But I stopped by on the off chance you'd still be here.

He stifled the urge to lift her face up so his eyes could catch hers. "You want to come over to the office? I can make you a cup of coffee. It's not Déjà Brew standards," he said, referring to the coffee shop on the beach, "but it's passable."

"Coffee sounds good. Thank you."

He led the way back to the trailer. Brooke followed close behind him, her breathing soft as she trailed him up the metal steps. Once inside, he closed the door behind her and took off his hard hat, watching as she did the same. He hung them both up as she patted her hair absentmindedly.

"Sorry about the hat." He gestured at her. "And for messing your hair up."

"My hair's already messed up. Dig in deep enough and you might find a few stray animals. I spend my life either washing it or tying it up. It drives my mom mad."

He could imagine. Lillian Newton's hair was never anything but immaculate. It never seemed to grow or change color, either. He couldn't imagine her ever agreeing to wear a hard hat – not if it might push a strand out of place.

Thinking of Brooke's parents left a bad taste in his

mouth. He walked over to the coffee machine and poured them each a mug, topping it with cream and carrying them back to her. "White no sugar," he said.

"You remembered." She smiled.

Damn. He'd forgotten to ask.

"You want to sit down?" He gestured at the conference table in the middle of the room. It was covered with blueprints and delivery papers. Brooke nodded and slid into one of the chairs, cradling her coffee cup with her hands.

"How's the dog you saved?" he asked her. "I meant to check with you over the weekend, but the party got so busy."

"She's fine. Not quite ready to be adopted out yet, but we're working on her. She needs training first." Brooke took a sip of coffee, her deep green eyes fixed on his.

"What happens if she doesn't respond to training? Will you euthanize her?"

"No." Brooke shook her head. "Definitely not. We don't kill animals at the shelter. We save them."

He should have known she would say that. "I feel like it's our fault she's homeless. Do you have a card? I'll speak to the director about paying for the dog's accommodation and vet bills."

"You will?"

Aiden shrugged. "It's the least I can do."

Her gaze softened. "That's very kind of you. The shelter always needs donations. Thank you."

"No problem."

She took another mouthful of coffee and swallowed it down hastily, before putting the cup on a small portion of the table not covered in paper. "Um, but that's not why I came to speak with you."

"It isn't?"

She shook her head and took a deep breath, squaring her shoulders. It reminded him of when she was a kid and went up against her parents. "There's something else I need to talk with you about."

⸻

This was the third time she'd been in his presence in ten days, and the impact he was having on her hadn't lessened any. It only seemed to grow, coating her skin and pulling at her muscles, making her heart beat faster than was physically comfortable. She was a grown woman, a mother of an eight year old boy, and yet every time she saw him she felt like the seventeen-year-old girl she'd once been. Besotted and aching, wanting him to notice her. Hanging on to his every word.

He was silent as he sat on the plastic chair opposite hers, his long legs stretching beneath the table. Though his clothes were covered in construction dust, she could still tell from their cut how expensive they were. But it was his face that drew her in. The chiseled beauty of his youth had been replaced by a masculinity which made her chest tight. There was a strength to his roman nose and square jaw that she hadn't seen a decade before. The teenager who had captured her thoughts as a young girl had become a man she couldn't take her eyes off.

"I don't know where to start," she said softly. She'd been practicing this for days, thinking of the right words – the ones to explain everything and not cause him to hate her. But they didn't exist. All that was left was the truth and it cut like a knife.

She wasn't sure who was going to bleed more.

"The beginning is usually the best place."

Looking up, her eyes met his again. Her stupid heart did a flutter. "You're right," she said, nodding her head. "But I'm not even sure where it began." Dropping her face into the palm of her hands, she let out a sigh. "I'm sorry, this is so stupid. I've been thinking about talking to you all week, and here I am, behaving like a dumbass." She lifted her face up. "And I know you're so busy. I'm sorry."

"Stop apologizing."

She sighed. "That's what I do. Apologize to everybody. I guess that's the way I was brought up."

Aiden shifted in his seat again. "We're all products of our childhood." He put his own cup down on the table. "But sometimes we have to break out of it."

"It's hard to break out when everything you do is scrutinized. And every move you make is watched like a hawk."

Aiden frowned. "Scrutinized by who?"

"My parents."

"Are you still living at home?" he asked her. "You and Nick never moved out?"

She felt almost relieved at his question. At least she didn't have to search around for her words. "We live in the bungalow out behind my parents' place. The one beyond the pool. Do you remember it?"

Three lines appeared across his forehead, as though he was thinking hard. "The one they used for staff?"

She nodded. "It's perfect for us. Once I finish my schooling, we'll be able to stand on our own two feet." Maybe if she talked for long enough she could ignore the elephant in the room.

"Are you studying to be a vet?" Aiden asked.

"Not quite. I'm training to be a veterinary technician. Like a nurse for animals. I couldn't afford the schooling to be a real vet."

"Your parents wouldn't help you?"

She shook her head. "Not with the tuition fees, no. They don't really want me to work with animals." Her eyes met his again. It was crazy how often it was happening. And each time it did her whole body heated up. "It's not their idea of what a Newton should do."

Aiden's face was impassive. "I guess not."

"And there's Nick. I want to finish up school sooner rather than later so I can get a job and we can move out and get on our own two feet. I don't want to live at home forever."

"He's a nice kid. You must be very proud of him."

Unexpected tears stung at her eyes. When was the last time anybody had seen her son as something to be proud of? "He is a good kid," she agreed. "He's funny, he's clever, and he is always really polite around people. I'm a very lucky mom."

And there was the lump in her throat again. This would be the perfect time to tell him, to finally get the truth out there. "How about you? Do you have any children?" Yeah, so much for letting it all out.

"No children."

She wanted to ask him about a wife or girlfriend, but really, what business was it of hers? And the fact was, she shouldn't be asking him anything. She should be telling him. Because she was the one who had all the answers.

Or one answer, at least.

Come on, Brooke, you can do this. "You must think I'm crazy, beating around the bush like this."

He shrugged. "I wasn't really thinking about that at all."

"The thing is," she said, taking another deep breath. "I wanted to tell you about Nick's father." She blurted it out, and it felt as though the words were hanging in front of her in a huge black arrow, pointing to the biggest loser in town.

"You did?" Aiden frowned. She couldn't blame him for being confused. "What about him?"

"I'm so sorry, it was such a big mistake. Not that Nick is a mistake. I'm really glad I have him, but it was never supposed to happen like this."

Was it her imagination, or did he lean back from her?

"It's none of my business," Aiden said. "What you do with your life is up to you."

"But it is your business, don't you see?" She leaned closer. Somehow she needed to make him understand. "You have every right to know the truth. And I should have told your mom years ago. I hate that she'll never know him. It's all my fault."

"Brooke, you're babbling. I have no idea what you're talking about." He lifted his hand, rubbing the back of his neck as though the skin there was on fire. "What the hell has Nick got to do with my mom? Or with me, for that matter? I've done the math..."

From the way her heart was banging against her ribcage, Brooke wondered if it was going to escape. She opened her mouth, desperately trying to find the words to make this okay, but they didn't exist.

None of them did, because it wasn't okay.

She blew out a mouthful of air, but still the ache in her body remained. "It has everything to do with your mom, and everything to do with you. Nick was her grandson, and he's your nephew." She squeezed her eyes shut, not wanting to see his response. "Nick is Jamie's son."

7

Aiden stared at her for a moment, as if he was trying to let the words sink in. His brow dipped, three deep lines forming as he stared at her with those dark blues. Her breath raggedly escaped her lips as she waited for his response. He must hate her right now. God knew she hated herself.

"You slept with my brother?"

Her throat tightened. She nodded but no words were forthcoming. Shame wrapped itself around her like a blanket.

"You can't be serious." His voice was ominously calm. It reminded her of the silence before rain began to lash down. So rare here in Southern California, and yet she could picture it in her mind's eye. She could smell the dampness in the air before the storm unleashed.

Anger formed on his face, and his head jerked back as he kept his gaze trained on her, as though he was looking for something – *anything* – to refute the words he was hearing. She felt herself paling beneath his scrutiny. She reached at the collar of her scrubs to pull them away. They felt like they were choking her even though the fabric was loose against her skin.

"I don't fucking believe this."

"I'm so sorry." She reached for him, but he shrugged her off, leaning back, as if he couldn't bare the thought of her touching him. He pushed himself to standing, walking over to the other side of the room. As if there couldn't be enough space between them.

Brooke followed him. Everything inside her wanted to take those words back. They might have been true, but she wished they weren't. So damn much.

"Please let me explain," she said, scrambling on her feet. She reached out for him and he shrank away.

"Don't touch me."

"Aiden, It isn't what you think. We—"

He put his hand in front of him, palm out, fingers splayed. "Stop," he said, his voice hoarse. "Don't say it. I don't want to know." He stopped short, blinking wildly. "Are you sure he's Jamie's son?"

She nodded silently.

"Well at least you kept it in the family." He laughed, but it sounded more like a growl.

The sound shot through her. Brooke could feel her body begin to shake. Dizziness took over her.

"Do your parents know?"

"No. I never told them." She laced her fingers, trying to still the way they were shivering. The coffee she'd drunk felt like a whirlpool in the pit of her stomach. Any minute it might come up.

"And Jamie. Does he know?" Aiden's lip curled down. He wasn't looking at her, unable to meet her gaze.

"I contacted him, but he wasn't interested."

A choking noise came from his throat. "And you didn't think to contact me?"

"And tell you what? That I'd been an idiot?"

"That you'd slept with my brother within a year of telling me you'd love me forever. I'm not stupid, Brooke. I can do the math."

A stray lock of hair fell from her ponytail, and she pushed it away from her face. Aiden turned to look out of the window, his broad back flexing beneath his shirt.

"I'm not a slut," she whispered. "I'm not." Even if people thought she was. And she could live with the whispers, with her parents' condemnation. But she couldn't live with Aiden's disgust. It tore at her, making her body feel inside out.

"I don't know who you are," he said, still looking away from her. "I don't know you at all."

She squeezed her eyes shut to try and push out the pain. All these years she'd dreamed about him, longed for his arms. Not once had she imagined how awful it would feel when he hated her.

"You should go," he said, his voice thick. "It's getting late. No doubt your son will be wondering where you are."

"His name's Nick. And he's not only my son. He's your nephew. Don't you want to know more about him?" she asked, her voice imploring. "He's your family, too."

"No." Aiden shook his head. His dark hair was short, revealing a thin sliver of tan skin between his hairline and collar. She knew how that sliver of flesh felt – the skin soft, the hair coarse. She'd run her hand around it enough times.

"Aiden..."

"You need to go." This time his voice was urgent. As though he was standing on the edge of something, trying not to fall off. His body tensed, his biceps flexing against the thin sleeves of his shirt. For the first time ever, Brooke felt the size difference between them. He'd never hurt her – not physically – but she felt afraid. Because if anything, he'd end up hurting himself.

"I'm going," she said breathlessly, stepping back to give them both some space. "I'm sorry. So sorry."

She didn't bother to reach for a hard hat. Right now she couldn't give a damn about health and safety. The need to get out of there outweighed everything else. It took a second to close the gap to the door, one more to reach for the handle and curl her fingers around it. As she pushed it down, she turned back to look at him one more time, but his back was still firmly to her.

"I'm sorry," she said again, though her voice was soft enough for him not to hear. Even if he had heard her, he made no response. Yanking at the door, she escaped onto the metal steps leading down to the path, breathing in a mouthful of air as she ran toward the gate.

But when she got there she realized she didn't know the code. Her breath was shallow as she reached for the handle anyway, making a futile pulling gesture which failed to move it one inch. The next moment she felt him beside her, his shadow long and dark as it stretched out on the dusty ground. He keyed in the code with six loud beeps.

The gate clanged as the lock released, and he pushed it open, holding it with his hand for as long as it took her to escape into the parking lot. Before she could turn to look at him she heard it bang close, and she was alone again once more.

Her car was one of the only ones left in the lot. She headed toward it, grappling in her purse to find her keys. It was only when she was safely inside, the driver's door closed and her hands resting on the wheel that she finally let herself go.

She'd done what she needed to do. She'd told him the truth. But right now, all she wanted to do was cry.

He waited at the gate until he heard her engine start up, and the rumble of her tires as she pulled away from the parking lot. Leaning back on the metal, he closed his eyes for a minute.

"*Damn.*" Her words had begun a maelstrom inside him, one he wasn't sure he was able to contain. He wanted to hit something – *anything*. But he wouldn't do that. Not now and not ever.

He wasn't *that* kid any more. Maybe he hadn't ever been. Yes, he'd been in a few fights in his time, but they usually involved standing up for somebody else. Right now the only person he wanted to fight was himself.

"Damn!" He shouted it this time, his words disappearing into the dusty air. His muscles contracted, not getting the memo he'd tried to send down from his brain. Because right now punching something felt preferable to thinking about what happened.

He stalked back to the office, his shoes leaving imprints in the dusty soil. And as soon as he walked into the office he saw her coffee cup resting innocently on the table. How long ago was she holding that? Ten minutes? Rage boiled up inside him as he reached out and swept it to the floor with his balled fist, the papers covering the surface sliding with his violent movement and scattering to the ground.

It didn't make him feel any better. In fact he felt worse, because now he was going to have to pick everything up and rearrange it so nobody knew what he'd done.

Taking another breath into his tight chest, he knelt down and slowly picked each blueprint and delivery receipt up. There were coffee droplets stuck to some of them, and he did his best to wipe them clean, though some stain remained.

When he was done he stood up and walked over to the window overlooking the site. But he didn't take in the half-constructed buildings, nor the yellow painted vehicles locked up for the night. All he could see was her, the way she'd been on Saturday night. Her hair long and flowing, her face bright, her arms wrapped around the son she so obviously loved.

Her son. and Jamie's.

He'd said it was none of his business, but his mind begged to differ. Because she'd slept with his brother, and they'd had a child together. She'd said she'd tried to contact Jamie, but did he even know about Nick? Surely he'd have told their mother? The one thing she'd longed for, before she died, was to have a grandchild. And all along they'd been a few hundred miles away from Angel Sands, from Nick.

There were so many thoughts swirling through his brain, it made his head hurt. He pushed down the little internal voice telling him he should have calmed down and actually listened to what she had to say. Because every word had felt like a knife stabbing at his heart. It hurt like hell.

In the distance the mountains were darkening, as the sun slowly made her way into the horizon. Any other day he would have thought it was beautiful, but right now all he could see was misery.

"I'm not a slut." Wasn't that what she said? He squeezed his eyes shut to try and force out the image of the hurt on her face. His disgust had obviously been written all over his as she'd told him the truth about her son.

Deep in his heart he knew she wasn't. She wasn't anything other than a girl who'd once taken his heart, and broken him up until he wasn't sure how to put himself back together again. It had taken years of hard work to forget her. To build himself back up and trust his own judgment. And now he was almost thirty years old. He'd achieved everything he wanted and more. The world was at his feet, and yet it felt like nothing at all.

He felt like nothing.

Because the woman he'd once adored had a son who carried his own blood, and at least some of his DNA. And yet he'd never be his.

That cut him to the bone.

8

The shrill blast of her doorbell woke her up. Groggily, Brooke checked the clock beside her bed. Eight A.M. Not even Nick was awake yet. There went sleeping in on Saturday morning.

Another push of the bell – enough to rouse Nick. "Mom? There's somebody at the door." He appeared in the hallway as she walked out of her bedroom. Stifling a yawn, she pulled her robe around her and ruffled her son's hair. "Who is it?" he asked.

"I've no idea." A glance in the hallway mirror told her all she needed to know. She looked like hell. And she should, too, after the almost sleepless night she'd had. She'd spent most of it tossing and turning. Remembering the way Aiden had looked at her when she'd told him the truth. As though she'd killed something sweet and dear to him.

Her morning mouth tasted of regret.

She finished knotting the robe belt around her waist, and reached out to open the door. Whoever it was, they were clearly impatient; even though she was on the other side of the glass, they pressed the bell a third time.

"Hell—. Oh, Mom, it's you."

"Is that any way to greet your mother?" Without being asked, Lillian brushed past Brooke and walked into the hallway. "Hello, Nick, how are you, my darling?" She took his hand and led him into the kitchen, sighing when she saw the blinds were still pulled. Brooke closed the front door, trying not to let out a groan. It was almost impossible when her mother was around.

"Brooke, why isn't the coffee on?" her mother called. "It's the middle of the morning."

"It's eight o'clock. Practically night time," Brooke pointed out, joining them in the kitchen. Nick shot her a smile and pulled the blinds without being asked. Thank goodness for him, he really was a good kid. "And unlike you, I don't have staff to put the coffee on. I do it all by myself."

Huffing, her mother opened and closed all the cupboard doors on the right hand wall. "I know how to make coffee, but I can't find the damn pot. Where did you put it?"

Brooke leaned down and pulled the canister out from the cupboard beneath the breakfast bar. "I'll do it. You sit down." One thing she'd learned from years of living with her mother, once she wanted something, she was almost impossible to divert.

"I don't want any. I've already had two cups." She glanced at her watch. "Of course I went to my yoga class first. The coffee's for you. You need to be bright eyed for today."

A sense of unease washed over Brooke. She turned to look at her mother, suspicion in her eyes. "Why?"

"We're going to Neiman Marcus to buy you a dress. Remember?"

No, she didn't remember, and that's because they'd never made any such arrangement. Another thing her mom had a habit of doing – having conversations in her mind and holding the real life people accountable. "I told you I already have enough dresses," Brooke told her, filling the coffee pot up with water. "I don't need another one."

"Don't be silly, everybody needs more dresses. And I've arranged for Nick to join your father on the golf course."

Nick's face lit up. "Grandpa's taking me golfing?"

"Yes." Lillian smiled at her grandson. "And afterward he's taking you out for lunch. A boys' day out, isn't that wonderful?"

Nick nodded, still smiling.

"You didn't ask me if we're free," Brooke grumbled.

Her mom's face took on a patient look. "I knew you would be. You don't have a shift at the rescue center, and I know for a fact Ally is working today. I called Ember to see if she'd like to join us, but she's busy." Her mom raised an eyebrow. "And don't bother trying to tell me about all this college work you have to do. You can do it tomorrow. You deserve a treat, and I want to give you one. I'm your mother."

Arguing with her mom was like pulling hard at a Chinese finger trap. The more you struggled, the deeper she pulled you in. Anyway, the thought of getting outside of these four walls held its own appeal. After yesterday's catastrophe, a change of scenery might be good for her.

"Okay," Brooke agreed, still wary. "I'll come, but you have to promise I can choose my own dress. I don't wear satin and I don't wear pink."

"Of course, dear."

"And I get to pay for lunch."

Lillian's lips pursed up. "I don't want to eat at McDonalds."

"That's rude. I can afford to buy us lunch at somewhere that doesn't give you a plastic toy with your meal."

"You can?"

"Yes. I'll even take us somewhere we get to sit down and order. How elegant does that sound?"

"You're teasing me." Her mom wrinkled her nose. "Aren't you?"

Brooke bit down a smile. "Yes, I'm teasing you. Now if you could do me a favor and get out of here, Nick and I would like to get dressed. We'll see you at the house in half an hour."

"Half an hour? Is that long enough?" Her mom looked pointedly at Brooke's hair. "Let's make it an hour. I'll have Laurence take us in the Mercedes."

Brooke put her hand on her mom's back, and steered her toward the front door. "Yep, whatever you say. I'll see you in an hour. Now go and get yourself ready, too."

"I am rea—. Oh, you're teasing me again." Lillian let out another huff. "I do wish you'd stop doing that."

Yeah, well sometimes it was her only defence against Lillian Newton. Brooke had an inkling she'd be teasing her mom a lot in the next few hours.

She'd never been a believer in retail therapy, but there was something to be said for getting lost in a good dress. Brooke stared at herself in the mirror, liking the way the light blue fabric clung to her upper body and flared out at the waist to a short, floaty skirt. It was sexy without being too obvious – and clearly very expensive. Out of her price range for sure.

"You look beautiful, dear." Her mom peeked around the curtain separating the changing rooms. "With your hair up, you'll look outstanding at dinner tonight."

Brooke whipped her head around. "Dinner? You didn't say anything about that."

"Oh, didn't I?" Lillian widened her eyes in innocence. "Silly me."

She wasn't even worth fighting with right now. Brooke

looked back at the mirror, a wistful expression on her face. Once upon a time she was the sort of girl who would wear a dress like this. One who would attend dances at the Beach Club, and let her parents pick out a suitable partner. One who did as she was told and made them both proud.

Hah! Look how *that* ended up.

And suddenly, the dam burst and all the thoughts she'd been blocking out came rushing in. The memories of yesterday. The way Aiden had looked at her when she told him the truth. As though she was the girl everybody said she was.

She could take it from all the others. But not from him.

Reaching behind her, she tugged at the zipper, arching her back to pull it all the way down. The dress fell to the floor in a lake of pastel blue. An assistant bustled in – Brooke hadn't even known she was there – and picked it up, sliding it onto the thick wooden hanger.

"Put it on my account." Lillian nodded at the assistant. "And have somebody take it out to my car, please."

"I don't want it." Brooke grabbed her jeans, shoving her legs into them. "It's pretty and all, but I can't afford it. Plus I have nowhere else to wear it to. It'll hang in my closet and feel sorry for itself."

"Clothes don't have feelings, dear." Lillian's voice softened. "Let me buy it for you as a gift, you don't let me treat you very often. You're my daughter, I'm allowed to buy you things once in a while."

Brooke chewed her bottom lip. Behind her, the assistant was wrapping the dress up in a thick plastic hanging bag, zipping it carefully to avoid snagging the fabric. She slid her mom's store card through the reader and handed the printed receipt to Lilian. It all made her feel about five years old.

"Thank you." Pulling her sweater over her head, and sliding her feet into the brown leather mules which had seen better days, Brooke grabbed her bag and walked out of the changing room. "And I definitely owe you some lunch now."

Her mom opened her mouth to say something, but closed it again.

"No, we're not going to McDonalds." Brooke answered her unasked question. "I've booked us a table at Gerard's."

Half an hour later, they were eating lunch – a caesar salad for her mom, with anchovies removed, and a club sandwich for Brooke, with every thing included. It almost felt normal. Like any other girl spending time with her mom on a Saturday. Brooke tried to remember the last time they'd done something like this – had a girly day of trying on clothes and spending time together – but she couldn't remember.

Had they ever done something like this?

"This is nice," she said, putting her half-eaten sandwich down on the plate. "I'm glad you asked me to come."

The fork her mom was holding froze in mid air, not quite making it to her mouth. "It is?" She didn't bother trying to hide the surprise in her voice. "You really like it?"

"Is it so hard to believe? Yeah, it's good to spend some time with you. We should do it more often."

"I've tried," Lilian said pointedly. "But you're always busy."

And there was the guilt again, made extra spicy because there was truth in her mom's words. All those time she'd asked Brooke to come with her to the salon, or the Beach Club, or even out for coffee, and she'd refused, not wanting to feel the pressure of parental expectation weighing down on her any heavier than it already did.

"I've got a lot going on," Brooke said quietly. It sounded pathetic out loud.

"I know you do, dear. And I don't want to add to your burden, I only want to see you once in a while. And Nick, too. Daddy was so happy to get to spend some time with him on the golf course today. He loves you so much, but being surrounded by us girls and not having a son has been tough on him. He always feels outnumbered." Lillian lifted her water glass to her lips, taking the smallest of sips.

"You don't add to my burden," Brooke said. Her throat felt scratchy, making her voice hoarse. "I'm grateful to you both. You gave Nick and me somewhere to live when you didn't have to. And you make sure he wants for nothing."

"We're his grandparents. It's our job. We want you all to be happy. But sometimes it feels like we're battling you all the way. Look at Maggie Richardson. She's always taking her daughters shopping, and they've joined our little book club, too. I wish we could do more together."

Okay, that might be taking it a bit too far. "Well we're here now," Brooke pointed out. "That's a good thing, isn't it?"

Lillian smiled. "Yes, it is. I'm very pleased we are. So why don't we talk about you? How are things going with school?"

"It's okay. There's lots going on at the moment. It's only a few months until graduation and there are so many assignments to finish."

"You work so hard. You'll do it, I know you will."

Brooke blinked a couple of times. Where had this cheer-leader mom been all her life?

"I hope so. And then there's Nick's extracurricular activities, and the shelter. I keep telling myself it will all be easier once I graduate. I'll only have one job to manage then, plus Nick."

"And you've been over to the Silver Sands Resort, too, haven't you?" Lillian pushed her half-finished salad away, clearly done with it. "Sally Mayweather said you were there. Fred told her."

Any appetite Brooke had dissolved with her mother's question. She should have known the word would spread in a little over a millisecond – this was Angel Sands, after all, not some metropolis. Funny how she used to love knowing everybody when she was a kid. But now the town was up in her business, and it felt as though the walls were closing in on her.

"What else did she say?" Brooke asked. Did her mom have any idea that Aiden was back?

The server came to clear away their plates. The two women waited silently as he stacked the half-eaten entrees in his arms, nodding when he asked them if they wanted the dessert menu.

"Not very much," Lilian said as soon as he'd left, balancing the dishes precariously as he walked. "Something about a stray dog. I have to admit I tuned out after that." Lillian laughed. "You know about me and animals."

"Did she tell you about Aiden?" Brooke blurted out. As soon as the words escaped she wanted to cover her mouth with her hand. What was she thinking?

"Aiden who?" It still hadn't sunk in. Her mother waved at a couple in the corner, a smile arching her painted lips. Lifting her hand into a strange impression of a telephone – thumb and little finger stretched out, she mouthed something about calling them next week.

Brooke considered changing the subject. Her mom was too preoccupied by whoever was in the corner to pay her any attention. She should take advantage of her distraction and end this before it started. Talk about Nick or her father, or even tonight's dinner, anything to get away from the one subject dominating Brooke's thoughts.

But that was precisely why she wanted to talk about him. She was desperate to. It wasn't only last night and his reaction that was getting to her, but the fact she actually cared about it. She cared what he thought about her – and that was the most frightening thing of all.

"Aiden Black. Joan's son."

Her mom slowly dropped her hand, the smile on her face

dissolving as her eyes widened. It wasn't often Lilian was silent, but for a moment all Brooke could hear was the low hum of chatter from the diners surrounding them, and the noise of traffic from the street outside. Beneath her perfectly-applied make-up, the color drained from her mom's face.

"What's he doing here?" Her voice was a whisper.

"I saw him at the Silver Sands site. He runs the business redeveloping the hotel there."

"Oh." Lillian's hand fluttered to her neck, pulling at the cameo bracelet pinned to her collar. "I didn't know he was back." She shook her head as if in answer to a silent question. "Why didn't anybody tell me?"

Brooke stared at her for a moment. Yes, the Blacks had left town in a hurry, but it didn't explain why her mom had turned so pale. Lillian lifted her glass and took a deep mouthful of water, closing her eyes for a moment.

When she opened them she seemed almost back to normal. The shocked expression was gone, replaced by her usual poise.

"Did you know Joan died?" Brooke asked her. "From cancer."

"That's very sad," her mom said evenly.

"Yes it is." Brooke was vehement. "Really sad. How long was she with us? Sixteen years or more? And we weren't even there to pay our respects."

"We hadn't seen her for years." Lillian kept her voice even. "And she wasn't a friend, she was staff. She wouldn't have expected us to be there."

Her mother's cool dismissal of a woman who'd meant so much to Brooke growing up rankled her. "She was more than staff," Brooke told her. "She *was* a friend. Practically family. She was the one who got me dressed in the morning, the one who took me to and from school."

"Because that's what we paid her to do," Lillian pointed

out. "I worry about you, Brooke. You have no idea what it takes to run a home or manage staff. When you do move into your own place, you'll need to learn very fast. Otherwise people will end up walking all over you."

The server arrived again, passing them each a leather bound dessert menu. Brooke took it gratefully, desperate to see the end of this conversation. She should have known talking about this with her mom would end up in them both feeling frustrated.

Lesson learned, she told herself as she opened the menu, taking in the sugary options printed on the page. Trying to talk to her mom about Aiden was a stupid idea. She wouldn't do it again.

9

"How much is this costing us?" Robert Carter asked, as he and Aiden watched the construction team moving the red Spanish tiles from the pallets they'd arrived in to the bungalows they were working on. "Twenty men, eight hours, all at double time." He winced. "Have you heard back from the suppliers?"

"They're willing to pay half the overtime," Aiden told him. "We'll have to cover the rest.

At seventy-five, Robert Carter was still as strong as an ox, and his sharp brain missed nothing. When Aiden first met him he'd found him as intimidating as hell. But Old Man Carter had seen something in Aiden which caught his interest – maybe the fact they were both born dirt poor and weren't planning to stay that way. Whatever it was, eight years of working together had taught Aiden that his boss's bark was way worse than his bite.

"Daylight robbery," Robert muttered, taking a tile and turning it, checking out the finish. "Still, they've got us over a barrel. What choice do we have?"

"We still have the contingency," Aiden said, his voice reassuring. "We've budgeted for problems like this."

"The contingency isn't bottomless. We're less than a year into the project, we shouldn't need it yet."

Aiden raised an eyebrow. He'd heard this lecture before, about a hundred or more times. "I'll go over the schedule, see where we can make some savings."

Robert turned to him. "You do that. And now you can tell me what's really on your mind; you've been distracted all morning." He looked around the site. His visit had always been planned, though neither of them had thought there would be any construction happening on that Saturday morning. He might have been head of the company, but Robert still liked keeping an eye on every project, driving down from LA early that morning to check out the Silver Sands Resort.

You could sum up in two words what was bothering Aiden. *Angel Sands*. It was that simple, wasn't it? And that was complicated, too. Because it was more than the town or the people who lived in it. It was *him,* and the emotions he'd been burying for years. The unfamiliar feelings rising to the surface.

And it was *her*, too.

"Maybe I shouldn't have come back," he said, turning to look at the man beside him. "There are too many bad memories here. I thought I could deal with them but..." Aiden shrugged. "I don't want my personal life to stop me from bringing my A game to this project. You gave me a job when nobody else would, you put your trust in me when everybody else thought I was a punk. I don't want to let you down."

"Your personal life, eh?" Robert pursed his lips. "And what personal life would that be? Last I heard you were married to this job."

"It doesn't matter."

"Yes it does. Because it matters to you. I can see that. And that means it matters to me. I'm not only your boss, I'm your friend. At least, I'd like to think I am. So what gives?"

Aiden picked up his coffee. It was lukewarm. "It's not what's the problem, it's who."

"Now this sounds interesting."

"Remember the girl I told you about? The one I left behind?"

"The one whose dad threw you out?" Robert asked. "Yeah, I remember." Realization crossed his face. "Is she still here? Have you seen her?"

"I've seen her three times in a little over a week," Aiden said. "I told you Angel Sands was small, but even I didn't know it was that small."

"And you want to leave because of that?" Robert shook his head. "I didn't take you for a coward."

Aiden laughed, though the sound was hard. "No, not because of that. I can handle her. It's the rest of it I can't manage." He took a deep breath, blowing the air out in a single burst. "She has a son, an eight year old son. It turns out he's my nephew."

"Whoa." Robert rocked back on his boots, folding his arms across his chest. "I have to admit I wasn't expecting that."

"Neither was I."

Robert cleared his throat. "So Jamie is the father?"

"Yeah."

"And this is the girl you loved back when you were a kid?"

"Yep."

It was Robert's turn to take in a big mouthful of air. He was quiet for a moment, staring into space. Shaking his head, he chuckled. "Jesus, we weave a tangled web, don't we? No wonder you're all messed up."

"Are you worried about my performance on the project?" Aiden asked him. "I'd understand if you were."

Slowly, Robert shook his head. "No. I trust you to keep your private life separate from your work. Anyway, now you have family here. Isn't that something you've been missing ever since your mom died? You should stay here and get to know your nephew. He's your flesh and blood, after all."

Robert's words stopped him short. *Flesh and blood.* Strange how that hadn't even occurred to him; he was so busy getting crazy over the thought of Brooke and Jamie, he hadn't even bothered to think about his own connection to Nick.

Aiden closed his eyes, picturing the way the kid had looked when they met at Lucas and Ember's house. His dark hair, his curious eyes. The perfect mixture of Black and Newton. His nephew had Brooke's goofy smile, and the same line of freckles across the bridge of his nose, but his hair and eyes came from the Black side of his family.

"I guess he is," Aiden said, opening his eyes and looking at Robert. The old man was staring at him.

"What would your mom want you to do?" Robert asked. "Would she want you to walk away, or would she want you to get to know him? To take care of him?"

She'd always said family came first. Wasn't that why they all left Angel Sands together? Even when Jamie's activities turned obviously illegal, she still held out hope that one day her prodigal would return home.

"She'd want me to get to know him."

"And how about you?" Robert asked. "What do you think you should do?"

Aiden tipped his head, thinking about his boss's question. When he'd imagined his return to Angel Sands, he'd always seen it as some kind of redemption. The local kid from the bad side of the tracks come good. He wanted to show them all – the doubters, the rich kids, the ones who'd shouted out insults as they'd driven past in the brand new cars their parents had bought them. They'd been kids, but now he was a man. He wasn't going to take any shit. Not any more.

He lifted his head and looked Robert Carter straight in the eye. "I want to stay," he said firmly. "And get to know my nephew. But first of all I need to get back to work."

Martin Newton was a man who commanded everybody's attention simply by walking into the room. His once blonde hair may have turned into an impressive full head of white that contrasted against his deeply tan skin, but he carried himself as though he was closer to thirty-years-old rather than sixty. Brooke watched as he dominated the dinner party conversation, his voice loud enough to be heard across the twelve foot table, his eyes constantly scanning the guests to make sure they were listening to what he had to say.

As a child she'd thought he was a superhero, the same way Nick did now. He lapped up the attention of children the way a cat licked up cream, always with a big smile on his face. It was in her teenage years when things started to sour – when she tried to assert her own opinions, and make her own decisions. As long as she went along with his wishes, she was fine. But if she went against them?

Well, she ended up here. And wasn't that a bitter pill to swallow?

"Your father's on good form tonight," the man next to her whispered, lifting his coffee cup to his mouth. "Where the hell does he get his energy?"

Brooke poured cream into her cup, stirring for much longer than necessary. "He likes being surrounded by people." Like vampires liked being surrounded by blood.

"I hope I'm like that when I'm older."

Brooke looked at the man sitting next to her. He was tall

and handsome, with thick blonde hair that made him almost Newton-like in looks. He'd already told her he liked to play racketball and golf, when he wasn't working. Which, by the sounds of it, wasn't very often.

And she was absolutely certain her mother intended to match the two of them together.

"I'm sure you will be."

He looked gratified, even though she hadn't meant it as a compliment, and she immediately felt bad. Alex had been nothing but a gentleman since she'd been introduced to him over cocktails. He'd asked her about her studies, about the animal shelter, about Nick. He even told her how much he liked kids. As though he'd been schooled by somebody who knew her well. It wasn't the first time Brooke had been paraded in front of eligible bachelors like a cow at auction. It didn't mean she liked it, though.

"Brooke, dear," her mother called out from across the table, "after you've finished with coffee, you should take Alex on a tour of the garden. He hasn't seen it before."

"It's dark," Brooke pointed out. "He wouldn't see much of it now, either."

Her mom's eyes widened and her lips pursed up. She knew that look. *Be quiet and do as you're told, otherwise I won't be happy.*

"I'd love to see the gardens," Alex said. He drained his coffee cup and placed it back on the saucer. "You have a beautiful home, Mrs. Newton."

"Thank you." Her mom tipped her head to the side, smiling widely at him. "You must come over for lunch and a swim some time. I'm sure Nick would love to meet you, too."

"Shall we go?" Brooke gave Alex a tight smile. Might as well get it over with. "But after the tour I need to get home. My babysitter wants to head out by ten." She stood without waiting for an answer. "Good night, everybody. It was lovely to see you all again." Amazing what she could say through gritted teeth.

"Oh. Of course." Alex stood up, pulling her chair back so she could step out. "I'll walk you back to your bungalow."

From the corner of her eye she could see her mom beaming widely. "It's okay, it's not exactly far."

"I insist. I couldn't let a lady walk alone."

"Fine." She gave him a tight lipped smile. "Let's go then."

Twenty minutes later she'd run out of things to show him. Though her parents house was set on two acres, most of it was laid to lawn, with palm trees and evergreens lining the borders. They wandered around the pool, the patio, and the rose garden that was her mother's pride and joy. She even pointed out her own house in the distance – the small one-story building which looked out of place next to her parents' mansion.

"I'm really sorry about my mom," Brooke said, as they walked toward her home. "She never takes no for an answer. It's really embarrassing when she tries to force people together."

"She means well," Alex said, gently placing his hand on the small of her back. The sudden contact made Brooke jump. "And I've got a lot of time for your father. I enjoy working for him."

"I want you to know it's nothing personal, but I'm not looking for a relationship." There, she'd said it. "And I know you probably aren't either, since you're newly divorced and all." Amazing what she could learn about somebody over a couple of hours at dinner.

A small smile curved Alex's lips. In the moonlight, his features looked more defined than they had in the dining room. As though they'd been carved from stone. "We were separated for two years," he said quietly. "I think I'm over it by now."

"I'm sorry to hear that. Break ups are never easy."

"I'm glad we didn't have kids. At least I haven't had to deal with that, too."

"I know what you mean. I'd hate to be parted from Nick. He's my life."

Adam smiled down at her. "I can tell, and it's lovely to see. You're clearly a wonderful mother."

Once upon a time people used to compliment her about her hair or her figure, or even her academic accomplishments. Yet none of them had filled her with warmth the way Alex's compliment did. "Thank you. That means a lot."

They were almost at the bungalow. The front windows were dark – no doubt Cora was in the sitting room at the back, and Nick fast asleep. Alex cleared his throat as they stopped at the steps to her front door.

"I've enjoyed spending time with you tonight," he said, turning so his body was facing hers. "I'd like to get to know you a bit more – as a friend. I know you're not ready for anything else, and that's okay by me. Can I call you some time? Maybe take you out somewhere?"

Brooke hesitated. In spite of his words, she really didn't want to give him the wrong idea.

"I'll tell you what," Alex said gently, as though he'd noticed her obvious reticence. "I won't push you this time. But think about it, okay? And when I see you again at a function somewhere maybe you'll have a different answer."

She tried to hide her sigh of relief. Disappointing people was never easy, especially when they were being as nice as Alex. "That sounds like a good plan."

"That wasn't a no," he said, smiling at her, his eyes sparkling in the moonlight. "So I'll take it as a win." He leaned down, brushing the hair from her face, and pressed his lips against her cheek. "Good night, Brooke. Sleep tight." He turned and walked back down the path to the house, stopping to give her one last wave before he disappeared into the distance. She stared out into the empty night for a moment, before pulling her keyring from her satin evening purse and running up the stairs to her front door.

But before she could slide the key into the lock, somebody stepped out of the shadows.

🦁 10 🦁

"Brooke?"

"Wha—? Oh my God." She stumbled on the top step, her high heels giving out beneath her. The figure reached out to steady her, his palm on her bare arm. As she lurched to the left, her hip smashed against the wooden stair rail, and for a moment she thought she was going to tumble right over the top. But he was holding her tight, pulling her to his chest, steadying her with the sheer force of his body.

Aiden's body. *Damn*.

"What are you doing here?" she whispered, her eyes widening at the sight of him. "It's late."

He looked down at her, scanning her dress, her bare legs, her high heels. Deep beneath his whiskey colored eyes, she could see something flash.

"Who was that?"

"Who was who?" He was still holding her. Was that right? Shouldn't she want to pull away from him? And yet there was something so deliciously warming about the way his hands were on her waist, his fingers digging deep so she could feel him through the fabric of her dress.

"That guy. Mr. Perfect. The one with the immaculate helmet of hair."

She wasn't going to laugh, not even if Alex's hair was unnaturally flawless. Like an astroturf field. It looked like hair, it felt like hair, yet it was too... yeah, perfect.

"Is he your boyfriend?" Aiden asked.

That took the wind right out of her sails. Any amusement she'd had suddenly vanished. She stepped back, out of his grasp, and watched as his hands fell down to his sides. "That's none of your business."

"Of course it's my business." Aiden shrugged. His eyes did a little movement again, as though he was checking out her legs. "I expect your mom and dad adore him, don't they? Bet he has a great job, and a 401k, and knows all the right people at the Beach Club."

Brooke licked her lips. They felt unnaturally dry. "What are you doing here?" she asked again, avoiding his question with one of her own. "How did you even get in?"

The corner of his lip lifted up. "You tell me your secrets and I'll tell you mine."

"You know what? I don't care." She pushed past him, searching in her small silver purse for her house key. "It's been a long day and I'm beat. I want to go to sleep."

"I came in the same way I used to."

That got her attention. She turned back, him only a few feet behind her. He was wearing dark pants, a white shirt, and a watch which must have cost thousands. The daughter of Martin and Lillian Newton knew quality when she saw it. "You climbed over the tree?"

"It's still there. It's taller, but I'm stronger now than I was back then."

She glanced to her left, to the edge of her parents' estate, where a copse of oak trees obscured the tall brick wall circling the land. For a moment she was a kid again, clapping wildly while she watched Aiden climb like a monkey over that thing. A young woman whose heartbeat sped at the sight of him shimmying down the trunk.

"Aren't you a tad old to be climbing trees?"

He was still half-smiling. It was infuriating. "I figured if I rang the bell I'd give your father a heart attack."

Giving up on opening the door, Brooke turned around, her keys folded inside her palm. The metal bit at her skin, but she ignored the pain. It helped remind her where she was.

Outside her house, where her son was sleeping. She wasn't *that* girl anymore. Though somebody needed to tell that to her racing heart.

"So we've figured out how you got in. Now maybe you can tell me why?"

"I want to talk to you about Nick." For the first time his smile faltered. He leaned back against the handrail, scratching his neck. "I'm sorry about the things I said to you yesterday. It was wrong." He brought his eyes up to hers. "*I* was wrong."

Strange how yesterday already felt like a lifetime ago. "Okay." She took a deep breath, feeling the air rushing into her lungs. How many times had she imagined seeing Aiden again? How many times had she fantasized that he'd come back to her, whisper words of love in her ear. Take her away from all of this to their happily-ever-after. But he wasn't here for her at all. He was here to talk about Nick, and she should be grateful for that.

"And I want you to know, whatever Nick needs, I'm happy to pay for it. School, clubs, clothes – you name it, you've got it."

"He doesn't need anything. I can take care of him." Her spine stiffened.

He looked around at her bungalow, his eyes narrow. "You mean your parents can."

"What?" Her head snapped up. "What's that supposed to mean?"

He looked shocked at her reaction. "It didn't mean anything. But if you're happy to accept their help, why wouldn't you want mine, too?"

A wave of fury washed through her. He really was like everybody else, assuming she couldn't make it on her own. "You know what? Yes, I accept some help from them. They let me have this place at a low rent, and they pay for Nick's medical bills. Apart from that, everything we have is what *I've* worked for. I do whatever it takes to put food on our table and clothes on our backs. So don't you *dare* come around here with your assumptions and your prejudice and tell me I should be grateful for anything you have to offer. We've survived perfectly fine for the past eight years without you." She took a breath, her chest aching from the rush of words. "And by the way, as a son of a single mom, I'd have thought you'd have more respect for a woman like me."

He recoiled, as though she'd slapped him. Even in the moonlight she could see the flush on his cheeks. They were both silent, staring at each other, the air between them loaded with emotions she wasn't sure she could identify.

"You're right. It was a stupid thing to say." He ran a hand through his hair, fingers raking it back. "It was cruel and wrong. You've always been independent, even when you were a kid." He tipped his head to the side, still holding her gaze. "If my mom heard me say something like that, she wouldn't have let me hear the end of it."

The thought of Aiden's mother softened Brooke's heart. Or maybe it was the lost look in Aiden's eyes. "You must miss her," she said softly, her throat feeling tight.

"So much."

The moonlight shone on his eyes. The residual anger disappeared, replaced by an empathy which made her want to reach out for him, hold him, let him listen to her heartbeat the way he used to. She curled her hands into fists, the metal of her keys digging further into her palm, to stop herself from doing it.

"I'm so sorry she never knew about Nick. It's one of my biggest regrets. The reason I told you about him – I don't want to rob you of any more chances."

"Can I see him?"

"Now?" She frowned. "He's asleep."

He shook his head. "No, I mean another day. Does he know who I am?"

"Not yet. I haven't told him." She hadn't told anybody. "I don't know where to start."

Aiden's face softened. "I understand. Maybe I can be a friend? Meeting up at the beach or for coffee. I'd like to get to know him, to spend time with him. I'd like for him to get to know me, too."

She nodded. "I'd like that, too. But I need to know you'll take it slowly. I don't want him getting attached to you, and have you disappear again." She blew out a mouthful of air. "Let's see how things go and I'll tell him the truth when I think he's ready. Not before."

Aiden flinched. "I'm not planning on going anywhere."

She tried to ignore the way he made her heart race. Her chest felt full of emotions. It was important for her that Nick got to know his family, this man who had been such a big part of her life for so long. That was all it was.

"Okay. So when do you want to start?"

"Is tomorrow too early? I thought maybe I could take you both to lunch."

She leaned back on the door, thinking of the pile of books on her kitchen table, and the papers she still had to mark. Of the laundry and the grocery shopping and maybe even getting some sleep at some point.

"Tomorrow sounds good. Let me know the time and the place and we'll be there."

This time there was no half-heartedness to his smile. It was big and it was breath-taking and it lit up his face so much brighter than the moon could. His grin used to make her go weak at the knees whenever she saw it, and it still made her legs shake now. It was making her smile right back at him.

But that was her muscles holding on to old memories. She could handle them, couldn't she?

"Where are you off to in such a hurry?" Lillian called out late the next morning as Brooke pulled open the car door.

She threw her bag on the passenger seat, and looked back to check that Nick's seatbelt was safely fastened. Her mom was standing at the corner of the driveway, her hand shielding her eyes from the lunchtime sun.

"Out for lunch at Delmonicos with friends."

"That's a shame. I was going to see if you wanted to join me for coffee." She rolled onto the front of her feet, checking to see that Nick wasn't listening. "I thought you could tell me all about Alex," she whispered.

"Nothing to tell." Brooke slammed the door shut, walking around to the driver's side. "I showed him around the gardens, he walked me home, we said goodnight. End of story."

She really didn't have time for this right now.

"Did you..." Lillian cleared her throat and pursed her lips, smacking them together.

"No!" Brooke wrinkled her nose. "Now honestly, we're late. Can we do this later?" Or preferably never.

"Whatever you say."

"Bye, Mom."

Within a minute, she'd drove out of the iron gates, separating the Newton estate from the road down to Angel Sands. To her right, the sun was glinting off the ocean, illuminating the white tipped waves and the warm blue water. As she followed the road into the town itself, she could see people were out in force – covering the sand with umbrellas and blankets, as surfers and body boarders threw themselves at the sea.

"Mom?" Nick asked, his voice carrying through from the back seat. "Where are we going again?"

"Out to Delmonicos on Paxton's Pier," Brooke said. "To see an old friend, remember?"

"The place that does the buttered noodles? And the cheesy garlic bread?"

"That's the one."

"Grandma hates it. She says anywhere with plastic table cloths should be banned."

Brooke tried not to laugh. That sounded *exactly* like something her mom would say. "Yeah, well she doesn't have to do the laundry, does she? Maybe she'd change her mind if she was constantly loading the washing machine."

"Grandma doesn't change her mind about anything," Nick pointed out. "She says only the weak minded do flip flops."

Maybe it was time to limit Nick's visits over to her mom's house.

"What's your friend's name?" he asked.

"Aiden Black."

"That's a strange name. Is she from your school?"

Brooke took the turn onto Beach Street, steering the car around a delivery vehicle outside the Fresh 'n' Easy. "She's a *he*. Aiden's a man's name. You've met him already. At Lucas and Ember's house when we went over the other week for a party, remember?"

Nick frowned, clearly not remembering at all. "Did you go to school with him, too?"

"No. He went to a different school. We knew each other when we were kids, though. His mom used to work for Grandma."

"How old is he now?"

"A few years older than me."

"Oh." Nick sounded disappointed. "Does he have any kids for me to play with?"

They'd reached the parking lot. The rocky ground was covered in sand, blown up from the beach on the other side of the building. She reversed her small car into a space, craning over her shoulder to make sure she didn't drive into the tall brick wall behind her. "No, he doesn't have any children. He likes children, though. He's really looking forward to meeting you."

"Is he tall?" Nick asked. "I can't remember what he looks like."

So many questions. But how often did she introduce Nick to a stranger – and to a strange *man*, at that? He was at the age where he was fascinated by men in general, and in the concept of fathers. He knew he didn't have one, but he didn't know why. And she knew that sometimes he felt left out.

"He's really tall. When he was a kid he used to climb the big old tree by the wall. It used to drive his mom crazy." And now it drove her crazy.

"He sounds like fun." He blinked, a smile curling at his lips.

She put the car into park and released her belt. "Well there's only one way to find out if he's any fun or not, right?" She got out of the car and Nick pulled his door open, unbuckling himself before he jumped down to the gravel. "Let's go say hi."

Aiden was sitting at a table on the deck, next to wooden steps leading down to the beach. The Sunday lunchtime crowd were out in full force – on the sand, as well as in the restaurant above. The air around him buzzed with conversation, as the smell of ozone mingled with the Italian food the harried waiters were carrying out, their huge silver trays balanced in the palms of their hands.

"This one's your table. Mr. Black is already here."

He looked up to see Brooke and Nick standing in front of him, along with the waiter. Instinctively, he got up and walked around the table, shaking first Brooke's hand, before looking down at her son.

She was dressed casually, a pair of slim jeans and a silk tank, her hair tied up, revealing her slender neck. The same neck he used to kiss, tease, and press his nose against to inhale her, as if she was all he needed to breathe.

Breathe. Yeah, that would be a good idea.

"Nick, this is Aiden." Brooke smiled down at her son. "I told you he was tall," she said in a mock whisper. She looked back at him and it felt like the sun had come out all over again.

The boy took Aiden's proffered hand. "It's good to meet you again, sir."

Aiden tried not to laugh at the boy's serious expression. "My name's Aiden, no need for sirs."

Nick smiled, although he still looked wary. As though he was afraid of making the wrong move. Aiden found himself wanting to reassure him, to tell him it was okay. How many times had he been in Nick's position – afraid of saying the wrong thing?

"I asked for a table by the beach," he said, nodding his

head at their seats. "In case you get bored of sitting with us for too long."

"He's used to it, aren't you, Nick?" Brooke gave him a small smile, before looking back at Aiden. "No grandson of Martin Newton would be allowed to run around the tables."

True story. Aiden remembered Martin Newton's iron rules all too well.

"Anyway, Delmonicos is our favourite," Brooke carried on, helping Nick scoot in his chair. As soon as she was done, Aiden pulled her chair out for her. She looked up at him in surprise. What was she expecting? That he would leave her to it?

"Why's that?"

"They're really great with Nick's food allergy. It can be a pain sometimes, eating out. But they're really flexible here. They know even a sniff of a peanut brings him out in hives."

"You have a peanut allergy?" Aiden felt his chest tighten. He should have asked her about allergies. He'd heard horror stories of kids not being able to breathe from reactions to peanuts.

"Yes, si— I mean Aiden." Nick nodded. "But it's okay. I don't have to go to the hospital too much."

He turned his head back to Brooke, who was sliding the children's menu in front of Nick. She looked so calm, so composed. When she looked up, catching his eye, she smiled at him, and it made his heart stutter.

"I'm glad to hear it." His voice was gruff. "Hospitals are no fun." He could still smell the one where his mother died. The sharp stab of bleach lingered in his nostrils long after he last walked through the sliding doors.

"It's pretty much under control," Brooke said, opening her own menu. "He's great – he knows what to look out for, and what to avoid. But sometimes those nuts can be sneaky little things. You'll find them in the strangest places, that's when we end up in the ER."

"At least they have a Playstation there," Nick said. "And Mom's allowed to stay with me if I have to sleep there."

It sounded awful. And expensive, even if her parents covered those costs. A flash of guilt hit him, as he realized how he could have helped them all these years. If she wasn't already high enough up there, Brooke rose a few rungs higher in his estimation. Her ears had to be popping by now.

"What job do you do, Aiden?" Nick asked, bored of talking about his allergy.

"I build hotels."

Nick's eyes got wider. "Like in Monopoly?"

Aiden laughed, shaking his head. "Kind of. Except I do it in real life. I work for a company that owns them all. It's my job to find new areas to build in. We're working on the Silver Sands Resort at the moment."

Nick looked impressed. "Do you use diggers?"

"Not personally, though it would be really cool. But we have a lot on our site."

"I love diggers. And tractors."

"Well maybe you can come and take a look at the site some time." He slid his gaze back to Brooke. "If your mom's okay with it."

Her eyes looked like mirrors. The sunlight was shining directly in them, and he could see himself reflected in their depths. "I'd be fine with it," she said, her voice thick.

The waiter slid a plate of garlic bread into the middle of the table, taking their order. For the next few minutes the air was filled with discussions about pasta, about drinks, and whether the arrabiata was better than the carbonara. Finally, the waiter went away, leaving Nick busy with the garlic bread, munching merrily at a slice.

"He's a good kid," Aiden said, leaning his head toward

Brooke. "You should be proud."

"I'm very lucky to have him. He's my life."

It was strange, seeing how the girl he knew – the one he'd loved – had turned out as a woman. As a teenager she'd been kind, loving, and of course, she'd been pretty. But this woman – because that's what she was now – her beauty could take his breath away if he let it.

But he couldn't let it. Look what happened the last time he gave into his feelings. And anyway, she wouldn't have him even if he wanted her. Not after the way he'd treated her when she'd told him the truth about Nick.

"Brooke?"

Somebody called from the sand. Aiden turned to see a man leaning on the wooden handrail separating the deck from the beach. A man, with perfect blond hair, and teeth too straight to be real.

The guy from last night. *Great.*

"Oh God." Brooke visibly paled. "What's he doing here?"

"Who is it, Mom?" Nick looked up from his garlic bread, turning his head to follow her gaze. There was no look of recognition in his eyes. Thank God. He wasn't Brooke's boyfriend, or at least if he was, he hadn't been introduced to her son.

He wasn't going to think about why that should bother him. *Not yet.*

"I'm so sorry, let me go say hi. I'll be right back." She lifted the paper napkin from her lap and placed it on the table, before walking over to the man who was still leaning on the rail. She was smiling at him, and that fact alone made Aiden frown.

"Who *is* that?" Nick asked again, this time directing his question at Aiden.

"I've no idea." Aiden shrugged. "Maybe one of your mom's friends?"

"Nuh uh. I know all of Mom's friends." Nick shook his head, helping himself to another slice of garlic bread. "Apart from you, that is."

"Does she have a lot of friends?" His throat felt tight. He swallowed a mouthful of water, but it didn't help. How old was Nick? Eight? It would be crazy to think Brooke hadn't had a boyfriend in that time. Crazy to think she didn't attract admirers like a flame attracted moths. He'd flown too close to the fire himself.

"Nope. She's too busy. She has Aunt Ally and Aunt Ember, plus Max and Ellie – he's the vet. He helps out at the shelter."

"But she knows everybody in town, right?" Aiden tried to keep his voice light. Nick was a kid, after all. He shouldn't be grilling him. It wasn't right.

"Yeah, Grandma and Grandpa have a lot of friends. They all know us."

And wasn't that the truth? Back in the day Brooke couldn't walk more than thirty yards without bumping into somebody her parents knew. God only knew how they'd kept their relationship secret for as long as they did. A mixture of clandestine meetings, and not being seen in public together. Maybe that was something he should have thought of before inviting her and Nick out for lunch at the busiest restaurant in town.

Brooke returned to the table a couple of minutes later. Her cheeks were flushed, although it was impossible to tell whether it was from the sun, or something else altogether.

"Sorry about that." She pulled her chair out and sat down, reaching across to wipe a crumb of garlic bread from Nick's chin. "Now, where were we?"

From the corner of his eye, Aiden could see the blond guy still watching them, even if he'd taken a few steps back from the railing. He gave her a smile – making it extra wide for their audience of one. "We were right here waiting for you."

"So let me get this straight, you've gone from having no guys interested in you, to having two guys vying for your attention at Delmonicos? Damn, girl, I didn't know you had it in you." Ally sat back on the sofa, lifting up her glass of wine in salute.

"She's a dark horse." Ember grinned at them both. "What were you doing with Aiden, anyway? Last I heard he hated your guts."

"He wanted to meet Nick," Brooke told them, carrying a bowl of chips into her living room. "It wasn't about me at all."

"That's bull." Ally never was one to mince her words. "He took you guys out to lunch, that wasn't only about Nick. And what's the odds on Alex happening to pass at the exact same time? I've never had two guys fighting over me. You're so lucky, Brooke." She faked a swoon, making them giggle.

"They weren't exactly fighting," Brooke pointed out. "Aiden stayed at the table with Nick, and Alex left after a quick conversation. The two of them never even met."

"Because if they did, they'd end up fighting," Ally said. There was no persuading her otherwise.

"What did Alex want?" Ember asked. She was painting her toenails with Brooke's Plum Princess polish. It wasn't often the three of them got together — thanks to their work schedules, Brooke's school work, and Nick. But when they did, it felt as though all the years had melted away, and they were back to being three best friends from school. Something about it warmed Brooke's heart.

"He claims he was passing by. Said something about taking a walk on a beautiful day." Brooke wrinkled her nose. The whole thing was weird. It made her spine feel all fizzy. As though somebody was shooting forty volts through it.

"He claims?" Ember repeated, grabbing Brooke's clear top coat. "You don't believe it?" She shook the bottle, making the tiny metal ball inside clink against the glass. "So why do you think he was there?"

"I think my mom must have told him where I was."

Ally grabbed a handful of chips. "She told him you were out with Aiden? Did she think he was going to hurt you or something?"

"I didn't tell her I was with Aiden. I told her I was going to lunch with some friends. She must have put two and two together and made seven. She probably thought I was with you two and it'd be cute for him to drop by."

"So all that stuff about him not pushing you for a date was a lie?"

Brooke grimaced. "I've got no idea. The whole thing was weird. And I was so embarrassed. I told Aiden there was nothing going on, and then he sees the guy twice in two days."

"Whoa, you're going to need to back up a minute." Ally lifted her hand up, waving a chip in the air. "You told Aiden about Alex?"

"He saw Alex walk me home on Saturday night."

Ember's mouth dropped open. "Aiden was here on

Saturday night?" She looked around as though there was some evidence of his visit to Brooke's bungalow.

Brooke frowned. "Yeah, that's what I was telling you."

"This is all out of sync. Let's start from the beginning. Last I heard, you told Aiden about Nick and he pretty much told you to screw off. What's happened since?"

For the next ten minutes, Brooke filled them in on the happenings of the previous weekend, stopping to answer their questions whenever they interrupted. Ember finished her toenails, screwing the cap back on the bottle, and sliding it onto the table.

"You reconnected with Aiden Black," Ally said, when Brooke had finished talking. There was a sigh in her voice. "Who would have thought it after all these years?"

"It wasn't about reconnecting," Brooke protested. "I was there to keep an eye on things."

"Whatever you want to believe." Ally took another handful of chips. "Man, these are good. I really shouldn't be eating them."

"So he wants to get to know Nick," Ember said, always the one who thought deeper about things. "How does that make you feel?"

Brooke leaned her head against the chair cushion. "I don't know," she admitted. "I'm pleased, of course I am. Nick deserves to know his family, and now that Joan's gone and Jamie is wherever he is, Aiden's all there is left. But it's like this part of my life I've managed to keep buried for so long has come back up. Everything was under control, and now it feels..." She trailed off, trying to think of the right words. "It's like when you have a bottle filled with three different colored liquids. They're all pretty and separated. Then somebody shakes it up, and they all swirl together into a brown mess, and you've got no idea if they're ever going to settle down again." It had taken years for her to get her life back, and she wasn't quite there yet – not until she finished her degree and got a full-time job. The future had seemed so clear, but now? It was as murky as that imaginary bottle.

Ember grabbed the wine, topping up their glasses and passing them to Brooke and Ally. "Did you ask your mom if she sent Alex over?"

Brooke shook her head. "I haven't seen my parents all week." She'd been avoiding them, not wanting to answer any questions about Alex – or, God forbid, Aiden. Who knew what Alex had told her mom and dad.

"And Aiden, what about him?" Ember asked, as though she could read her mind. "Did the two of you talk about his relationship with Nick? Where he sees it going?" Have you decided when you're going to tell Nick he's his uncle?"

"We haven't discussed it properly." Brooke glanced over at the closed living room door. There was no way she wanted Nick to hear this conversation. Not yet. If or *when* she told him about his father and the Black family, it wasn't going to be like this. Thankfully, he'd been asleep for hours, long before Ally and Ember had arrived, and he always slept like a log. "Nick was with us at lunch on Sunday, and he'll be there when we visit the resort tomorrow."

"You're seeing him again?" Ally's eyes widened. "Doesn't that make it two weekends in a row?"

"He promised to show Nick the diggers on the construction site. He can only do it on the weekend – when there's no building work going on. It's too dangerous otherwise."

Ember smirked but said nothing.

"What's that expression for?"

Ember shook her head, the smile still curling her lips.

"You think there's something more going on?" Brooke asked. "Because there isn't. I know we had a thing years ago, but that's old news."

"Yep, sure. You keep telling yourself that. And if you

believe it, you're more gullible than I thought. You guys were in love. It was the romance of the century. He disappeared and you could hardly drag yourself out of bed for weeks. We were so concerned about you, weren't we, Ally? We used to call each other every night, and discuss our concerns for you. About how you hadn't eaten anything and were fading away to nothing. So don't tell me this is old news, because some things are way too huge to die."

Brooke's mouth fell open. "You guys used to call each other and talk about me?" Tears stung at her eyes. "You're so lovely."

"You're our friend," Ember said, taking her hand. "Jeez, how long has it been now? More than twenty years since we first met."

"And because we're friends, we can tell you when you're lying to yourself," Ally pointed out. "Even if it makes you hate us a bit."

"I don't hate you," Brooke said. "I think you're seeing something that's not there. And even if it *is* there, I need to ignore it. My life is complicated enough as it is. I don't need anything else to worry about right now."

"Be careful," Ally warned. "The last time you said something like that, you ended up pregnant with Nick."

A curve ball like that was *exactly* what Brooke was afraid of.

"This is wonderful," Brooke said, as she watched Nick climbing into the cab. "Thank you so much for organizing this. When you said you'd show him the diggers I thought he'd be looking at them. I had no idea he'd be able to drive one."

Aiden shrugged. "When I told Paul about Nick and his

fascination for the machines, he offered to demonstrate. He's fully trained and a good guy. He won't let Nick do anything to put him in danger."

"I know that." Brooke nodded. "He's so excited. I'll never hear the end of it. You're fast becoming his favorite person." She turned her head to look at him. He was smiling back at her, the skin around his eyes crinkled up. And that's when it hit her like a sandstorm in a desert.

They were standing close. *Too close.* And it was firing up all the nerve endings beneath her skin, making her flesh tingle. Even that night on her deck they hadn't been this close to each other. Their arms hadn't been touching, his hand hadn't brushed against hers. But now they were and it was as though all the years were melting away. He only had to smile at her and she was a sixteen-year-old girl again, giddy and high on the first flush of love.

Stop it, Brooke. She took in a deep breath of air, but it did nothing to calm her overheated skin. From the corner of her eye she could see him still looking at her, and it made her heart race.

This was all Ember's fault. Ember's and Ally's. That stupid talk last night when they'd raised their eyebrows at her coming here. They'd told her there was more to this day than she'd thought. That the old news between her and Aiden might not have been so old after all.

Paul started the engine up, the digger rumbling noisily as he showed Nick which levers to push. Beneath his small, yellow hard hat, her son looked delighted. He laughed with joy when he managed to make the scoop rise up.

And for a moment she let herself smile, too. Even let herself imagine what life might have been like if Aiden *really* had been Nick's father. Would they have been standing here together before driving home and making lunch. Maybe they'd read him a story every night, and Aiden would pour her a glass of wine and they'd drink it on the deck, exchanging stories of their day before heading up to bed.

To bed? Damn, she really was blushing now.

She was being stupid. Of all people, she should know where day dreaming got you. Because he wasn't her husband and he wasn't Nick's father. She was the girl who'd spun off the rails so fast they were all still barely hanging on from it.

"This place is really coming along," she said, her voice wobbly. "How long until you think it will be ready?"

Everywhere she looked they were surrounded by building materials. Blocks of sandstone bricks piled high, pinned into place by wire fences. Sacks and sacks of bond and concrete. And a whole load of red roof tiles covered in plastic sheeting, waiting to be moved to the right place.

"It's going to take a while," he admitted, shielding his eyes from the sun. "We had some delays with orders, so we've eaten into our contingency time. I'm hoping to have it ready to be open before next Christmas."

"Next Christmas?" she repeated. "That's eighteen months away. Will you stay here until it's ready?" The thought of it made her heart gallop.

He shrugged. "I'm not sure; I go where I'm needed. We've got a new development starting in Florida later in the year. I might be sent there."

She felt her mouth go dry. "You wouldn't stay here after the hotel is built?" Had she managed to hide the disappointment in her voice? She'd hoped so. "To manage it or something."

He bit down a smile. "Not any more. I served my time as a manager, but I prefer this end of the job. Planning projects, overseeing them. We have a great team of people who run the hotels and resorts like clockwork. I trust them to do their jobs."

"I always imagined you'd go into finance or something,"

she murmured. "What made you want to do this?" She looked up at Nick, who was staring intently at the dashboard of the digger, listening carefully to the driver. He was so busy up there, he hadn't looked at her for the past couple of minutes.

Aiden cleared his throat. For the first time, he looked uneasy, as though he couldn't quite find the words he was looking for. "After we left Angel Sands, I needed a job," he said quietly. "I started working at a local hotel while I was going to school. It was hard for mom to find anything without references."

"But she had references," Brooke said. It felt as though somebody was pouring ice water down the back of her top. "And why did she leave if she had no job lined up?" She frowned. "Mom said Joan had gotten an offer she couldn't refuse, and that's why you all left so quickly."

"What?" His smile dissolved. "They told you we left because she had a new job?"

"Didn't you?" Her heart was beating a bit too fast. It was like she was on the cusp of something big, waiting for it to hit. She dug her fingernails into her palms to try and ground herself.

His eyes shifted around her face, as though he was searching for something. Whatever it was, he seemed to come up short. He lifted his hand, raking his fingers through his hair, until the strands were going this way and that. The same way they used to when she couldn't keep her hands off him. "Did you really think we left because she had a new job?" His voice was as gravelly as the shale surrounding them.

Goosebumps broke out on her skin, in spite of the warmth surrounding her. She tried to swallow, but her mouth was too dry. "You left after Daddy found us..." she trailed off. Best not to go into that. "He said your mom decided you needed a new start."

His laugh was humorless. "And you believed them? You believed I'd leave without even trying to talk to you?"

She lifted her shaking hand to her mouth. "Yes," she whispered. "Yes, because you never tried to contact me again. You left..." She shook her head. "And you didn't come back."

"Because they fired my mom. And even worse, they accused her of stealing from them. Said they had evidence to take to the police. We had a choice; either we stayed and she faced prosecution, or we left and they'd drop it all."

She could hear his words, but they weren't sinking in. "Your mom stole from them?" Her voice wavered. It was hard to imagine Joan doing any such thing.

"No. She didn't steal a goddamn thing." He was vehement. "But they had the ability to frame her. They would have done it, too. Anything to make us leave."

It was as though the whole world was shaking around her, and everything was off-center. "But why would they lie?"

"Mom! Look at me!" Nick shouted from the digger. "I'm scooping up dirt, see? I did that."

She pulled her gaze from Aiden's, her mind still as fuzzy as before. "That's amazing," she called up to her son. "Look at you. You're a real builder." When she looked back at Aiden, his brown eyes were still trained on her, and he looked as confused as she did.

"I've no idea why they lied to you, Brooke," he finally said. "Maybe you should ask them that."

12

Nick had been antsy all evening, as though he sensed Brooke's turmoil. She tried to put the bad thoughts out of her mind – unsuccessfully – as they worked their way through their evening routine. After a dinner of grilled cheese sandwiches and soup, wolfed down by Nick, and ignored by Brooke, the two of them walked down the hallway to the bathroom, where she pushed in the plug and started to draw him a bath.

Recently he'd begun to insist she wait outside while he bathed – he was becoming conscious of the differences between their bodies. She still missed sitting next to him while he splashed in the water, making a white beard with the bubbles she'd poured for him. Instead she leaned against the wall, listening through the partially opened door, making sure he was still alive.

By eight o'clock he was exhausted, fatigue making his eyelids heavy and his body floppy. In spite of his protests, he climbed into bed, huffing as she tucked the blankets around him. "I'm not tired," he said, his voice heavy.

"I know. But I want you to try sleeping anyway, okay? You've got school tomorrow."

And she had somebody she needed to talk with. Two somebodies, actually. And since Cora wasn't available to come babysit at short notice, this particular conversation was going to have to take place on the deck.

"Today was a good day," Nick said, letting his head fall back on the pillow. "I like Aiden. He's cool."

It was strange how she was seeing the likeness between them more each day. As though by breathing the same air, the Black in Nicholas was coming to the forefront. The dark hair, the strong nose, they even had the same mannerisms. It made her heart clench to look at him.

For so long it had been only her and Nick. From giving birth at the age of nineteen, they'd somehow become a family, in spite of her parents' anger and the town's condemnation. He'd been such a good baby – sleeping lots and batting his deep eyes at her, his love for her almost as strong as the emotions she felt for him. Now he was growing up so fast, and she could see hints of the man he would become. And she knew it would be somebody she was going to be proud of.

"He likes you, too," she told him. Nick's lips immediately split into a grin. Because Aiden's opinion of him mattered. Brooke swallowed in spite of her dry mouth, because she was going to need to tell her son the truth soon. She owed him that – they all did.

It wasn't only him she'd been hiding the truth from. As far as her parents – and nearly everybody in town – knew, the father was somebody who'd passed on by. By the time she'd discovered she was pregnant, Jamie Black was long gone. Though she'd eventually tracked him down using a private investigator, it was clear from his response that he wanted nothing to do with the child she was having. If she was really honest, she was relieved he felt that way.

It was bad enough she was single and pregnant as a teenager. Telling her parents Nick was Jamie's son probably would have killed them. As difficult as their relationship was, she never wanted that.

"Can we see him again?" Nick asked her. "Maybe tomorrow?"

"Not tomorrow, sweetheart. It's a school night. But soon, okay?" She had a feeling Aiden would insist on it.

"Okay, Mom." His voice was heavy with sleep. "Love you." He reached his arms up and she dipped her head, kissing his cheek as he hugged her close. By the time he released her, his breathing was even, his mouth slack as sleep overtook him.

"Love you too, sweetheart," she whispered. "Sleep tight."

It was after eight when she heard the soft knock on her door. Brooke wrenched the door open, seeing her parents standing on the wooden deck surrounding the bungalow, both dressed in their Sunday best.

"This won't take long, will it, darling?" her mom asked, attempting to walk past Brooke and into the living room. "We have cocktails at the Spencers' this evening. Is Nick still up?"

Brooke blocked her way, making Lillian stop short. "He's asleep. Let's talk outside."

"But I want to say good night to him. Or at least look in on him. It's been too long since I saw him last."

"Stay on the deck." Brooke's voice was so much stronger than she felt. Flicking the lock onto the latch, she carefully pulled the door behind her, hearing it softly click shut. "I don't want him hearing this conversation." She pointed at the wooden chairs laid out on the far corner, overlooking the lawn leading down to the cliffs. "Sit down."

"Well there's no need to be so rude about it," Lilian huffed.

"Hush up," her husband told her. Turning his head to look at Brooke, he asked her, "Now what's all this about? Your mother's right, we're due at the Spencers' in half an hour."

"It'll take as long as it takes."

"I don't like your tone." Her father's voice was brusque. It reminded her of those terrible days all those years ago. When he left her in no doubt she'd let him down completely.

Brooke watched in awkward silence as her parents sat down on the dark wood chairs. Her mother's nose wrinkled up as she brushed the seat, trying to get rid of the dust settled there. In the distance, the sun was sliding down, almost past the cliffs, casting a long dark shadow on the land beyond the bungalow.

"I want to ask you about Joan," Brooke said, pulling out a chair and settling herself on it.

"Oh, did I tell you she died?" Lilian asked, turning to her husband. "I probably forgot, you know me, I'm an airhead."

Brooke's stomach contracted at her mother's dismissal of Joan's death.

"She did?" Her father's voice was even. "That's a shame." He glanced at his watch, his face impassive.

Another silence. This one felt thicker than the last. Full of recriminations Brooke had no idea how to voice.

"Was that all you wanted to talk about?" Martin asked her, raising a silver eyebrow.

"No." Brooke shook her head. "I want to ask you why she left."

"What do you mean? Why are you dragging all this up again? Come on, Lillian, we'll be late." Her father went to stand up.

Brooke put her hand on his arm. "Sit. *Down*."

He looked shocked at her vehemence. "What on earth?"

"Why did she leave?" Brooke asked again, through gritted teeth.

"Brooke, your father's right. This is silly. You know why she left. After everything that happened she wanted a new start. She knew she'd done wrong to encourage you and Aiden in your little... fling." She wrinkled her nose again. "She got a job offer in LA and she took it."

"That's not what Aiden says."

Her father looked up at her, his eyes narrowed. "Your mother told me he was back in town."

So she'd admitted that much. Clearly Aiden's reappearance was more important to her than Joan's death. Brooke swallowed, hating the way the thought tasted in her mouth.

"Yes, he is." Brooke's head felt like a balloon. Light as air, but full at the same time. It was dizzying. "And he told me why he left. Why they all left."

"Honey, please, stop dragging this up. It's old history." Lillian reached out, trying to grab Brooke's hand. Brooke pulled away sharply, curling her fingers into fists. "We're your parents, we love you. Nothing else matters."

"Did you threaten to have Joan arrested?" Brooke asked. "Did you make her take Aiden away from me."

Like an IED ticking over from inactive to explosion, her father's face turned puce. "We're going, Lillian." He stood up. "I don't need to be spoken to like this."

"That's right, walk away," Brooke said, standing too. He was at least half a foot taller than her, but right now she felt as mighty as she ever had. "You're many things, Dad, but I never thought you were a liar. Not until now."

They stared at each other, her father's nostrils flaring. His eyes were narrow as he tried to intimidate her. But she stood firm and silent; if one of them was going to break, it wasn't her.

"Yes, we made them leave," he finally admitted, his voice

carrying across the still night air. "That boy took advantage of you. I should've had him arrested. Had him thrown in jail for what he did. That dirty little shit, the thought of him touching you makes me sick. That family got off lightly."

Tears stung at Brooke's eyes, the same way they always did whenever her dad shouted. It was scary and it hit nerves she'd long since forgotten about. Made her feel like a child being rebuked, not the woman she was.

"You lied to me."

"It was for your own good," Lilian told her, revealing her complicitness in their cover up. "Your father's right. He took advantage of you. All those years we had welcomed that family into our home, and look what he did."

"That's not true. He didn't take advantage of me. We were in love."

"That wasn't love, that was sex." Her father's voice was still harsh.

"Oh Brooke, of course it must have felt like love. Everything does when you're a teenager. But it wasn't – how could it have been? You were completely unsuitable for each other." Her mom reached out for her, but Brooke stepped away.

"In what way?" she asked, though she already knew what their answer would be.

"You want her to spell it out?" her father spat. "He was scum, and you're a Newton. There's no comparison."

"You think the Blacks were scum?"

"I don't think it, I know it," her father said. "And I don't care if Aiden Black is back in town, driving some expensive car and wearing tailored suits. You can't buy your way up the social ladder. He's simply well-dressed scum now. I forbid you to see him."

She would have laughed, if it hadn't been so crazy. "I'm an adult. I can see who I want."

"Not while you're living in my house, you can't."

Her father may have lacked many things, but generosity wasn't one of them. Not once in all the years since she'd had Nick had he ever threatened to take their home away from them. The shock of it made her hands start to shake. "You don't get to tell me who I can and can't see."

"You're my daughter. I can tell you whatever I want to. And if I hear you've been near that man again, you'll be out of this place before you can even blink."

"You'd really throw us out?" she asked him, incredulous. "You'd let me and Nick be homeless?"

"Nick will always have a home with us. I wouldn't punish him for your decisions. But we've protected you for long enough. If you're stupid enough to see that man again, it's your choice, but don't expect us to pick up the pieces this time." He reached for his wife's hand. "Come on, Lilian, we're going to be late."

Her mother stood, sliding her hand into his. "Darling, we were only thinking of you."

Brooke blinked back the tears trying to escape from her eyes. "I never expected you to pick up the pieces," she said, her voice wobbly. "I never expected you to interfere in my life, either. I'm a grown adult. I'll see who I want to see." She sucked in a deep lungful of air, but it did nothing to ease the burning in her chest. "And so will my son."

❧ 13 ❧

Ally passed a mug of coffee to Brooke, squeezing her fingers as she took it. "So what did they say?"

"Dad started shouting again. His face was so red I was afraid he was going to have a heart attack. In the end, Mom dragged him away, but not before he'd called me every bad name under the sun." Brooke took a sip of coffee. "That's when I called you."

"It must have come as a shock to them. Remember how shocked Ember and I were when you told us Aiden was back. Give them time to get used to it."

"There's not much else I can do," Brooke said, looking around the beach house Ally shared with her fiancé, Nate and his daughter, Riley. "Thanks for taking us in." Though it was spacious enough – with a beautiful spare bedroom more than big enough for Brooke and Nick, she couldn't help but feel uncomfortable at imposing on her friend. "It's only for one night, I promise."

"You stay as long as you need to," Nate told her, carrying a trayful of coffee into the living room and setting it down on the smoked glass coffee table. "There's plenty of room here. Plus Riley's having the time of her life with Nick."

It was early on Monday evening. Brooke had picked Nick up from school and brought him straight to Nate and Ally's – thanks to their kind offer. The thought of staying one more night in the bungalow, knowing what her parents thought of her was too much. She needed to put distance between them, to sort out her thoughts. And more importantly, to get control of her anger.

They'd manipulated her and lied for all these years. The thought of them forcing the Black family to leave town in the dead of night made her heart hurt. For Joan, for Aiden – even for Jamie. But most of all for her and Nick. She'd been so in love with Aiden it had hurt, and when he left it was as though she'd been torn in two.

"I need to start standing on my own two feet," Brooke said, her voice resolute. "I want to find somewhere Nick and I can put some roots down. It's been a long time coming, after all."

Her eyes met Ally's. More than anybody, her friend understood the need to call somewhere home. It made Brooke feel so happy to see Ally in love with Nate Crawford. Their love story had been unexpected but so right. And now they were living together, engaged to be married, and so happy they lit up the air around them.

"I've never left home," Brooke said, her voice soft. "And I'm almost twenty-eight-years-old. What does that say about me? And more importantly, what kind of message am I sending to Nick? I'm the biggest failure."

"You're nothing like a failure," Ally protested, frowning. "Look at you. You've managed to bring up your son to become a fine young man, you're studying for your degree, and you're single handedly keeping the animal shelter going.

Who raises more money for that place than anywhere else? Brooke Newton, that's who."

Brooke's eyes stung at her friend's passion. "You're too sweet to me."

"No, that's not true. I'm only telling you what's obvious to everybody else. You're amazing, Brooke, and I wish you could see it for yourself."

Brooke wished she could, too. She felt anything but amazing. She was homeless, and even worse, Nick was too. He deserved stability and happiness, and she needed to make sure he had it.

"We meant it when we said you could stay as long as you need," Ally said. "You've always been there for me whenever I've needed you. Let me do the same."

Brooke reached for Ally's hand and squeezed it tightly. Their eyes met in deep understanding. The kind you only got when you'd had your friend's back for a long, long time. There was a bond between them – between the three of them – deeper than family ties. They would do anything for each other. Through thick and thin, no matter what.

"Mom, can we go to the beach?" Nick asked, breathless, as he ran into the living room. Riley was close behind him, a grin on her face which made Brooke wonder what they'd been up to.

"Sure. Let me get my swimsuit on, okay?"

"Can Riley come, too?" he asked, looking up at the older girl. Riley shrugged, trying to remain cool, but the expression on her face showed she wanted to join them. Like Nick, she was an only child, and at almost seventeen, she was eight years older than him, but the two of them often sought each other out when Ember, Brooke, Ally, and their friends were all together.

"Sure. The more the merrier." Brooke stood and looked at Ally and Nate. "You guys want to join us?"

"Why not? It's a beautiful evening." Ally glanced at her fiancé.

"Yup. Let's do this thing."

Nick ran out of the living room, chatting excitedly with Riley about surfing and the waves and how he loved to swim. Thank goodness he was so adaptable.

"You okay?" Ally murmured, walking to join her by the living room door.

"Yeah. I was thinking about what to tell Nick about moving out."

"Maybe leave that until tomorrow," Ally suggested. "You've had enough to deal with today. Anyway, he's going to be fine. You both are."

Brooke opened her mouth to answer, but the shrill ring of her phone swallowed her words. She pulled it from her pocket, wincing when she saw her mom's name flashing on the screen.

"You going to get that?" Ally asked.

"Not right now. I've got nothing to say to her." Brooke winced. "Or nothing good, anyway."

"What if she wants to see Nick?"

Brooke took a deep breath. "I'm not going to stop my parents from seeing him. He loves them and they love him. It's me who's mad at them, not him. I'll message her tomorrow, but only to talk about him. Everything else is off the table until I cool off."

"Mom, can we go now?" Nick ran out of the guest room with his swimshorts on. "I want to swim before it gets dark."

Brooke grinned, her eyes shining with love. "Of course, sweetheart," she said. "Give me two minutes, okay?"

It was time to relax and have fun with her son and forget about her problems for a while. Yes, she was practically homeless and no, she wasn't speaking to her parents, but at least she and Nick had each other.

Everything else could wait until another day.

The construction site lay silent as the day was drawing to an end. Aiden walked up the steps to the trailer office, intending to finish up his emails for the night and head home for some long-awaited rest. Not that he'd been sleeping much recently. His mind was too full of Brooke's revelations and his brand new relationship with his nephew to do that. A glass of something alcoholic and a plate full of pasta would work wonders. Even if it was bound to be past nine in the evening before he ate it.

"I've been calling you," his secretary said as he walked into the main reception. "There's somebody here to see you. You didn't answer your phone."

He pulled it from his pocket. Dead. The battery was on its way out, it wasn't holding a charge at all.

"Who is it?" Aiden asked, glancing at the clock. It was almost seven. "And you should head home, I'm only going to be here for a few minutes longer. Your family must be wondering where you are."

She leaned forward as though she didn't want to be heard. "It's Martin Newton, of Newton Pharmaceuticals." Her eyes widened, as though it was a big deal. "I didn't want to leave until you got here. I told him I had no idea when you'd be back, but he insisted on waiting."

Aiden followed her gaze to the closed door of his office. A strange sensation washed over him. It wasn't that he was afraid – he'd long since stopped fearing the influence Brooke's father exerted. He might have been a big deal in Angel Sands, but in the wider world he was nobody. It had taken Aiden a while to realize that. Even longer to face the ghosts of his past and understand the only person who had power over him was himself.

He wasn't a kid anymore. Martin Newton couldn't hurt him.

"You can go home," Aiden said, smiling at her even though it took some effort. "I'll speak with Martin and leave right after."

He didn't have to ask twice. His secretary was standing and grabbing her purse before he could take a second breath. "I'll be in early tomorrow," she told him. "We have a delivery, remember? Plus Mr. Carter's arranged a meeting for seven."

Of course he had. Old Man Carter found it hard to sleep these days, and had a tough time understanding that other people could. A six A.M. meeting wasn't unheard of.

Aiden rolled his shoulders and his neck, releasing the tension there. It wasn't as if he hadn't been expecting this. Ten years ago, Martin Newton had told them in no uncertain words they shouldn't come back to town. Ever. And he was a man who hated to be disobeyed.

The man standing in the corner of his office turned around. He didn't look very different to how Aiden remembered him. Still held himself ramrod straight, with eyes that seemed to drill right through your skin. His hair was a lighter silver, his face more lined, but those were the only physical changes Aiden could discern.

"Martin." No more Mr. Newtons from him. Those had disappeared along with his childhood. "I wasn't expecting you. You're lucky I'm still here."

Martin stared at him for a moment. Not because he was lost for words nor because he wanted time to regroup. Aiden understood the man more than he realized. He always liked to have the advantage and Aiden had stolen it from him by walking in with an agenda. Martin was working out how to swap their roles.

"Sit down," Martin said, gesturing at the chair.

"After you, please." Aiden turned to the refrigerator plugged in by the door. "Can I get you a drink?" he asked. "Water, soda, or I can make you some coffee."

"I don't want a drink. What I have to say won't take long."

Aiden turned back to look at Martin. He hadn't sat down. He was still standing exactly where he'd been ever since Aiden had walked in. "I want to talk to you about my daughter."

"I don't think there's anything to say. You said enough the last time I saw you, and nothing's changed since."

"That's where you're wrong. You leaving town was the best thing that could have happened. You shouldn't have come back." Martin placed his hands flat on Aiden's desk, leaning forward. "This place has been perfectly fine for years. But then you walk back in and everything goes to hell. You tell lies to my daughter, you make her leave home with my grandson—"

"Wait. What?" Aiden frowned. "Brooke's left?"

"As if you didn't know. You probably told her to do it. She always was easily persuaded, especially by an asshole like you."

Aiden opened his mouth to respond, but closed it again sharply. He didn't know what the hell was going on, but he sure wasn't going to say anything without speaking to Brooke first.

"Is that all you wanted to tell me?" he said, his voice deceptively soft. "Because I have a lot of work to do. It was nice to see you again, Martin. Thanks for dropping by. Don't forget to wear a hard hat on your way out."

"You throwing me out, boy?"

Aiden squared his shoulders. "Let's get one thing straight. I'm not your boy. I never was. I don't owe you anything, and I sure as hell don't want to spend my evening talking to you. So

I'm suggesting you leave before you say something we both might regret."

"You think you can waltz back in here and mess my family up? Well you've got another thing coming. You were scum when you were a kid and you're still scum now. Though you learned to dress better." Martin shook his head, his eyes narrowing to slits. "You don't want to get on the wrong side of me. You should remember what I'm capable of."

"You're capable of terrorizing women and kids until they leave town? Well excuse me if I don't cower at the thought. I'm not that boy anymore, Martin. I'm here to build a resort and I'm not planning on going anywhere."

"I'm important in this town. I know people, *influential* people. I can cause you more problems than you'll know how to deal with. You don't want to get on the wrong side of me, and I'm pretty sure your boss wouldn't want to either. Maybe it's him I should be talking to." His voice wavered, as though he had no idea what to do next.

"Go ahead." Aiden walked toward Martin, leaning over the desk to pull out the drawer. "Here's his business card. I think you'll find he gives as many flying fucks about your influence in Angel Sands as I do." His laugh had no humor in it. "You're a big fish in a very small pond, Martin. Outside these town limits nobody gives a damn what you think."

Martin's jaw was so tight Aiden could see a twitch where he was biting down. He shook his head again, nostrils flaring as he took a breath in. "I'm leaving," he announced, as though it was completely his idea. "But you listen to me, boy. You mess with my family, you mess with me. Leave my daughter and grandson alone. You're nothing to them, and you should keep it that way."

In that moment, Aiden realized he had absolutely no idea they were his family, too. No inkling that Jamie was Nick's father. He could announce the fact right now, and watch as the realization washed over Martin's face, relish the way it would cut him like a knife.

But something stopped him. It wasn't his secret to tell.

"Goodbye, Martin," he said firmly, watching as the older man stalked to the door, yanking it open, and stepping into the main office. He didn't say another word as he made his way out of the cabin and down the metal stairs, heading toward the gate to the parking lot.

He'd forgotten his hard hat. Aiden didn't bother to call after him. Maybe a piece of falling masonry was what he needed now. Grabbing the phone, he called the night time security guard, asking him to let Martin Newton out of the gate. Sighing, he walked back into his office.

He had so much work to catch up on, so many project plans to read and emails to respond to, but his head was reeling.

There was only one person he wanted to talk to, and it had nothing to do with the resort at all.

———

"I'm going to finish up here and I'll be right home," Brooke told her son, cradling her phone on her shoulder as she poured food into each cat's bowl. "Are you being a good boy for Ally and Nate?"

"Of course." Nick sounded indignant at the thought he might not be. He was growing up so fast. Only a few years until she had teenage tantrums and exaggerated eye-rolls to contend with. Brooke bit down a sigh. Part of her wanted to keep him exactly like this – her little boy. Although Nick would hate the description. In his mind, he was already big. Her arms ached to hold him and protect him from the outside world.

"Mom, can I go now?" Nick asked, bringing her attention

back to the phone call. "Riley's home, and I want to see if she'll come to the beach with me."

"Okay, baby, but give Riley a bit of space. She might need it after a day at school."

"Ah, he's gone." Ally's voice echoed down the line. Nick must have handed her back the phone. "And don't worry about Riley, she's loving having him around. He's like the little brother she never had."

"Well thank you. For everything. I mean it."

"No need to thank me," Ally said, her voice light. "We're friends, we do things for each other. God knows I owe you enough. Oh, and Nate's planning on cooking shrimp tonight. Will eight be okay?"

Brooke checked her watch. It was a quarter after seven. "Yep, that's great. But you've got to let me do the cleaning up."

Ally laughed. "Whatever. See you soon."

Brooke slid her phone into the pocket of her scrubs and gave food to the last of the cats. Everything else was ready for the shelter to close. The dogs had been exercised, the smaller animals were safely in their cages. And the larger ones – the goat and the sheep that would be rehomed that weekend – were safely out in the paddock. Clara was in her office, ready to take the night shift. All Brooke had to do was lock the front door.

She was about to slide the bolts across the top, when Brooke noticed the door knob turning. Blinking, she pulled it open, fully expecting to see another animal being brought in.

But instead there was Aiden, his dark eyebrows pulled down, his hand raking through his thick dark hair like a comb.

"Aiden? Are you okay?"

"I was passing. I saw your car." There was the strangest expression on his face. A mixture of confusion and something else – but she wasn't sure what. "Can I talk to you for a minute?"

"Sure. I'm about to close up. You want to come in?"

He nodded, stepping in and waiting as she closed the door behind him. "Are you alone here?" he asked her, the frown still furrowing his brow.

"No, Clara is here. She's taking the night shift. I can't do it because of Nick." Brooke glanced over at the closed office door. "I want to make sure everything's clean and ready for tomorrow before I leave." She bit her bottom lip. "I usually say goodnight to them all," she admitted. "I don't want you to think I'm crazy or anything."

"Don't let me stop you." He gestured toward the pens. His eyes softened as he looked toward the dogs behind the Plexiglass doors. "Hey, is the dog you rescued from the resort still here?"

"Perdita? Yeah, she's going to be with us for a while. We need to train her before we rehome her." Brooke inclined her head, and he followed her gaze toward the light brown medium sized dog laying down in her pen.

"She looks different," Aiden said.

"She cleaned up well. And luckily she's healthy too. Now she needs to learn a few manners." Brooke raised her eyebrows.

"Perdita," Aiden murmured. "The lost one. Did you name her?"

"I liked it. It seemed fitting."

"It does."

His eyes caught hers, and she felt her heart leap. Strange how he still did that to her after all these years.

"I had a visitor myself this evening," Aiden told her. "I thought you should probably know." He leaned on the counter, tipping his head to the side as he looked at her. "It was your dad. He came to warn me off. Told me it was my fault you've left home."

"Oh God." Brooke squeezed her eyes shut. "I'm sorry. This has nothing to do with you. He shouldn't have involved you."

"Of course it has something to do with me. You left because of what he did to us. He's right, this is my doing."

She opened her eyes. He was closer. Close enough for her to see the brown flecks in his irises. Her fingers were trembling, so she laced them together to still them.

"You should have called me when you left. Where are you staying?" Concern softened his words.

"With Ally. But only for a couple of nights. I'm going to start looking for somewhere tomorrow, as soon as I drop Nick off at school."

"Let me help you look. I know a good realtor. I used her to find my place."

"There's no need, it doesn't take two of us. And anyway, haven't you got to work? From what I hear, the whole site would shut down without you," she teased.

He grinned back at her. "Nobody's irreplaceable, Brooke."

"That's pretty much what my dad hinted at."

"What do you mean?"

"He said something about Nick living with them if I'm homeless." She paused, thinking about his words. "Do you think he could make that happen?" she asked, alarmed. "Could he take Nick away from me?"

"I wouldn't let him." His words were like oil on troubled water. "Don't worry about what hasn't happened. He was probably spouting off."

"But he did it before, didn't he?" she asked softly. "He made sure he got his way by forcing you and your family out of town. Who's to say he wouldn't do it to me, too, if I was standing in the way of what he wanted?"

"Your father loves you, Brooke. I might not be his biggest fan, but not even he would steal a child from his mother. That would be crazy."

She leaned back on the counter, her arm an inch away from his. She could feel the warmth radiating from him. "This is such a mess. And I'm sorry, I shouldn't be offloading it all on you. You didn't ask for this."

"I want to help. That's why I'm here."

Her father would have said it was a typical Brooke move, expecting other people to help her with the mess she'd created. And maybe he'd be right. For too long she'd relied upon other people, expected them to clear up her mess. She could argue all she liked about her circumstances being bad, and not having the choices she wanted. But at the end of the day, she was luckier than most. She'd lived a life of privilege, and she knew it.

"You shouldn't have to," she told him. "It's not fair you have to pay the price of my decisions again."

"I never paid the price of your decisions," he told her. "I loved your decisions." He cleared his throat. "Back when we made them together, they were the best decisions ever."

She tried to ignore the way her heart flipped at his words. It was only muscle memory, wasn't it? "You always know how to say the right thing."

He smiled. "Not really. But I always know how to say the truthful thing, so maybe that helps."

"Will you let me know if he causes you any problems?"

"I can handle him, Brooke. I'm not afraid of your father. The only hold he ever had over me was my mom, and... yeah. He doesn't have that any more."

Another heart lurch. She was almost getting used to them. "Even so, let me know, okay?" She was feeling stronger. Amazing how he always knew the right words to say. It had been way too long since she'd heard them, though.

"Okay," he agreed. "And I'll meet you at the school in the morning."

"Are you sure you don't mind?" She liked the idea of him coming with her. Maybe too much.

"Yes, I'm sure. As long as you're okay with it." His voice was warm, soft. Like a blanket she wanted to wrap herself in.

She took a deep breath. He wasn't asking her to marry him, he wasn't asking her to give up her firstborn. He wasn't asking for anything at all. They were two adults looking for a space she could call home. "Yes," she said, smiling at him. "I'd like your help with apartment hunting."

"In that case, I'll see you in the morning."

❧ 14 ❧

He could tell by the slump in her shoulders this apartment was the same as the last. He didn't even need to step inside to take a look – it was a bust. He watched as the realtor pointed things out to Brooke, and she nodded, her face taking on a look of polite interest. But he knew her, and he knew what she looked like when she was getting dejected. No wonder. With the little money she had available, she could never afford anything better than this.

"And you're certain your father couldn't help with the lease?" the realtor asked for the second time. "With his backing, you'd be able to secure something better. I have a few new listings which might interest you."

"No, I want to pay for this on my own." Brooke looked around the tiny living space, her expression neutral as she took in the gouges on the walls, the threadbare stained carpet, the kitchen cupboard doors hanging off. "I'm sure with a bit of work I can make this look like home."

Aiden couldn't stand it anymore. For the past two hours he'd tried to be silent as they looked at apartment after apartment, watching as she slowly began to accept exactly *what* her wages could get them. A home far worse than the one he'd grown up in. No place for a child to live.

"Brooke, can I talk to you for a moment?" He glanced at the realtor. "In private?"

The realtor nodded. "I'll be outside. Come and find me when you're ready."

A moment later she closed the door behind her, leaving them alone in the fleapit masquerading as an apartment. Brooke looked around again, this time letting the dismay pull at her expression, her bottom lip trembling as she took everything in. "Can you believe this is at the top range of my budget?" she asked him, her voice quiet. "I feel so stupid. Like a poor little rich girl finally mingling with the masses."

His laugh was small but genuine. "You're hardly that. Why would you know how much rent cost if you hadn't needed to before?"

"Because I'm an adult. And I'm a mother, too. I should know these things. Especially if I've made my son homeless." She bit her lip. He hated the way she looked so sad. He wanted to pull her into his arms, make everything okay.

There went his knight in shining armor complex again. He should trade his Mercedes in for a prize steed.

"You know the price of a loaf of bread, right?" he asked her.

She looked up at him, confused. "Yes."

"And a gallon of milk?"

"Yeah. But what does that have to do with anything?"

He took a step toward her, wanting to cut through the space between them. "It means you're not out of touch with reality. There's no possible reason for you to study the real estate market unless you were planning to dive into it. And until this week, you didn't have those plans."

"I never intended to live with my parents forever," she

told him. "I was always planning to move out as soon as I got a job after graduating."

"There you go." Aiden shrugged. "And by that point you would be able to afford something better."

She let out a big sigh. "I guess. And until then we'll have to settle for a place like this."

"No." He shook his head. "Not this place."

"Why not? It's as good as the others we looked at. I'm sure I can do something with it." She didn't sound very certain, though.

"You can't make the area any better than it is, though. It's not safe."

"*You* used to live around here."

He raised an eyebrow. "That's how I know it's not safe."

She tugged at her ponytail, letting out a sigh. "So what do I do? Apart from go back to my parents with my tail between my legs. And seriously, if I do that, I might as well give up. I'd be admitting I'm never going to grow up."

"You *are* a grown up," he told her. "But even grown ups need help sometimes." He moved closer, until there were only a couple of feet between them. Her breath was shallow, making her chest rise up and down rapidly. He started to reach for her, but pulled back.

No, he couldn't touch her. Not if he wanted to stay sane.

"Let me help you," he said. She looked up at him, her eyes wide, but she said nothing. "I can put a deposit down for you. I have the money."

She took another shallow breath, the air rushing between her lips. "I can't ask you to do that."

"You're not asking, I'm offering. That's different."

She blinked a couple of times, still staring at him. Two deep lines formed in her brow. "It's not different, it's the same. It's me relying on other people when I should be able to support myself. Don't you see, Aiden? I've spent too long letting people control me. I can't do that any more."

"You think I'd control you?" he asked her. Even the suggestion of it made him angry. "You think that's what it's about?"

Her eyes widened. "No, not at all. I know you wouldn't. But I can't keep doing this."

His heart was pounding and he had no idea why. Being this close to her was like flying too close to the sun, beautifully blinding, and yet you knew it was going to kill you. "Nicholas is my nephew," he said, trying to keep his voice even. "And you're my friend. Let me help you until you can stand on your own two feet. How long is it until you graduate?"

"Three months, that is if I get my practicals finished on time."

"And then?" he asked her. "What are your plans for afterward?"

"I've been offered a job at the local veterinary clinic. The pay's not great, but it has good medical insurance and I need to have that for Nick." Her face paled. "Oh shit, what if my parents stop his insurance too?" She lifted a hand to her mouth. "Jesus, what if he isn't insured any more?"

He reached out and curled his fingers around her wrist, gently pulling her hand away from her face. But he didn't let go. Instead, he slid his palm down until her hand was folded in his, their fingers threading together without either of them saying a word. He stared down at them – at her slim, elegant fingers – remembering the time he'd kissed every one of them as they promised each other forever. The times she used to touch him, hesitant at first, then bolder, making his skin break out in a rash of goosebumps.

"It's going to be okay," he told her softly. "He'll be

covered. If not by your parents, then by me. I'll cover him. Stop panicking."

"I can't help it." She squeezed his hand tightly. "I had a plan. I only needed to get through graduation. And now it's all messed up, and it's my fault. I've put Nick in danger. He's got no home and he might have no insurance." She looked up at him, her eyes glassy. "I'm a terrible mother. I should let him stay with my parents, shouldn't I?"

He grabbed her free hand with his, interlinking them together. Now he was holding both of her hands. "You're an amazing mother, Brooke. I've seen you with Nick, he's your world and he knows it. Everything you do is for him. If you hadn't gotten pregnant you wouldn't still be here now. So stop saying those things, I don't want to hear them. Not from you."

A single tear escaped from the corner of her eye and ran down the sharp line of her cheekbone, to the corner of her mouth. It stayed there for a moment, before the slightest movement of her head allowed it to continue its route to her chin.

"Don't cry," he whispered. "I can't stand to see you cry."

He never could. Not with any woman, but especially not with Brooke.

He tugged at her hands, pulling her closer until their bodies were touching, her chest pressed into his abdomen. Releasing her hands, he slid his arms around her shoulders, holding her closer still.

He'd forgotten how good she felt in his arms. Forgotten how slim her waist was, how warm her skin was, how she smelled of sunny days. She was the final piece of the jigsaw, slotting into place after all these years, and it made his head spin.

"Let me help you," he whispered again. "Until you get a job. I want to take care of you and Nick. I need to."

He could feel her trembling in his arms, and when she looked up, her face was wet with tears. He reached out to wipe them away. But when he touched her, it was like being shocked by a thousand volts. It took every ounce of strength he had not to jump away.

"I'll pay you back." Her voice was muffled by his chest. His shirt was thin enough for him to feel her breath through the cotton. It sent a shot of pleasure through him, one he had no right to feel. And yet it was good. So good.

"You don't have to. Consider it backpayment for child support."

She looked up at him, her eyes fierce. "No. If I accept your help, I need to know it's a loan. You're not Nick's father. You don't owe him anything."

Her words hit him like a fist in the gut. He wanted to double over. Protect himself. Nick wasn't his son, he was Jamie's. Damn if the reminder didn't hurt more than a punch.

"Okay, it's a loan. I'll even get my lawyer to draw up an agreement if you want."

Her expression softened. He wasn't sure which Brooke he liked more – the angry kick ass one, or the kind, soft spoken one.

Both. He liked both, and way more than he should.

"He's asleep."

Brooke walked out of the room Ally had made up for Nick and headed into the living room where Aiden was waiting for her. Ally and Nate were out with his daughter for a school meeting followed by dinner, and the house had been empty when they had arrived back from apartment hunting.

Aiden was by the open glass doors, staring out at the ocean as it gently lapped against the evening shore. While she'd helped Nick get ready for bed, Aiden had gone outside to return some phone calls he'd missed during the day. He must have come back in while she was reading Nick a story. It was strange to see him like this – so casual and at ease. He looked more like the Aiden she remembered from all those years ago – the intense student with a muscled body. Her friend. Her lover.

"Is he okay? If you want me to drive to the store, to pick anything up for him, I can."

"He's good. Kids don't need a lot. A roof over their head, some food to eat. Somebody who loves them." She flashed him a smile. "He was asleep before I even left the bedroom."

"He's lucky to have you as his mom." Aiden's eyes were dark as they settled on her. She wondered what he saw. The perfect girl he'd once known or the flawed woman she'd become.

After they'd finished apartment hunting, they'd picked Nick up from Ember's place and the three of them had played on the sand for a while. She could already see where the sun had caught Aiden's skin and turned it into a deeper tan. Her own skin felt tight from the sea salt carried in the gentle breeze.

"I guess I'll head home. Now that I know you're both okay."

Brooke blinked. "There's no rush. Ally and Nate will be out for at least another hour with Riley." She pulled at her bottom lip with her teeth. "Unless you'd rather go."

"I can stay."

"Let's go and sit on the deck," she suggested, gesturing at the rattan sofa and table Nate had set up out there. "Would you like a drink?"

"No, I'm good."

The beach was practically empty – this far up the bay it was mostly used by locals. There were too many rocks to make it useful to surfers. The ocean moved back and forth, like one of those penny pushers at the arcade, its constant rhythm soothing to her ears. Above it, the sun was slowly slipping down the sky, casting an orange glow above the horizon. If the sunset had looked beautiful from her bungalow on the cliffs, down here it was achingly perfect.

Sitting beside him, she leaned her head back against the cushions, breathing in the salty ozone. She'd always loved Ally and Nate's house. It felt so peaceful.

"I called the realtor a while ago," Aiden said, stretching his legs out in front of him. "They have all the details for the lease. If everything goes to plan you should be able to move in next week."

"Next week?" She blinked, even though the sun wasn't dazzling. "I thought it might be sooner. I hope Ally won't mind too much."

"You can always move in with me."

She turned her head to the side, looking at him. "You've already done enough for us. I can't ask for anything more."

"You're not asking, I'm offering."

"Same difference."

He laughed. "I'd forgotten how stubborn you were."

"I'd forgotten how persistent you were." She stretched her own legs out, resting her feet on the edge of the coffee table.

"I guess there's a lot we've forgotten," he said, glancing down at her legs. She was wearing shorts – she nearly always did in the summer, especially in the evenings. Her skin glowed in the light of the setting sun.

He looked up at her, and she liked what she saw. His stare sent shivers down her spine. As though he was seeing inside her, to the truths she hid in there.

"There's a lot I remember, too."

He shifted on the sofa, until there were only inches

between them. Beneath the denim, she could see his muscles flex. He'd always been the strong one. Working manual jobs as a kid to make sure his family had enough money. Playing sports until he collapsed to get the scholarship he so desperately needed. And that summer, when it had felt like they were the only two people in the world, she'd shown him how much she appreciated his body. The same way she'd fallen for his heart.

"Do you ever wonder what it would have been like if I hadn't left?" He scanned her face, as though her expression had all the answers.

"Only in the abstract," she whispered. His closeness was making her feel breathless. She could smell him mixed in with the fragrance of the ocean. It was intoxicating. Her blood pulsed to the rhythm of the waves, as though the two were connected. "If I thought about it too much, I'd have to think Nick away. And he's the best thing that's ever happened to me."

He didn't look upset at her answer. Instead he looked interested. "And you've never regretted your decision?"

"Not for a minute. Being a mom is the greatest privilege I've had. He's my life. I'm so thankful to have him."

Aiden stared at her for a moment, his eyes dropping to look at her lips. For a second she wondered if he wanted to kiss her, but then she wanted to laugh at herself. Of course he didn't. Look at the two of them – he was the success, she was the one trying to get through the day. They had nothing in common, not any more.

Except Nick. They had Nick.

"I think it's time we tell him you're his uncle," she said. "I don't want him finding out from anyone else, and he has the right to know." She looked up at him, trying to gauge his reaction. "That is if you're okay with it?"

Aiden's eyes glowed. "I'd be more than happy with that.

As long as you think he'll be fine. I don't want to do anything to upset him."

"He'll be ecstatic. He's never had an uncle, and I know he's always jealous of his friends with big families. It's hard on him sometimes at school events. He has my parents, and of course they've been as supportive as they can. But on sports day and Father's Day he always misses out."

Aiden looked down. "I hate the thought of him not having someone there for him. The next time there's an event like that you tell me and I'll be there."

Unexpected tears stung at her eyes. She blinked them back, embarrassed. "You don't have to do that." Her voice was thick, low. She lifted a hand to cover her mouth, scared she was going to say something stupid.

Gently, he pulled her hand away, folding it in his own. "I want to. I want to be there for Nick. I want to be there for you." He squeezed her hand, and threaded his fingers through hers. "Since Mom died, I've been... I don't know... missing something. Being part of a family, taking care of people. Knowing where I belong. And now you're telling me there's this connection, this boy who shares my blood along with yours. And I want to be part of his life. I want to take care of him. I want to make sure he doesn't miss out on anything."

A sob escaped her lips. She tried to pull her hand from his, but his grip was too tight. "I'm sorry," she said, biting her bottom lip. "I'm being stupid."

"There's nothing stupid about you."

She took a deep breath, trying to ignore the way her chest felt so tight. "I'm not used to this, you know? I've tried so hard to make up for him not having a dad. Tried so hard to be the best mom I can be. But it's so difficult sometimes, being a single parent. I second guess everything I do. I worry and fret and there's nobody to talk to about it. Mom and Dad have never been the sharing types. And Ember and Ally don't really understand, even though they care about us both." As she talked about it, he realized how lonely it could be.

"You're an amazing single mom," he said, his voice gentle. "I'm the product of a single mom, too, remember? I saw what she went through trying to bring us up, keep a roof over our heads. I've got nothing but respect for you."

The way he was looking at her made her skin tingle. If she wasn't careful, she was going to do something she'd regret. Pulling her hand from his, she ran her hand through her hair. "Let's tell him tomorrow."

"Okay." The warmth in his eyes confused her. He was a friend, but she found herself wanting so much more. And when he smiled at her, and those dimples appeared on his unshaven cheeks, she had to ball her hands into fists to stop from touching him.

Because this man with his strong muscles and a kind heart was almost impossible to resist.

❦ 15 ❦

Brooke left the Faculty of Veterinary and Animal Sciences Building, heading down to the parking lot where she'd left her old Nissan. She blinked as she emerged onto the front steps, the brightness of the sun causing momentary blindness. Slowly, her vision reappeared, her eyes focusing on the steps in front of her.

Her mom stepped forward, making Brooke jump. Her face was a mask of determination. "We need to talk," she said, folding her arms across her designer jacket. Brooke knew that look all too well.

It was too late to dart back inside, through the safety of the security doors. Too late to pretend she hadn't seen her, and veer to the left to avoid another awkward conversation.

"Not now, Mom. I'll be late to pick up Nick."

"We can talk in the car. Frederick is over there." Her mom pointed at the black town car, so out of place among the old compacts and newer sporty numbers, depending on which social strata the local college students found themselves in. "I've been calling you for days, and you won't pick up. So I called Ember and she wouldn't tell me where you're staying."

Lilian lowered her voice. "You're not staying with *him*, are you?"

Brooke sighed. She so wasn't ready to have this conversation. Especially on the stairs of the university building, surrounded by students she studied with every day. "I can't come with you in the car," she said, her voice patient in spite of her frustration. "My own car's in the lot. Plus Nick has swimming lessons today, so we're heading straight there." She started to walk down the stairs. Her mother followed her, a step behind. She could see her shadow moving.

"At least tell me you and Nick are okay. I've been worried to death about you. We both have. The way you left was so childish. I can't understand you putting your son in danger like that."

Brooke stopped short. "I'd never put Nick in danger. *Never*. We stayed with friends for a few days, and now we have our own place. We're both fine." And she'd already said more than she intended to. Damn, her mother was good.

She took long strides across the concrete path, her mother's shoes clicking as she struggled to keep up. This was so stupid and embarrassing. She felt about five years old.

"Where are you living? We need to know for insurance purposes. And what if something happens to you? Who's going to help you?" Her mom was panting between words. "Will you slow down for a minute? Let me talk to you, for goodness sake."

Dear God, she wasn't going to let it go, was she? Biting back a groan, Brooke stopped and turned to look at her mom. She was standing about five feet away, her hands on her thighs, trying to catch her breath. Brooke tried to ignore the guilt tapping at her brain, pushing all the buttons her parents installed from birth.

She's your mother, she demands respect.
He's your father, he knows best.

You're a child, Brooke. Let us make the decisions.

Dammit, they were like fruit flies, buzzing around, distracting her. Impossible to swat away.

"We're both fine. We're in an apartment near Silver Sands. It's clean, it's nice, and it's close to the bay. What else do you want to know?"

"How are you paying for it?"

"That's none of your business."

"But it *is* my business. You're my daughter, and Nick is my grandson. If you're getting into debt, it could reflect badly on us. Or if you're doing something..." she lowered her voice, "illegal or immoral."

Brooke laughed, shaking her head. "Are you asking me if I'm turning tricks to pay the rent?"

"Brooke! Stop it." Lilian looked around to see if anybody was listening. "You shouldn't make jokes like that."

Funny thing was, she wasn't really joking. She wouldn't put it past her mom to suspect that. Everything about this conversation was making her want to scream.

"What illegal or immoral things do you think I'm up to?" Brooke asked her.

Lilian shook her head. "Stop evading the question. How are you paying for your apartment?"

"With the money I've saved from working every spare moment I've had." There, she'd said it. And she was annoyed at herself all over again.

"And the furniture? How did you pay for that?"

"It's a furnished apartment."

Lilian frowned. "You didn't choose the furniture? Have other people used it? Oh, Brooke." She scrambled in her purse, pulling out her wallet. "At least let me buy you some new beds. You don't know who's been laying on them."

Brooke could feel her jaw begin to ache from biting her tongue for too long. "Mom, I don't need furniture. I don't need anything. We're fine. Thank you." Her words were like rifle shots, staccato and loud.

Lilian blinked, as though the sun had caught her eyes. She had exactly the same expression on her face Nick got when he was reprimanded. Sad, innocent, hurt. "I'm sorry," she said softly. "I only want what's best for you."

Brooke felt her shoulders slump. It was almost impossible to be mad at her mom when she had that expression on her face. She wasn't a bad person. Okay, so she made some bad decisions – helping her dad kick the Black family out of town was one of them – but she had kindness inside her, too.

"I know you want what's best for us," Brooke said. "And I understand you worry about us, but you don't need to. I'm a grown up. I'm perfectly capable of taking care of myself and my child." She licked her lips, trying to ignore the guilt still tugging at her stomach. "I'm really grateful for everything you and Dad have done for me. For us. But it's time I started standing on my own two feet, and making my own decisions."

It was an echo of what she'd said to Aiden, but this time it came out as a plea. Why was it so hard for her mom to understand? All her friends were treated like adults by their parents. Sometimes too much – like when Ally's dad left her to bail out his failing business. But every time Brooke tried to pull away, her parents held on tighter.

Not anymore, though. It was time to cut the ties.

"But the decisions you make aren't always good ones, darling." Her mom pursed her lips, shaking her head sadly. "First, that time with Aiden, and then when you got pregnant with Nick. You were supposed to go to college, to enjoy your teens. But everywhere you went you made wrong choices."

Brooke's mouth felt dry. "But they weren't the wrong choices, because they led me here. They gave me Nick. And look." She gestured at the buildings behind her. "I'm still in school. I'm still achieving what you wanted me to."

"But what about this boy? Ever since he came back you've changed. You won't listen to us, you shout at us. It's all his fault, isn't it?"

"Aiden isn't a boy." And wasn't that the truth.

"Whatever you want to call him, he's a bad influence. He was then, and he is now. You're throwing everything away, Brooke, and it's his fault. He should never have come back here. You would never have talked to Daddy and me the way you did if it wasn't for him."

"This has got nothing to do with Aiden. It's about *me*. My need to live my own life. And yes, he might have been a catalyst for this, but I would have gotten here on my own. You stifle me. You tell me I'm not able to make decisions without you, but you're wrong. I'm an adult. Why can't you let me be one?"

She couldn't look at her mom. She couldn't. Because if she did, she knew she'd see the hurt there, and she'd fold. She'd feel guilty and apologize, and she couldn't bear to do that.

Couldn't bear to let herself be dragged back to the life they wanted her to live. Couldn't bear to give up this future she'd created for herself.

"I'm late to pick up Nick. I need to go. Goodbye, Mom."

"I've had all of the paperwork you requested drawn up." Mark Johnson, Aiden's lawyer, pushed a buff envelope thick with paper over to him. "This is your copy. I want you to read through and let me know if you have any questions. You told me the father is absent, and the mother has primary custody, right?"

"That's correct."

"And have you talked this over with her? You say you want

the child to benefit from the trust at the age of eighteen. Is she happy with that?"

Aiden glanced at the envelope in front of him. "I haven't discussed it with her."

Mark raised an eyebrow. "Is there a reason for that?"

"She doesn't like the thought of me helping her. Said she wants to stand on her own two feet. But if something happens to me, I want to know they're both taken care of."

"And that's where your will comes in. The draft of that is in the envelope as well."

Aiden nodded. "Thank you. And what about the other matter?"

"Your brother?" Mark pushed his glasses up the bridge of his nose, and pulled a green cardboard file folder toward him. The man preferred paper to virtual documents. "As requested, we engaged the services of a private investigator. From what he's ascertained, your brother is still in Clapman Prison. They're considering him for parole next month. Though we have no idea whether it will be granted or not, but all indicators show he's kept his nose clean while he's been incarcerated."

"So there'll be no reason to deny him?" Aiden's chest felt tight. Apart from seeing him at their mom's funeral, he hadn't heard from Jamie in years. Hadn't wanted to. There was nothing between them except DNA, and he preferred to keep it that way.

"Did you look into his rights as a father?" Aiden asked. Mark cleared his throat, looking through the piles of paper on his desk. "The first thing I did was check the birth certificate. There's no father listed. But all he'll need is a simple DNA test to assert his rights."

Aiden felt his blood run cold. "And what exactly are those rights?"

"As a father, he has the right to petition the court for

custody. Whether it's every other weekend, joint, or full. He also has the right to make decisions on medical treatment, welfare, and educational matters."

Aiden shook his head. "You can't be serious. We're talking about an eight year old kid who's never laid eyes on this man. You're saying my brother has rights even if he's never bothered to meet him? Even if he's been in jail for years?" He couldn't believe that was true. There had to be a mistake.

"He could argue that the exact reason he hasn't seen the child was because he was incarcerated," Mark pointed out. "Courts in California look at what's in the best interests of the child, and usually that best interest includes having both parents in their lives."

"Even if one parent is a drug dealer and a felon?"

Mark shrugged. "They'll take that into account, but they'll also take into account the fact he's paid for his crime and has been rehabilitated into society. Just because you're a criminal doesn't mean you're a bad parent. I'm sorry, Aiden, but that's the law."

The thought of Nick having to spend time with Jamie made Aiden want to hit something. The last time he'd seen his brother before he was arrested, he'd come around begging for money. When Aiden had refused, Jamie had come back later, and begged their mother for help instead. When she'd told him she had nothing to give him, he'd ransacked the house like a madman, stealing her jewelry and phone. Everything he could find.

And the courts might give a man like that access to Nick? It made him want to vomit.

"So what can I do to stop him?" Aiden asked.

"Honestly? You're best off waiting and seeing. He probably won't want anything to do with his child. After all, he's not bothered to contact the mother at all in the past eight years. There would be no reason for him to do so now."

Unless he heard Aiden was around. Or stopped to consider that Brooke had access to her parents, who were the richest couple in Angel Sands.

"And if he does come here and demand his son?"

"If he does, you can come back and talk to me," Mark said. "I can't promise anything, but I'll help you and the mother fight it all the way." He lowered his voice. "But you have to be prepared that he'll get some level of custody, and he'll definitely get the right to make decisions. Your best hope is that he doesn't come around, or if he does, he signs away his rights."

Aiden slumped back in his chair, defeated. If Brooke knew any of this – if she even had an inkling that Jamie might come back – she'd panic like crazy. She'd been bad enough when she'd thought they were homeless. God only knew what her reaction would be if Jamie asserted his rights. Damn, she'd be a mess.

He couldn't let that happen.

"I want you to keep the PI on retainer. Ask him to monitor the parole board, and let me know the outcome of any application for release. And if Jamie gets out, I want to know every move he makes. I can't take the risk he might come back here."

Mark scribbled a note on the legal pad in front of him, and nodded, looking back up at Aiden. "Of course. When he gets out, you'll be the first to know."

❧ 16 ❧

Brooke leaned back on her chair and looked out toward the ocean. The coffee shop was bursting with customers, and Ally was behind the counter, her face beaming as she dealt with every order. It was such a change of sight compared to that of a few months ago, when the Beach Café had been like a ghost town. But thanks to Ally and Nate's hard work, the newly renamed Coastal Coffee had become a big meeting point in Angel Sands – and finding a table on the deck like this one was like discovering a shining nugget in the gold rush.

"There you go. A latte for you and an Americano for me." Ember slid the tray onto the table and pulled out a chair. "Ally's swamped in there, but I've never seen her happier. Isn't Nate a great guy?"

He really was. Since the day he'd walked into town having bought the Beach Café from Ally's dad, he'd transformed their friend's life. Although both Nate and Ally had fought against the attraction between them, their getting together had been inevitable as far as Brooke and Ember were concerned.

"Talking of great guys, how's Lucas?" Brooke asked.

"He's working today. But off tomorrow." Ember grinned. "He has this idea we're going to spend all day in bed, but I've already written us a to-do list."

"I've got a feeling he's gonna put that list where the sun don't shine."

"I'd like to see him try."

Like Nate and Ally, Ember and Lucas were a great couple. Brooke felt warmth wash over her as she saw how content her friend looked. They both deserved happiness, and she was delighted for them.

Even if sometimes it made her feel a little lonely herself.

"So I got you a gift." Ember leaned down and pulled a prettily-wrapped square from her purse. "For the new apartment."

"You shouldn't have." Brooke's eyes were warm as she looked at Ember. "But I love it already."

"You don't know what it is."

"Doesn't matter. You always have good taste."

Ember raised her brows. "Don't tell Lucas that. You'll give him a big head."

Brooke grinned as she opened the gift. Her favorite set of candles – blue and white and smelling of the ocean. "It's perfect. Thank you."

"I thought you deserved a moving in gift, after everything you've been through." Ember moved closer. "And how's Uncle Aiden doing?" She wiggled her eyebrows. "I hear he's smitten."

"I think Nick's smitten, too," Brooke admitted. "Especially now that he knows Aiden's his uncle."

"You told him?" Ember leaned forward, her eyes wide, her chin propped onto her upturned palms. "When? How? I need details."

"A couple of days ago." Brooke blew out a mouthful of air.

She still wasn't over the anxiety of it all yet. "We took him out for ice cream and explained that Aiden is his daddy's brother." She pulled her bottom lip between her teeth as she remembered the conversation.

"You know my daddy?" Nick asked.

"Yes. But I haven't seen him in a long time," Aiden said, his expression serious. "He's not a good man."

Nick had blinked, two lines appearing on the bridge of his nose as though he was concentrating on something. "But you're not bad, are you?" He glanced over at Brooke. "Aiden's good, right, Mom?"

She nodded. "Yes, sweetheart, Aiden's a good man. And he wants to be a good uncle, too, if you'll let him."

Nick had stared at her for a moment, before his solemn gaze moved to Aiden. "I've never had an uncle before. I don't know what they do."

Brooke could see Aiden trying to bite down a smile. "Lucas is like an uncle," she said to her son. "He plays with you, he talks with you. He loves you."

"I love Lucas, too." He nodded slowly. "Does that mean I can call you Uncle Aiden?"

"Yeah." Aiden's voice was gruff. "But only if you want to."

"I think I do." Nick dipped his spoon into the mound of pink and white ice cream piled in his bowl, scooping it up and lifting it to his lips. "Mom, where does the sun go at night?" he asked before closing his lips around the spoon.

She glanced at Aiden who was staring straight at her. Shrugging, she brought her attention back to her son. "It doesn't go anywhere," she said, trying not to grin at his abrupt change in conversation. She knew her boy well enough to understand he'd had enough information about his family, at least for now. He wanted time to take it in before talking about it again. "The sun stays in the same place, it's us who moves."

"How did he take it?" Ember took a sip of her coffee and placed the cup down on the table.

"He was fine. He's asked a few questions since, but nothing more. I think he's still taking it all in."

They both turned to look at Nick, who was drinking soda from a cup and straw, as he sat on the beach next to one of his school friends. The two of them were in deep conversation, their heads so close to each other their hair was touching.

"And what do your parents have to say about it?"

Brooke caught her friend's eye. Ember knew the Newtons well. She'd spent enough time at Brooke's house over the years. From birthday parties and sleepovers, to dinner dates and cocktail parties, the Newton house had been like a second home to Brooke's friends. And though both Ally and Ember had the Lillian Newton seal of approval, they both knew Brooke's parents weren't always as supportive as they could be.

"They don't know yet," Brooke admitted.

"That you've told Nick?"

Brooke slowly shook her head. "I haven't told them a thing. Not about Jamie being Nick's dad, or Aiden being his uncle."

"Oh." Ember brought her hand to her mouth. "Brooke, don't you think you should tell them? Now that Nick knows..."

Brooke nodded her head. "I know I should. But there hasn't been a right time."

"Maybe the wrong time will have to do." Ember wrinkled her nose. "If I know your mom and dad, it will be a hundred times worse if the news comes from somebody else but you."

"I know." Brooke lowered her head into her hands. "None of this was planned. A few weeks ago I thought I had everything covered. I was going to graduate, move out with Nick, things were going to be easy." And then Aiden came along and her world was tipped upside down. All the secrets she'd buried for so long were rising to the surface, demanding to be heard. She lifted her head and took a deep breath. "Anyway, they're away on vacation, so there's no way of telling them. And as soon as they're back it's the Charity Gala. I'll tell them after that."

"I'd forgotten all about the gala. I need to choose a dress." Ember grimaced. She'd never been one for dressing up – preferring shorts and a t-shirt to an evening gown.

"On the plus side, at least you'll get to see Lucas in a tux," Brooke pointed out. Ember grinned at her words. "And if you can't find anything, I have hundreds of dresses still hanging in my closet back at my parents' house. I'm pretty sure they'd fit you perfectly."

"How are the arrangements going?"

"Good I think. Clara has it all under control. All the tables are sold and we have some amazing auction items. Hopefully we'll be able to raise a lot of money for the shelter."

"It'll be a fun night," Ember said, though her tone wasn't as certain as her words.

Brooke laughed. "Yeah, sure. Keep saying that and we both might believe it."

"At least it's for a good cause."

"That's why we're going. And afterward we won't have to think about it for another year."

A dark shadow passed over the deck, landing on the metal table in front of them. Brooke looked up to see who it was, and felt herself blush as she recognized the man.

He was dressed in a suit again, the dark wool complimenting his warm complexion. His tie was loose, his top button unfastened, and his sunglasses were pushed on his head.

"Speak of the devil and he will appear," Ember said under her breath.

But he didn't look like a devil. He looked glorious. There weren't many men who could carry a suit off as well as he did. There weren't many men who could carry casual off like Aiden, either. Brooke tried to calm her racing heart, annoyed at herself for the way she reacted to him.

He was Nick's uncle. That was all.

"Hey." He looked bemused to see them both staring up at him. "Everything okay?"

"Hi." Brooke smiled at him, the corners of her eyes crinkling. "What are you doing here?"

"I've got a meeting with Nate. We're talking about opening a Coastal Café in the resort." Aiden glanced inside the coffee shop. "I thought I'd come over here instead of him coming to the resort since they're so busy." He looked around the deck. "Is Nick here?"

"He's on the beach with a friend."

Aiden followed her gaze. His entire stance seemed to relax when he saw the two of them building a sandcastle. "I'll say hi on my way out." He turned to Ember. "Hey, how are you doing?"

"I'm good." She shaded her eyes from the sun as she looked up at him. "And you?"

"Yeah, great." He looked totally at ease as he stood there, talking to her friend. As though he was another one of the gang. Brooke felt her heart ache at the thought – she wanted him to be exactly that.

Slowly, he turned to look at Brooke, blinking when he realized she was staring straight at him. And there was a fizzing in the air again. A frisson of excitement only the two of them could feel.

"Are you and Nick free tomorrow?" he asked her.

"Um, yeah. I think so." She bit the corner of her lip, trying to stop her blush from deepening. Over his shoulder she could see Ember smiling widely. "I'm pretty much unpacked, and I'm not due at the shelter until Monday."

"Great, I'll pick you guys up at nine. Wear layers, it could get cold out there."

"Out where?"

He shook his head, grinning. "It's a surprise."

"For me or for Nick?" She met his gaze, feeling a smile break out on her face, mirroring his. "Because I promise not to tell."

"For both of you. Be ready at nine, I'll do the rest." He glanced at his expensive silver watch. "I'd better go. I'm already late for Nate. I'll see you tomorrow, okay?"

She nodded, trying to ignore the excitement in her stomach. "Okay."

He leaned forward and kissed her cheek. Her breath caught in her throat as he stepped back. She couldn't help but lift her hand to her face, feeling the hot skin burning beneath her palm.

He walked into the coffee shop, the door tinkling behind him. Brooke stared through the window, watching as he walked toward the counter where Nate was waiting for him. The two of them smiled at each other as they shook hands. Brooke watched as the movement pulled his shirt tight across his back, revealing the strength of his muscles. She had to work hard not to sigh.

"Nothing going on at all between you two, huh?" Ember said. "Let's see how long that lasts."

Aiden closed his laptop down and drank the last dregs of coffee, not noticing it was only lukewarm. While he was working the sun had set, only a thin line of light remained on the horizon, as the day lost its battle against the encroaching night.

He lifted his hand to the bridge of his nose, pinching it to try and relieve the pressure in his head. Ever since his meeting with Mark Johnson there had been a persistent ache in his temples, and neither painkillers nor sleep seemed to ease it. There was that feeling in the pit of his stomach, too, and it always seemed to get worse whenever his brother's name was mentioned.

Jamie. The thought of him touching Brooke – beautiful, perfect Brooke – felt like a knife jabbing at his skin. Where Brooke had always felt like the sunshine of his life, Jamie had been the darkness, casting a shadow over everything. For all his life he'd believed they were in completely separate compartments, never coming close to each other.

How wrong he'd been.

The girl he should never have fallen for and the brother he couldn't stand. And now there was Nick to think about, too.

He lifted his head, his gaze falling on the silver photograph frame perched on the corner of his desk. Behind the glass was an image of a young woman with dark hair and eyes that seemed to sparkle in spite of the life she'd had to lead. Her right hand was resting on her swollen stomach, her left lifted in a wave to whoever was taking the photograph. His father, maybe? Aiden found it hard to believe. When he was alive, his father didn't have a sentimental bone in his body – and no time for things such as photographs. He was too busy drinking and fighting to care about memories.

Anyway, he'd never seen his mom smile at his father the way she was smiling in this picture.

Damn, he missed her. He closed his eyes for a moment, trying to imagine her expression if she'd known Nicholas was her grandson. She'd always loved Brooke – even after Martin had thrown them out, she wouldn't hear a word said against them. The Newtons were like gods to her. She'd probably have thought she wasn't worthy to be a grandparent to a Newton child.

"But you were worthy," he whispered, his voice thick with emotion. As far as he was concerned, she was more worthy than any of them. There was more goodness in Joan Black's bones than in the whole of this town.

Apart from Brooke.

God, he'd wanted to hate her as much as he hated her parents. He hadn't banked on her being more beautiful than he remembered, nor on her being kinder and brighter, too. And all those emotions they'd felt as teenagers – the ones that had led to long evenings with her curled up in his arms as she'd talked about school and he'd told her about college and they'd made plans for a future which could never exist. They were coming back, but this time they were adult emotions. Not the sweet whispers of adolescence. Every time he saw her there was this pull toward her, and he wasn't sure how long he could hold out against it.

He wasn't sure if he wanted to, either.

❧ 17 ❧

"We're going whale watching?" Brooke looked up at the big wooden boat ahead of them, *The Ocean Explorer* painted in blue and red on the bright white hull. It was bobbing softly in the water, the side occasionally crashing against the metal gangplank connecting the boat to the harbor. Beside her, Nick gasped, and she looked down to see his wide eyes and even wider smile.

"Whales? Sweet! Are they killer ones?"

Aiden lifted his mirrored aviators from his face, and grinned at his nephew. "Maybe, but there are no guarantees. There should be plenty of humpbacks and orcas, though. And they say the dolphins practically climb on board to say hello."

"That's so cool."

"Is this okay?" Aiden asked quietly, so only Brooke could hear. "I checked the safety details and we should be fine. The rails are high, and all the kids get a lifejacket to wear. I won't let anything happen to him."

"It's more than okay. Nick loves whales. How did you know?"

"We were talking about them the other night. He said he'd love to see them close up. I wanted to make it happen."

"You're fast becoming his favorite uncle."

"I'm his only uncle." His lips pulled up into a smile.

"Then you're doing fine." She grinned right back at him.

As they climbed on board, Griff came to greet them. He'd been captain of the whaling boat for the past five years, taking over from his father before him. She couldn't remember a time when there hadn't been whale tours launching from Paxton's Pier. They were as much a part of Angel Sands as Frank Megassey's hardware store.

As soon as he saw her, Griff leaned forward to hug her, pulling at her pony tail to mess with her. He high-fived Nick, who was already overwhelmed by the boat – being in contact with the captain made him turn silent for a minute.

"How're you doing?" Griff asked her. "Long time no see. They must be working you too hard at school." Griff had never gone to college. He'd been a surfing prodigy and had done the circuit for a few years, before settling back in Angel Sands. Nowadays he surfed for fun.

"I'm busy as always." Brooke grinned at him, so pleased to see a friendly face. "Do you remember Aiden from Lucas and Ember's party? He's a friend of mine."

"He's my uncle," Nick said, finally finding his voice. "My *Uncle Aiden*."

Griff reached his hand out to Aiden. "Yeah, I remember. It's good to see you again. You work at the resort, right?"

"That's right." Aiden took his hand, shaking it firmly.

Griff touched the peak of his captain's hat. "Well it's good to have you on board. Now go and get yourselves comfortable, and little guy, you need to put this on." He handed Nick a bright yellow life jacket. "We'll be pulling out in about ten minutes. Once we're on our way, how about you come and sit in the pilot's seat with me?"

"Can I?" Nick's face lit up. "Is that allowed?"

"I'm the captain of this ship. If I say it's okay, then it is." Griff winked at him.

Twenty minutes later they were leaning on the rails, feeling the warm salty air blow against their faces. Behind them, Angel Sands was disappearing into the distance. The sun was casting a thick line of gold across the blue ocean, as the occasional wave broke the peaceful water. Motoring out of the harbor, they'd already seen sea lions and harbor lions, as well as a fat otter lazing out on a rock. Nick's eyes were searching this way and that, taking everything in. She could feel the excitement vibrating out of him.

"We need your help, folks. One of the first signs of a whale is the blow spout," the tour guide told them. "Keep searching for it, and if you see it, shout. We'll turn the boat toward it."

That was music to Nick's ears. He took it as a command, refusing to do anything but scan the water.

"This was a great idea. Thank you." She shot Aiden a smile. He'd perfected the casual look; with a pair of jeans, a black t-shirt, and a pair of aviators. With the ocean breeze in his hair he could be part of a cologne commercial. She wasn't the only one who noticed, either; there was a group of girls – tourists – in the corner who hadn't been able to take their eyes off him. Every time he turned, she could hear them giggle.

"I've got a few years to make up for. You can expect more trips like this." He looked down at Nick, who was still rapt, staring at the ocean, before he glanced back at Brooke. "If that's okay with you."

"You don't need to keep asking. He's your family, too."

Aiden's smile grew wider. She liked what she saw.

There was another boy on board, a few years older than Nick. From the looks of it, he was with his father. "Dad, is that a blow hole?" he shouted, clearly excited by what he could see.

"Nope, only a wave."

Nick frowned, turning his head for a moment. It was the first time he'd stopped looking at the ocean. He turned to Aiden and took his hand, folding his small fingers around Aiden's longer ones. "Uncle Aiden, will you look with me? See if we can spot a whale?"

Aiden's eyes were soft as he hunkered down next to Nick. "Sure. Let's see what's out there."

Brooke stood back for a moment, watching as the two of them scanned the ocean ahead. Their heads were pressed together, dark hair mingling with dark hair. Aiden had his arm casually slung around Nick's back as he pointed something out with his free hand, talking softly so only Nick could hear.

Seeing them together was the most delicious torture she'd ever felt. As though everything she really wanted was so close – near enough to almost taste – and yet it was an illusion. She wanted to pick it up and play with it, twist and pull until it became real.

She shook her head, trying to bring herself back to reality. Nick called out, his entire body shaking as he jumped up and down. "I see it, I see it. Look!" She followed his arm, pointing to a blow spout in the distance. The water puffed up, as if by magic, no sign of the majestic animal beneath.

"You got it, little buddy," the tour guide said, high fiving him. She moved her radio up to her lips. "Captain, we spot humpbacks at ten o'clock."

It was late afternoon by the time the boat headed back

toward the bay. Nick was laying on the bench seat in the cabin of the boat, exhausted from a combination of excitement and the heat of the sun, not to mention the salty ocean air. Brooke was next to him, with Aiden on her other side. Like Nick, she could feel her body starting to soften and relax.

"He had such a good time," she told Aiden. "I'm not sure what he liked most, spotting the whales or Griff letting him steer the boat." Or being with his uncle. She was liking that part, too.

Aiden stretched his arm along the backrest, until it was behind her. Without thinking, she leaned into him, feeling his hard body against hers. She heard his breath catch for a second, before he curled his arm around her, his palm strong against her shoulder.

"I'm glad he enjoyed it. I would have loved to come out and look for whales at his age. We used to do it from the shore all the time."

"I wish I'd known. I'd have bought you a ticket."

He chuckled. "You were a kid, too. And by the time I was a teenager, I had my mind on other things."

She could feel her heart start to speed up. "I guess we all did when we were young. I blame the hormones."

He was stroking her arm, his finger moving up and down her bare skin. It was making her entire body tingle. Did he realize what he was doing, or was it an absentminded gesture? She couldn't bear to look up, or move, for fear he would stop. It felt way too good for that.

"I kind of liked the hormones," Aiden said, his voice low. "They made me brave. Made me do things I would have been too scared to do otherwise. Made me flirt with girls who were out of my league."

She licked her lips, dry and salty from the sun. "You never told me about them."

Another chuckle made his body shake. "That's because you *were* them."

"You thought I was out of your league?" she asked, shocked.

"Brooke, you were out of my stratosphere."

She felt giddy at his words. As though she'd stepped off a rollercoaster and the world was still spinning. His fingers were still tracing lines up and down her arm, leaving a trail of fire behind them. "I always thought you were the one who was too good for me. I was this annoying kid, following you around everywhere. I must have been infuriating."

"Yeah, but that was before *that* summer. I came home and you were all grown up. And I didn't mind you following me around any more. I wanted it, the same way I wanted you."

Was it possible for a body to explode? The way her chest ached – as though it was so full of emotion it could burst – made her think it might be. Sitting there against his hard, strong body she felt like a teenage girl again, the one who followed the college boy around, asked him questions about his classes, and asked for his help with her horses. Anything to keep his attention.

Until he noticed her. *Really* noticed her.

And she hadn't been the lovesick puppy any more. She was a girl in love with a boy so much it made her heart sing. She'd been obsessed with him the same way he'd been with her. And that summer it was as though there was nobody else in Angel Sands except Aiden Black. They'd made the town their own, sneaking down to the cove to make out on the rocks, buying separate tickets for the movie theater, then snuggling down together inside. Making eyes at each other across the counter at the Beach Café, neither of them saying a word.

There were times he'd sneak into her room. Climbing over that damn tree and using the blanket of night to find her. He'd held her in his strong arms as they talked for hours, making up stories about their future, stories she really thought would come true. And when the words ran out, the kisses would begin. Soft at first, then heated, until her whole body felt like it would burst into a ball of flames. And she'd begged him to finish what he'd started, to make her his the only way he could. To seal their promises with the one thing they could never take away. But he'd resisted, telling her they should wait, they shouldn't have their first time in her parents' house. That he wanted to be certain she wanted him as much as he wanted her. Somehow, his chivalry had only deepened her love for him. It hadn't stopped her from trying, though.

Until that heartwrenching night when everything changed.

"Mom, can I stay over at Uncle Aiden's tonight?" Nick's sleepy voice brought her out of her thoughts. Aiden's hand froze on her arm. "Owen always goes to his dad's on Saturdays. They call it boys' night. I want a boys' night."

For the first time since he'd started touching her, she turned to look at Aiden. His eyes were dark, his expression serious. Their stare lasted a second too long, enough to send her heart pounding once again.

"I don't know..."

"He can stay if it's okay with you." Aiden's voice was rough. "I have a spare room."

Her body was still stuck in the after-effects of their conversation and his touch. Pulses of electricity were shooting beneath her skin, making her feel tender and raw. "It's okay with me."

"You can drink beer, if you want," Nick said, suddenly awake. "Owen's dad does. And they eat pizza and watch movies. His dad's really cool. Like you."

Reluctantly, she pulled away from Aiden's embrace, her

skin turning cold where he'd been touching it only a moment before. She took a deep breath, trying to center herself. "I'll pack you a bag with your things," she said, smiling at Nick. "But you have to promise to do what you're told. When Aiden says it's bedtime, it's bedtime. No messing around, okay?"

Nick was the picture of innocence. His eyes were wide, his bottom lip dropped open. "Of course," he agreed, sneaking a smile at Aiden. "Anything you say, Mom."

❧ 18 ❧

B rooke sat at her compact kitchen table, legs curled up underneath her, as she reached up to check her messy bun. After dropping Nick's bag off at Aiden's house, she'd come home and showered, pulling on an old pair of shorts and a t-shirt, since she wasn't planning on going anywhere. Her latest assignment was in front of her, and she was going through her tutor's comments with a pen in her right hand, scribbling notes on the lined pad beside her.

It was getting harder to concentrate. She was so tired, yet she couldn't switch her mind off. Each time she tried, he'd claw his way into her thoughts again. She remembered the way his fingers had felt as they caressed her skin. Did he know he was setting her on fire? He had to, right? You didn't touch somebody like that without meaning it.

She tapped her pen against her lip, remembering what he'd said. That she was out of his stratosphere, but he wanted her anyway. She couldn't help but think the tide had changed now. She was the one who was punching above her weight – the poor student batting her eyelashes at the rich businessman. She was the one doing the wanting, too. She could feel the tingles right down to the tips of her toes.

It was clear she wasn't going to get any work done, so she pushed the books closed, piling them up on each other to put them away on the shelf. As she was about to close down her laptop, her phone began to buzz. Glancing down at the vibrating device, she saw Ember's picture appear on the screen and she picked it up, swiping her finger to accept the call.

"Hey."

"Hey, how did today go?"

She'd forgotten Ember had been there when Aiden had made arrangements for today. "It was really good. We went out on a whale tour. Nick went crazy over it."

"I know." Ember sounded smug. "Griff told me." She cleared her throat. "Well, he told Lucas who told me, which is the same thing."

"What else did Griff say?" Brooke asked. The grapevine seemed to be working faster than usual. A glance at her watch told her it was only a few hours since they'd left the boat, yet word was already spreading. She felt her cheeks heat up at the thought of being the subject of gossip.

Been there, done that. She didn't want to do it again.

"Only that you and a certain... um... old flame were looking mighty close. His exact words were 'you couldn't pry them apart with a tire iron'."

Brooke didn't know whether to laugh or cry. How she and Aiden had kept things quiet all those years ago, she'd never know. Maybe technology had been their friend – or rather the lack of it. Nowadays you were only a swipe of a finger away from having your secrets unleashed on the world. "We're friends. We have Nick in common." She wasn't ready to admit her feelings to her friend. She was barely ready to admit them to herself.

"That's not what Griff saw."

"You'd believe him over me? I'm devastated." Brooke traced the pattern of wood on the table in front of her. "It doesn't matter anyway. There's no future in it, even if either of us was interested. We have nothing in common."

"Apart from Nick."

"Yeah, apart from him."

"And your shared history."

"Okay. That, too."

"And the fact you're both clearly itching for each other. Every time you're together I can practically hear the fireworks exploding."

Brooke sighed, leaning back in her chair. "Has the shine worn off you and Lucas? Are you so bored you're looking for romance when it's not there? Maybe I should call him and suggest he visit a certain, um, website. Spice things up a bit."

"Well since you ask..." There was a smile in Ember's voice. One which made Brooke sit up straight and take notice. "There's another reason I called you."

"What reason? What's happened?"

"Lucas asked me to marry him. And I said yes, of course." Ember's words tripped over themselves in a breathless tangle. "It was so romantic, Brooke. He got down on one knee in the sand as the sun was setting out over the water. You should see the ring, in fact you probably can see it, it's that big. Look out the window and you'll see the moon reflecting on it."

Brooke laughed. "I'm so happy for you." She really was. The warmth enveloping her had nothing to do with embarrassment this time, and everything to do with pure delight for her friend. "You and Lucas are such a great couple; you're made for each other. Do you know when you're going to do the deed?"

"I'm thinking over winter break. That will give us enough

time to have a short honeymoon too. And of course I want you and Ally to be my bridesmaids."

"Does Ally know?"

"Yes. I was worried I was stealing her thunder, since she isn't getting married until next year. But she promised me I wasn't." There was a pause. "I'm not, am I? I don't want to upset anybody."

"Of course you're not. Ally and Nate always said they wanted a long engagement. They aren't going to rush anything because of Riley, remember. Whereas you and Lucas don't have to worry about any children..." Brooke trailed off, a thought occurring to her. "Unless there's something you're not telling me?"

"I'm not pregnant, you goof." Ember chuckled. Brooke could picture her shaking her head. "Not yet, anyway. Maybe some time."

"You'll make awesome parents. I can picture it now, Lucas will probably get your children surfing before they can even walk."

"We're talking about Mr. Safety here. I don't think he'll ever let them surf." Ember's voice was warm as she talked about her fiancé. "Oh, Brooke, I'm so happy. I didn't think getting engaged would change anything but it has. It's made me feel more in love with Lucas than ever. No wonder Ally always has a smile on her face." After another pause, Ember added, "I wish you could have this too."

"Hey, I'm happy enough. I have my work, and Nick. That's all I need."

"Is it?"

Brooke blinked, thinking over her friend's question. A few months ago she would have answered 'yes' right away. Her life was on the up. She'd finish her degree soon and be able to work as a veterinary technician. Nick was settled and enjoying school. Independence from her family was only a breath away.

But now? She felt like the ocean after a rare storm – full of sand and water all mixed up and murky. She couldn't see through it, but she had to keep swimming, hoping for the best. It would be stupid to pretend Aiden wasn't a big cause of her confusion. Having him back in her life was such sweet agony.

"Yes," she replied to Ember.

"Oh honey, when are you going to do something about Aiden?" It was as if Ember was completely ignoring Brooke's words, only concentrating on the tone underlying them.

"I'm not, I can't."

"But he's gorgeous and he's available and he's into you," Ember blurted out.

"Look where that got me last time." Her phone beeped, alerting her to another call. Frowning, she pulled it away from her ear, glancing at the screen to see who it was.

"Ember, Aiden's calling. I need to take it. Nick's with him."

"No problem, I'll talk to you later."

"Is he okay?" Brooke was breathless when he opened the door. "I got here as soon as I could." She hadn't needed to knock or ring the bell, the sweep of her headlights across the darkened room as she pulled in was enough to alert him to her presence. And now she was standing on his front step, wearing an old pair of shorts and a t-shirt that was way too big for her, her hair pulled away from her face revealing freshly scrubbed skin. She smelled of summer fruits – sweet and edible – as though she'd stepped out of the shower.

"He went back to sleep." Aiden grimaced. "I swear he was

inconsolable. Kept talking about his nightmare and the sharks eating you. He wouldn't rest until I called you."

Her face fell. "He fell asleep? Should I leave?" The full moon was shining down on her, making her face look almost ethereal.

"No." His response was almost immediate. "You should come in. He might wake up again."

She rolled her lip between her teeth, nodding. "I *would* like to check on him, if that's okay with you." Aiden stepped aside, letting her pass him in the doorway. She brushed against him, and his body responded to the soft touch. Did she know she had this effect on him?

Nick was in the first bedroom on the left. She peered around the doorway into the gloomy space, lit only by a nightlight on the far corner. Aiden stopped behind her, resting his hand lightly on her shoulder. Her breathing was still rapid, as though she still hadn't caught it yet. He could feel her lean back into him, her slight body pressed against his muscled torso. "I'm sorry if he's been a pain," she whispered. "He doesn't normally have nightmares."

"He's not a pain," Aiden whispered, his lips close to her ear. "I felt bad because I couldn't console him. He wanted you."

"He'll be devastated if he can't stay over again. He was so excited to spend 'man time' with you."

"Why wouldn't he stay over again?" Aiden frowned.

She turned to look at him, her body twisting against his. "I thought he might be too much for you. He doesn't have a lot of sleepovers. Only with a few friends. I know kids aren't easy, and you haven't had much experience with them. Plus there's the peanut allergy. That additional responsibility always puts people off." She grimaced. "Not everybody has your patience."

Aiden winced. "There's only one way to get experience,

and that's by doing it. I like having him over. I like spending time with him. He's family."

Her face softened, the same way it always did when she spoke about her son. "He likes spending time with you, too."

He could feel the muscles in his arm twitch. He wanted to hold her, to touch her the way he'd touched her on the boat. The sensation of her soft skin against the rough pads of his fingers had felt like heaven.

"Would you like a cup of coffee?" he asked her, his voice low and rough. "Maybe you could hang around for a bit to make sure he doesn't wake up again? That's if you have the time."

"Coffee sounds great." She followed him to the kitchen, where he filled up the coffee pot and pulled out white ceramic mugs he kept in the cupboard over the stove top. From the corner of his eye he could see her lean on the counter, her eyes hooded with worry. He wanted to smooth away the lines between her brows. She worried constantly about her son, he knew that much. Maybe it was time somebody took some of the burden off her.

He gestured for her to go through to the living room while the coffee pot spluttered away. By the time he'd poured the hot liquid into the mugs – followed by a dash of cream, the way she liked it – she was sitting on his cream leather sofa, her bare legs curled up beneath her. She was staring out of the window to the beach beyond, her eyes taking on a faraway look.

He slid the mugs onto the coffee table, sitting down next to her. Was he too close? It was hard to tell, especially when he never felt close enough.

Aiden wasn't sure when his interest in Brooke had gone from being purely friendly to wanting more since their reunion. Maybe it had never been about friendship. From the moment he'd seen her saving the dog it had been as though something inside him was switched back on. A long-neglected fire that had somehow sparked back into life. And now it was burning him from the inside out, and the only person who could stop it was her.

"I love this view," she said, her voice soft, as she lifted the mug to her pink lips. "You must sit here and stare out of it all the time. It could never get boring."

Aiden shifted in his seat, following her gaze. "I'd forgotten how beautiful the coastline is. Funny how being away for so long can dull things in your mind. Like a faded photograph."

She took a sip from her cup. "Did you miss this town when you left?"

He felt his stomach tighten. It was hard to think about those days, let alone talk about them. "There were aspects that I missed, yes." He looked at her over the rim of his coffee cup. Her eyes were trained on his, her lips pressed together. "But I was angry."

"At my father?" she asked.

"Mostly, yeah. But at the whole town, too, even though it hadn't done anything wrong. But growing up on the wrong side of the tracks, it gives you a chip on your shoulder, you know? Too many people look at you as if you're worth less than the dirt on the soles of their feet."

"I never looked at you like that."

He tried to swallow down the lump in his throat. He never talked about this stuff. *Never.* Now he was breaking all the rules. "I know you didn't. And I never blamed you, not for one minute. But if we'd stayed and your father had told everybody what he was threatening to, they all would have believed him. My mom did nothing wrong, but he was going to make her pay the price for our mistakes."

Her eyes glistened. "I wish I'd known. I never would have let him do that to her. Or to you."

He shook his head, feeling the fire light up again. "You wouldn't have been able to stop him. Nobody could. He has this sense of entitlement that lets him mess up other peoples lives."

"The way he messed up mine," she whispered.

That stopped him in his tracks. He put his empty coffee cup down on the table, turning to face her. A lock of hair had fallen over her eyes. Without thinking, he brushed it from her face, tucking it behind her ear. "He did what he thought was best for you."

"He sent you away," she said, her voice strained. "He lied to me, he hurt me. If it hadn't been for him..." She squeezed her eyes closed for a moment. "God, I won't go down this path. Not again."

Her lip was trembling. It took less than a second for him to reach out, and trace the plumpness of her mouth with his thumb. He expected her to pull him away from her, to stop him from stroking her. Instead, she pressed his palm to her mouth, kissing the rough skin there. The sensation shot straight through him, sending a shiver down his back. She looked at him, her eyes wide, and a single tear formed in the corner of one, threatening to spill over.

"Don't cry." He moved his finger up to wipe away the drop. "Please, don't."

She closed her eyes again, breathing his skin in. "Stay here for a moment. Let me pretend..."

Pretend *what*? That he wanted to touch her, feel her, have her? There was no pretense in that. He leaned forward, needing to inhale her the way she was doing to him. His face was only an inch away from hers. He could feel the warm sweetness of her breath against his skin, could see the way the corners of her lips curled up at his closeness. Her eyes suddenly opened, and he could see the deep blue of her irises, eclipsed by her dilating pupils.

"Aiden..."

He didn't say a word. Instead, he closed the gap between them until the bridge of her nose was against his. She was too close for him to focus. Too close for him to do anything but breathe her in as though she were his last gasp of air.

"Don't move," he said, his voice rough. "Just pretend..."

Her chest hitched. He curled his hand around her neck, feeling her hair still damp from her shower. He ran his thumb slowly up and down, taking in the sensation of skin against skin, enjoying the way the air caught in her throat.

"I'm not pretending," she whispered.

"Nor am I." His voice was strong and sure.

He waited a moment, taking in the overwhelming sensation of her closeness. Every sense he had was full of her. She was the sweetest overdose.

He pulled his hand back to her jaw, running his finger along the edge of her face. He held her, angling her head until his nose slid along hers, and their lips touched with the briefest of touches. She was looking at him, holding her breath as he waited. For what? Her agreement? The way she was looking at him, he knew she was more than willing for him to kiss her.

Maybe it was Aiden who felt afraid. The need for her clawing at his chest felt insatiable. One step further and he'd have been gone. The way he'd been when he was a kid. She owned him, she always had. Even if she didn't know it.

Her mouth parted beneath his, and that was all it took. He pulled her closer, his lips clashing with hers, skin on heated skin. She kissed him back, all strawberries and sweetness, her body arching until her chest pressed against him. She moaned into his mouth, lips trembling, and threaded her arms around his neck. The feel of her body sent a shot of desire straight through him, making him hard, wanting, needing.

"Aiden?"

It only took a moment to realize it wasn't her calling his name. The voice was too young, too distant.

"Are you there?" Nick sounded fearful.

They jumped apart. "Yeah, and your mom's here too. We're coming." He looked back at Brooke. Her eyes were wide, glassy. She lifted a finger to touch her already swollen lips. "We're on our way, honey," she called out. The two of them got up – Brooke shaking as she did – and hurried to Nick's room.

He caught her hand, folding it in his. Before they made it to the bedroom he spoke, his voice raspy and low. "This isn't over."

She glanced at him, her expression questioning.

No, it wasn't over. Not by a long shot. And this time he'd make sure of that.

❧ 19 ❧

"I had a phone call from a guy named Martin Newton last week. He had a lot to say about you." Robert Carter folded his arms across his chest as the two of them stood in the middle of the construction site. Dust swirled around their legs, lifted into the air by the breeze blowing up from the ocean. Not that you could hear the ocean right now – the noise of the diggers and compactors drowned out the crashing waves. They both had to shout to get themselves heard.

"I thought you might," Aiden said. Nine years ago that would have sent him into a tailspin. But he wasn't afraid of Martin Newton any more. The man had no hold over him.

"He told me he could send a lot of business my way if I agreed to let you go." Robert smirked. "That guy really doesn't like you, does he?"

"What did you tell him?"

His old friend shrugged. "Not a lot. I've learned the best way to deal with bullies is to ignore them. And its not as if I need his endorsement. We're not aiming at the business market, we're looking at luxury. That man's small fry."

Aiden tried not to smile at Martin Newton being described like that. The very sound of it would make him throw a fit. Every kid in Angel Sands grew up knowing who he was, after all. Owner of Newton Pharmaceuticals, big cheese at the beach club, a man with a finger in every pie he could find.

But not this pie, apparently. And that made Aiden like his boss even more than he already did.

"I don't want to make any trouble for you. He knows a lot of people around here. Probably could influence the zoning committee. It could end up costing us money."

Robert lifted his dark sunglasses from his face, looking Aiden straight in the eye. "I thought you knew me better than that, son. I don't take bribes and I don't cave to threats. Seems to me like this Newton guy is trying to do a bit of both. I've seen his kind before – a little guy thinking he's king of the castle. But, he's all bluster and no substance. He wants to make an enemy of me? Bring it on." He slid his sunglasses back down. "But I *am* interested in what he had to say about his daughter."

Aiden tried to ignore the dryness in his mouth. "You are?" His voice came out raspy.

"Yeah, is it true you've brainwashed her? Because if I knew you had those skills I would have put you to work years before."

Aiden laughed. "I can tell you've never met Brooke Newton. Nobody could make her do something she doesn't want to do."

The corner of Robert's mouth lifted up. "It sounds as though she might be the one brainwashing you. Want me to call her dad for you?"

Aiden smiled. "I think I can handle her myself."

"Those are famous last words, son. I said the same thing

the day I met my Mary. Turned out she was the one handling me." His boss grinned. "And I loved it."

"Yeah, well there's nothing going on between me and Brooke. I like spending time with her and my nephew. That's all."

"Sure it is."

Aiden tried to bite down the smile pushing at his facial muscles. Robert Carter knew him too well. Because that wasn't all, not by a long shot.

As far as he was concerned, the best was yet to come.

"Did I show you where the mugs are?" Brooke asked, trying to fix the thin gold hoop in her ear as she walked into the kitchen. Cora was there, helping Nick with the assignment he'd forgotten to do.

"You look pretty, Mom," Nick said, looking up at her. His eyes widened as he took her in. "You never wear your hair down. It's nice."

"Gorgeous, as always. That's a lovely dress." Cora's face was beaming.

Brooke looked down at the pale blue sundress she'd put on. Aiden hadn't given her any idea of where they were going. She had no idea whether she should dress up or be casual. At least she could dress this down with a pair of flats and a sweater if she needed to. "Thank you kindly." She gave a mock curtsey. "Are you sure you have everything you need?"

"I really do," Cora said, nodding at her. "And if I can't find something, I'm sure this young man will show me. Now go and have a good evening."

But Brooke lingered for a moment longer. The nerves in her stomach were flying around like butterflies on amphetamine. Maybe because it was the first time Nick had been left with a sitter since they'd moved in here. Or was it the thought of this date with Aiden?

She opened her mouth, taking in a lungful of air, but it did nothing to dampen her nerves. It had been years since she'd been on a first date – even longer since it had progressed into a second. Being the single mother of a small child made relationships difficult.

"Call me if you need anything." She pressed her lips to Nick's head, kissing him in spite of his protests. "And you do what Cora tells you to, okay? Bedtime by nine."

"We'll be fine. Now go," Cora told her.

"I won't be late."

"Be as late as you like. I've got nowhere to be. And it's double time after midnight." Cora grinned. "Seriously, we're all set. Have a lovely time."

"Where are you going again, Mom?"

Brooke opened her mouth to tell him the truth but closed it. She didn't want to give him hope, or to worry him, either. "Out with a friend."

"Have fun."

"I will." She blew him a kiss and grabbed her purse, sliding her feet into her flat sandals. As soon as she reached for the door, her heart started to pound. Agreeing to dinner with Aiden had seemed so simple when he'd asked, but now that she was faced with the reality of it, nerves had taken over. Maybe this date wasn't such a good idea after all.

She'd asked Aiden to pick her up outside, and he'd agreed readily, not asking her why. Maybe he understood more than she thought.

By the time she'd made it out of the apartment building, his dark grey Audi was idling by the sidewalk. As soon as he spotted her he climbed out, a smile lighting up his face. And those damn butterflies started multiplying, making her whole body shiver.

"Hey."

"Hey you." He walked toward her. "You look beautiful." He reached his hand out for her, palm facing upward, his eyes trained on her face. She lay her own hand on top and he folded his fingers around it, his skin warm and rough.

"Are you ready to go?"

She nodded, letting him lead her to the car. He opened the passenger door and she slid in, sitting on the cool leather seat. Closing the door behind her, he walked around and got into the driver's seat. Less than a minute later, they were driving away.

"Is Nick okay?" Aiden asked her.

"He's good. Excited to see Cora again."

"Cora?"

"She's my babysitter. She's known him since he was a baby. I call her my lifesaver sometimes – I'm lucky to have her."

"Didn't your parents babysit when Nick was a baby?" he asked.

"They barely babysat *me*. Why would they babysit my child?" She frowned. "They love Nick, but they don't love babysitting. Luckily, Cora does."

"My mom would've helped if she'd known," he said softly.

There was a lump in her throat. "I know she would have. And I wish she could have. Nick would have loved her."

The air around her suddenly felt melancholy, as though it was full of atoms too heavy to be ignored. She sighed, shaking her head. Tonight wasn't a night for regrets, even if she had way too many. "Where are we going? I hope I'm dressed okay."

From the corner of her eye she saw him glancing down at her legs. "It's a small restaurant on the coast. After, I thought we might go for a walk."

Thank God for the flat shoes. "Sounds lovely."

She looked at him again, taking advantage of the fact he

now had his eyes on the road, steering the car around the curves leading to the cliff top. She could never get enough of looking at him. For years he'd been a ghost in her memory, a man frozen as a boy. But now he was here, and so much better looking than she ever remembered. Time had been kind to his looks – sharpening them, lending them a strength which made her feel protected. His nose was strong, his jaw defined, his cheeks dark with evening growth.

"Are you looking at me?"

She bit her lip, trying not to smile. "I was looking at the view, you happened to be in the way."

"The view's out your window, not mine," he pointed out.

"Do you talk to all your dates like this? Surely you should be flirting with sweet words, not accusing me of staring."

He pursed his lips, eyes still on the road. "Do *you* talk to all *your* dates like this?"

"I don't have a lot of dates."

His eyebrow lifted. "Why not?"

"Because I'm a single mom. Even if that doesn't put guys off, the logistical problems mean I can't get out very often. Plus there's my parents to contend with. It's amazing how many guys turn around at the electric gates and decide it's not worth the effort."

"Their loss."

"That's what I like to think."

"And my gain."

"Is that right?"

Ten minutes later he pulled the car into a graveled lot, outside of a white stucco building, built into the sides of the cliffs. Fifty feet below, the ocean swirled and eddied over brown rocks, the dark water frothing into a white foam where it broke. Within moments he was out of the car, and walking around to open her door, offering his hand as she climbed out.

"You always did have good manners," she said, as he pulled her to standing.

"My momma taught me well."

"That she did." She felt breathless.

"I hope this place is okay. I drove past it the other day, and wanted to try it out."

"It's beautiful. And far enough away from Angel Sands, too."

He grinned. "Yeah, I thought that might help. Didn't want to be bumping into people we knew."

"Not on a first date."

He tipped his head to the side. "Is that what this is? A first date." Three lines appeared on his forehead, as he thought on her words. "It can't be, can it? We've dated before."

"We were kids before. We couldn't afford to date. Not somewhere like this anyway." It wasn't quite the truth. She could have afforded it, but she also would have had to ask her father for the money.

The thought of it made her shiver.

"Dates aren't about affording it. Or money. They're about being together."

"Like those picnics we used to have at the cove." She smiled, remembering the bag full of subs and Cokes.

"Yeah, like those." His voice was soft. He frowned again. "Would you rather do that? Than eat here, I mean?"

"Go to the cove with subs and Cokes?"

"Yeah. Well it doesn't have to be subs. I can ask them to prepare us some food and we can take it down there. That's if you want…"

It was strange to hear him so unsure. And yet it touched her, deep inside. He cared about what she wanted. It had been a long time since anybody had done that.

"I want." Brooke nodded firmly. She couldn't think of something she'd like better.

The sun was almost below the watery horizon by the time their food was prepared and they'd driven back to the cove. Aiden parked the car and grabbed the bag of food, along with the plastic glasses and plates the restaurant had given them. Hands full, they made their way down the steps carved into the rock, leading to the cove below.

"It still amazes me how empty this place is," he said, as they laid the food out on one of the flat brown rocks at the far end of the sandy plain. "You'd think more people would come here. Yet every time I drive past it, it's empty."

She looked up at him, her eyelids heavy. "Maybe they know it was our place."

"Our place?" he murmured. "Yeah, I guess it was. We should put up a sign or something. Trespassers not permitted." He grabbed the bottle of wine from the bag. "White okay?"

"Yes please."

He poured her a glass, and filled his own with water. "Cheers."

She lifted the plastic glass, touching the rim to his. "Cheers."

By the time they'd finished eating, the sky was dark, and the cove lit only by the candles he'd placed on the rock. The flames flickered and danced, swaying to a barely perceptible breeze. She wiped her fingers on a paper napkin, chasing the food down with a mouthful of wine. When she looked up at him, he was staring at her, his eyes as black as the night sky.

"You look beautiful in candle light." His voice was low. "As though you've swum up from some underwater palace."

"Like a mermaid?" she asked him.

"More of a siren. You always were impossible to ignore."

His words were like a shot of adrenaline to her veins. "And you always did know how to sweet talk me."

"I only said what I knew to be true."

And what did he think now? The way he was looking at her – with dark, narrowed eyes – left her reeling. "Sometimes I find it hard to believe you're really back," she whispered. "Like maybe you're a figment of my imagination."

He swallowed, his throat undulating in the gloom. "I can't believe I stayed away for so long."

She pulled the soft skin on the inside of her lip between her teeth. "I'm glad you're here now."

"So am I." He reached out, running his hand down her arm. The same way he had on the boat. But this time it was the two of them and the ocean, and she allowed the shiver he caused to wrack her body. "I never should've left." He traced the inside of her wrist with the pad of his finger.

"Aiden..."

"No, hear me out." He'd reached the delicate skin on her wrist, tracing the tangle of blue beneath her flesh. "I left for the right reasons – what I thought were the right reasons – but I should have refused. I should have fought harder for you. For us. I should have told your father where to go."

"We were so young, so afraid. And you had your mom to think about. I'm glad you protected her, and kept her safe. That proves you're the man I always thought you were."

He ran his fingertips along the lines on her palm, stroking each finger in turn. Lifting her hand to his mouth, he kissed it. She gasped as she felt the warmth of his lips brushing against her sensitive skin. Slowly, he kissed his way up her arm, setting her nerves alight, and she froze, waiting to see where he'd go. His mouth brushed her wrist, the inside of her elbow, making her gasp.

"Do you ever think about that night?" He looked up at her, his eyes heavy-lidded.

"Our last night?"

"Yeah."

"All the time," she admitted. "I wonder what would have happened if my dad hadn't been out so late. If he hadn't been driving past the beach. If he hadn't seen my car there."

"I still remember what you were wearing."

"I wasn't wearing much by the time he found us."

Aiden smiled. "I remember that, too. I've never seen anything as beautiful as you were that night. Your skin lit by the moonlight, your body warm against mine."

They'd been close, so close, and it had taken her breath away. Over the years she'd tried to rationalize it. To tell herself that all teenagers feel those heightened emotions. But she could never forget the way his muscled thighs had felt between hers, or the way he'd asked if she was sure about a hundred times.

She'd been certain.

"I was so in love with you," she whispered.

Pulling at her hand, he moved her closer until her thigh was pressing against his. With his free hand, he reached out, brushing her curtain of blonde hair over her shoulder, exposing her neck, her shoulder, her chest. The moment he pressed his lips to her throat her body responded. He moved his lips upward, kissing her jaw, her cheek, the corner of her lips. His mouth lingered there, his breath warm, his lips soft. She opened her eyes to see him staring at her, eyes still as dark as coal. She tried to swallow but the dryness of her mouth stopped her.

When she was sixteen, their kisses had been plentiful. They'd given and taken without knowing their relationship had a sell-by date. But now, as his lips moved slowly, achingly along hers, she knew this kiss couldn't last forever.

Aiden cradled her jaw in his palm, and pressed his lips to hers. His kiss was slow, exploring, his tongue sliding slowly against hers. Her heart began to pound as he pushed her backward, until her back was against the rock. He slid his hand underneath, protecting her skin from the rough edges, and kissed her again. He moved with her, his body hard and muscular when he pressed into her, her thighs opening as he slid his hard, thick leg between them. She looped her arms around his neck, pulling him closer, needing to touch him, feel him, taste him. She couldn't get enough of him. It was as though something inside her had been unleashed, and it was aching to be fed. She kissed him back, hard and needy, her soft moans leaving him in no doubt how he was making her feel.

Holding her breath, she felt his mouth against the sharp jut of her clavicle, and the soft dip of skin below her throat. His lips brushed over the swell of her breasts, making her nipples hard and achy, and when he reached up to brush the fabric covered peaks with his thumb, she sighed out loud.

Lifting her easily, he brought her down to the ground, her hair splaying out on the golden sand as he leaned into her. His legs were between hers, his hands holding his weight above her. When he kissed her again, she wrapped her legs around his waist, her hips undulating to the rhythm of need he was building inside her.

"Is this okay?" he murmured, his fingers stopping at the thin straps on her shoulders.

She nodded, and he pulled at them, letting them dangle over her arms as he dipped his hands beneath the fabric, cupping her swollen, tender breasts, the warmth of his hand radiating through her bra. Brooke arched into him, her breath short, telling him with her body what she couldn't say with her lips. Then he pushed her dress down, and her white lace bra with it, exposing her pale skin to the night. His lips followed his hands, kissing the swell of her breasts, the dark red of her areola, and finally the hard, needy peak of her nipples. She let her head fall back, moaning louder as he sucked her in, her fingers grabbing at his hair as he sucked her into his warm, velvet mouth. She rocked her hips again, feeling him hard and thick against her, needing the friction it created.

Blood rushed through her ears, drowning out the sound of the ocean. Aiden moved his hands down, stroking her waist, her stomach, her hips, pushing the hem of her dress up, exposing her smooth thighs and white lingerie. His fingers were touching the damp scrap of silk covering her core, eliciting another loud moan from her lips.

"Aiden..."

"Shh, let me touch you." He kissed her again, swallowing her sighs as he stroked her, his fingers maddeningly gentle as he moved them back and forth. She arched her back, pressing herself into him, begging with her body for more.

"Please don't stop."

He pushed his hand beneath the light fabric, his fingers pressed against her warmth, skimming against her as he pulled her panties aside. She could feel the burn begin, deep in her belly, swirling and growing until it was impossible to ignore.

Her breath was escaping in tiny gasps, a staccato burst that echoed her pulse, as the pleasure inside built into an unstoppable force. She tightened around him, her body arching until she was barely touching the sand, her toes digging into the smooth grains, trying to keep her grounded. She was flying, convulsing around him, the ecstasy lighting her up like a beacon in the night. He held her as she soared, his lips capturing hers, tasting her pleasure he coaxed from her.

She never wanted him to let go.

20

Though the candles were still flickering, they were almost burned down to the wick. The flames turned her face orange and yellow, a contrast to the blackness of the sand and sea beyond her. He could see the sparks in her eyes as she stared up at him with the same innocent yet sexy-as-hell look she always had. The one that made him want to protect her from whatever hurricane was coming.

And there was *always* a hurricane.

"It's getting late," he said, his voice low. "We should go."

There was disappointment in her eyes. "I guess. I don't want to, though. I'd happily lay here with you for hours." She smiled at him, her lips pink and swollen from their kisses. He loved the way she looked right now – content, sated. As though every muscle in her body was relaxed.

He did that to her and it made him feel ten feet tall.

"We might have a bit of explaining to do if we stay here." He winked. "Let me take you home. We can come back another day."

"But you didn't..." She looked down, biting her lip. "You know."

"This wasn't about me." He was still hard, but under control. There was a cold shower back home with his name on it.

"I'm sorry, I didn't mean to be like that. So quick. It's been a while."

He was amused at the way she was talking around the subject. As though she was afraid to say the right words. "How long?" She'd piqued his interest.

She blinked, her eyelashes sweeping down as a frown formed on her face. "Um, yeah. Quite a long time." She laced her fingers together. "Like a really long time."

Now he was curious. A half smile formed on his lips. Normally, he wasn't the possessive sort, but the thought he'd reawakened something in her made him want to do it all over again. "A year?" he asked.

She shook her head, still not meeting his gaze. "Longer."

So she was making this a game of higher or lower. He could handle that. "Two?"

"Longer."

He tipped her chin up with his fingers, needing to see her eyes. "How long?"

There was something going on behind those pretty eyes – a struggle that made him want to reach out and calm her. Though he couldn't tell in the candlelight, he thought she was blushing. "I can't." She shook her head again, her lips twisting together. "It's so embarrassing."

"Don't be embarrassed. It's just us. Nobody else. I don't care about your past, though I'm interested in it. I want to know your story."

She relaxed against the sand, pulling her hands apart. "I haven't had sex since I got pregnant with Nick."

He tried to keep his shock under control, but failed miserably. His eyes widened. "Seriously? You haven't had sex in nine years?" Damn, so much for not caring. He tried to temper his tone. "Why not?"

"It's hard being a single mom. Even getting to go out was a miracle, and don't forget I lived on my parents' estate. I couldn't exactly bring guys home, even if I'd wanted to. Which I didn't."

The way she looked away from him made him sense that wasn't the entire story. "Okay. That's understandable. You had Nick to think of."

"And I guess, you don't miss what you haven't had."

He tipped his head. "Can you explain that? I don't quite understand."

"I've only had two experiences of sex in my life, and both times ended with consequences. There was us that one night that we got caught..." She waved her hand. "And then you left." Her voice trembled. "Then there was Jamie." She sighed. "Which led to me being pregnant."

His stomach tightened. He hadn't expected that. "You've never had a good experience of sex." He shook his head, trying not to frown too hard. "That's terrible."

"As I said, you don't miss what you haven't had." She shrugged. "Though if tonight was anything to go by, maybe I should miss it."

"Tonight was a only a taste. Sex isn't only about orgasms or even about the act itself. It's about connecting, loving, wanting to give each other pleasure. It's about feeling naked skin on naked skin, warm and delicious. It's about the two of us and nothing else."

"You sound like you've had a lot of experience."

"Some." He didn't want to talk about other girls. Didn't want to talk about his past. He was too busy thinking about hers. "Enough to know how good it can be." He traced his finger along her jaw, lingering at her mouth. "Let me show you."

Her eyes widened. "Here?"

He chuckled. "No, not here. When we make love it's going to be under a roof, maybe in a bed, where nobody else can see us."

"Maybe in a bed," she repeated. "Where else would you want to do it?" He could feel her muscles form into a smile. Her eyes were sparkling.

"We'd start off in bed, but maybe we'd need a shower, or maybe we'd lean against the wall. I can promise you once we've done it the first time, it will never be enough."

It never would be for him. The thought of showing her what she was missing, of teaching her things that would rock her world, was enticing. It took every piece of self control he had not to start right here, right now.

Her chest hitched. "When?"

"When what?" He raised his eyebrows.

"When can we see each other again? When can you show me what I've been missing out on?"

Her enthusiasm gratified him. "As soon as you arrange for a sitter. An all night one. Because once you're in my bed, I'm not going to want to let go of you until morning."

She nodded slowly, braver now, keeping her eyes on his. "In that case, it's a date."

"Are you guys free on Saturday?" Brooke asked. "I need a sitter for Nick, and I was wondering if he could stay over."

Ember raised an eyebrow, pouring cream into her coffee. Behind them she could hear Ally talking to a customer, taking his breakfast order. "Yeah, we haven't got anything planned. What are you up to?"

"Aiden's asked me out again." Brooke couldn't stop the smile from pulling at her lips.

"Mmhmm." Ember nodded. "This is the guy who isn't interested in you, right?"

"You can stop it. I concede. You were right and I was wrong. Happy now?" Brooke's tone was teasing.

"I can tell *you're* happy, which is the most important thing. So I'm guessing the first date went well."

"It was heaven." She sighed, a smile pulling at her lips.

Ember leaned forward, her elbows on the formica table. "Heaven? Tell me more."

"Ugh, I swear this day can go take a jump off the boardwalk." Ally pulled a chair out, slumping dramatically on the table. "How the hell am I supposed to serve breakfast when we don't have any eggs?"

"No eggs?" Brooke winced. "There goes our order."

"What happened?" Ember frowned. "Did your delivery not come?"

"Nope, and Nate's spitting buckets. I heard him on the phone earlier, reaming out the supplier." Ally sighed. "I had to remind him I'm the manager of this place and it's up to me to do the reaming."

Brooke tried not to grin. Despite Ally's shaking head, she and Nate made a great team. He owned coffee shops all down the West Coast, but it had been her idea to brand the beachside ones differently. She'd even thought of the name – Coastal Coffee – and from the looks of how busy the shop was, her idea was going down a storm with locals and tourists alike.

When Nate had asked her to come and manage the shop, he'd promised that she'd have free rein. After all, he had a huge business to run. But he was also hugely protective of Ally and looked after her the way she deserved. Including ranting at suppliers when they didn't do their job.

"Talking of spitting buckets, your mom came in to the café yesterday." Ally raised her eyebrow at Brooke.

"She's back from vacation? I didn't know."

"I'm surprised they haven't been camping outside your door," Ember murmured. "They'll want to see Nick, won't they?"

"I'd guess so." Brooke frowned, and looked down at the table. She wasn't ready to have a conversation with them yet. Especially not when she had to tell them the truth about Nick's father. They were going to go crazy when they found out he was related to Aiden and his family. Squeezing her eyes shut, she tried to get the image of her father's angry red face out of her mind.

There was plenty of time to tell them. Maybe she'd find the guts to do so over the next week.

"There's no need to look so scared," Ally told her. "She wasn't that bad."

Brooke finished the last of her coffee, feeling the warm liquid slide down her throat. "What'd she say?"

"She wanted to know about your new place, asked me if I'd seen it yet. Whether it was as 'low rent' as she was led to believe."

"Did you give her any answers?"

"I told her you and Nick were doing fine. Then she asked me if I'd noticed something..." Ally lowered her voice, "different about you. Whether you were having some kind of breakdown."

Well that was a new one. "She thinks I've lost it?"

"She can't understand why you won't come back home." Ally shrugged. "I told her you're happy, and that's all that mattered."

"You're a good friend." Brooke reached out and squeezed her hand. "When did our parents get so complicated? I swear they're causing us more trouble now than they did when we were teenagers."

"Are you sure about that?" Ember winked. "They were

pretty difficult when we were younger, too. And so was Ally's dad. We've grown up. We're strong enough to stand on our own two feet. I don't think your folks like that much."

Brooke shot her a smile. "I guess they'll have to learn to live with it."

"I know they drive you crazy, but they love you," Ember said. "They'll adjust to your new situation." She shrugged.

"Yeah, I guess." Brooke closed her eyes and breathed in, tasting the salt in the air. The sound of the ocean echoed the beating of her heart.

"Don't worry," Ally said, reaching for her hand. "They'll come around. They love you and Nick. But sometimes they forget you have your own lives to live."

Brooke tried to smile. "Yeah, sure." They'd only been away for a week but she'd already felt freer than she had in a long time. Now that they were back, she felt a feeling of wistfulness wash over her – the same feeling they used to get as kids when summer started to fade into fall, school started back up, and they had to leave the beach and their school vacations behind.

Things were changing, and her life was moving on whether they liked it or not.

If only she could find the strength to tell them that.

𝕤 21 𝕤

Brooke pulled her car into the driveway leading to Aiden's rented house. Once she turned off the ignition, she leaned forward on the steering wheel to rest her head. Looking down she could see her bare legs stretching forward – her feet still touching the pedals – and the hem of the pink dress she'd taken hours in choosing.

She felt weird. As though she was turning up for a booty call. Not that she'd ever done that before. What would Aiden be expecting? For her to march in and head straight for the bedroom? She wasn't sure she had the confidence to do that.

Who was she trying to kid? She wasn't sure she had the confidence to even get out of the car. Her hands were still gripped around the wheel, anchoring her to the stationary car.

Lifting her head up, she saw herself reflected in the glass of the windshield. Glaring at her mirror image, she shook her head, silently berating herself. How had she managed to get so worked up over this? It was supposed to be fun, wasn't it? A little touching, a little loving, and then she could walk away with her head held high. Aiden would never hurt her – not intentionally. He wasn't Jamie, he wasn't any randon guy. He was *him*.

Her rock; or at least that's what he'd used to be.

She breathed in, her chest expanding, as she reached for the door knob. Here went nothing. Or something. Damn, she needed to get her confidence back. She was a strong woman – a single mother, a student, a soon-to-be veterinary technician. She could tame wild animals with a few words. Surely she could do this.

Dammit, she *wanted* to do this. Her face heated up at the thought of what lay ahead.

Within thirty seconds she was knocking at his door. It swung open almost immediately – far too quickly for him to be doing anything other than waiting for her. The thought sobered her up. Maybe she wasn't the only nervous one.

"Hey. I wondered how long you'd be sitting out there." There was a shy smile on his lips. "I was thinking I'd have to drag you out of the car."

She tried to ignore the blood rushing to her cheeks. "I was listening to the radio." She winked at him, putting on an air of bravado. "I wanted to hear the end of the song."

He tipped his head to the side. "What song were you listening to?"

Oh hell. She wrinkled her nose, thinking for a minute. "Um, the Beach Boys." Lame, so lame.

He coughed out a laugh. "Good Vibrations?"

She rolled her eyes.

With a grin on his face, he stepped back, motioning for her to come in. As soon as she walked inside the door, he took her hand, pulling her close until her body was touching his. She was struck by the hard warmth of his body, the pine fragrance of his cologne. She'd not bothered to wear high heels today – she'd figured she'd kick her shoes off as soon as she walked in – and their height difference was marked. She leaned her head against his shoulder, her cheek pressed to the top of his chest, closing her eyes for a moment. His arms encircled her, his hands pressed to the small of her back. She could hear his breath – soft and low – as he leaned his cheek against her hair.

She could smell something else, too. The most delicious aroma of food wafting out from the kitchen. She couldn't remember the last time she'd eaten.

"You cooked?" she asked him.

"You sound surprised." There was a smile in his voice.

"I didn't expect you to."

He stepped back, his hands sliding up to her shoulders. Their eyes connected. "What did you think I was going to do? Drag you straight into the bedroom and have my wicked way with you?"

This time she laughed. He was way too close to the truth for comfort. "I don't know." She shook her head. "It smells delicious."

He grabbed her hand and led her into the kitchen, where two pots were boiling on the stove. "I made pasta, something quick and easy. Slow release carbs to give you stamina."

Her mouth dropped open.

"I'm kidding. Well not about the pasta, because that's what we're having. But I didn't plan on a slow release." He squeezed her hand. "Try to relax. This is supposed to be a date. Let's eat and talk and see where things go. No pressure. We don't do anything you don't want to, okay?"

She licked her lips. "Am I that obvious?" She hated being so uptight.

"Only to me. I was watching you out of the window. You looked scared to death. And I don't want you to be scared. I want you to be Brooke. Cool, calm, with an edge that drives me crazy." He slid his arms around her waist. "The girl I can't get out of my mind."

"Okay." Her voice was soft. She could be *that* girl, couldn't she? Sure she'd taken some hits to her self-esteem, but she had confidence. As a mother, as a student, even as a teacher. She needed to show it here.

"I've set the table on the deck. Go sit out there and watch the sun go down." He grabbed a wine bottle from the refrigerator, pouring her a glass and passing it to her. "I'll bring the food out in a minute."

She took the glass, feeling the condensation against her skin. "Don't be too long."

"I don't intend to."

"Good, because I'm hungry." She grinned at him, the action feeling easier now. He knew exactly how to make her feel comfortable. Another thing she remembered from years ago. His words were like Prozac – soothing to the soul.

"The sooner you get out of here, the sooner I can feed you."

She was still smiling when she walked through the white gauze curtains and onto his deck. The sun was slip-sliding down the horizon, the sky surrounding it layered in orange and purple. Whispy grey clouds were dotted here and there. The air was so still it was almost ethereal.

Growing up in Angel Sands, she'd become accustomed to the daily sunsets, but whenever tourists visited they always remarked upon their beauty. It was as though mother nature was putting on a daily performance, taking her evening bow against a painted backdrop.

She sat for a moment, letting the stillness of the evening wash over her. Taking a sip of the wine, she savoured the cool crispness of the grapes as the liquid danced on her tastebuds. The beach was deserted, the pale yellow sand turning grey as night descended, the dark water slowly ebbing and flowing against the grains. The waves sounded like a mother's heartbeat as they gently washed to shore. Slow, steady, reassuring.

"You look beautiful, by the way." Aiden walked across the deck, two plates of pasta in his hand, the wine bottle tucked under his arm. "Especially in moonlight."

She turned to look at him. He didn't look bad himself. In fact, he looked as mouthwatering as the food he was carrying. Dark jeans, bare feet, and a white shirt with the sleeves rolled up. Funny how she didn't feel so hungry any more. Not for food, anyway.

"I didn't know you could cook," she said, as he slid the plate in front of her.

"How do you think I've survived all these years?" he asked, his voice teasing. "Man can't live on takeout alone."

"I don't know." She shook her head. "I guess sometimes I still think of you as a college student. But you're not, are you?"

"Definitely not." He twisted a forkful of tagliatelle with an expert touch, raising it to his mouth. "I like cooking. It's restful. Things take as long as they take, and you can't rush them. It's very different to the rest of my life."

The pasta was delicious. The noodles were perfectly cooked – al dente – and the cream sauce was smooth without being heavy. She closed her eyes as she tasted it – letting the hint of garlic and oregano linger for a moment before swallowing it down. "Remember the time you tried to cook the fish you caught?" she asked him.

He smiled, his eyes lighting at the memory. "As I remember you were impressed. You wanted to run away and live in the cave while I went out and hunted your dinner every day."

"You forgot to gut the damn thing. It tasted rancid." It was funny, though, remembering how she'd watched him make a fire on the beach, creating a makeshift rotisserie with some old driftwood and sticks. She'd been amazed right up until she put the first morsel into her mouth.

"Hopefully I've learned a lot since then." He twirled his fork into the pasta again. Amazing how a simple act could send shivers down her spine. He was a magnet – she was drawn to everything he did.

"Well this definitely doesn't taste like an nineteen-year-old boy cooked it." She took a sip of her wine. "It's delicious."

"The Fresh 'n' Easy's finest." He winked.

"You got this from the Fresh 'n' Easy?" She grimaced. The local supermarket wasn't known for the quality of its produce. "Wow."

"I got the ingredients from there. It was either that or drive out of town, and I had a dozen meetings today." He shrugged. "I figured you wouldn't want to wait until midnight to eat.

"No, I wouldn't have wanted that." She met his gaze again, laying her silverware on the now-empty plate. "Thank you, that really was lovely. I can't remember the last time somebody cooked for me." That was, if you didn't count the formal dinners she had to turn up to at her parents' house. But she so rarely actually ate that food – her mom had always told her not to. *Better to skip the eating and entertain, dear.*

"It seems like you've missed out on a lot of things. I guess you had to grow up fast."

"I don't mind. I like cooking, as long as I have the time." She swallowed her last mouthful of wine. Her glass was barely empty before he was filling it up again. "Next time I'll cook for you."

"Next time?" A smile played at his lips.

"What, is this a one time thing?" She didn't need to hear his answer. She knew it already, the same way he knew hers.

"That depends on you."

She looked at him, her eyelashes sweeping down and obscuring him for a moment. "It does?"

"Yeah. I told you, I'm not going to push you. Not for anything. Whatever happens tonight is on your terms."

"What if I want you to push me?" She ran a finger around the rim of her glass. "What if I want you to take the lead? To show me what your terms look like?"

He was close, yet too far away. The table between them felt like a barrier, and she wanted it gone. He must have wanted the same thing, because the next moment he was up and closing the distance, offering his hand to her. She slid her palm inside his, letting him pull her up to standing. His touch was enough to set her on fire – her skin fizzed with anticipation. He pulled her close, his finger tipping her chin up until her eyes locked with his. They were dark, narrowed, taking her in.

"I'll take the lead if you want me to." His voice was thick. "But if you want me to slow down, or stop, or..."

She put her finger on his lips, feeling the softness of his skin there. Such a contrast to his face, where his beard was already pushing through. "Hush. I don't want you to stop, and I won't want you to slow down. I only want you."

* * *

Her words were like paraffin poured over an already-burning fire. They set his body alight. How long had he thought about this moment? About having this woman offer herself up to him, the same way she'd laid herself bare a decade ago? For so long she'd been a memory – a thought in the breeze he'd successfully ignored. But now she was here, in his home, and it felt as though every dream he'd ever had was coming to life.

"You've got me." He brushed his lips across her temple. Her skin was warm and soft. She looked up at him, her eyes wide and inviting, and the innocence he saw sent a shot of pleasure down to his groin. He'd been hard since they'd started eating – it was impossible not to be when she kept sliding the pasta into her mouth, her lips parting the same way they parted whenever he kissed her. Even with the table between them he could feel the heat of her, see the need in her. To know he was the guy she wanted to sate that need made him feel ten feet tall.

He kissed her cheek, her jaw, the corner of her lips. Her throat undulated as she swallowed at his closeness. With his hand still beneath her chin, he angled her face, the tip of her nose sliding along his until they fit right together. Her eyes were closed, her lips slightly open. She was waiting for him. And though they'd kissed before, this felt different. He could taste the anticipation wafting from her.

Because this wasn't only a kiss, it was a beginning. The appetizer for what he had planned. As his lips hovered above hers, he could feel her arching her body into him, all softness and curves and warm flesh. The kind of body a man could lose himself in, again and again. The kind he'd never get enough of no matter how hard he tried.

He ran the tip of his tongue along her bottom lip, tasting her gasp as she opened up to him. He kissed her, his mouth demanding, his hands sliding down her back to press them closer together. He was hard against her belly – pulsing at her closeness. She lifted her hands, threading them in his hair, her nails digging into his scalp as she tried to get them closer still.

She was as responsive as hell, her lips moving and loving as their tongues slid together. Guttural noises came from deep in her chest as he cupped the back of her neck, his fingers sliding through her smooth, blonde hair. She might have asked him to lead, but right now *she* owned him. Owned his body, his responses, the aching need that pressed into her. And she was the one who led him to his bedroom, her fingers threaded through his as she kept looking back at him. He could see the desire in her eyes, making them sparkle. Her lips were swollen from their kisses. Her breath gave away her desire, pushing her breasts up with short little gasps, as though she couldn't get enough air into her body.

He followed her into his room, his eyes scanning her body. Her dress clung to her, accentuating the dip of her back, and the rise of her behind. Her hips curved in perfect symmetry, into a waist so small he could span it with his hands. How was it possible a woman like this had never experienced good sex?

"Take your dress off." His voice was low. He'd barely finished speaking before she was sliding the pink fabric up her thighs, slowly revealing more of her tanned skin, a contrast to the white g-string she was wearing. He dragged his lip between his teeth as she lifted it up further, revealing her stomach, her breasts, and finally her face. Her hair dropped down around her shoulders – light gold on bare skin – and he bit harder to hide his moan.

Damn, this woman was beautiful. And it wasn't simply the way she looked, but who she was. The way she was looking at him, like he was king of the goddamned castle. It made him want to be everything she needed. Everything she wanted.

"Let me see you for a minute." He nodded at her. She stood still, like a statue. But she didn't look embarrassed or afraid. Maybe it was the way he was staring at her, the heat in his eyes. The need made every cell in his body pulse.

"You like?" she asked him.

"Yes I do. Very much."

"So touch me." It wasn't a beg. Not even a command. The sentence made complete and utter sense. You couldn't look at perfection without wanting to touch it.

He stepped forward, closing the gap between them. His hand slid down her side until he was cupping her waist. His fingers pressed into the soft skin, feeling the flare of her hips beneath them. Still holding her, he dropped to his knees and pressed his lips to her stomach.

"Oh!"

He looked up to see her head tipped back before he kissed her again, with an open mouth. He licked her skin, tasting her. Imagining what she would taste like when he moved to her core.

"Take your bra off."

He felt her move her arms to unhook the clasp. The scrap of white fabric fell to the floor. He lifted his head, taking in the way her breasts lifted up from her chest, tipped with perfect pink nipples.

With his hands still spanning her waist, he pushed her back to the bed. Her knees buckled as she sat, her breasts at the perfect height as he kneeled in front of her. He moved his hands up, feathering her ribcage, feeling the soft swell of her skin as he reached her breasts. He moved his thumbs, feeling the peak of her. Hearing her moan as he stroked again and again. He leaned in, inhaling the scent of her, and pressed his lips to her sensitive skin. Her nipple was hard as he pulled it between his lips, sucking and licking until she let out a deep moan. He moved to her other breast, worshipping it in the same way, loving the taste of her, and the way she responded to his touch.

Her legs opened as he leaned in closer still, her bare thighs grazing against his torso. He unbuttoned his shirt, needing to feel his skin on hers, needing to feel their chests pressed together. As he shucked it off, he leaned forward, pushing her until her back hit the mattress. His chest molded against hers, his lips kissing her lips, and her thighs hooked around his hips as she began rocking against him.

Her hands moved down, in between them, desperately seeking his belt. She tugged at it, missing a couple of times before she finally unclasped it, and pushed the thick metal button of his jeans through the fabric and unzipped him.

He was straining against his boxers, hot and hard as she

slid her hand inside his waistband. Her hand circled him, her fingers stroking his overheated erection, her thumb brushing against his swollen tip.

"Let me touch you." His voice was rough, his breath as ragged as hers. "I want to make this good for you." He moved back, her fingers falling from him, before he tugged at her panties until she was bare. It was impossible to move his eyes from her – she was as perfect there as everywhere else. Pale skin covered with scant blonde hair, glistening in the half light.

As soon as his fingers grazed her, she arched her back from the mattress. She was wet and swollen, her nerve endings sending her body into overload whenever he touched her. He could tell she was already on edge – even though he'd barely moved his fingers – and the thought made him throb with need. He rolled his thumb in a circle, and her hips gyrated in the same rhythm, her breath getting shorter and shorter until there was no breath at all. A moment before she reached her peak, he slid his fingers inside, never letting up on the circles with his thumb. He felt her tense, her muscles rigid around him, her body freezing the same way the air stills before a storm. A moment later she convulsed around him, a long drawn out moan escaping from her lips. He pulled his fingers out, his slick hand tugging at his jeans and boxers, pulling them all the way off. She opened her eyes, reaching for him, and he climbed above her, grabbing a condom from the nightstand next to the bed.

"Are you okay?" He tore the foil, hesitating to hear her reaction.

"More than okay." Her voice was low. Full of need.

"You want me to stop?"

She shook her head. "I never want you to stop." Her eyes were heavy, her muscles relaxed. "I need you inside me."

Damn, he needed that too. Like she wouldn't ever believe.

He rolled the condom on and leaned over her, his elbows resting on each side of her, caging her in. She reached for him again, her fingers circling him in tight heat, moving slowly up and down in a way that made him ache with desire. She rubbed his tip against the heat of her core, and his whole body jumped at the sensation. He slid against her, her legs widening to welcome him, her muscles relaxing to engulf his tip.

He closed his eyes, savouring the moment, before slowly pushing the rest of his way inside. She was warm and tight, squeezing at him as he entered. Her breath as short as his with the pleasure of it all. Her thighs pressed into his hips, encouraging in a rhythm they both needed to find, as her palms pressed against his ass cheeks to increase the friction. Her lips sought out his, kissing him fast and hard, her mouth vibrating with tiny moans he swallowed down. Every time he withdrew, the root of him ground against her, coaxing out her pleasure, making her tighter still. She stopped kissing him, her head falling back, her eyes squeezed shut, her nipples hard against his chest as he continued to move. Then she was coming again, pulsing around him, dragging him in until he couldn't tell where her pleasure ended and his was beginning. He stilled, closing his own eyes, letting his orgasm crash out of him. His sighs were deep and low as he spilled his release.

When he opened his eyes, still resting on his elbows, she was staring straight at him, her green eyes wide. He inclined his head, brushing his lips across hers, unwilling to move because he didn't want to pull himself out of her.

"That was…" She smiled, the corners of her eyes crinkling.

"It was…"

"So good."

"Yeah." He hadn't quite caught his breath. Hadn't caught ahold of his thoughts either. They were swirling around his brain, not quite making sense. And yet one thing made perfect sense – her laying beneath him, her muscles still holding him in. Brooke and Aiden, and nothing else. "It was a long time coming." Ten years. Jesus.

"Not for me. I think you'll find I came quickly. Twice." She grinned. There she was again, the Brooke he remembered so well. Funny, mischievous, never afraid to tell him what she thought. "Still, we've got a lot of time to make up for."

It was his turn to smile. "Give me five minutes and I'll take you up on that."

❧ 22 ❧

"Well you look like a woman who's freshly..." Ember trailed off as Nick appeared next to her in the doorway, his face splitting into a smile as he spotted Brooke standing on the front step. "Fresh. I mean you look fresh."

Brooke bit down a laugh. "Hey, Ember." She crouched and mussed her son's hair with her palm. "Hey bud, did you have a good time?"

"Yep. We made pizza and watched a movie. Lucas let me play on his Xbox. It was cool."

"I made sure it was 'R' rated." Ember winked, and lowered her voice. "Unlike your night."

"Did you play Xbox, too?" Nick asked. "With Uncle Aiden?"

Brooke shook her head, sending Ember a dirty look. "No, honey. Aiden doesn't have an Xbox, remember?"

"He likes playing though, right?" Ember was still grinning.

"Aaaand, that's my cue to leave. Have you got your stuff ready?"

"Hey, not so fast. We made you breakfast, didn't we, Nick?

Plus Lucas needs Nick's help in the backyard." She winked at him.

"They've got table tennis out there." Nick's eyes were wide. "It's so cool."

"Toys for boys." Ember rolled her eyes. "He's out there waiting for you."

As soon as Nick ran up the hallway, she turned back to look at Brooke. "Well?"

"Well what?" Why did she feel like she was walking into an ambush.

"How was your night? I noticed you only messaged me once to check on Nick, about two thousand less times than you normally do. Which makes me think you were busy. *Very* busy." The two of them were walking up the hallway, toward Ember's kitchen. "How many times were you busy?"

"Can you pour me a cup of coffee before we get into specifics?" Brooke asked her. "I seriously need a caffeine fix."

"Yeah, you do look tired. Glowing, though. Like a woman who spent the night doing anything but sleeping." Ember grabbed a mug from the cupboard, pouring in the dark coffee from the pot. "Seriously, you look happy. That makes me happy, too."

"We had a nice evening." Brooke smiled, remembering the rest of their night. Lots of cuddling and talking, not to mention great loving. She couldn't have asked for more than that.

"So are you seeing him again?"

"Every other Saturday, when he picks up Nick."

Ember sighed. "I mean are you *seeing* him again. As in a date?"

"I think so." Brooke leaned on the countertop, her hands cupped around her coffee mug. "He got a business call first thing, and then had to rush off to work after that. He said he'd call me."

"Oh." Ember grimaced. "That's, um..."

"Don't worry. I don't think he meant it like that." And if he did? She was a big girl, wasn't she? She'd coped with worse and survived.

"Come on, I need more details. How does he feel about you? How do you feel? Should we be preparing Nick to become a big brother some time soon?"

"Ember!" Brooke shook her head. "I'd expect these questions from Ally but not from you."

Biting down a grin, Ember pulled her phone from her pocket and unlocked it with her thumb. Slowly she turned the screen around to show a message from their friend.

Remember to ask her everything. Okay?

"Well at least we can count on her," Brooke said, raising her eyes to meet Ember's. "Predictability is good, right?"

"And she'll kill me if I don't get some details. So give me something to work with. How many times?" Ember batted her eyelids and made Brooke laugh again. In the distance she could hear the rumbling of Lucas's voice as he spoke with Nick. Way too far away to hear this conversation.

"Okay. Four. Is that enough for you?"

"The point is, was it enough for *you*?"

Brooke couldn't help but laugh at Ember's question. "Yeah. It was enough. For now."

———

Aiden looked up from the report he was holding. Two thin pieces of paper – the typing double spaced. Not a whole lot of information for the amount he was paying the PI up in Northern California.

"Sorry for springing this on you over the weekend," Mark said. He was wearing a polo shirt and chinos – the perfect lawyer-at-leisure attire. He looked as though he'd run out in the middle of a round of golf.

"I appreciate you coming to meet me," Aiden replied, still holding the report. "Especially on the weekend. I hope I didn't drag you away from your family."

The lawyer shrugged. "It's fine. I knew this couldn't wait until Monday."

He looked down again, his eyes scanning the typed words. "I can't believe they gave him parole so soon. Do we know why?"

"They don't have to give a reason. They can just grant it." Mark shrugged. "There are no limits on his release either. Your brother's free to come and go as he pleases."

Aiden felt his stomach drop. Mark had called him as Brooke was leaving his place. They'd been talking about their next date when Aiden's phone started to ring. If it had been anybody else he would have ignored it, but Mark never called unless it was important.

And yeah, this was definitely important.

"So he can come here without us knowing?"

"He can go anywhere. He'll have a Parole Officer he'll need to check in with regularly, but apart from that, his time is done."

"Shit." Aiden shook his head. "If he comes near Brooke or Nick I'll..." he trailed off. He'd what? He had no goddamned right to stop his brother from seeing his son. Damn, this was so messed up.

"Is there any reason he might come here?" Mark asked. "You know him better than anybody. What's the first thing he'll do when he gets out?"

Aiden swallowed, though his mouth was as dry as the desert. "He'll want money. I guess he'll look for me first. Now that Mom's gone, I'll be the obvious person to tap."

"And if he doesn't find you?"

"I'm not exactly hiding." Aiden felt his body slump. "Fuck, I'm going to lead him straight to her, aren't I?"

"Not if we get to him first. How do you feel about being pre-emptive? Maybe offer him a payment to leave you alone?"

Aiden leaned his chin on his hand, thinking. "Would that work?"

"It's worth a try. If all he's after is easy money, we can do that. I'll ask my guy on the ground to approach him once he's out of jail. I can even get some papers drawn up."

"What kind of papers?"

"The kind of papers that buy his silence. We could pay him to rescind any claim on his son, if you think it might work."

"No." Aiden shook his head, his voice short. "He doesn't know much about Nick, and I'd like to keep it that way. This thing should stay between him and me. I don't want Brooke knowing anything about this."

"So we'll make it a geographical thing. Money in exchange for him staying away from Angel Sands. You think he'll take it?"

"I don't know. It's been a long time since I was around him outside of our mom's funeral." Aiden sighed. "I want the whole damn thing to go away, you know?"

"I know." Mark's voice was sympathetic. "And if it makes you feel any better, the likelihood is he'll be back in jail before the year's out. In my experience, guys like him don't stay clean for long. But in the meantime, we'll approach him and make the offer."

"When does he get out?" Aiden's hands tightened around the report, his knuckles bleaching.

"In a few days. Our man will follow him from the gate. Offer to buy him lunch, show him a friendly face. And if he has the cash on him, I can't see Jamie turning that down, can you?"

"How much are we talking about?" He knew a couple of hundred wasn't going to cut it.

"I'll ask him for an opinion, but I was guessing around thirty thousand. Enough to set him up for a few months. It should buy you some time if nothing else."

Still holding the report, Aiden leaned back, a sigh escaping his lips. It wasn't as if he was short of money. Nowadays he could lay his hands on a sum like that immediately. It didn't make it seem any less dirty though. Like he was bribing a competitor or something.

But what choice did he have? There was no way he wanted Jamie coming anywhere near Angel Sands. The thought of him getting within breathing distance of Brooke and Nick made his blood turn cold.

Only a few hours ago she was laying in his arms, her body curled against his. He'd stared at her as the early morning light started to haze through the windows, watching her face as she slept. Her skin was soft, unlined, still so young in spite of the years they'd been apart. Maybe that's what he liked the most – she was still the same person he'd known, yet somehow so much more.

"Okay, I'll get the money wired over today. I want our guy all over this." Aiden waved the report in his hand. "I need to know if my brother so much as takes a piss in a toilet that isn't his. Every move he makes I want to know about. Doesn't matter how much it costs."

He was still holding the report as he walked out of the office building, heading over to his car parked alone in the lot. Like the inside of the building, the outside was deserted.

Throwing the file onto the passenger seat, he climbed into the car, pulling his phone out of his pocket to check for messages. There were the usual – overtime reports from the site foreman, a quick update from Robert about his plans to visit next week – but nothing from her. He quickly pulled up her number and pressed 'call'.

"Hey." Brooke answered before it had even started ringing. It made him smile.

"Hey yourself. What are you doing?"

"We're walking into the apartment. I'm going to make Nick lunch and get some work done. How about you?"

He looked up at the tall glass office building. "I've been in a meeting. Going to head over to the site to check things out."

Her voice was teasing. "You really are a workaholic, aren't you?"

Yeah, he was. Or he used to be. But now he was less sure. Glancing in the rear view mirror, he saw the corner of his reflection. He looked like the same man, he sounded like the same man, but inside he wasn't so sure any more.

A taste of her and he was changing. His body reacted to the memory of her, of her soft skin and warm breath, of the way she felt when he slid inside her.

"You're working too, remember?" he replied, a smile playing at his lips. "Sounds like the pot calling the kettle black."

"We're two peas in a pod. Made for each other."

He liked that. *A lot*. Liked hearing her saying it even more. There was something growing between them, something new and precious, and it felt like it was his job to protect it.

"So we never talked about our next date. What are you doing tomorrow?"

"I'm working at the shelter."

"If it's me against the animals, I know I'll lose. How about Monday?"

He heard her sigh. "I'll be free after ten. I'm helping Clara get everything ready for the gala next Saturday. Everything's getting crazy at work."

"Maybe I can help. Come in and lick envelopes or whatever the hell it is you're doing," Aiden suggested.

"You'd do that?" Her voice was soft.

"Of course. I want to see you."

He heard her breathe – long and deep. "In that case, I have something else to ask you."

This was intriguing. A smile played at his lips. "Shoot."

"Did you want to be my plus one for the gala?"

He felt his throat go dry. "On Saturday?"

She hesitated for a second before answering him. "Yeah. It's at the Beach Club. You don't have to come if you don't want to. In fact, maybe we shouldn't. My parents are going to be there."

"I want to come."

"You do?" Her voice softened. "Are you sure? People will talk."

"People always have." Maybe this time they wouldn't talk about him being trash like his brother. In fact, it would be his chance to show this whole town who he'd become, no thanks to them. And if he got the chance to rub his relationship with Brooke in Martin and Lillian Newton's faces? Well that would do him fine.

"I'll be there, Brooke. In fact, I'll pick you up. And in the meantime, I'll see you at the shelter Monday."

He glanced over at the file folder in the seat next to him. The report with details of Jamie's parole. For a moment he felt his chest tighten at the thought of Jamie, at the thought of how the Newton's thought he was the same as his brother.

Yeah, well he wasn't. And maybe he finally had a chance to prove it.

❦ 23 ❦

The animal shelter had descended into chaos. A cat they'd rescued the previous day was giving birth to a litter of mewling kittens, whose unexpected arrival had caused all the other animals in the shelter to be on edge. They'd spent the best part of the afternoon in surgery, helping the cat as each tiny kitten emerged. Each one had been born alive and healthy, thank God.

"Well, I need to get back to work," Max said, when the final kitten had arrived. All five of them were now nestled against their mother, taking in her milk. He pulled his scrubs off and stuffed them into the laundry chute, before washing his hands and grabbing his battered leather bag. "You did good here," he told Brooke, looking over his shoulder at her. "I'm looking forward to you joining my team."

"Me too." Brooke gave him a tired smile. "If I graduate that is."

"Of course you're going to graduate. I gave you a good write up on your practicals, and I know your written work is good. I checked it over, remember?"

She did, and she was forever grateful. It was only a couple

of months until she finished college – and until she would get an honest-to-god paycheck every few weeks. The limbo she and Nick were living in would disappear. She couldn't wait.

The shelter director walked into the operating room, the open door letting in the wails and barks of all the animals in their pens. Clara glanced at Brooke. "You look about as beat as I feel. Let's get on with the gala preparations and maybe we'll be out of here before midnight."

"That sounds like my cue to leave." Max grimaced.

"But you'll be there on the night, right?" Brooke asked him.

"Of course. I'll see you there." He pulled his jacket on and turned to Clara. "From the looks of the kittens they're settling in nicely. They've all fed and their mother is keeping them warm. There's a small one I'd like to keep my eye on, but I'll check in with you tomorrow."

"Of course."

"Brooke did great. She didn't even need me here today." He winked at her. "You'll be doing me out of a job soon."

A loud rapping on the door cut through the sound of the animals and Max's conversation. Clara frowned and glanced at the clock. "Please God don't let it be another animal. We've no space left."

"It's okay. It's a friend of mine. He's offered to help with the gala preparations," Brooke said quickly. Did she sound breathless? She felt it. The thought of seeing him again made her stomach erupt with butterflies.

She walked over to the front door and slid open the locks, turning the key to unlock the handle. "Hey," she said, smiling as she saw him. Aiden was still in his suit – no doubt he'd come straight from the resort – and the contrast between his elegant perfection and her just-helped-a-cat-give-birth disarray couldn't have been starker. But it was hard to be embarrassed when he was staring at her with those warm, brown eyes in a way that made her heart stutter.

A slow smile pulled up at the corner of his lips. "I've missed you."

Her heart wasn't stuttering anymore. It was galloping like it was at the Kentucky Derby. "I've missed you, too."

"Who's this?" Clara asked, standing closer to Brooke than she'd realized. Brooke jumped and turned around, her eyes wide.

"Um, this is Aiden Black. He works at the Silver Sands Resort site. He's the one who found Perdita."

Clara tipped her head to the left, as though she was scrutinizing him. "Hmm. I don't suppose you'd like to adopt her, would you?"

It was hard not to laugh out loud at Aiden's expression, but Brooke managed it anyway. Mostly by biting down so hard on her lip she almost broke the skin.

"Um, I don't think I have the time to devote to a dog."

"How about a python? They don't take too much care. Or we have some amazing rodents which only need food and company."

Aiden looked ready to vomit.

Okay, it was time to put him out of his misery. "Don't panic, she's not going to force you to look after a snake." Unable to hide her grin any longer, she looked over her shoulder at Clara. "Okay, where do you want us to start?"

"That's the last one," Brooke told him as Aiden carried a large cardboard box full of brochures out to the van. Which was so full he had to stack the box on top of a basket full of menus, before he stood and closed the double doors. At some point in the past couple of hours he'd abandoned his suit jacket and slid off his tie, rolling it up and stuffing it in his pocket, unfastening his top few buttons to give himself some air.

It was a warm, still night. Even at almost ten o'clock the temperature was high enough for him to break out into a sheen. Without the ocean breeze he'd become used to it was almost stifling.

"Thank you so much," Clara said, giving him a beaming smile.

"It was my pleasure. And I meant what I said, any time you want out of this place, there's a job for you." He winked at her. It had been a running joke all night. She was so organized, so prepared. He knew she'd fit in well at Carter Leisure. Not that she'd ever leave the animals. Like Brooke, he could tell she had a connection with them. She cooed and talked to them all whenever they passed the glass pens.

"You can head off now." Clara glanced at them both. "I'll drive the van over to the Beach Club tomorrow. One of the stewards will help unload it and put the boxes in the storage area until Saturday."

"And then the fun really begins." Brooke smiled, and it lit up her face. Aiden wasn't sure he'd ever get over how beautiful she was. Every time he looked at her it made him want to touch her.

Who was he kidding? The thought of her made his fingers ache with the need to feel her soft, smooth skin. He couldn't get enough of her. Not after she'd spent the night at his place, their limbs tangled around each other and the sheets.

"Well, goodnight. See you tomorrow, Brooke." Clara turned to him. "And if you change your mind about that python..."

"I'll be sure to let you know."

He watched as she let herself back into the shelter, ready to hand over care to the night manager who'd be keeping a special eye on the new kittens. He could tell Brooke was already getting attached to them. She'd picked one of them up to show him, and the sight of her holding the tiny bundle of fur had made his chest feel like a python was squeezing it tight. Was it possible to want to kiss somebody and shelter them from the world at the same time?

It made him realize he'd done the right thing, sending money to pay his brother off. She didn't deserve to have to deal with Jamie, not after everything she'd been through. There was too much goodness in her to let it be squeezed away by his brother.

"Do you want to grab a coffee at mine?" she asked him. "I have to get home and pay Cora, otherwise she might not babysit for me on Saturday night."

He nodded. "Yeah, sure."

"We'll have to be careful, though. Nick sometimes wakes up in the night."

"I promise not to touch you at all," he said, his voice solemn.

She laughed. "Let's not go too far. It's been hard enough having this distance between us all night, I'm not sure how much longer I can keep doing it."

Knowing she felt the same way was enough to propel him forward. Her eyes were wide as she stared up at him, those same moss green pools that always kept him mesmerized. Slowly he lowered his head to press his lips against hers.

God, her mouth was soft. His tongue slid against hers, warm and velvety. He could feel himself react within seconds, and as she pushed her body against his, he couldn't help but let out a moan.

"I take it back," he whispered against her lips. "I can't not touch you."

"I'm glad." She wrapped her arms around his neck. "Because I never want you to stop.

"I wish you could stay all night," Brooke said as she snuggled into his side. Her warm body pressed against him as she lay her head on his chest. The two of them were in her living room, Cora having long since gone home. Nick was out for the count in his bedroom, but they were still fully-clothed. Neither of them wanted to risk him seeing something he shouldn't.

Aiden kissed her hair. "I wish I could, too. There's nowhere else I'd rather be." He still had to pinch himself sometimes, knowing he was with the girl he'd fallen for all those years ago. She was everything he wanted – warm, soft, kind – and this time he was determined not to let her go.

"I never knew how good cuddling could be." There was a smile in her voice as she traced the seam of his pants along the side of his thigh. Even when her touch was dulled by a layer of denim, it still felt electric. "No, strike that, I did. It was one of the things I missed most when you left. Not being able to hold you anymore." There was a catch in her voice, and it cut him to the quick. He held her tighter, wanting to show her he wasn't going to leave her again. As far as he was concerned, she was his, and nothing would tear them apart.

Not this time.

"Was it hard when we left?" he asked, his voice soft.

She let out a sigh. Her blonde hair brushed against his lips. For a moment all he could hear was her breath and his heartbeat.

"It was a bad time for me," she told him, lifting her head to catch his eye. He could see the truth there, written plain. The memory of her pain was enough to make him wince.

"I was heartbroken. I couldn't sleep, couldn't eat. I barely cared about getting out of bed in the morning. I kept waiting for you to contact me, to let me know you were thinking about me, but you didn't."

His chest felt physically painful. "Christ, I'm sorry."

"It wasn't your fault. I know that now. But then I didn't. I thought you didn't care, thought you didn't love me. I thought I was unlovable." Her voice cracked as she finished her sentence.

His heart ached for her. "That's so untrue."

"I don't know how I got through those first few months without you. They're a blur. I can remember getting into huge trouble for not handing in assignments, and hearing Mom and Dad having worried conversations about me outside my bedroom door. But I didn't care." She tried to smile. "I guess they thought I was some kind of melodramatic teenager. Maybe I was."

"You were hurting. We all were."

She bit her lip. "And the following summer, I heard Jamie was in town. I was so damn excited to hear that."

He waited for her next words, his throat so tight he couldn't move at all.

"I was so desperate for news about you, so I sought him out. It took a while, but eventually I found him staying in somebody's apartment on the other side of town." She glanced up at Aiden. "He'd been dealing from there."

He looked down to see his hand curled into a fist. It took everything he had to unfurl his fingers.

"There were so many people coming and going he wouldn't pay any attention to me. People buying stuff and shooting up, a whole circle of people smoking. And when I tried to get his attention he said he'd only talk to me if I bought something from him." She took a deep breath. "So I did, and that's when he told me you'd met somebody else."

"What?" A ball of fury formed in the pit of his stomach. "He told you that?"

She nodded.

"And you believed him?"

Her eyes were watery. "I didn't want to, but I wasn't in a good place. And it explained a lot..."

"I hadn't. I would never have done that to you so quickly. It took me a long time to *want* to date again."

"But I still believed him. So I took the joint he'd rolled up for me, along with a bottle of vodka he'd shoved in my hands."

"He got you high?"

"No." She shook her head. "I got *myself* high. And drunk as a skunk. That bit's on me. What happened after... not so much."

"What did he do?" His voice was sharp. It made her blink. "Sorry." He kissed her brow. "It's not you I'm angry at, it's him."

"It's all kind of hazy. I remember kissing him, and I didn't hate it. As awful as it sounds, I was so low. Any attention felt good."

"And you slept with him?"

Brooke nodded. "I barely remember it, but yeah, I did. Once. It wasn't until a few months later I realized I was pregnant."

Aiden tried to remember back to those days. Jamie was hardly ever home by that point, and he'd liked it that way. It made his and Joan's lives so much easier.

But if only he'd known where he was wandering to.

"I was almost six months along before I realized I was pregnant. He'd been out of town for almost as long." Brooke rubbed her eyes with the heels of her hands. "Half of me didn't want to contact him at all. But it didn't seem right. And maybe there was a part of me that wanted any contact I could get with your family. So I hired a PI."

"You did?"

"Yeah. It didn't take the guy long to track your brother down. When he heard I was pregnant he told the investigator I should get rid of it and not to contact him again." Brooke looked down at her hands. "So I didn't."

"Why didn't you contact me?"

"What would I have said? Hey, I'm crazy in love with you, and guess what? I'm having your brother's baby!" Brooke grimaced. "I was so ashamed. I never wanted you to know. Every way I looked at it I was screwed. So I decided to have the baby without any support." She smiled at Aiden, as though she finally felt lighter. "And I'm so glad I did."

"Jamie never told me. And I can't believe he never told Mom, either. She would have insisted on seeing you both."

"I know. I hate that Nick never had the chance to know his other grandmother." Brooke looked at him with those wide, pretty eyes. "I'm sorry."

He swallowed hard, ignoring the ache in his chest. "It's not your fault. None of this is. The more I hear the more I realize you were everybody's victim. I should have been here to take care of you, and I wasn't."

"You were taking care of your mom."

"Yeah, I guess."

She turned, her body brushing against his as she scrambled to her knees, cupping his strong jaw between her warm palms. "You told me this wasn't my fault, well it wasn't yours either." Lowering her head, she let her brow rest against his. He could feel her breath soft against his lips. "It's all in the past," she whispered. "There's no point in dwelling on it. I have Nick and I wouldn't have it any other way." Her voice dipped. "I also have you, and I'm so happy about that." She brushed her lips against his, and he felt a jolt of pleasure rush through him. "So let's stop talking about the past and start concentrating on the present."

He curled his arms around her back. "That sounds good to me."

•••

It was almost midnight by the time he'd left Brooke's apartment. The town lay silent, the only noise he could hear was the gentle crashing of waves a few blocks to the west. He was still smiling from the memory of the evening – the way they'd kissed like crazy after she'd opened up to him. No more secrets, no more lies. Just the two of them laid bare.

Walking across the blacktop parking lot, he scrolled through the messages he'd missed for the past few hours. It wasn't like him not to check his emails and texts incessantly. Maybe it was like him now, though. He felt like a different man. Taller, stronger, more complete.

He deleted the usual marketing messages, taking note of a couple of work emails he'd need to tackle in the morning. That's when he saw the email from the Private Investigator his lawyer had retained. The man tasked with making Jamie an offer he couldn't refuse.

Thank God he'd agreed to pay Jamie off. The thought of him seeking Aiden out and finding Brooke and Nick was enough to send an ice-cold shiver down his spine. A wave of protectiveness washed over him as he glanced back at her apartment building. He wouldn't let anything happen to them. He couldn't. They were too important to him.

He used his thumb to scroll down to read the message. He'd reached his car and leaned on the driver's side, his eyes trained on the email.

Dear Mr. Black,

•   •   •

Your brother was released from prison earlier today. I met him at the gates, and discovered he doesn't currently have a registered home, though he has been supplied a list of local shelters with spaces for him. I explained who I was, and offered to drive him to a local motel and pay for a night's accommodation, which he agreed to. He also agreed that I could pick him up tomorrow morning in order to buy him breakfast, and take him shopping for some clothes.

He is aware that I am acting on your behalf, and that you will be funding the accommodation and any clothing purchases. I also explained that you would like to set him up for the longer term, and we will discuss it over breakfast tomorrow. He did ask about you a number of times, and I explained you were out of state on business.

I will send a further email to you tomorrow outlining the results of our discussion. Your brother seems likely to accept whatever help we can offer.

Yours,

Richard Neville
    Private Investigator

Aiden slid the phone into his pocket and climbed into his car, half his mind on the email, the other half on Brooke. The fear of his brother contacting Brooke or Nick waned, enough to let him relax back into the driver's seat as he turned on the engine. It came to life with a reassuring growl, cutting through the night air. Allowing himself one last glance at Brooke's place, he put his foot on the gas and accelerated out of the parking lot.

After all these years, it felt as though everything was finally slotting into place; and it felt pretty damn good to him.

"I'm sorry. I know I'm late. But I brought you all coffee." Ally breezed her way into the Heavenly Hair Salon carrying a cardboard tray filled with insulated coffee cups. She handed one each to Brooke and Ember – who were already in their seats, staring at the mirrors in front of them – and passed the rest to the stylists who were hovering around them.

Brooke grabbed her cup and took a long mouthful of Americano. After all these years, Ally knew exactly how she liked it – dark with some sweetness, and only a splash of warm milk. Truth was, she needed the caffeine kick.

"Sit down." The third stylist pulled out a chair and Ally slumped onto it. Within moments she was wrapped in a black gown and Marie was running her fingers through her golden locks, asking her questions about how she wanted her style. When they'd finally agreed, she took her off to wash her hair.

"Hurricane Ally," Ember said, grinning at their friend. "She never changes, does she?"

"Would we want her to?" Brooke asked.

"No way."

In the past few years, having their hair styled together before the gala had become a tradition. Usually Brooke's mom would join them, making a fourth along the wall of mirrors, but her seat was conspicuously empty.

"She's not coming?" Ember asked, following Brooke's gaze.

"I don't think so." Brooke swallowed. "I tried to call her last night but she didn't answer. I left a voicemail."

"And she hasn't returned it?" Ember's expression was full of sympathy. "That's hard."

Brooke nodded. "I guess I'm getting a taste of my own treatment. One way or the other I'll see her tonight."

"Do you think she'll come?"

"Of course. It's one of the biggest dates in the Angel Sands calendar. She wouldn't miss the opportunity to catch up with everybody. Plus it's for a good cause. She might not be talking to me, but she still does a lot of work for charity."

"She'll talk to you. I know she will." Ember reached out from under her hairdressing cape and grabbed Brooke's hand, squeezing it tight. "She loves you."

"What did I miss?" Ally asked as the stylist brought her back over, a black towel wrapped around her head like a turban. She slumped into the chair again and grabbed her coffee.

"We were talking about Brooke's mom."

"Oh thank God. I thought you might be talking about Aiden without me here to listen."

Brooke shook her head as Ember coughed out a laugh.

"Seriously. I need all the details. How are things going between you? Have you slept with him again?"

"Ally!" Ember looked around. Nobody was listening except the stylists, and everybody knew they took all secrets to their graves.

"Too much?" Ally asked.

"Yep."

"In that case, you can at least tell us how you feel about him."

Wow. She wasn't expecting that. In a weird way the question felt more intimate than asking her if she'd slept with him again. Because while the sex was good – okay, amazing – her emotions were all over the place.

"I really like him," she whispered, already knowing those

words weren't strong enough. She loved him. She could feel it in every cell of her body. Loved the way he took care of her, the way he looked at her, the way he had a special smile he gave only to her. Every time she saw him it was as though the two of them were in a bubble nobody else could penetrate.

"She loves him," Ally said to Ember, who nodded and earned herself a squeal from her stylist.

"Yep."

In the mirror she could see her own stylist nodding in agreement. Traitor.

"Have you told him?" Ember asked.

"No!" She wanted to shake her head, but knew it could end in disaster.

"Why not?" Ally said as the stylist combed through her hair, making her grimace every time she hit a knot.

"Because it's too soon. And it's too messy. I haven't even told Nick we're seeing each other, and I haven't told my parents that Aiden's Nick's uncle. It doesn't feel right saying those three words until everything is out in the open."

"Then you better start talking to people."

All three stylists nodded in agreement. If she wasn't feeling so nervous, Brooke would have laughed.

"I tried. I called my mom, remember?" Brooke sighed. "I'll call her again after the gala. That's not a conversation to have at the event."

"And you'll tell Nick about the two of you being a couple?"

Brooke met Ember's gaze in the reflection of the mirror. "Yeah, that's the plan."

"The plan?" Ally asked, her voice rising up an octave. "You have a plan?"

"Aiden and I talked about it. He wants us to tell Nick together. It'll be a lot for him to take in, and we want him to be able to ask Aiden anything he wants to."

"Oh my God, why didn't you say so?" This time Ally was

definitely squealing. Her stylist wisely put the scissors she'd been holding on the little shelf in front of the mirror. "That's better than an 'I love you' by far. It means he's serious about you."

"You think?"

"He wants to tell Nick about you being together, and we all know how much he cares about Nick, so yeah, I really do think."

The hope budding inside of her began to bloom in her chest. Yes, her life was complicated, and getting more so by the minute, but whenever Aiden was around everything felt so good. As though she could conquer any mountain she tried to climb.

"That's fantastic," Ember said, giving her a warm smile. "If anybody deserves a happily-ever-after it's you."

24

Brooke stared at herself in the small bathroom mirror as she combed the mascara wand through her lashes, her mouth forming an 'o' as she concentrated on not smudging it everywhere. When she was happy with the effect, she slid the tube back into her cosmetic case and grabbed the MAC lipstick she'd worn to a stump, this time spreading the dark pink hue across her mouth.

"You make strange faces when you put on make up," Nick said, peeking around the door.

She turned to him and stuck out her tongue. "I didn't know anybody was watching."

"You look pretty," he said, taking in her long silver dress. Her hair was swept into the messy updo her stylist had created earlier. All she needed were her earrings and her evening purse and the look would be complete.

"Thank you, darling."

"And Cora is here. She told me to tell you."

"You opened the door?" Brooke's good humor disappeared. "What have I told you about that? If the doorbell rings you call me."

He blinked, as though he was holding back tears and she immediately felt bad. "I knew you were busy. I was trying to help."

Her hands shook as she put the lipstick down on the ceramic sink and turned to look at him. Her beautiful boy, with his dark hair and whiskey eyes. Growing to look more and more like a Black every day.

"I'm sorry, honey," she said softly. "I know you were. There are some bad people out there and it's my job to protect you from them. I can't do that if you're opening the door without my knowledge."

He nodded, his expression serious. "I only opened it because I could see Cora. I wouldn't have done it otherwise." His bottom lip was still trembling. Picking up the hem of her skirt to stop it from getting caught under her feet, she walked over to him and squatted down, reaching out to brush the hair from his face. He was already dressed in plaid pajamas. Beneath his nose was a hint of a milk moustache. Her heart clenched at the sight of him.

Her son. Her love. The thought of anybody hurting him made her fists want to curl up. It was her job to protect him, always.

"Will Uncle Aiden be at the gala?" Nick asked.

She took another ragged breath in. Secrets and lies – she hated them all. They were ropes binding her up until she couldn't move a muscle. She was going to cut them off her, one by one, and break free.

"Yes, he's taking me."

"Like a date?" Nick frowned, but she knew it wasn't because he was upset. She recognized that expression – it was one he made when he was trying to work things out. She saw it all the time when he was doing his math homework.

"Sort of." She nodded. "Is that okay with you?"

Nick tipped his head to the side and pondered her question. "Yeah," he said after a moment. "I'm good with that."

She ruffled his hair with her outstretched fingers. "So am I."

"Mom?"

"Yes?"

"Do you love Uncle Aiden?"

The question hit her like a bullet to the chest. Her head lifted so she could look right into Nick's eyes. The frown was still lingering as he stared at her, but more than anything she saw complete trust there. Whatever she told him he'd believe, because she was his mom and therefore his world. The same way she'd believed her parents when they'd told her why Aiden and his family had skipped town. All along she'd felt powerless in the face of her family, her choices, her life, but right now the burden of power overwhelmed her. She had the power to shape her son's reality, and it was both a burden and an honor.

"Yes, sweetie," she said, her voice soft. "I love him a lot."

"So do I."

That was all he said, and she was relieved. She and Aiden would tell him more when this damn gala was over. But for now, he seemed content with what she'd said.

Circling her arms around him, she pulled him close, breathing in the scent of his soap and shampoo, and the hint of milk lingering on him. How long would he smell like this? Her little boy. How long did she have to make him be the kind of man she wanted him to be?

Not long enough.

"I'm going to see Grandma and Grandpa tonight," she told Nick, leaning back to glance at his face.

He looked surprised at her mention of them. "You are?"

"Yes. And I'm going to speak to them and tell them about

everything I've told you. That Aiden's your uncle and that we love him."

A smile burst out on Nick's face. "They'll love him too, won't they? Maybe we can bring him the next time we go to dinner."

"I don't know how they'll take it," she told him. "But it's always good to tell the truth, no matter how hard that is sometimes."

He hugged her again tightly, and she didn't give a damn how much he was crushing her dress, or whether her make up was smudging as she dropped her face to his hair to breathe him in one last time before she left.

And when he released her and ran back into the kitchen to Cora, she found herself standing up and not even bothering to glance at herself in the mirror. She didn't care how she looked, because she was finally in control of her life. And it felt absolutely amazing.

"Everybody's staring."

Aiden followed her gaze. They were standing at the double wide entrance to the ballroom, looking in to where the tables were already filled with guests. She was right, most people were staring, but not with malice on their faces. The expressions they wore were intrigued and interested, and from the way they turned to talk to each other, Aiden and Brooke were going to be the main gossip point of the gala.

"Let them." He turned to smile at her. "Have I told you how beautiful you look tonight?"

"About ten times." A smile played at her lips. "And as I told you before, you're the beautiful one. Have you noticed it's mostly women staring at us?"

He could never get enough of her. Everything about her

was luminous. From her silver evening dress that skimmed every curve, to the glow of her exposed skin, from her chest right up to her long, elegant neck. When he'd picked her up from her apartment, he'd felt every nerve ending in his body come alive. The need to touch her, feel her, and breathe her in was almost overwhelming. He was counting down the hours until they could get out of this place and be alone again.

"They're staring because they like to gossip."

"You know them too well."

He took her hand, sliding her fingers between his, and held her tightly. "It's going to be okay," he told her. "By this time next week we'll be old news. Things move fast in Angel Sands."

They stepped inside the ballroom, and the warm, breezy atmosphere enveloped them. The orchestra was playing a slow song, low enough so the chatter coming from the tables could easily be heard. On the far end of the room the wall of glass doors were pulled back to let the warm evening air inside, framing a perfect view of the dark blue ocean as the sun began to slide below the horizon.

"My parents aren't here yet," Brooke said softly.

He looked at the table by the stage – table number one, of course. Sure enough it was full save for two empty seats.

"Maybe they're not coming."

She gave a small laugh. "That's wishful thinking. They like to make an entrance. They've probably already told the kitchen not to serve any food until they arrive."

"It's going to be okay."

"How do you always know the right thing to say?" she asked him, her eyes shining beneath the glow of the crystal chandeliers.

"Because I know what you're thinking." He smiled at her.

"I'm not sure whether to be pleased or afraid."

With his hands still in hers, he steered her toward their table – on the other side of the room to where her parents would be sitting. Six people were already seated there – Ally and Nate, Ember and Lucas, plus Lucas's friends, Griffin and Jackson. They all stood to greet Brooke and Aiden as they approached, and Aiden reluctantly let go of her hand in order to shake everybody elses'.

"You look amazing," Ember was telling Brooke. She side-eyed Aiden, and he nodded, still knowing exactly what she was thinking.

"That's what I said."

"Yeah, well you don't look so bad yourself," Ember added. "Who knew you guys would all look so handsome in dinner jackets? I've told Lucas he's going to have to wear one every day now."

"That'll be a real help when I'm climbing ladders," Lucas said, shaking his head at her. His smile was only for her.

Once they'd said their hellos, Aiden pulled Brooke's chair out and watched as she sat down. She looked as good from the back as she did from the front. The dress exposed her from the top of her neck to the base of her spine, and his lips tingled with the need to kiss every inch of her skin.

As he slid into the seat next to her, he watched as her back stiffened. He didn't need to glance over at the doorway to know her parents had finally arrived. Her chest rose as she took in a mouthful of air, and dropped as she blew it out.

"It's okay," he murmured, covering the back of her hand with his palm. "Relax."

"They're looking at us," she said, repeating her earlier words.

"Let them look."

Casually, he slid his arm around her shoulders, letting the tips of his fingers caress her skin. She said nothing, but she leaned into him, and he felt the warmth of her against his body.

From the corner of his eye he could see Martin and Lillian walk toward their own table and greet their guests. With a final glance toward their daughter, they sat down and the food began to be served.

"Come and dance with me," Aiden murmured, reaching his hand out for her to take. Brooke looked up at him. His face was constantly in her thoughts. His high cheekbones and strong nose, above those full, full lips that made her legs tremble. He must have shaved right before he picked her up – the usual evening shade on his jawbone was absent. Brooke let him take her hand and help her up, before he led her to the dancefloor.

"I've never danced with you before," she said, as he slid his arm around her waist and pulled her body against his. She could feel the hard planes of his stomach on her abdomen.

"We danced at the beach when we were kids."

"That was a fast dance. We've never danced with you holding me."

She felt his chest rise with a laugh. "Do you know why?"

"Because you can't dance?"

This time his laugh was louder. "No. Because I didn't trust myself to not want more."

"You silly boy. I wanted you to want more."

Shaking his head, he began to sway to the music, moving their bodies in time to the rhythm. She let her head fall against his chest as she closed her eyes, feeling the crisp cotton of his shirt on her cheek. It did nothing to disguise the heat of his body, or the hardness of his chest muscles. She felt him press his lips to her temple, and it sent a shiver down her spine.

"Nick was asking about us," she told him as they swayed slowly toward the middle of the dance floor.

"What about us?" There was no shock or worry in Aiden's voice; more idle curiosity.

"Whether this was a date."

"What did you tell him?"

She looked up at him, the action crushing her breasts against his shirt. "I told him the truth."

"Good. That always works."

It was impossible not to smile. "That's what I said. I know we said we're going to tell him about us together, but I didn't want to lie to him."

"You don't have to explain it to me. I want everybody to know." His glance slid over toward where her parents were sitting, waiting for the dancing to end and the auction to begin.

They were looking right at her and Aiden.

"They're next," she murmured. "As soon as I find the gumption."

"You've got the gumption, Brooke. You always did. But you have to believe in yourself, too."

Maybe he was right. Whatever it was, she felt more sure of herself than she had in a long time.

When the music ended and the MC gave a five minute warning for the auction, Aiden led her back to the table where her friends were all milling around. Ally reached for her hand, grinning. "I'm heading to the bathroom. You coming?"

"Wait, I'm coming, too," Ember said, blowing a kiss at Lucas who was shaking his head. "What? You think I'm going to miss out on the gossip? The bathroom is always where the real party's at."

There was a huge line for the restroom. The three of them stood and waited patiently, trying not to look enviously at the lack of queue for the men's room.

"Have you managed to speak to your parents yet?" Ally murmured as they inched their way toward the front of the line.

"Not yet, but I've had plenty of eye contact from them. I'm planning on speaking to them once the auction is over."

"Good idea. Let them spend their money first. That way they'll be more generous."

Ember laughed. "You're mercenary."

"Hey," Ally protested. "I'm a business woman. Anyway," she turned back to Brooke, "you and Aiden looked amazing out there. Like you're made for each other. I swear I saw electricity flowing between you."

"Your parents will accept him eventually. The same way they'll accept Nick being related to him."

Brooke pressed her lips together, thinking about the conversation she'd be having in less than an hour. "You know what?" she said. "It doesn't matter how they react. I have no control over that. What matters is I tell them the truth. That I'm happy Nick is Aiden's nephew, and I'm delighted Aiden and I are dating. Either they deal with it or they don't. That's up to them."

"Wow." Ally's mouth dropped open. "I'm so proud of you. What happened to quiet little Brooke?"

"She became a raging river," Ember said, grinning.

They'd made it to the front of the line, and one by one they went into the stalls. When Brooke came out, Ally and Ember were already at the sinks, washing their hands as the MC announced the auction was about to begin. "Okay, we're going to need a debrief tomorrow," Ally said as the three of them made their way back to the table. "Meet me at the café at nine."

"Um, I may be having breakfast in bed with a certain fiancé of mine," Ember said, shaking her head with a smile.

"Hey, if I have to get up for work the least you can do is come and entertain me. Just for a half an hour, okay? We didn't get quality bathroom time in there, and I need my girl talk."

"Okay, okay. I'll see you at nine."

Brooke bit down a laugh at her friends' exchange. She knew she'd be up – Nick never slept in on the weekends. Nine o'clock would be like a second breakfast for them.

"Ladies and Gentlemen, please take your seats for the auction."

Brooke glanced at the table and realized Aiden wasn't there. She frowned. "Is Aiden in the bathroom?" she asked Lucas once they got to the table.

Lucas shook his head and stood to pull Ember's chair out. "No. He's talking to some guy." He inclined his head toward the bar. Brooke followed his gaze and spotted him, his broad back facing her.

She saw the man he was talking to and her heart nearly stopped. It might have been almost nine years since she last laid eyes on him, but she'd know that face anywhere.

Her breath caught in her throat and her legs began to tremble as if she'd run a marathon.

What the hell was Jamie Black doing in Angel Sands?

❧ 25 ❧

She'd never seen Aiden hold himself so still. He had a lethal edge to him that sent a shiver down her spine. Brooke swallowed in spite of her dry mouth and looked at Ally and Ember, who stared back at her with wide eyes.

"Is that who I think it is?" Ally whispered.

"Shit." Ember was only echoing what all three of them were thinking.

"Is everything okay?" Lucas frowned. "Is Aiden in trouble?"

Brooke shook her head and looked over at the bar once again. "No, he's not in trouble. He's talking to his brother." She could see the auctioneer climbing up onto the stage. She should be standing with Clara, helping spot the bidders and take down the names of the winners. Instead she was staring at her biggest mistake and it made her want to scream. "I'm going to talk to them."

"Is that a good idea?" Ember reached for her. "Brooke?"

Maybe it wasn't a good idea, but she had no idea what else to do. From the way Aiden was standing, his hands fisted by his side, she was afraid if she didn't intervene there was going to be carnage. With her breath caught in her throat, she covered the distance between the table and the bar, the calls of the auctioneer ringing in her ears.

She stopped about four feet away from where the two of them were standing. Aiden's voice was low and dark, but she couldn't hear what he was saying. Slowly, she brought her gaze to the man he was addressing. He had shaved dark hair, a scar running through his eyebrow, and a neck covered in tattoos.

As if he could feel the heat of her scrutiny, Jamie looked up at her. He blinked as though there was sand in his eyes, his scarred eyebrow rising up.

"Brooke?" he asked, his eyes squinting. "Brooke Newton?"

Aiden immediately turned around and caught her eye. "Go, Brooke," he said, his voice imploring.

"I'm not going anywhere."

"Brooke Newton," Jamie said again. A half smile curled his upper lip. "Jesus Christ you're prettier than I remember." He pushed his tongue against the inside of his cheek. "Did you know I've had her?" he asked Aiden.

"Shut. Up."

"Not a great lay. She'd been out of her mind on alcohol. But sex with a Newton is always sweet, isn't it, bro?"

Brooke stiffened. "What are you doing here? I thought you were in prison."

"There's this thing called parole. I served my time." He tipped his head to the side and licked his lips. "How's my kid doing? Is it here tonight?"

The way he was grinning at her made her want to scream. She'd spent the last nine years protecting her precious boy from pain. And now his birth father was here and she couldn't handle it.

"He's not here."

"We had a boy?" He raised his eyebrows. "Congratulations

to us. I guess I'll see him another time." Jamie shrugged as though he was a friend inviting himself around for coffee.

"No you won't." Aiden moved so he was in between Brooke and Jamie, shielding her from him. "You'll leave and not come back. You're not wanted here."

"What's the matter, bro?" Jamie's voice was low. "You seem real jittery right now."

"You were supposed to stay in Sacramento." There was something off about Aiden's words, but Brooke couldn't place it. She was too caught up in the disaster waiting to happen. Behind her the auction was continuing, but she couldn't hear a word of what they were saying.

"But I came down here instead. I've got a kid here. I have rights, you know."

It was as if a veil had descended over her. No, not a veil, a suit of armor. One that riled her up and made every muscle in her body tense. She was in fight mode, a lioness protecting her cub, and Jamie Black had no idea what was about to hit him.

Aiden reached for her arm, but she shrugged him off and walked around him. She stopped right in front of Jamie, her eyes at the same level as his thanks to her stupidly high heels. Slowly, she raised her arm and pressed the pad of her finger against his chest, feeling the heat of him through his thin t-shirt. Jamie blinked but didn't move.

"Don't you *dare* claim any rights over my son. Don't you dare come here and tell *me* anything about my boy. You've never met him, you've never cared for him, you've never spent a dime on him. You're a sperm donor, that's all, and neither of us want you here."

Jamie lifted his hands up as if to ward her off. "Hey, cool it."

"Don't you tell me to cool it."

"Babe, I'm not interested in our son. I'm more interested

in my brother's cash. I want a few more dollars from him and I won't bother you again."

"What?" She turned to look at Aiden, confusion making her head feel woolly. "What's he talking about? Why would he want a few dollars more?"

"You didn't tell her?" Jamie asked, laughing loudly.

"Tell me what?"

"Brooke, go back to the table. I'll explain it all later." Aiden's voice was urgent. "Go, please."

"What's he talking about?" she asked him again. "What cash?"

"He paid me off. Offered me thirty thousand dollars to keep away from you and your son. I've come down to reopen the negotiations."

"You knew he was out of prison?" she asked Aiden. "Why didn't you tell me?"

"Yeah, bro, why didn't you tell her?"

"Shut the hell up," she said to Jamie. Her world famous patience was wearing thin.

"You didn't need to know." Aiden reached for her again, folding his hands around her elbow. "He's my problem and I'm sorting it out."

"Talking about me like that could hurt my feelings," Jamie pointed out, looking like he was enjoying himself a little too much.

Ignoring him, Brooke asked, "Aiden, what have you done?"

"He's sent me a bribe. That's what he's done. Thirty thousand dollars to keep away from you and your kid." Jamie pushed his lip out in a mock-pout. "What's up, Brookey, don't you think you're worth more? Because I do."

The champagne she'd drunk earlier swirled around in her stomach, making her throat contract with a need to throw up. Why would Aiden have done that without speaking to her first? What gave him the right to make decisions about her life without her input?

"Were you ever going to tell me he was out?" she asked Aiden. "If Jamie had taken your bribe would you have kept silent forever?"

The look on Aiden's face told her all she needed to know.

He'd planned to keep this a secret forever.

"What about telling the truth always?" she asked him. "What about no more secrets, no more lies? What about letting me take control of my own life?"

"Brooke..."

"No." She put her hand up. "I need to think this through."

"What's going on here?"

Brooke turned to see her father standing a couple of feet away from Aiden, and next to him was her mom, staring at the three of them with wide eyes.

Dear God, could this get any worse?

"Mom, Dad, can I talk to you about this later?" Brooke asked, though she knew it was futile. Her father wasn't going anywhere, she could tell by his expression.

"Hey, it's Grandpa and Grammy. How you doing?" Jamie swaggered toward her dad, holding his hand out. Her father looked at him with distaste.

"I see you brought the rest of the scum with you," Martin said, staring right at Aiden. "What is this, the Black family outing?"

"Well, not *all* the family. One of us is missing." Jamie winked at them. God, how had she ever let herself get near him? He was odious.

"I heard about your mother. My condolences."

"I wasn't talking about my mother. I'm talking about my son."

Time froze. Brooke's breath caught in her throat as everybody went silent around them. Even the auctioneer had stopped calling out, as though realizing there was a far better show happening stage left. Slowly she turned to look at Aiden, whose mouth had dropped open. She began to count down in her head – five, four, three, two, one second to disaster.

"You have a son? I didn't know." It was the first thing her mother had said. Brooke turned to look at her. She was surrounded by her usual air of grandeur, her body held straight in a way only years of yoga could maintain.

"Oh, I'm pretty sure you know him very well."

"Jamie, shut the hell up." Aiden closed the gap between himself and his brother, squaring his body up.

"Hey, I'm talking to Marty and Lil. We're practically family, after all."

"What's he talking about?" Lillian said, frowning at his shortening of her name. "Brooke?"

Brooke opened her mouth to say something, but no words would come out. They were all frozen on her tongue. She couldn't breathe, couldn't move. It was like seeing a train heading straight for you and being caught on the rail.

"Come on, as if you didn't know." Jamie's eyes sparked as he moved his gaze from her father to her mother. "You must have known, right? We're related, after all. Your grandson is my child."

26

Aiden couldn't stand the look of betrayal on Brooke's face, her eyes full of tears. This woman, the one who dominated everything in his life, he'd hurt her and it was killing him. He reached for her, wanting to pull her into his arms and protect her from the world unraveling in front of her.

But she stepped back and lifted a hand up to wipe away the tears from her cheek. "No lies," she whispered, her words cutting through him like a knife. "That's what you promised. You should have warned me. I could have been prepared. I could have done something..."

"Brooke, is this true?" Martin's voice was low. Menacing. "Did you sleep with this scum?"

"Takes one to know one, Marty."

"Dad, I..."

"Brooke," he roared, silencing the room. "Tell me what the hell is going on."

Her face crumpled. Aiden couldn't stand the way she looked at him with helplessness in her eyes. He'd betrayed her the way her parents had. Made decisions without believing she had a right to make choices too.

"I need to go," she whispered.

"You're not going anywhere," Martin commanded. But she was already backing away, her hand fluttering at her throat. A moment later, she turned on her heel and ran toward the door, holding her skirt with one hand as she tried to keep herself stable with the other. Aiden turned to follow her when a soft hand touched his shoulder. Ember. Worry was etched on her face.

"Let her calm down," she said. "Don't follow her. Sort this out first."

He followed her gaze to Brooke's parents and his brother. They were glaring at him, every one of them looking at him as if he had all the answers.

But he didn't. Not a single one.

Ember was right. He couldn't leave his brother here with the Newtons. Jamie was too much of a liability for that. Aiden could do nothing but watch as Brooke disappeared through the open doors onto the ocean front, her hair flying in the breeze.

She was gone and he felt empty. So empty. He took a breath and felt the emptiness fill with a whole new emotion.

Cold, white anger.

At Jamie, at Martin and Lillian, but most of all at himself. Because his crappy decisions had led to this confrontation, and the very person he'd been trying to protect had borne the brunt of it.

"Was it something I said?" Jamie was still grinning. For the first time Aiden wondered if his brother was on something. Surely he wouldn't be so stupid...

Of course he would.

"You," Aiden said, glaring at the man who shared his blood but nothing else. "Keep quiet."

He turned to Brooke's parents. For once Lillian was silent, and Martin was too. But his eyes were full of accusations waiting to come out.

"You should know Brooke was going to tell you everything," he told them, his voice low. "None of this is her fault."

Martin's nostrils flared. "Of course it is. You lay with scum you end up becoming scum."

There was a gentle hand on his arm again. "That's not true," Ember said, her voice sounding stronger than he felt. "She's your daughter. She's made mistakes. But Nick isn't one of those. He's a joy to everybody." She looked straight at Brooke's parents, her eyes wide and true. "I know how much you love him."

Lillian lifted her hand to her throat, in a gesture that reminded him of Brooke. "I don't know what to think."

"No wonder she never told us who the father was," Martin spat. "She would have been thrown out before she even finished her sentence."

"Why? Because of his family?" Ember gave Aiden a side glance, as though to tell him to remain silent. She was probably right. If he opened his mouth his fist would almost certainly follow, and the last thing Brooke needed was her father floored by her boyfriend.

If that's what he still was.

"But don't you see," Ember continued, leaning closer to Brooke's parents, "Nick is part of their family, too. If you hate the Black family, you hate your grandson. And I know you could never do that."

There was silence as Lillian took those words in. Martin's face was still mutinous, as though he wanted somebody – *anybody* – to blame for this.

"I need to think." Lillian looked up at her husband. "Martin..."

"What?"

"Let's get a drink and talk about this sensibly."

"I want answers."

She ran her hand down his tuxedo-clad arm, and slid her fingers into his. For the first time, Aiden could see a hint of Brooke in her mother. In the soft way she was dealing with her husband, defusing him like a bomb about to implode.

"Come on, darling," she said, looking up at him. "Let's go and talk this through."

Martin swallowed, his adam's apple bobbing above his crisp, white collar. He might have had twice the strength of his wife, but he still allowed her to pull him along and away from the fracas.

Ember had discreetly left, too. Only Aiden and Jamie were left standing there, staring at each other. Without an audience, the smirk had dissolved from his brother's face.

Aiden opened his mouth to speak, but had no idea what to say. A memory washed over him, of when he was maybe four or five-years-old and the two of them were cowering at the top of the stairs while their father beat their mother for not keeping his dinner warm. Jamie had slid his hand into Aiden's and squeezed it as the tears rolled down his cheeks. "It's okay," Aiden had whispered. "He'll fall down and go to sleep in a minute."

Where had it all gone wrong? Had Jamie tired of being Aiden's brother, and inhaled whatever it took to forget about his life? Or was Martin Newton right, did the bad run through each of them like a fault in the earth – waiting for the fissure to happen?

"Go outside," Aiden said to Jamie. He was fidgeting, moving from one foot to the other like he was dancing a jig. "I'll meet you out there in a moment."

Jamie blinked, as though he wasn't sure what to do next. "Will you bring money?"

"No." Aiden shook his head. "But I won't bring the cops either if you leave quietly. Wait for me in the parking lot."

When he returned to the table only Ember and Ally were there, the two of them staring at him with worry as he reached for Brooke's wrap and his own wallet and keys. Beneath her wrap was her small silver evening purse. He hadn't realized she'd left without it.

"I tried calling Brooke, but her phone is still here," Ember said, inclining her head at the purse in his hand. "Lucas and Nate have gone out to look for her."

"And Griff and Jackson are by the door, keeping an eye on your brother," Ally added, giving him a sympathetic smile.

His stomach dropped. The thought of Brooke out there all alone without any money or her phone alarmed him. She couldn't have gone far. Nate and Lucas would probably be walking back in with her by their side any minute. He could talk to her then.

If she'd listen.

"Christ, I've messed up."

Ember gave him the smallest of smiles. "Yeah, you have," she said kindly.

"What do I do?" he asked them. "Tell me. How do I make this better."

Ember and Ally exchanged a glance, and turned their heads to look at him. "You know what to do. You've been doing it for most of the time you've been back," Ember told him. "Except for this one thing."

"I was trying to protect her. Jamie's my problem. She shouldn't have to worry about him."

"But she didn't want your protection. She wanted your partnership." Ember glanced over at the table on the far side of the room where Lillian and Martin were leaning in toward each other, both of them talking rapidly. "She's had people making decisions for her all her life. Her father thought he was protecting her by sending you away. Her mother thought she was protecting her by lying to her. She trusted you, Aiden. She thought you believed in her enough for her to make her own decisions. But you didn't."

"That's not what I wanted."

"But it's what you gave her. You took her choices away from her and made them yourself."

"I'm no better than her father," he said slowly, as realization washed over him. "No wonder she hates me." He needed a drink. Because every damn word Ember was telling him was true.

"You're better in one respect," Ally said, her eyes soft. "You're listening to the truth, and taking it all in."

"Give her time," Ember urged. "And space. And if she comes back to you, grovel like hell."

"And in the meantime, you should probably go and talk to your brother." Ally nodded toward the door. "I'm not sure how long Griff and Jackson can stand to watch him."

Jamie was pacing up and down the blacktop of the Beach Club parking lot when Aiden arrived outside. The coolness of the night time air caressed his skin. Griff and Jackson gave him a nod and walked back inside, leaving the two brothers alone once again.

Aiden took a deep breath of ocean air. He'd come back to this town in a blaze of glory, determined to show Angel Sands how he'd changed, come up in the world, become *somebody*. And yet somehow, in their eyes he was still that kid from the wrong side of the tracks. The scum who'd messed with Martin Newton's golden girl.

Yeah, well fuck them. He didn't have time for their opinions right now.

Noticing him standing by the door, Jamie stopped walking and came to a halt in front of him. Aiden eyed him warily, waiting for the anger he'd felt inside the Beach Club to descend. But it didn't. Instead a deep, dark exhaustion clawed into every bone.

"Why are you here?" he asked Jamie.

"To see my brother." Jamie grinned. "I missed ya, kid."

"Cut the bullshit." Aiden's voice was low. "Why are you really here?"

Jamie's mouth twisted as he lifted his hand to wipe at his nose. "Thirty thousand dollars," he said slowly. "Is that all I'm worth to you?"

"That's what my peace of mind was worth to me. But I shouldn't have paid it to you anyway."

"I need more."

"No." Aiden shook his head. "You're not getting another dime from me."

Jamie's lip twitched. "I need it. Thirty thousand isn't going to get me very far. I owe people money. I need somewhere to live..."

"So get a job like the rest of us."

"You think it's so easy, don't you? With your pretty suit and shiny degree. Not all of us came out of this thing unscathed, *brother*. Some of us still bear the scars."

As if he didn't have scars, too. He might not have borne the brunt of his father's beatings, but his skin had enough evidence to show they'd happened. "You want to talk about this stuff?" he said, raising an eyebrow. "Then go to therapy."

"I could make trouble for you. I saw how you look at her. I can make things bad between you and Brooke. I have rights.

I have a son. I could fuck up his life the way Dad fucked up ours."

Aiden's gut clenched. The thought of Nick going through what they'd gone through made his heart hurt. Jamie was a loose cannon, and the need to shield his nephew – and Brooke – from him was so strong Aiden could almost taste it.

"Sure. Hang around and see how much you enjoy it. Rights bring responsibilities. You ready for Brooke to sue you for child support? I'm pretty sure you must owe a lot."

Jamie blinked but said nothing.

"Keep the thirty thousand," Aiden said. "But you won't get another dollar from me. We're done here." He leaned forward, his eyes connecting with his brother's. "And if you think you can hurt Nick, you're mistaken. His mother wouldn't let you. She's a wolf. She'd eat you for breakfast."

Disbelief flooded Jamie's face. "Yeah right."

"Try her. See what happens."

As though he couldn't stand the closeness between them, Jamie stepped back and ran a hand across his head. "Yeah, well, I wanted some money. That's all."

"And you're not getting it."

The door of the Beach Club swung open. Aiden glanced toward it, expecting to see elegantly clad couples leaving and heading home. But instead he saw Ember, her face unnaturally pale as she held her phone tightly in her hand. Her eyes sought his out and he could see panic in them, as her chest rose up and down to keep up with her breathing.

"You need to come with me," she said, her voice breathless. "There's been an accident."

27

Brooke ran onto the beach, stumbling as her heels sank into the soft, pliable sand. She yanked her shoes off, holding them in her right hand as she held her skirt up with her left, desperate to put as much distance between herself and the disaster she'd left behind at the gala.

It was a disaster of her own making. But that knowledge did nothing to calm her racing heart, or clear the messed up haze in her mind. It was almost impossible to think straight.

Air. She needed air. She stopped running and bent over, resting her hands on her thighs as she gasped mouthfuls in. The Beach Club was in the distance, lights spilling out from the ballroom, but it still wasn't far enough away. She needed more space, more air, more time to think. Standing up, she sucked in another breath and followed the coastline until Angel Sands was only a cluster of buildings in the distance, and grass grew in the dunes as the coast turned the corner into Silver Cove.

Before the beach expanded into the half-built resort, there was a tiny cluster of rocks. She brought Nick here sometimes, and they'd run into the ocean and pretend there was nobody else in the world.

It was Aiden who'd first shown her this place. *Their place.* The one spot her father couldn't reach them, where she could be herself and not only a Newton. And it was here that she stopped and sat on one of the rocks, dropping her shoes onto the dusty sand before she lowered her head into her hands.

Was it her fault people made decisions without asking her first? She'd grown used to it from her parents. But Aiden? She'd stupidly thought he believed in her. Enough for her to make her own decisions, regardless of how tough they were.

But he hadn't. And it hurt. Because he saw her the way everybody else did. As something fragile to be protected, not as a partner.

Her chest felt hollow, as though somebody had scooped out her heart and lungs and laid them gently on the sand, leaving an emptiness where they used to be. She squeezed her eyes shut, her mouth trembling as she remembered her parents' expressions of horror, Jamie's laugh, and Aiden's shock at everything being exposed.

It had been humiliating. Practically everybody she knew was at the Beach Club right now and they'd unwittingly purchased first row seats to the scene Jamie had created. They were probably all talking about her. *Again.* About how she'd brought humiliation down on her parents, how her lies ran so deep nobody knew what the truth was any more. She closed her eyes, trying to shut out the embarrassment.

"There you are."

Lucas and Nate were walking along the beach toward her. Even in the darkness of the night they were a sight for sore eyes, dressed up in black tuxedos and white dress shirts. Brooke tried to smile at them but it came out as a grimace.

"I'm sorry. You didn't need to come and search for me. I was going to come back as soon as I composed myself."

"Hey, you don't need to apologize." Lucas sat and stretched out his long lean legs in front of him. "I was happy to get out of there. I'm not one for dressing up." As though to emphasize his words, he pulled at his neatly knotted bow tie, letting the ends fall down as he unfastened the top button of his shirt. "Anyway, Ember was worried about you. We said we'd make sure you're okay."

Nate sat down on the other side of the rock, giving her a soft smile. "You doing okay?" he asked.

"I'll be fine." Maybe if she said it enough it would be the truth. Looking up, she caught his eye. "I had to get out of there for a while. I'm so embarrassed."

"There's no need to be embarrassed. You're not the one who made a fool out of themselves." Nate was older than Lucas – older than all of them – and had been a single dad for a while before he'd met Ally and they'd fallen in love. That was something he and Brooke had in common – bringing up a child under difficult circumstance. He'd always been more than kind to her. "Nobody's talking about you. Well not many people. They're too busy talking about Aiden's brother."

"Jamie." Even saying his name made her throat feel tight. "I had no idea he was back in town." She shook her head, trying to hold her tears in check. "I never wanted anybody to find out like that."

"It's not your fault," Lucas said, his voice low. "You were blindsided, anybody could see that."

"Aiden should have told you his brother was out of jail," Nate agreed. "He messed up."

"He thought he was protecting me." Brooke sighed, looking down at the sand. "But you're right, he should have told me. I'm not some delicate girl who faints at the first sign of trouble."

Something splashed out in the ocean – close enough for

the sound to carry to where they were sitting, but far enough so she couldn't quite see what caused it. A dolphin, maybe.

"I thought he knew I was strong," she continued. "I thought he saw me as an equal. But he doesn't."

Thinking about it felt like a knife to the place where her heart used to be.

"He messed up," Lucas agreed. "But we all make mistakes sometimes. And you know, a big part of loving somebody is about wanting to protect them. Nobody wants the person they love to get hurt. I'm like that with Ember all the time. Reminding her to fill up on gas, or checking under her hood to make sure she has enough oil. And when the three of you go out for the evening I'm on edge all night until she comes home."

The smallest of smiles crossed Brooke's lips. "You're really good to her, I know that. But you've never hidden something important from her."

"I didn't tell her I loved her when I knew I did."

Brooke tipped her head to the side. "Why didn't you?"

"Because I was scared. And maybe Aiden's scared too."

In her rush to escape from the Beach Club, some of her hair had fallen out of her updo and lay around her shoulders. The ends tickled her skin. Sweeping it away, Brooke looked at Lucas, her eyes meeting his. "What does he have to be afraid of?"

"You want to take this one?" Lucas asked, turning to Nate.

Nate shook his head. "You're doing a fine job."

"Thanks," Lucas said, raising his eyebrow as he turned back to Brooke. "I'm not an expert on relationships. And I'm pretty sure Ember would agree. But from what I can see, Aiden's head over heels for you. And when a guy falls hard for a woman it can mess up his thinking. I'm not making excuses for him, the guy needs to pull his head out of his ass, but being afraid of losing the person you love the most can make you lose your mind."

"You think he's in love with me." She swallowed hard, finding it hard to believe.

"I can pretty much guarantee it."

She looked at Nate, who was nodding in agreement.

"But he hurt me."

"Yeah, I know. I'm not saying you have to do anything about it."

The tide was coming in. The rocks in front of where they were sitting were slowly submerging. A few minutes more and the ocean would be kissing her feet. "I don't want love if it means lying to me. My parents have done enough of that. The kind of love I want is equal. Taking care of each other but always being honest."

Lucas's phone started to ring. He pulled it from his pocket, the screen lighting his face as he swiped his finger across to accept the call. "It's Ember," he told them. "Hey, babe. Yeah, we found her." He listened as his fiancée talked, lines appearing on his forehead as his face pulled into a frown. "Um. Okay. We'll meet you there."

His eyes met Brooke's as he ended the call, and she knew from the expression on his face that it was bad. The hole where her heart used to be began to expand until it felt as though every breath was being pushed out of her body.

"What is it?" she whispered.

Lucas swallowed hard. "I'm really sorry, Brooke. Nick's been taken to the hospital."

Lucas swung his truck into the hospital parking lot, not bothering to find a space. Driving as close to the double glass doors as possible, he hit the brakes and turned to look at

Brooke. "You go in," he told her. "I'll park and follow you. Ember said she'll be waiting for you in the family room."

"Thank you." The words came out like a whisper. Her chest was so tight it was a surprise she could say anything at all. After Lucas got the call from Ember, all three of them had run back to the Beach Club, Nate picking her up twice when she'd stumbled over her bare feet. Her heart was racing so fast it hurt.

Nicholas. Tears stung her eyes at the thought of her baby in pain. God, she couldn't stand this. She never should have left him, and she damn sure shouldn't have left the Beach Club without her cellphone. That thing was almost a part of her body, she took it with her everywhere in case of a situation like this.

Except for the one time she needed it.

If she'd answered Cora's call, she would have been here at least twenty minutes earlier. Nick had to be so scared, in pain, wondering where the hell she was. What kind of mother was she to be so late?

"Can I help you?" the receptionist at the front desk asked her.

"My son's been brought in with anaphylactic shock. His name's Nicholas Newton."

With an allergy as serious as his, Nick had more than his share of ER visits. But the anaphylaxis had never been as bad as Cora had described. His babysitter knew to inject him with epinephrine as soon as he showed signs of a reaction, but the little vial would only be enough to keep him going until he got to the hospital.

The nurse tapped on the keyboard, staring at the monitor in front of her. "Ah yes, he's in a triage room. Go on through. Your family's already in there." As soon as the nurse pressed the button, Brooke pushed her way through the doors, and into the waiting room lined with blue plastic chairs.

Before she'd even scanned the room, Cora was running over to her, throwing her arms around Brooke. "Oh God, Brooke, I'm so glad you're here. He kept asking for you."

"Where is he?" Brooke's need to see Nick overrode any other thought. She'd comfort Cora later. Right now she needed her son.

"In room three. Doctor Westbrook is with him."

Brooke swallowed, trying to keep the tears at bay. Nick didn't need her to break down, he needed his mom. Somehow she had to stay strong. "Was it bad?" she whispered.

Cora nodded. Tears were pouring down her face. "He couldn't breathe."

A wave of nausea passed over her – so strong she could taste it on her tongue. The door opened and a nurse walked in, a clipboard in her hand. She scanned the room, blinking as she took in all the people. "Nicholas Newton's family?"

Half the room stood up. There was Ember and Ally – and Nate and Lucas who had recently arrived – along with her parents, and Max and Ellie.

Then there was the man in the corner. Aiden was leaning against the wall, in his dress pants and crisp white shirt. His hair messed up as though he'd been raking his fingers through it. His jaw was clenched, a muscle jumping in his cheek. One of his hands was clasped around the wrist of his other arm, running up and down his exposed, warm skin.

His head was angled down as though he couldn't bring himself to look at her. She swallowed hard, her heart so full of words she didn't know how to say. There was no time to say them anyway.

"I'm Nicholas's mother," she said to the nurse. "How is he?"

"He's stable. Would you like to see him?"

Brooke nodded. The nurse led her in the direction of the treatment rooms, her voice low as she explained his treatment so far. "He's got an oxygen mask on and an IV in for fluids."

Brooke could barely take it in. The nurse stopped talking as she pulled the door open to Nick's room, standing aside so Brooke could walk in.

He was hooked up to fluids, with a oxygen mask strapped across his mouth and nose. His chest was rising up and down rapidly, his breathing labored as they tried to get as much oxygen into him as possible. He was hooked up to a monitor – showing his blood pressure was low – and in the other arm he had a catheter stuck into his hand, pumping fluids into him, in an effort to stabilize his vitals.

It felt like a knife to her heart.

"Miss Newton?" a woman in a white coat asked. In her mid-thirties, with short blonde hair and a smile, the doctor walked toward Brooke, holding out her hand. "I'm Doctor Westbrook.

Brooke took her proferred hand and shook it. "Can you tell me how Nick is?"

"Of course. You're aware of his anaphalaxis, right?"

"Yes. We've been here a few times before."

"Okay. From what we can tell, Nick ate a cookie and had an immediate reaction – worse than usual from your babysitter's account. We're doing what we usually do in this situation, making sure we can open his airways, and trying to get his blood pressure up. He's dealing with it like a champ. I wish all my patients could be like this." She inclined her head at Brooke's son. "You can go sit with him. He's awake."

Nodding, Brooke walked over to the empty spot beside Nick's gurney, gently laying her hand over his. "Hey baby, I'm here. It's going to be okay."

Nick looked up at her, his face pale. Almost immediately his body relaxed. He couldn't say anything – not with his heavy breathing, and the mask covering his face – but his expression told her all she needed to know.

He was relieved she was here. He knew he was going to be okay. She'd make things better, the way she always did.

The fact she should have been here twenty minutes earlier felt like a weight on her shoulders. She'd been so selfish, so caught up in her own problems, and he'd waited longer than he should've for her. She felt sick at the thought of him being alone and scared.

The blood pressure cuff at the top of his thin arm inflated automatically, deflating once the reading appeared on his monitor.

"We're going to give him another steroid injection in twenty minutes, and then let him rest. I'd like to keep him in overnight, but if he improves the way I think he will, you can take him home tomorrow."

Home. There was nowhere else she wanted to be right now. Taking care of this little kid who meant everything to her.

"Can I stay with him tonight?"

Doctor Westbrooke smiled. "Of course."

"You hear that, honey?" she said softly, hunkering down so she could whisper in Nick's ear. "I'm staying right here with you tonight, and you're coming home tomorrow. Everything's going to be fine."

She slid her hand into his and he squeezed it tightly as she sat down in the chair beside Nick's bed. The hem of her silver evening dress rode up, revealing her ankles and feet covered in sand. What a mess she was. Right now she didn't feel fit to be a human, let alone a mother.

It was going to be a long, long night.

❦ 28 ❦

A distant noise startled her. Brooke's eyes flew open, her body stiffening as she woke from her fitful slumber, her evening dress crumpled around her body. It took her a moment to realize where she was. She blinked, her blurred vision slowly focusing on the bed beside her, and the monitor beside the bed, and her palm still wrapped around her son's smaller hand.

The clock on the wall told her it was going on three in the morning. They'd moved Nick up to a private room in the children's ward a few minutes after midnight. Brooke had gone with him, holding his hand as the orderly pushed his gurney to the elevator, talking softly with him as he stared up at her with his oxygen mask still on. When the night staff came into their shift at ten, Doctor Westbrook had come up to the ward to say goodbye, and had authorized the mask to be taken off and for the drip to be stopped. Now the only thing he had connected to his body were the pads on his chest hooking him up to the monitor. They didn't seem to be bothering him much. The combination of the shock and the treatment had sent him into a deep sleep, and she knew from experience he wouldn't be waking up any time soon.

Her body ached from sitting in the chair for too long. Gently letting go of Nick's hand, she stood and stretched, lifting her arms up above her head and rolling her shoulders, moving her neck from one side to the other.

There was a huge glass window on the other side of Nick's room, opening to the hallway and nurses' station. A movement caught her eye and she turned to look. On the other side of the glass she saw Aiden, still wearing his dinner suit.

She twisted to look at him, but he hadn't seen her yet. She took the chance to take in his messed up dark hair and the wrinkles in his clothes from where he'd been sitting in one position for too long. His white shirt was crumpled and untucked, and there were creases on his cheek from where he'd been leaning against the wall. He looked as unkempt as she felt.

His gaze snapped to hers, and his eyes widened in recognition. For a moment they stared at each other. She could feel the heat radiating through her, as though somebody had lit a match and thrown it onto the paper of her stomach. He took a step toward the glass between them, and without thinking it through, she did the same.

"Hi." He mouthed the word. She couldn't tell if he'd voiced it too – the glass was too thick. "You okay?"

She nodded, swallowing hard. "He's good. Asleep."

Aiden frowned. "What?"

She mouthed it harder. "He's asleep."

On the other side of the glass, Aiden shook his head and frowned. Taking another glance at Nick – who hadn't stirred at all – she walked over to the door, slowly pushing the handle and stepping out of the room.

"He's asleep," she whispered. This time Aiden nodded.

"How's he doing? Is there any improvement?" He sounded panicked.

"He's so much better. They've taken him off the oxygen and fluids. The doctor said he should be able to come home tomorrow."

Aiden closed his eyes and let out a mouthful of air. An orderly walked past with a cart and they stepped aside to let him through. As he disappeared around the corner of the corridor, Aiden lifted a hand to his hair, raking his fingers through it.

"Thank you for being here," Brooke said, her voice low. "You really didn't have to stay."

"The nurses have told me to leave about a hundred times." Aiden shrugged. "But where would I go? There's no way I could sleep without knowing you're both okay."

"Did everybody else leave?"

"Yeah. Your mom and dad were still arguing on their way out. I'm pretty sure it's going to be a long night for them. And Ember and Ally told me to give you their love and call at any time." A ghost of a smile pulled at the corner of his lips. "They'll all be back first thing in the morning. You should get some rest."

She opened her mouth to tell him he could go home, but closed it again. There was something reassuring about having him here, only the two of them and Nick in the dark, silent hospital. It made her feel less alone. "You want to get a coffee?" she asked him. "The café's open twenty-four hours a day."

"Is it okay to leave Nick?"

"Yeah, for a few minutes. I'll ask the nurse to keep an eye on him. He won't wake until morning. Not after everything that's happened tonight." And coffee sounded heavenly. She couldn't remember the last time she'd had liquids. Her thoughts turned to the gala before she turned them resolutely away again. She wasn't sure she had the energy to dwell on that.

After a brief discussion with the nurse, they rode the elevator in silence, both of them too stuck in their own thoughts to say much.

The café was deserted, apart from a couple of nurses taking their break in the far corner. The barista took their order, and methodically filled up the espresso machine with coffee beans, pulling handles and moving cups until he slid their two mugs of latte across the counter. Aiden grabbed them both, leading her over to a table next to a window, looking out across the night time bay, the darkness occasionally broken by flashing beacons flooding light across the surface of the ocean.

Brooke took the chair opposite Aiden's. Lifting the cup to her lips, she took a sip, then baulked at the heat searing at her tongue. "Ouch." She grimaced, putting the cup back down.

"Too hot?"

"Way too hot."

When she lifted her gaze she saw him staring right at her with those warm, whiskey eyes that saw right inside her.

"I'm sorry," he said, leaning back in his chair. "None of this should have happened."

He clearly wasn't talking about the burning coffee, even though her tongue was still stinging from the onslaught. Her fingers were trembling, like leaves fluttering in a breeze. The shock of tonight's events made everything seem hazy – like an old movie she could barely recall.

"I don't think I can talk about this now," she told him. Her voice cracked at the end of her sentence. "I'm so tired and scared, and part of me is still pissed about everything that happened tonight. I can't go there right now."

"I understand." Aiden pulled his gaze from hers, swallowing hard as he looked out of the huge window. She watched as his chest lifted and dipped with his breaths. How easy it would be to walk over to him, to let him hold her, console her, tell her it was all going to be okay.

But she couldn't. That was something the old Brooke would have done; sought out comfort where it was offered, given up her own need for control to somebody else. For so long she'd doubted herself and her decisions – and yes, some of them had been absolutely terrible – but some of them had been amazing, too. To sweep tonight under the carpet would be to disrespect herself and the woman she was becoming.

She couldn't let people make her decisions anymore. They were hers, and hers alone to make.

"Can I tell you one thing?" Aiden asked her. His voice was deep. Caressing.

She nodded.

"Jamie's gone. He's left town."

She slowly licked her lips. Her tongue was still hurting, but the nagging of her thirst overrode the pain. Taking another sip of the coffee – this time thankfully cooler – she let the liquid coat her mouth.

"Okay."

"He left of his own free will. I didn't ask him to leave and I didn't ask him to stay. I realized a little too late it's not my place to make those calls."

The sadness in his tone made her heart clench. She had no idea what to say to him. She was torn between trying to make everything better and somehow standing up for herself.

"What happens next is between you and him. And Nick, I guess." He ran the tip of his finger around the rim of his coffee cup. "There's a lot more I want to say, but this isn't the time or the place."

"I guess not…"

"I'd still like to see Nick if that's okay."

She looked up, surprised at his words. He wasn't going to

fight for her. Brooke wasn't sure how to feel about that. Part of her was disappointed, wanting to see him beg and plead and show her how much she meant to him. The other was relieved – she hadn't lied about being too tired to talk about this stuff tonight.

"Of course you can still see him. He loves you. I'd never take him away from you, no matter what."

"Thank you."

In the gloom beneath the night-time cafeteria lights, the resemblance between him and her son was so strong. Those warm whiskey eyes and dark, dark hair. Even the way he was staring at her was so familiar it hurt.

"Have you finished?" he asked, nodding at her coffee cup.

"My tongue tells me I have."

The corner of his lip quirked up. "I'll walk you back to Nick's room and head home. It's been a long night for all of us. We should both try and get some sleep."

"Oh. Okay."

He pushed himself up from the table and she followed suit, letting him take the lead as they walked across the cafeteria and back toward the bank of elevators at the end of the hall. And as he pushed the button to call the car, she leaned against the wall, a wave of exhaustion washing over her, along with the strangest feeling that, in spite of everything, she wasn't in control at all.

When she opened her eyes again, daylight was streaming in through the window next to Nick's bed. He was still asleep, but his lips were moving as he murmured words she couldn't quite hear. It didn't disturb her though – she'd gotten used to his sleeptalking over the years. In twenty minutes or so he'd most likely be wide awake.

The sound of a throat clearing made her turn in her seat, her muscles complaining at the sudden movement. They were coiled and tight from where she'd been curled up on the chair, unwilling to stretch unless she forced them.

"*Mom?*" she said, frowning, shock evident in her voice.

Lillian was standing in the doorway, her face twisted as though she wasn't quite sure whether to walk in or leave. Her watery blue eyes met Brooke's.

"Is Nick okay? I couldn't sleep and you weren't answering your phone. I wasn't sure whether to come or not." Lillian stumbled over her words. There was no sign of her usual assurance. "I know I'm probably the last person you want to see."

Brooke's chest felt tight. It took her a moment to realize she'd been holding her breath. She let the air out. "It's okay. I'm sure he'll be pleased to see you when he wakes up." She circled her head to loosen the tendons in her neck.

Her mom took a tentative step inside. "Did you get any sleep?" Her bottom lip stretched, as though she was trying to force it into a smile.

"A little. Not much."

"I brought you a change of clothes. Just in case you needed them." Her mom held out a white bag. "And some toiletries, too. I hope you don't think it's too forward of me."

Brooke couldn't remember the last time she'd seen her mom so hesitant. It felt strange. And yet there was something conciliatory in the way Lillian waited for Brooke to decide whether or not she wanted the bag. In past times she would have shoved it in Brooke's hands and told her to get changed right away before somebody saw her.

But now it seemed like a kind gesture.

"Thanks. I'd love to get out of this dress." Brooke met her mom's eyes, and gave her a grateful nod. A moment later she took the bag from her hands. "Will you sit with Nick while I change in the bathroom?"

"I'd like that." This time her mom's smile was big. She walked over to where Nick was fitfully sleeping and sat down on the chair Brooke had just vacated. With a glance back at them, Brooke headed for the bathroom with the white leather bag her mother had given her.

She wasn't sure what she expected to be inside the bag – but a simple pair of worn jeans and a t-shirt wasn't it. Brooke blinked, trying to recall when she'd last seen her old grey tee with the pink Angel Sands logo on it. Years ago? When she pulled it on it was tighter than she remembered, but it was still a million light years preferable to the dress she'd been wearing since last night.

"Mom, where did you find these clothes?" Brooke asked as she walked back into the hospital room. On catching sight of her son, she smiled. "You're awake."

He nodded. "Grandma told me you were getting changed."

"How are you feeling?" she asked him, walking to the far side of his bed and taking his hand. Her eyes met her mom's, and she could see her own relief reflected in the light blues.

"I'm good. Can we go home now?"

Warmth flooded her veins. The fear and panic from last night had left her body feeling on high alert, but she was slowly beginning to calm down. "Once the doctor's taken a look at you and gives the all clear."

"Can Grandma come too?" he asked. "And Grandpa?" The hope in his voice reminded her how much he'd missed them. It hit a tender spot in her heart. "Can you, Grandma?" Nick asked again.

"I'm... I'm not sure. Your mom will be very busy."

"You're welcome to come over," Brooke said, her voice strong. She might not have liked what they'd done to her –

both last night and all those years ago – but they were still her parents. They thought the world of Nick, and he idolized them both. It would take a long time for her to begin to trust them again, and longer until she could let go of the pain they'd caused her, but they still had more in common than they had differences.

They loved her. Even if they sometimes had a strange way of showing it.

They were welcome to come over. It didn't mean she'd forgiven them, but she knew in her heart she'd get there. And until she did, she'd get through it for her son's sake.

What mother wouldn't do that?

29

It had been a long week. Aiden lifted his head from the computer screen in front of him, finally admitting to himself the numbers on the screen meant nothing. They were floating there, little dots of ink among the white, and he was sick of looking at the damn things.

For the hundredth time he picked up his phone and checked his messages. One from his boss, a couple from some contractors, but nothing from the person he wanted to hear from the most.

And it stung like a bitch.

The door to the office opened, and Brecken Miller walked in, taking his hard hat off and smoothing his hair with the palm of his hand. "The crew have finished for the night. No overtime needed this weekend – we're back on track." There was a grin on his face, and no wonder. He and his team had worked like Trojans to catch up after all the delays they had. Normally, Aiden would have been the first to celebrate their achievement – keeping to the schedule had a big effect on the bottom line, after all. This was a prestigious project – the success or failure of which would be laid firmly at his door.

And in his business life he'd been nothing but successful.

His personal life was the complete opposite. He'd made such a goddamn hash of it all. The thought of it made him sick. He'd lost her and it was all his fault.

Breck said something. Aiden frowned and looked up at him. "Sorry, Breck, I missed that."

"You okay?" Breck asked, sitting down in the chair on the other side of Aiden's desk.

"Yeah, I'm fine."

"You still not heard from her?" Breck inclined his head at the phone laying in Aiden's upturned palm. It came as no surprise to him that Breck knew exactly what was going on. Not because Angel Sands was a small town, either. But he was also best friends with Lucas Russell, who happened to be engaged to one of Brooke's best friends.

This place was way too connected.

"No, I haven't heard from her." For a moment he considered asking Breck if he knew anything, but shrugged the thought off. Partly because he didn't want to make himself vulnerable, but mostly because he didn't want to know. Not if it was bad, and let's face it, it would be. Why else would his phone be silent?

"You heard from your brother?"

News really did travel fast. "No. But the PI I hired says he's back in Sacramento. I don't think he'll be coming back down here for a while."

Breck didn't blink at the mention of a private investigator. "That's good to hear. I remember Jamie from when we were kids. He was bad news even then."

"Yeah, well he's worse now." Aiden's mouth dried at the thought of his brother, and the claim he tried to stake on Nick and Brooke. The claim he could still pursue if he had the energy or motivation, and thank God he didn't right now.

"You've had a crazy few weeks. I bet you're glad it's all

calmed down now. If things keep going like this we might even finish ahead of plan." Breck grinned at him. "Wouldn't that be good?"

"It would for you." Aiden raised an eyebrow. As project manager and head of the construction team, Breck's contract had a nice little bonus written into it on completion. Finishing ahead of the agreed date would lead to it being doubled.

"It's a win-win, right?"

"Yeah. It sure is."

"Man, she's really messed you up, hasn't she?" Breck said. "You want to talk about it?"

"Not really."

"I didn't think so."

"What's there to say? I made decisions without her, I hid things from her, and now she doesn't want to know me. Who can blame her?"

"Nobody."

Aiden rubbed his jaw with his fingertips. "Maybe I should call her. Do you think I should?"

Breck's eyes were wide with surprise. The irony of their conversation didn't escape Aiden's notice. For a guy who didn't want to talk about it, he sure was saying a lot. It felt good, to finally get it out. Like somebody uncorking a bottle, he could feel the pressure slowly release from him.

"Why haven't you already called her?" Breck asked. He pulled up a chair and sat down, crossing his legs in front of him.

"Because I've made enough decisions for her, I don't want to make any more. I don't want to pressure her into talking to me. I want her to make the choice to do it willingly."

"That sounds fair enough."

"Yeah, but it's killing me."

Breck laughed. "I can see that, man." He shrugged. "But

for what it's worth, I think you're doing the right thing. I'm no expert on relationships, but I can tell you've thought this through. You're not playing games. You're handing back control."

"And I freaking hate it."

"You're giving her the time and space to think things through. You're a good guy, Aiden. She'll realize it eventually."

Good guy, bad guy, at the end of the day it didn't matter. He'd ended up treating her the same way she'd always been treated. No wonder she didn't believe him when he'd said he was different.

But he'd do whatever it took to be the man she wanted. Even leave her alone if that was her choice. It would hurt him like nothing had ever hurt him before, but he'd still do it.

Because he loved her, and right now it was the only thing keeping him going.

Brooke flicked on Nick's nightlight and pulled the door closed behind her, walking back into her small living room. "He's finally asleep," she told Ember and Ally, who were sitting on her sofa looking up at her. Three insulated cups of coffee were on the table in front of them – Ally had finished her shift at the coffee shop and had brought them over with her, along with some pastries that looked delicious.

"I've got one for Nick, too," Ally said, pointing at the paper bag next to the cups. "I thought he could have it for breakfast. It's completely nut free, I promise."

"Thank God for that." Brooke wasn't quite up to smiling at the situation yet, but she still appreciated Ally's levity. It was so good to have her friends with her. For the past few days she'd taken time off work and her classes to stay at home with Nick while he recuperated. He was itching to get back to school, and the doctor had given him the all clear to start back on Monday.

But for now, all she wanted to do was keep him home and hug him tight.

"Nick's teacher asked me to give you this," Ember said, pulling a large envelope from her bag. "His classmates made him a get well soon card."

Brooke took it, pulling the large white card out of the envelope. Each child had drawn a self-portrait on it, and beneath their drawings they'd written their names in varying degrees of scrawl. Opening it up, she smiled as she read the words.

Get well soon, Nicholas. We miss you.

"That's so sweet," Ally said, leaning over Brooke to read the message inside. "I didn't think of bringing a card."

"You brought coffee, which is even better," Ember pointed out.

"Talking of coffee, your mom came into the shop today," Ally said, glancing at Brooke from the corner of her eye. "She said she and your dad came to dinner here yesterday."

"I didn't know you were talking to them again," Ember said, leaning forward with interest. "Tell me more."

"It's still early in repairing the relationship," Brooke said slowly, remembering the awkward politeness of the previous night. "And they're probably not going to be talking to me for a while after I fed them chicken nuggets and mashed potatoes, but it was Nick's choice and they got what they were given."

"I'd pay good money to see your folks eating chicken

nuggets," Ally said, trying to suppress a grin. "Did they really eat it?"

"Every last morsel," Brooke said, biting down a smile. "I guess they really wanted to spend some time with Nick."

"And have you heard from Aiden?" Ally asked.

"No. Not a word." She tried to hide the disappointment from her voice, but it didn't work at all. "Actually, that's not true. He messaged on Wednesday to ask how Nick was, and to see if he was up for staying with him on Saturday." Brooke licked her dry lips. "I said it would be fine. End of conversation."

"He didn't talk about your relationship?"

Brooke shook her head. "No."

"Maybe he'll say something tomorrow when you drop Nick off?" Ember said, frowning at Brooke's words.

"Maybe." Brooke tried to ignore the taste of disappointment on her tongue. "But wouldn't he have said something already if he was still interested? Maybe my running out of the gala and being all high maintenance has put him off."

"Your reaction was understandable. You discovered he was lying to you." Ally crossed her arms in front of her.

"Yeah, but he'd done it with good intentions," Ember said. "He never meant to hurt you. He was so upset. But as soon as you ran out of the Beach Club he realized his mistake. I've never seen him so shaken."

"So why hasn't he called?"

"I don't know." Ember pressed her lips together, her eyes soft as they met Brooke's. "And you won't either, unless you ask him."

"Oh this is such a mess." Brooke dropped her head against the back of her chair and closed her eyes, pressing her palms to her face. "I wish Jamie had never come back."

"Have you heard from him?" Ally asked.

"No. Thank goodness." He was the Black brother she

could do without talking to. "I know all children have a right to know their fathers, but I really don't think he'll bring anything good into Nick's life. Not unless he cleans his act up massively."

"I don't think he'll ever do that," Ally said, her voice solemn. "Does Nick know about him?"

"Yeah. I told him on Wednesday."

"What did he say?"

"Nothing, really. He was thoughtful for about five minutes before he asked me to get him some ice cream and completely changed the subject. I guess I'm taking my lead from him. I'm ready to answer his questions when he has them, but I'm not going to push him to talk about it until he's ready."

"You're such a great mom." Ember gave her a warm smile.

"Yeah, sure."

"You are. I wish you had more confidence in yourself. Look at you, you have motherhood cracked, you're almost finished with your studies, and you're one of the mainstays of the animal shelter. All of Angel Sands thinks you're fabulous."

Brooke looked over at her friend. There wasn't a hint of humor on Ember's face. It was as though she meant every word. But she couldn't bring herself to believe it. Because right now it felt as though everything she touched turned to dust.

"I know of at least one person in Angel Sands who doesn't think I'm fabulous," Brooke said, her voice thick. And damn if he wasn't the one person whose opinion mattered most of all.

"You sure about that?" Ally asked, raising an eyebrow. "Maybe you should ask him first, before you come to any conclusions."

30

"Mom, will my dad be at Uncle Aiden's?" Nick asked as Brooke turned the car onto Beach Drive. He was a ball of pent up energy after a week of being cooped in their apartment. Brooke glanced in the mirror and saw him fidgeting in his seat. It was as if his body had no idea how to contain his excitement. He'd been talking about having 'guy time' with Uncle Aiden all day. She loved seeing him so happy, but there was still a tender spot in her heart which hurt every time he said Aiden's name.

Maybe she needed some guy time, too.

"No, sweetie, he doesn't live around here, remember? He's in Sacramento."

"Is that far?"

"Quite far. A few hundred miles." She smiled at his reflection in the mirror, and he grinned back. "Sacramento is right at the top of California, and we're near the bottom."

"So I won't be seeing him, will I?"

"Not unless you want to." She took a deep breath in. The two of them were booked for family therapy next week, and as far as Brooke was concerned, it couldn't come soon enough. She needed all the help she could get in answering his questions as truthfully as possible, while making sure he didn't get hurt. Lies weren't an option. Ever.

"But he's Uncle Aiden's brother, right?"

"Yes."

"I wonder what it's like to have a brother," Nick mused, as she turned onto the new development where Aiden's beach house was. "It must be kind of cool."

"Your guess is as good as mine. We're both only children, kiddo. Though I think sometimes you make your own family."

"How do you make your own family?" Nick frowned.

"You build it up, person by person. First you start with the family you have, and then you add some friends. And one day you wake up and you know you can rely on those people, no matter what happens."

"Like Ember and Ally?" he asked.

"That's right. And Lucas and Nate, plus Max and Ellie. They're like family, too."

"And Uncle Aiden," Nick added.

The mention of his name was enough to make her feel warm inside. "Yeah, though he's your blood family as well."

"But not yours," Nick pointed out."

"No, not mine." She pulled into the empty space next to Aiden's Audi and switched off the engine. "Right, have you got all your things?" she asked, glad to change the subject.

"Yup."

"So let's go."

She wasn't sure whether she was dreading this or desperate for it. It had been a week since the gala and almost as long since she'd last seen Aiden. Her whole body ached at the thought of seeing him again. The tightness in her chest was making it hard to breathe.

She had no idea what she was going to say to him.

"Can you stay in the car and I'll go in on my own?" Nick asked. "That's what Owen does when his mom takes him to his dad's house. She said if she had to talk to that, *you-know-what*, she'd end up smacking him in the face."

Brooke grimaced. Owen's parents' divorce was legendary in its toxicity – not exactly a model she wanted to follow. "No, I won't sit in the car. I'd like to make sure you get in safely." To prove her point, she climbed out, and opened the back door, grabbing Nick's bags as he scrambled out. "And anyway, you have too many things to carry yourself."

Nick ran ahead, his tennis shoes barely touching the steps up to Aiden's front door. She smiled, wondering if Aiden knew what he was in for. Within a minute of Nick's first over-enthusiastic knock on the door, the man himself was opening it, a grin lighting up his face as he saw Nick standing on the porch.

"Hey bud, how are you feeling?" He stepped aside to let Nick in, reaching out to ruffle his hair. Nick glowed at the attention.

"I'm good. Do you have any soda? I'm thirsty. Can we go swimming? I got my shorts somewhere." He turned to look at Brooke. "Mom, have you got my shorts?" He was still barking out orders as Brooke made it up the steps. Almost immediately, Aiden caught her eye.

"There's juice in the fridge," he called out, as Nick ran past him into the house. Turning back to Brooke, he leaned against the door jamb. "I guess that means he's feeling better."

"He's been going stir crazy cooped up at home." She smiled apologetically. "I think you're going to bear the brunt of it."

Aiden shrugged. "I've spent the week arguing with ten angry builders. I think I can handle it." He tipped his head to the side, scrutinizing her. "And how are you doing? You recovered from Nick's reaction yet?"

"I'll tell you after tonight. It's the first time I've been on my own since it all went down. I'll either sleep for a thousand hours, or I'll break down." She shrugged. "But I'm guessing sleep will win out."

"You haven't got anything planned?"

"Nope. Ember and Lucas have a date night, and it's game night at Nate and Ally's. They invited me but I'll pass. They're way too competitive for their own good." She raised an eyebrow. "So it's me, the sofa, and a chick flick."

He was still looking at her with those deep whiskey eyes. "You're welcome to stay here with us."

"Don't say that in front of Nick. He's made it very clear to me it's *Guys' Night*. I believe that means there are no moms allowed." She laughed. "I don't want to cramp either of your styles."

"You'd never cramp mine."

Oh! How few words it took to light the little flame of hope inside her. He only had to offer the smallest of olive branches and her mind started to race with possibilities. She needed to stop speeding ahead.

"Aiden, can we go to the beach now?" Nick reappeared, a small carton of juice in hand. "I can see some of my school friends out there. I wanna tell them about the hospital." Nick came to a stop beside him. "Oh, hey, Mom." He looked surprised to see her still there.

Maybe if she'd been another kind of mom, she'd feel upset at him wanting her to leave him with Aiden. Jealous, even. But she couldn't help but feel her heart swell at the sight of Nick standing next to his six-foot-two lookalike, knowing their relationship was filling the holes in Nick's soul Brooke never could.

"I'm about to leave," she told him. "Have a good time and

do what Aiden tells you to. And brush your teeth, otherwise they'll rot with all that sugar."

Aiden looked at Nick and then back to Brooke. "Are you sure you're okay?"

She nodded, keeping the smile plastered on her face. "Yep, I'm all good. I'll see you tomorrow."

"Bye!" Nick waved absentmindedly and dropped to his knees, rifling through his bag, no doubt looking for his swim shorts.

Aiden caught her gaze one last time. There was a question behind his eyes she didn't know the answer to. A softness, too, and it made her want to melt. She needed to go, before she made an idiot of herself. Time to head home and pour herself an ice cold glass of water – or take a cold shower.

"Goodbye honey. Bye Aiden." Lifting her hand in a brief wave, she turned and all but ran back to her car, not sure whether to be happy their first encounter had been so civilized.

Her apartment was eerily quiet. The small table she and Nick ate their meals at – and she did her work on – was completely bare. Her project was finished, and all the housework was done. For the first night in forever she had absolutely nothing to do.

It should have felt like heaven. Wasn't this what she'd been longing for? Some peace and quiet, time to relax without the pressure of her academic work bearing down on her? But now that she had it, she felt so lonesome it actually hurt. As though there was a hole inside her nothing could fill.

Leaning on the kitchen counter, she wondered what Nick and Aiden were doing now. It was almost nine – Nick should have crashed and burned, in spite of him wanting to stay up as late as he could. Maybe Aiden was sitting out on the deck, staring out at the ocean as the sun slowly slipped below the water line, leaving the inky black night to creep in. Or maybe he was watching a movie – not the chickflick sort she'd intended to watch; he'd always preferred action to words.

She'd planned on leaving whatever happened between them up to fate. But what if fate made the wrong decision?

Had it been fate that pulled them apart after her father discovered them in a compromising position? Was it fate that led her to being pregnant at the tender age of eighteen? Or was it their decisions, as bad as they were, which led them to the spot they were in now?

Her thoughts felt as though they were punching at her skull, trying to force their way out into the world. She started to pace her small living area, from the kitchen space to the glass windows at the other end of the room and back again.

Hadn't she been complaining about not being trusted to make her own decisions, first by her parents and then by Aiden? So, why was she afraid to make a decision about the two of them now? Because leaving it to fate was pretty much removing herself from the equation. Giving control over to somebody – or something – else.

Did she really want to do that? She was only beginning to take control of her own life.

Leaning her head against the cool glass, she stared out of the window and into the encroaching night beyond. Through the ghost of her reflection in the glass she could see the lamplit streets and the dark outlines of houses with their yellow square windows, lit from within like a child's Christmas scene. She pulled her phone from her shorts pocket and swiped it on, smiling as the photo of Nick playing at the beach flickered to life.

She'd asked for control, she'd demanded to make her own decisions. It was time for action.

Pulling up her message app, she quickly found Aiden's contact, and swiped her finger across the keyboard like a pro.

I wanted to check that everything's okay with Nick. And with you. I miss you. xx

---

"I didn't expect to see you here on a Sunday." Brecken Miller craned his head around the office door.

Aiden looked up from the spreadsheet he'd been working on, his eyes blinking against the sudden onslaught of daylight flooding through the open door. "I could say the same thing about you."

"I left a couple of tools here, and I need them back at the house," Breck told him, leaning on the side of the door. "I saw some movement up here. Wanted to make sure we didn't have a break in."

"I need to get these projections over to the head office before tomorrow." Aiden inclined his head at the laptop screen.

"And you can't do them at home on your deck?"

"There are too many distractions there."

The truth was there weren't enough. After Brooke had picked up Nick this morning, he'd been unable to sit still. He'd tried to talk to her, to ask her about the message she'd sent him – and the fact she missed him – but she'd smiled and told him she'd see him soon.

It was killing him not to call her, and if he stayed at home he probably would. But he'd made a promise that he wouldn't take control from her and make any decisions for her, and he intended to keep it. Even if he had to sit on his hands all night.

"Yeah, well I'll leave you to it. Try not to work too hard." Breck shot him a smile. "And if you finish working before dinner time, drop over. I'll be heating up the grill around seven."

"I might do that." Anything to avoid his empty house.

As Breck clattered his way down the metal steps leading to the building site below, Aiden picked his phone up again. No new messages. His heart dipped. Right now he'd take any morsel of hope she had to offer.

He pressed on the message icon, wanting to read the one from last night again, when Breck's footsteps on the metal staircase got suddenly louder. He quickly slid his phone into his pocket and looked up, frowning.

"Did you forget something?" he called out, right as the door to the outer office opened. Five footsteps across the space to his own door, and Breck was pushing it open.

Except it wasn't Brecken at all.

"Brooke?"

"Hey. I've been looking for you all over." She smiled at him, lingering in the doorway. "I tried the house, and scoured the beach. I was going to give up after trying here and call you."

"You could have messaged." He raised an eyebrow, enjoying the way her cheeks flushed at his words.

She slowly shook her head. "Not for this. Some things should only be said face to face."

For a moment he wondered if she planned to give him the brush off. But then he thought of that message. "They should? What kind of things?" He stood up and walked around his desk, resting on the front of it, his long legs stretched out before him. He wanted to walk over to her, to pull her close and drag whatever it was she'd come to say out of her.

Stop. He needed to let her take the lead.

"I wanted to say thank you for keeping Nick last night."

"That could definitely have been said in a message." He tipped his head to the side. "Where is he anyway?"

"Ember came over to watch him for a while. He had a good time last night, by the way. Though when I asked him what you did, he told me 'what happens at Aiden's stays at Aiden's.'" She narrowed her eyes in a mock-frown.

"We swam, ate crawfish, and watched *The Lego Movie*. It was wild." Aiden winked. "But you know, you could have joined us. You're always welcome."

"I wanted to." She took a tentative step forward. He grasped tightly onto the desk to stop himself from doing the same. Christ, she really was killing him.

"What stopped you?"

"I didn't know if you were only being polite."

"Polite? That's a new one on me. I'm not sure anybody's called me that before." He tapped his fingers as they still held the wooden desk. The muscles in his legs flexed, as though they were ready to walk over to her, whether he liked it or not.

"I don't want to give Nick the wrong idea, either." Her fingers twisted together. "Though I'm not sure what the right idea is." She laughed nervously. "Am I making any sense to you? I don't feel like I am."

He looked at her for a minute. At her silken hair falling in waves past her shoulders, at her flushed face and her tan skin. She couldn't be any more adorable if she tried. He was literally clinging to the table right now. "You don't know what idea Nick might have," he repeated. "About us."

"Yeah. Exactly."

"But you don't know what the idea is." His voice was deadpan.

She bit her lip. "When you put it like that, I make no sense at all."

He stood taller. "One thing I've found in business is if you want something you have to be clear. Let the other person know in no uncertain terms." Was he leading her? Controlling her? He hoped not.

"That sounds like a good idea." She sighed. "This would've been so much easier to do by text message."

"But this sort of thing can only be said face to face," he said, reminding her of her own words. "Whatever it is."

She took another step forward, her eyes wide like a scared colt. "Do you still care for me?" she asked him, her voice trembling.

He nodded. "Of course I do." It took every ounce of strength he had not to ask her if she felt the same.

"So there's hope?" she asked him, not quite meeting his gaze. "For us, I mean?"

"I haven't stopped hoping." His biceps flexed as he fought against himself to run to her. "And I won't stop, not until you say there's no hope."

Her chest rose as she took a deep breath in. She moved again, the minutest of steps. She was right beyond arm's reach now. One step and he could have her against him.

Finally she looked up, her eyes scanning his face. "I hope. I hope so much it hurts."

Damn it. Within a second he'd let go of the desk and took a single stride toward her. Her eyes widened as she saw him approach, her lips opening to take in another gasp of air. He stopped short of her, only inches between them. She looked up at him, her eyes wide and shining – like a piece of green glass rubbed smooth by the sea. "Have you changed your mind?" His voice was rough. "About us?"

"I've never changed my mind about you," she told him. "You were always the one. It was me I needed to work on." Her smile was as tentative as her voice. "I've done a lot of thinking over the past few days. Having Nick at home meant

I didn't have much choice. And I realized something important."

"What is it?"

She licked her lips, the pink tip of her tongue moistening her plump skin. "There's a difference between somebody caring for you and somebody wanting to control you. When I walked into the hospital and saw you all there for Nick and me, I knew it wasn't about control. It's because you care for us." She took another fast breath. "And there's no point in having total control if it means you push away the ones who care for you the most."

"Caring seems too weak a word," he told her, reaching out to brush his finger tips along her heated cheekbone. It was the softest of touches, yet it sent a shudder through her. "I love you."

Her smile grew until it lit up her face. She grabbed his hand, pressing his palm to her face. Closing her eyes for a moment, she kissed his palm, her breath dancing against his rough skin. "Another thing I've learned," she told him. "Control can be overrated."

"It can? Tell me more."

She rolled onto her toes, trying to lessen the distance between them. He looked down at her, taking her in. His heart ached at the sight of her.

"For example, if I was to lose control and kiss the hell out of the guy who runs this resort site, in his office, would it be a bad thing?"

He slowly shook his head. "I don't think so, no."

She rested her hands lightly on his shoulders, her fingers brushing against his neck. It was his turn to shiver. She inclined her head until her lips were only a breath away from his. He could taste the anticipation in the air, soft and sweet, exactly like her. The next moment she was pressing her mouth to his, her arms around his neck, and he was kissing her back like his life depended on it. His arms circled her waist, pulling her as close as he could, until her body melted into his. Her mouth was warm and welcoming, opening up to him when his tongue slid along the seam of her lips. His hands were moving up, tangling in her hair, and his heart clattered in his chest in response to her boldness.

Control was definitely overrated. He'd had precious little since he met her, and had even less now.

And he wouldn't have it any other way.

EPILOGUE

How could she be late today of all days? Brooke ran up the courthouse steps, smoothing her hair from her face, grimacing at the way her hands still smelled of dog no matter how many times she'd scrubbed them. It had been a hell of a morning at the veterinary clinic, with three emergency cases being brought in, the last involving a sock, a Labrador, and a twisted gut. The Labrador won, thankfully.

If it hadn't been for this court date looming, she'd have loved every minute of it.

"Can you help me?" she asked the clerk in the main lobby once she made it through the small line at security. I'm looking for Case 2114. Newton vs Black."

"Courtroom Three. They're about to start."

Damn. She flew across the lobby to the door labeled three. Taking a moment to steady her breath, she pushed it open and walked inside, trying to ignore the way the sound of her heels hitting the wooden floor echoed through the courtroom.

Her lawyer gestured at her, and Brooke slid into the seat next to him. She could feel the heat of a hundred eyes searing against her skin. Twisting her neck, she saw her family and friends filling the seats in the gallery, along with a man whose warm, brown eyes were staring at her in question. Slowly he raised his brows.

"Work," she mouthed. He smiled and shook his head. In the months since she'd graduated and become a veterinary technician, work had made her late more than once. Emergency call outs, surgeries going wrong, and of course there were always animals who needed her attention. Between that, and making sure Nick was always taken care of, she was amazed she'd found time to nurture a new relationship.

"I love you," he mouthed back, and it made her heart heat up.

"I love you, too."

"This court is now in session. All rise for the Honorable Judge Lawrence McCafferty," the clerk called out. The courtroom echoed with the sound of shoes against the wooden floor. Brooke glanced at the table next to hers. The defendant's table. Only a solitary attorney sat there.

The judge took a seat and everyone else followed. When he'd unfolded his glasses and got them settled on the bridge of his nose, he lifted the paper up before him. "Case 2114, Newton versus Black." He peered over the rim of his glasses. "I presume you're Newton?" he said to Brooke.

She nodded. "Yes, Your Honor." Her heart was beating like crazy against her chest, which was stupid because her lawyer had talked her through every step. Maybe it was the pressure of being in a real live courtroom – she'd never even seen inside one before today. Combined with the adrenaline from this morning's surgery, she was surprised she was still able to breathe, let alone speak.

"And I see Mr. Black won't be attending?" This was addressed to the attorney at the other table.

"That's correct, Your Honor."

"Okay, well let's begin. In the matter of Newton versus Black, request to terminate parental rights, how does your client wish to plead?"

"No contest, Your Honor. My client confirms he wishes to rescind his rights."

It was over in less than twenty minutes. The judge had reviewed their statements, asked a few questions, and granted Brooke's petition. The fact Jamie was in complete agreement with it hadn't hurt their case. As far as the law was concerned, he was no longer Nicholas's father.

As far as Brooke was concerned, he never had been.

"I'll have the paperwork finished and over to you by the end of the week," her attorney said as they stood and waited for the court to empty. "Good luck, Miss Newton, not that you need it."

"Thank you for all you've done." She shook his proferred hand and grabbed her purse, slinging it over her shoulder. The attorney gave her a nod, and headed over to talk with Jamie's attorney, leaving Brooke alone in the courtroom.

Another deep breath. What a day it had been. She'd saved a dog and protected her son all in the matter of a few hours. Biting down a smile, she headed toward the door to the lobby, pushing it open to see everybody waiting there for her.

Her parents were the first to congratulate her. Though things hadn't returned to the way they had used to be between them, they were civil enough. Her mom gave her a quick hug, and her father patted her back. She'd had to turn down his offer to fund this lawsuit three times – thank God he didn't offer again.

"I'm so happy for you both." Ember was the next to hug her, quickly followed by Ally who was almost jumping up and down with happiness. And as they parted, she saw Aiden waiting for her, wearing a dark blue suit that took her breath away.

"Hey." He took a step forward, reaching out to cup her cheek. From the corner of her eye she saw her parents leave the lobby. There was still no love lost between them and Aiden, but she couldn't bring herself to care. They were polite to each other, and that's all she asked for.

"Hey." She felt breathless, the way she always did when he touched her. He took another step closer until his body was only inches away from hers. With his stature and build, he dwarfed her, and yet he never made her feel anything less than his equal.

Usually, he made her feel so much more.

"Congratulations," he whispered, brushing his lips against hers. "How do you feel?"

She closed her eyes for a moment, breathing him in. Her heart skipped like an excited puppy to have him so near. "I feel..." She frowned, trying to think. "The same. Nothing's changed, really, has it?"

He laughed. "No, it hasn't."

"Jamie was never Nick's father, not really." She opened her eyes, inclining her head until her gaze met his. "As far as he's concerned, *you're* his father."

He'd been calling Aiden 'Dad' for the past couple of months. Last week, he'd made him a Father's Day card and given it to Aiden with a beaming smile on his face. Aiden had turned his face away so Nick hadn't seen the tears forming in them, but Brooke had seen them.

And they'd made her want to cry too.

"Like I said at therapy last week, as far as I'm concerned he *is* my son." He ran the pad of his finger across the sharp plane of her cheekbone.

She smiled at the memory. She and Nick had been seeing

a family therapist ever since she'd told him the truth about his father, and in the past couple of months Aiden had joined them. They were becoming a family in almost every sense of the word.

"I'd like to make it official, if you'll both have me," Aiden murmured, as though he could read her mind.

"Official?"

"Yeah." For the first time he looked uncertain, and it made her love him even more. She was used to his raw confidence, his strength, but it was his vulnerability which made him complete. "I was going to save this for another time. When we were alone." He glanced behind her, presumably at her friends. "But I'm not sure I can wait any longer." He pushed a hand into his pocket and pulled out a small blue velvet box. "I've been carrying this around for weeks."

"What is it?" She was grinning because she already knew. And his smile told her he *knew* she knew.

He opened the lid, and she stared down at the contents with wide eyes, blinking with recognition. A simple oval emerald set in an elegant yellow gold setting. "This was your Mom's," she said, looking up at him. "It's beautiful."

"I had it reset," he told her. "But with the same design. Her fingers were much bigger than yours."

"I love it. It's perfect."

"I wasn't sure if you would. We can go and look for a different one if you'd prefer?"

"Are you kidding?" she grinned as he slid the ring onto her left finger, and held it up to watch the stone catch the light. "You can't give it to me and then take it away. And anyway, I love that it was your mom's. It makes it even more special." She caught his eye again. "I wish she could have been here."

"So do I."

"Maybe she is. And maybe she's happy for us, too."

"I forgot to ask you," he said, an undeniably sexy grin forming on his lips. "Brooke Newton, will you marry me?"

"Um..." She swallowed a laugh. "Okay."

"There's something else I want to ask."

"There is?" This time she was stumped. What else could there be?

"I want us to be a family. A *real* family. Once we're married, and if you both agree to it, I'd like to adopt Nick."

Tears formed in her eyes. "Of course I agree. And although we'll ask Nick, I know he will too. He loves you so much," she said, looping her arms around his neck and hugging him tightly. "And so do I."

He wiped the tears from her cheeks with the pads of his thumb, and pressed his lips against her damp skin. "You've made me the happiest man alive," he told her, brushing his mouth against hers and making her shiver. "Thank you."

It had been ten long years between their first kiss and this last one. Those years of heartbreak had finally led to this moment of pure joy. And as he held her tightly and kissed her until she was breathless, Brooke knew the wait had been worth every minute.

They were partners. Equals in every way. And together, their future looked perfect.

DEAR READER

Thank you so much for reading Aiden and Brooke's story. If you enjoyed it and you get a chance, I'd be so grateful if you can leave a review. And don't forget to keep an eye out for **JUST A KISS**, the fourth book in the series.

To learn more, you can sign up for my newsletter here: http://www.subscribepage.com/e4u8i8

I can't wait to share more stories with you.

Yours,

Carrie xx

ABOUT THE AUTHOR

Carrie Elks writes contemporary romance with a sizzling edge. Her first book, *Fix You*, has been translated into eight languages and made a surprise appearance on *Big Brother* in Brazil. Luckily for her, it wasn't voted out.

Carrie lives with her husband, two lovely children and a larger-than-life black pug called Plato. When she isn't writing or reading, she can be found baking, drinking an occasional (!) glass of wine, or chatting on social media.

You can find Carrie in all these places
www.carrieelks.com
carrie.elks@mail.com

ALSO BY CARRIE ELKS

STANDALONE
Fix You

ANGEL SANDS SERIES
Let Me Burn
She's Like the Wind
Sweet Little Lies
Just A Kiss
Baby I'm Yours

THE SHAKESPEARE SISTERS SERIES
Summer's Lease
A Winter's Tale
Absent in the Spring
By Virtue Fall

THE LOVE IN LONDON SERIES
Coming Down
Broken Chords
Canada Square

ACKNOWLEDGMENTS

Thank you to my gorgeous family, Ash, Ella, Olly and Plato the pug. You guys rock my world.

As always, so many thanks and much love to Meire Dias, my agent and my friend. Your unstinting support is amazing. To Flavia, Hannah and Jackie at the Bookcase Agency, thank you for all you do. I'm so proud to be represented by you.

To my editor Rose David and my proofreader, Mich, thank you for helping me to clean this book up and make it shine.

Najla Qamber is a kick-ass designer, and she hit this cover out of the park. You're amazing, lady!

Bloggers have always been such an important part of my book journey. Thanks to each and every one of you who shows me support in so many ways – sharing covers and release days, promoting sales, reading and reviewing books. You're the engine that keeps the book world going, and I appreciate you so much.

Finally, to my lovely facebook group members (The Water Cooler - if you want to join!), thank you! We have so much fun – you make Facebook a great place to be. You help with ideas, inspiration and most of all you put a smile on my face. Thanks for being so amazing.

Printed in Great Britain
by Amazon

C000115584

Cooking for Dogs

Published in 2007 by New Holland Publishers (UK) Ltd
London • Cape Town • Sydney • Auckland
www.newhollandpublishers.com

Garfield House, 86-88 Edgware Road, London W2 2EA, United Kingdom

80 McKenzie Street, Cape Town 8001, South Africa

Unit 1, 66 Gibbes Street, Chatswood, NSW, Australia, 2067

218 Lake Road, Northcote, Auckland, New Zealand

ISBN 978 1 84537 739 7

Editor: Ruth Hamilton
Designer: Ian Sandom
Illustrator: Coral Mula
Production: Hazel Kirkman
Editorial direction: Rosemary Wilkinson

10 9 8 7 6 5 4 3 2 1

Reproduction by Modern Age, Hong Kong
Printed and bound by Craft Print, Singapore

Cooking for Dogs

fun recipes for your favourite friend to enjoy

Marjorie Walsh

New Holland

Contents

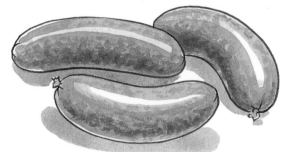

Introduction

When I looked at the nutritional information on commercial pet food and saw by-products, fillers and derivatives I decided that I didn't want to feed that to my dogs. I wouldn't eat these things so why should our dogs? I started out by just making extra when cooking the family's meals so that our dogs ate what we ate. Because I wanted to get it right, I did a lot of research and invested in some nutritional software. The end result is happy, healthy dogs with coats like velvet, plenty of energy and hardly any pooping.

There is no mystery or magic to feeding your pet well. A review of just a few of the books that are available on feeding your pet and the nutritional information on commercial dog food packing shows that the experts don't really know what makes the perfect dog food. Breeders and vets will have their favourite foods, too. So, how do you know?

Dogs are like humans: all different. Some can eat anything and everything. Some have sensitive tummies and some specific breeds have their own problems. For example, deep-chested dogs like Newfoundlands can be prone to twisted gut, a serious condition. For larger dogs it is much kinder to put their feed bowl in a stand adjusted for their height so that they are not stooping to eat their food. A side bonus is that their bowl stays in one place and they don't have to push it round the floor to get that last morsel.

Then it is a matter of trial and error to find foods that eliminate any possible health problems. Try different foods and different food combinations until you find one to suit.

For all dogs, just be guided by your pet. If he or she is happy, with a glossy coat, bright eyes, active and with regular, firm stools then you're feeding the right food. And if you can feel the ribs, you are feeding the right quantity.

The only golden rule is to add calcium to every meal, approximately $\frac{1}{8}$–$\frac{1}{4}$ teaspoon should be sufficient. In most foodstuffs the phosphorous to calcium ratio is inverse to needs, this means that the phosphorous element usually exceeds the calcium level. If we don't adjust this imbalance not only are we not getting enough calcium but over time, the excess phosphorous will leech calcium from bones making them brittle and prone to breaks.

How to you get calcium? Two ways: if you like eggs, simply save the eggshells, wash and bake in an oven at 180°C/350°F/Gas mark 4, for about 30 minutes. Then reduce to a powder form either in a food processor or with mortar and pestle. If you want it really fine put it through a coffee grinder after the food processor. Otherwise you can just buy calcium tablets from a health food store and crush them finely.

All of the recipes in this book are made with foods that humans eat. In theory then, you can make any of these meals for your own dinner and then take a portion for your pet, add calcium and hey presto, with one cooking session everyone in the family is fed. You will also see that some of the recipes contain a small amount of liver. This to ensure that your doggie gets his or her B12 requirement.

Please check the nutritional information. Some of the recipes can be used for regular feeding but others should only be offered occasionally. We think of dogs as meat eaters but actually they are omnivores and don't need as much protein as is commonly believed. As a guide, their meal should consist of 25% protein, 30% fat and 45% carbohydrates.

The nutritional information is based on the needs of an average 22kg (50lb) dog, that is a house pet with regular outdoor activity. If your pet is smaller just reduce the portion size accordingly. For example, for a dog of 11kg (25lb) either halve the recipe size when making or simply halve the portion size given. For a larger dog, increase similarly. For a working dog or lactating bitch double the portion size. For older or infirm dogs give them portion sizes that keep them happy.

Serving sizes are based on two meals a day; breakfast and an evening meal, with a little room left for a small snack. If you don't have time for breakfast in your house, just increase the serving size for the one meal.

So, armed with this information you can actually share your evening meal with your pet, remembering to add calcium to their portion. Dogs also need fat for energy so their meat should not be too lean and don't get too hung up on calories. Just be guided by your pet. And, as we all know, just because a dog keeps looking for food does not mean that you are not offering enough food. Like some humans, some dogs are just food focused and always on the look-out for something to eat.

How easy is it? Well just cook extra, either from one of the recipes or your own evening meal. Divide into portions and either refrigerate or freeze for later use so you have ready-made meals on hand when you have run out of dog food.

Go on, give your pooch a change from the tin or dried food packet!

MARJORIE WALSH

Nutrition primer

A dog's life, then and now: a brief history of feeding

When dogs were wild, they devoted much of their daily activity to hunting. For about 3,000 years after domestication, dogs ate whatever food was left for them at the end of a meal. It was a scrappy, tough existence. In 1922, a group of American businessmen started a new industry. Horsemeat unsuitable for human consumption could be converted into dog food. Gradually, complex formulas and elaborate ingredients came into vogue. Generally speaking, modern dog food is well balanced. Although today's dog no longer must search out food, mealtime remains a central aspect of his/her life. From the person in charge of feeding to the diet itself, routine is one of the most important factors affecting a dog's behaviour. Routine helps to ensure a good appetite, digestion and regular eliminations.

Did you know?

A diet consisting 100% of meat is entirely inadequate. Meat contains no calcium, so a diet of all meat will cause a deficiency of this mineral which is essential for bone and muscle health. Low- or no-fat meat is missing the dog's best source of energy. This causes protein to be used as an energy source, which means the dog feels hungry all the time. To aid digestion, all types of carbohydrates need to be boiled, baked or toasted before feeding to a dog. Starches from oats, corn and potatoes in particular are difficult to digest unless cooked. On the other hand, white and whole-wheat bread are two of the best natural foods to include. Actually minerals are most critical for canine health, especially calcium and phosphorus. Dogs often require some supplement of these in part because commercial food ingredients (meat, meat by-products, soybeans, casein and eggs) contain low levels of both, in the wrong ratio. Milk and bone meal are excellent sources to supply calcium and phosphorus, as well as magnesium, in easily digested form.

Energy

A dog needs energy more than anything. And for that, s/he needs calories. Lots of them. This is one of the most important, fundamental requirements. It relates directly to how much food the dog must consume every day. This is critical for a dog owner to keep in mind. Most people think of calories as something to be avoided as much as possible. But a calorie is a measurement of energy potential. That means, in simplified terms, that the more calories in your dog's food, the greater energy potential it contains (more on this later). If the food is high in calories – 'high caloric density' – then your dog doesn't need so much food to supply its daily need for fuel (energy).

Table scraps

Dogs existed for thousands of years eating table scraps. It's logical to think that table scraps would be an ideal way to improve the overall nutritive value of a dog's diet. However, just as dog food has changed over the years, so too has the food at our tables. With the advent of commercial dog food, fewer dogs eat table scraps. As human food has become more commercially prepared, its suitability as dog food has declined. Table scraps have plenty of calories, but with little else that is usable by the dog's body systems. Table scraps can improve the palatability of commercial food, but they must be finely chopped and blended together.

- **Fact:** Most table scraps are composed of fats and carbohydrates, with lots of calories, but little else in the way of nutritional value.
- **Fact:** Dogs often prefer the taste of table scraps to their more balanced commercial food. If not mixed well together, the dog may eat the table scraps and not the other.

Choosing the right food

The most reliable way to judge the nutritional value of a dog's food is to see what happens when s/he eats. Is s/he always hungry? Coat dull or glossy? Active or uninterested and lethargic? Of course, these are only a few indicators and can signal other problems. Your dog is your best guide to deciding on the right food. And for starters, you can eliminate:

- tinned food containing more than 78% water
- any food whose guaranteed calcium content is less than 0.30%
- any food without at least one cereal grain

Digestibility

Digestibility is the reason for all this information about types of food and ratios. A dog food may contain the exact balance required, but if the ingredients used for that food are indigestible, the dog will starve. On the other hand, when a dog's food is made well, from ingredients approaching full digestibility, s/he may produce a stool only two to three times a week. When the digestive system can break down a food completely, and absorb all its nutritive content, there is little to no waste. In general, animal food sources are more digestible than plants. However, most carbohydrates come from plants. And cellulose, which makes up a large portion of plant carbohydrate, cannot be digested. Dogs' digestive systems do not contain the right enzymes for the job. Thus alfalfa, which contains virtually every nutrient a dog needs, is useless because the dog cannot digest it. Yet gelatin is equally unsuitable because, while it is highly digestible, it lacks two essential amino acids.

Teasing the palate

The commercial food industry tends to overlook food palatability from a dog's standpoint. Flavours and odours are far more likely to be negative, rather than positive, factors in a dog's interest in food. Additionally, dogs care about the texture of their food, and some studies have shown that a low-salt diet is preferred almost two to one. Freshly made food is often sold frozen, but this should not be considered a negative selling point. On the contrary, frozen food will retain its fresh flavour longer and tends to be rated highest by discerning dogs. Frozen food is both highly digestible, tasty and desirable to the dog. Frozen food should be served at room temperature.

Recommended daily allowances: Calories 1350kcal; Protein 48g; Carbohydrates 186g; Fibre 18.9g; Fat 42g; Calcium 2700 mg

Breakfasts

This section contains recipes for healthy breakfasts, occasional treats, some for the calorie conscious and some for those with intolerances. Egg is almost the perfect dog food so dish up these recipes knowing that you are giving your pet something good.

Slimline cereal

Preparation time: 5 minutes • Cooking time: 0 minutes • Servings: 1

A slimline breakfast that gives bulk with few calories.

Ingredients

1 Weetabix or 5 Tbsp equivalent cereal

⅛ tsp calcium

240ml/8fl oz/1 cup skimmed milk

120ml/4fl oz/½ cup water

Method

- Place the Weetabix or equivalent cereal in the dog bowl.
Add the calcium. Pour over the milk and water mixture. Serve.

Note: slightly warm the milk or use warm water so that the breakfast
is just like comfort food; warm and moist.

Nutritional info per serving: Calories 153kcal; Protein 10g;
Carbohydrates 26g; Fibre 2g; Fat 0.95g; Calcium 682mg

Light scrambled egg

Preparation time: 5 minutes • Cooking time: 5 minutes • Servings: 1

You can add cereal and replace the skimmed milk with

full fat milk to increase the calories in this breakfast by a third

to the full breakfast version.

Ingredients

2 eggs

140ml/5fl oz/⅔ cup skimmed milk

⅛ tsp calcium

Method

• Break the eggs into a non-stick pan over medium heat, add the milk and stir until cooked. Pour into a dog bowl, add the calcium and mix in. Let cool to room temperature and serve.

Nutritional info per serving: Calories 256kcal; Protein 19g; Carbohydrates 10g; Fibre 0g; Fat 15½g; Calcium 615mg

Smoked haddock and eggs

Preparation time: 5 minutes • Cooking time: 5 minutes • Servings: 1

A breakfast for pooches who are lactose intolerant, on dry food and who need a high number of calories. If your pet doesn't need this many calories then this quantity will make two servings. Also perfect if you don't want to feed your pet meat. Dogs love fish: the smellier, the better!

Ingredients

55g/2oz smoked haddock, flaked

1 tsp sunflower oil

3 eggs

1 English muffin, toasted

¼ tsp calcium

Method

- Poach the haddock in water or milk for 5–10 minutes. Heat oil in non-stick pan. Break eggs into pan, add flakes of fish and stir until cooked.

- Toast muffin. Put egg and fish mixture into dog bowl. Tear muffin into bite sized pieces, add to egg and fish. Add calcium and mix well. Serve.

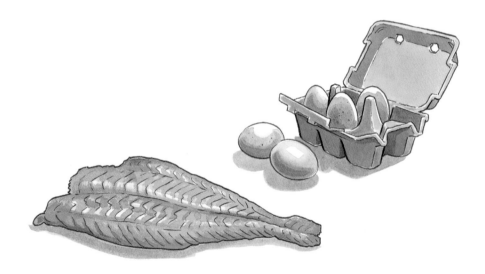

Nutritional info per serving: Calories 675kcal; Protein 45g; Carbohydrates 57g; Fibre 9g; Fat 30g; Calcium 1181mg

Eggs and sausage

Preparation time: 5 minutes • Cooking time: 12 minutes • Servings: 1

A breakfast you can share with your pet, this is a meat recipe

for a lactose intolerant pet. If not lactose intolerant you can add a

little milk (about 80ml/2¾fl oz/⅓ cup) to make it more moist.

Talk about chop lickin'!

Ingredients

1 sausage (about 2oz/55g)

1 tsp sunflower or corn oil

2 eggs

1 slice wholewheat bread, toasted

¼ tsp calcium

Method

- Grill sausage, cut into bite-sized pieces and leave to cool.

- Heat oil in non-stick pan. Break eggs into pan (add milk,
  if using) and stir until cooked. Stir in cooked sausage.

- Place egg and sausage mixture into dog bowl and while it is cooling,
toast bread. Tear into bite-sized pieces and stir into the egg and sausage
together with the calcium. Serve at room temperature.

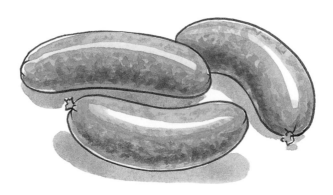

Nutritional info per serving: Calories 460kcal; Protein 27g;
Carbohydrates 15g; Fibre 2g; Fat 32g; Calcium 800mg

Bacon, avocado and cheese omelette

Preparation time: 10 minutes • Cooking time: 6 minutes • Servings: 2

A very special breakfast that you can either share with your pet or serve as a birthday treat. This is a substantial breakfast in terms of calories so if you and your pet are weight-watching serve half (or halve the ingredients to make 1 small omelette). Avocado is great for a shiny coat.

Ingredients

75g/2½oz fresh tomatoes, chopped

2 Tbsp fresh coriander, chopped
or 1 tsp dried coriander

1 Tbsp fresh lime juice

3 rashers bacon

1 small avocado

4 eggs

2 Tbsp water

1 Tbsp sunflower or corn oil

50g/2oz/½ cup Cheddar cheese,
grated

½ tsp calcium

Method

- In a small bowl mix chopped tomatoes, coriander and lime juice to make a dog-friendly salsa. Grill bacon and leave to cool. Peel the avocado. Remove the stone and cut the flesh into 1cm (½in) pieces. Cut the bacon into bite-sized pieces.

- In a bowl, whisk the eggs and water. In either an omelette pan or non-stick frying pan heat the oil. Pour the egg mixture to cover the bottom of the pan. Cook until almost set. Over half the egg mixture, put the bacon, avocado and cheese. Fold the other half of the egg over the top and cook until set.

- Allow to cool to room temperature and serve together with the salsa. Cut the omelette into pieces if your pet is small.

Nutritional info per serving: Calories 650kcal; Protein 26g; Carbohydrates 13g; Fibre 7.5g; Fat 56g; Calcium 1000mg

Speedy Meals
and Fast Food

We all know that there is little time to cook fancy evening meals. All of the recipes in this section can be ready in 30 minutes or less. And in some cases, you can reduce the time even further by using canned or frozen vegetables or pulses, pre-cooking rice and using leftover cooked meat. And there are a couple of vegetable dishes that you can use with any meal which is predominately protein, from any of the other chapters.

Honeyed chicken

Preparation time: 10 minutes • Cooking time: 5 minutes • Servings: 1

This recipe has been designed to make use of cooked chicken but you can use fresh chicken (see method for details). Add a portion of the Stir-fried bean salad (see page 32) to make the perfect meal. The nutritional information is based on the chicken dish with the Stir-fried bean salad on the side.

Ingredients

1 Tbsp olive oil	120g/4oz cooked chicken, diced
2 garlic cloves, crushed	6 anchovies
3 Tbsp honey	¼ tsp calcium
Grated lemon rind	240ml/8fl oz/1 cup chicken stock
1 tsp dried rosemary	Stir-fried bean salad (see page 32)

Method

- Heat oil in pan, sauté garlic for 1 minute. Add honey, lemon rind and rosemary and stir until the honey is liquid. Remove from heat. Stir in chicken, anchovies and calcium. Add chicken stock and mix well.

- Place in dog bowl, add portion of 'Stir-fried bean salad' and serve at room temperature.

Note: if you want to use fresh chicken, cut into bite-sized pieces and sauté in a pan with garlic until cooked through (about 5 minutes) then follow recipe as for cooked chicken.

Nutritional info per serving: Calories 1298kcal; Protein 84g; Carbohydrates 141g; Fibre 21g; Fat 45g; Calcium 1745mg

Lamb with spinach

Preparation time: 10 minutes • Cooking time: 6 minutes • Servings: 1

If your pooch has adventurous tastes then this lamb with a

Japanese twist will go down a treat.

Ingredients

1 Tbsp sesame oil

2 garlic cloves, crushed

1 apple, cored and cut into
bite-sized pieces

¼ tsp ground mixed spice

280g/10oz spinach

3 Tbsp rice wine, white wine
vinegar or cider vinegar

1 tsp cornflour, dissolved in
1 Tbsp water

250g/8oz cooked lamb,
cut into bite-sized pieces

½ tsp calcium

540g/20oz/3 cups pasta or rice

Method

• Heat oil in wok or frying pan. Add garlic and stir-fry for 1 minute.
Add apple and stir-fry for a further minute. Stir in ground mixed spice.
Add spinach and stir-fry for 1 minute or until just wilted. Add rice wine and the
cornflour mixture to wok. Stir-fry for 1 minute. Remove from heat, add lamb and
calcium and stir until well mixed.

• At the same time, bring a pan of water to the boil and cook pasta or rice
according to the instructions. Drain and run under cold water.

• Put pasta or rice into the dog bowl, add lamb mixture and mix well.
Serve at room temperature.

Note: if you want to use fresh lamb, stir-fry it with the garlic for 2–3 minutes.

Nutritional info per serving: Calories 1412kcal; Protein 84g;
Carbohydrates 143g; Fibre 20g; Fat 55g; Calcium 1800mg

Stir-fried bean salad

Preparation time: 10 minutes • Cooking time: 8 minutes • Servings: 3

A vegetable and pulses dish that can be divided into three servings and eaten as a whole meal or smaller servings can be used as a side dish.

Ingredients

170g/6oz green beans, cut into 3cm (2in) pieces

170g/6oz runner beans, cut into 3cm (2in) pieces

140g/5oz mangetout

2 Tbsp olive oil

2 cloves garlic, crushed

450g/16oz tinned red kidney beans, drained and mashed

425g/15oz tinned cannellini beans, drained and mashed

340g/12oz tinned sweetcorn, drained

225g/8oz Cheddar cheese, cubed

3 Tbsp fresh parsley, chopped

¾ tsp calcium

Method

- Half-fill a saucepan with water. Bring to the boil, then add green and runner beans and simmer for 2 minutes. Add mangetout, bring back to the boil and then drain and rinse under cold water.

- Heat oil in a wok or frying pan. Add garlic and stir-fry 1–2 minutes. Stir in kidney beans, cannellini beans and sweetcorn. Stir-fry for 3 minutes. Remove from heat. Add cheese, parsley and calcium and toss everything together to mix.

- If serving as main meal, put one-third into dog bowl and serve at room temperature. Put the remainder in a bowl, cover and refrigerate. Use within 3 days.

Note: you can use any vegetables that you have on hand: fresh, canned, frozen. If you do not have fresh parsley either omit or use 1 tsp dried parsley.

Nutritional info per serving: Calories 1120kcal; Protein 63g; Carbohydrates 131g; Fibre 34g; Fat 38g; Calcium 1544mg

Greek-style vegetables

Preparation time: 10 minutes • Cooking time: 4 minutes • Servings: 1

A low protein dish that can be a meal on its own or divided into

3 servings and added to other meals.

Ingredients

2 Tbsp oil	½ tsp dried oregano
1 clove garlic, crushed	1 Tbsp balsamic vinegar
340g/12oz red or yellow cherry tomatoes	50g/1½oz/½ cup feta cheese, crumbled
675g/1½lb broad beans, frozen or fresh (shelled)	½ tsp calcium

Method

- Heat oil in wok or frying pan. Add garlic, tomatoes, broad beans and oregano. Stir-fry 3–4 minutes over medium heat until beans are tender. Stir in balsamic vinegar. Stir-fry for a further minute.

- Remove from heat, add cheese and calcium and toss to mix. Serve at room temperature in a dog bowl.

Nutritional info per serving: Calories 1265kcal; Protein 65g; Carbohydrates 154g; Fibre 41g; Fat 47g; Calcium 2108mg

Paw lickin' pizza

Preparation time: 10 minutes • Cooking time: 20 minutes • Servings: 2

Don't wait for pizza delivery; whip this one up for your loved one! The
recipe has been divided into two servings but if your pooch can't resist
and needs some special treatment let him/her eat the whole pizza!

Ingredients

70ml/2½fl oz/⅓ cup
tomato purée

70ml/2½fl oz/⅓ cup water

1 Tbsp corn oil

¼ tsp garlic powder

½ tsp calcium

1 shop-bought pizza base

50g/1½oz mixed vegetables,
cubed

110g/4oz cooked beef,
cut into small cubes

25g/¾oz/¼ cup Cheddar
cheese, grated

Method

• Preheat oven to 200°C/400°F/Gas mark 6. Mix the first five ingredients together and spread over the pizza base. Place vegetables and beef on top and sprinkle the cheese over. Bake for 20–25 minutes or until top is golden. Leave to cool then slice.

Note: you can make your own pizza base if you wish but using a shop-bought pizza base means that this dinner can be whipped up in next to no time.

Nutritional info per serving: Calories 905kcal; Protein 42g; Carbohydrates 125g; Fibre 7g; Fat 25g; Calcium 900mg

Chompin' chicken nuggets

Preparation time: 10 minutes • Cooking time: 20 minutes • Servings: 2

Yummy, yummy, yummy. A special treat only, as while this is low in

protein, it's quite high in fat. You can add your own vegetables or use

one of the vegetable recipes from the book as a side dish.

Ingredients

2 chicken breasts	1 egg
140g/5oz/1 cup wholewheat flour	250ml/8½fl oz/1¼ cups milk
	8 Weetabix (or equivalent cereal)
1 tsp garlic powder	120ml/4fl oz/½ cup corn oil
½ tsp calcium	

Method

- Cut the chicken breasts into small cubes. Mix together the flour, garlic powder and calcium. Whisk the egg and milk together and add to the flour mix to make a batter. Crush the cereal.

- Drop the chicken cubes into the batter, then roll in the cereal.

- Shallow fry in the oil for about 20 minutes. (They can also be deep-fried.) Serve cool.

Nutritional info per serving: Calories 1240kcal; Protein 53g; Carbohydrates 108g; Fibre 16g; Fat 68g; Calcium 1411mg

Hound dog hamburger

Preparation time: 10 minutes • Cooking time: 20 minutes • Servings: 1

A healthy hamburger which looks pretty spectacular and which your

doggie will love – he/she won't wait to appreciate the look of it!

Ingredients

3 large sweet potatoes

225g/8oz minced beef

½ tsp rosemary, dried

½ tsp calcium

2 Weetabix, crushed or
8 Tbsp equivalent cereal

½ tsp cod liver oil

60g/2oz frozen peas or sweetcorn
or mixture of both

Method

- Peel and cut potatoes. Boil until tender and then mash. Leave to cool.

- While potatoes are cooking, mix remaining ingredients together in a bowl. Form into one large pattie. Grill until cooked through, approximately 20 minutes.

- Divide cold mashed potatoes in half. Shape each half into a large pattie. Place one potato pattie on the bottom, add the hamburger and top with the second potato pattie. Serve at room temperature.

Note: if you don't have any cod liver oil in the cupboard substitute sunflower or corn oil.

Nutritional info per serving: Calories 960kcal; Protein 75g; Carbohydrates 122g; Fibre 19g; Fat 18g; Calcium 1638mg

Fish 'n' chips

Preparation time: 5 minutes • Cooking time: 10 minutes • Servings: 1

A perfect midday snack or a light evening meal. Preparation time
depends upon how far away the fish and chip shop is from where you
live or whether you make the home-made version!

Ingredients

2 pieces battered cod	280g/10oz/2 cups flour
1 medium portion chips	2 pieces of cod (or other white fish)
OR	120ml/4fl oz/½ cup oil
2 eggs	1 medium portion frozen chips

Method

- Go to fish and chip shop and buy lunch or dinner for all of the family. Allow to cool to room temperature before serving

OR

- Beat the eggs and pour into a bowl. Put the flour into another bowl. Coat the cod with the egg and then dip into the flour, coating both sides.

- Heat the oil in a frying pan and fry the cod until cooked through, about 3–4 minutes each side. Cook the chips according to instructions on packet. Let cool. Break the cod into bite-sized pieces and place in bowl with chips. Serve at room temperature.

Note: you could replace the chips with fried cooked potatoes – a good use for any leftover potatoes.

Nutritional info per serving: Calories 506kcal; Protein 12g; Carbohydrates 60g; Fibre 5g; Fat 25g; Calcium 30mg

Poochie's potatoes

Preparation time: 15 minutes • Cooking time: 15 minutes • Servings: 2

A side dish for Chompin' chicken nuggets (see page 38)

or for adding to any other meat dish.

Ingredients

500g/17oz cooked potatoes, diced

1 Tbsp mixed vegetables, frozen, canned or fresh

50g/2oz/½ cup cottage cheese

1 Tbsp brewers yeast

2 Tbsp diced carrots, cooked

⅛ tsp calcium

60ml/2fl oz/¼ cup milk

1½ tsp corn oil

50g/1¾oz/½ cup Cheddar cheese, grated

Method

- Preheat the oven to 170°C/350°F/Gas mark 4. Layer the first six ingredients in a casserole dish. Pour the milk and oil over. Sprinkle with the grated cheese.

- Bake for about 15 minutes at until the cheese melts and the top is slightly brown. Serve cool.

Note: You can substitute the potatoes with 500g/17oz/3 cups cooked oatmeal or cooked brown rice

Nutritional info per serving: Calories 497kcal; Protein 21g; Carbohydrates 53g; Fibre 5g; Fat 23g; Calcium 478mg

Special Occasions and Exotic Meals

All the major holidays are represented, although for pooch's own birthday you will need to go to Snacks and Treats for a delicious cake. All of these recipes can be made with fresh ingredients or you can use up food left over from your own holiday celebrations. There is also a selection of delicious Mediterranean dishes when you want an exotic, but healthy, meal.

Valentine love apple cake

Preparation time: 10 minutes • Cooking time: 1¼ hours • Servings: 10

What is a love apple? The French originally called tomatoes *pomme d'amour*, or love apples, so this gorgeous dessert is a great addition to a pooch's Valentine party. Each serving should be about 75g/2½oz.

Ingredients

1 tin condensed tomato soup

1 tsp baking soda

2 eggs

½ tsp calcium

35g/1¼oz/¼ cup brown sugar

280g/10oz/2 cups wholewheat flour

1 tsp ground cinnamon

½ Tbsp ground cloves

1 small bottle or tin of maraschino cherries

strawberry, raspberry or black cherry conserve, optional

Method

• Preheat oven to 160°C/325°F/Gas mark 3. In a mixing bowl, stir baking soda into the soup. Lightly beat eggs and add to the soup mix. Then combine the rest of the ingredients, except conserve, and mix thoroughly.

• Pour into a 15-cm (6-in) heart-shaped cake tin or a 23 x 13 x 8-cm (9 x 5 x 3-in) loaf tin. Bake for 55 minutes–1¼ hours or until a toothpick comes out clean when inserted in the centre of the cake.

• Cool for 5 minutes in the pan; then remove and place on wire rack to cool completely. If you want to make it really special for Valentine's, spread a little strawberry, raspberry or black cherry conserve on the top before serving a slice in a dog bowl.

Nutritional info per serving: Calories 178kcal; Protein 5g;
Carbohydrates 26g; Fibre 4g; Fat 7g; Calcium 169mg

Pumpkin cauldron

Preparation time: 20 minutes • Cooking time: 55 minutes • Servings: 1

A yummy Halloween treat, especially for young dogs. How much food you will get will depend upon the size of the pumpkin. The nutritional analysis is based on 5–6 cups of cooked mixture, which will be equal to one serving.

Ingredients

1 pumpkin	3½oz Tbsp flour
2 chicken breasts	570ml/1 pint/2½ cups chicken stock
2 Tbsp olive oil	1 cinnamon stick
2 red peppers	1 bay leaf
55g/2oz bacon	2 Tbsp fresh parsley, chopped
1 clove garlic, crushed	½ tsp calcium

Method

- Pre-heat oven to 190°C/375°F/Gas mark 5. Cut the top off the pumpkin to make a lid. Scoop out the seeds. Cut the flesh from the insides, being careful not to cut the skin. Cut flesh into bite-sized pieces.

- Cut the chicken into bite-sized pieces. Heat the oil in a frying pan and fry chicken until golden but not cooked through. Remove. De-seed the peppers and cut into bite-sized pieces. Cut the bacon into bite-sized pieces. Add the garlic, peppers and bacon to the pan. Cook for 2–3 minutes. Stir in the flour and cook for 1 minute. Add the stock and bring to the boil. Add the chicken, pumpkin, cinnamon stick and bay leaf.

- Pour the mixture into the pumpkin, put lid on and bake for about 45 minutes or until the chicken is cooked through. Stir in the parsley and calcium. Spoon some into the dog bowl (without the cinnamon stick and bayleaf!) and serve at room temperature.

Nutritional info per serving: Calories 1316kcal; Protein 86g; Carbohydrates 102g; Fibre 20g; Fat 67g; Calcium 1676mg

Turkey cranberry stew

Preparation time: 10 minutes • Cooking time: 6 minutes • Servings: 1

A yummy way to use up that leftover turkey at Christmas to give your pet

a dog-licious dinner.

Ingredients

225g/8oz sweet potatoes

225g/8oz squash or pumpkin

110g/4oz celery

250g/8½oz cooked turkey, diced

240g/8⅓fl oz/1 cup turkey stock

2 Tbsp flour

55g/2oz cranberries,
fresh or dried

½ tsp calcium

Method

• Peel and dice potatoes and squash, cut celery into bite-sized pieces. Boil in a saucepan for 3–4 minutes, until just starting to go soft. Add cooked turkey to the saucepan.

• Whisk the flour into the cold turkey stock. Add turkey stock to the pan and simmer for 10 minutes, stirring occasionally. Add cranberries and mix well. Remove from heat and place in dog bowl. Stir in calcium and serve at room temperature.

Nutritional info per serving: Calories 1090kcal; Protein 88g; Carbohydrates 120g; Fibre 18g; Fat 30g; Calcium 1717mg

Dog nog

Preparation time: 10 minutes • Cooking time: 40 minutes • Servings: 8

A special Christmas treat for your pet.

Ingredients

1 chicken breast

1.4 L/2½ pints/6 cups water

140g/5oz/1 cup wholewheat flour

2 eggs, beaten

⅛ tsp parsley, dried

Method

- Boil chicken breast for about ½ hour and remove from water to cool. Add flour to chicken water and beat out any lumps. Add beaten eggs. Cook on low heat until mixture has thickened. Mince chicken in food processor and add to the gravy. Add a little more water if needed to get a pourable liquid.

- Place in dog bowl, sprinkle with parsley and serve at room temperature.

Note: To reduce preparation and cooking time, use leftover cooked chicken.

Nutritional info per serving: Calories 90kcal; Protein 7g; Carbohydrates 11g; Fibre 2g; Fat 2g; Calcium 18mg

Roasted root vegetables

Preparation time: 15 minutes • Cooking time: 30 minutes • Servings: 2

The recipes that follow in this section do not have any vegetables, so this dish is the perfect addition to any of them. Alternatively, add 285g/10oz cooked turkey, diced, and 2 tsp calcium to make it a complete meal of its own.

Ingredients

950ml/1⅔ pints/4 cups fruit juice (apple or cranberry)

225g/8oz carrots

225g/8oz sweet potatoes

225g/8oz turnips

225g/8oz swede

225g/8oz parsnips

3 Tbsp butter

Method

- Boil juice until it is reduced to 1 cup, about 30 minutes.
Pre-heat oven to 220°C/425°F/Gas mark 7.

- Peel and dice root vegetables and place in roasting pan. Whisk the butter into the reduced juice and pour over vegetables. Toss to coat. Roast until vegetables are golden and tender, stirring occasionally, about 30 minutes.

- Allow to cool to room temperature and serve with a main dish.

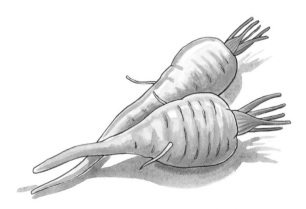

Nutritional info per serving: Calories 486kcal; Protein 6g;
Carbohydrates 80g; Fibre 18g; Fat 18g; Calcium 2270mg

Mediterranean prawn casserole

Preparation time: 10 minutes • Cooking time: 35 minutes • Servings: 1

We know that Mediterranean dishes are healthy. Watch this get woofed down and know that you are giving your loved one super goodness.

Ingredients

250g/8½oz wholewheat pasta	140g/5oz tomato sauce
3 garlic cloves, crushed	170g/6oz cooked prawns
560g/1¼lb tinned plum tomatoes, chopped	1 tsp dried dill
70ml/2½fl oz/⅓ cup fish stock	95g/3½oz/1 cup Asiago cheese, grated
	¼ tsp calcium

Method

- Preheat oven to 200°C/400°F/Gas mark 6. Bring a pan of water to the boil, add pasta and par-boil for about 6 minutes. Drain and set aside.

- Add the garlic, juice from tin of tomatoes and fish stock to the pan. Bring to the boil, reduce heat and simmer for 5–7 minutes until most of the liquid has evaporated. Stir in the tomatoes and tomato sauce. Bring to the boil. Add the prawns, pasta, dill, half the cheese and calcium. Mix thoroughly.

- Transfer to a lightly greased shallow baking dish. Sprinkle the top with the rest of the cheese and bake for 15–20 minutes. Allow to cool to room temperature and serve.

Nutritional info per serving: Calories 1206kcal; Protein 85g; Carbohydrates 128g; Fibre 22g; Fat 41g; Calcium 1744mg

Rice pilaf

Preparation time: 10 minutes • Cooking time: 30 minutes • Servings: 1

Full of goodness. You can also substitute the beef stock with chicken stock and the beef with chicken and omit the garlic to make a tummy-friendly meal for your pet.

Ingredients

360g/13oz/2 cups brown rice

475ml/16½fl oz/2 cups
beef stock

2 garlic cloves, crushed

110g/4oz hummus

¼ tsp cinnamon

110g/4oz tinned
black beans, mashed

110g/4oz cooked beef, cubed
(or any other meat)

½ tsp calcium

Method

• Bring a pan of water to the boil and par-boil the rice for 10 minutes. Drain.

• Add the stock to the pan, then add the garlic, hummus, cinnamon, black beans and rice. Stir to mix. Bring back to the boil, reduce heat and simmer for about 30 minutes, stirring occasionally, until the rice is cooked and the liquid has evaporated. Add more liquid as necessary.

• Allow to cool, stir in the beef and calcium. Place in dog bowl and serve.

Nutritional info per serving: Calories 1046kcal; Protein 66g; Carbohydrates 127g; Fibre 22g; Fat 30g; Calcium 1626mg

Tuna polenta

Preparation time: 10 minutes • Cooking time: 50 minutes • Servings: 2

Fish isn't just for cool cats! It's for hot dogs as well! Add

a vegetable side dish from any of the chapters and you've got

the perfect dinner.

Ingredients

1½ L/2¾ pints/6½ cups water	2 tsp cod liver oil
325g/11oz/2 cups polenta	30g/1oz liver, chopped
285g/10oz tinned tuna	1¼ tsp calcium
4 eggs, beaten	180g/6⅓oz/1 cup cooked brown rice
50g/1¾oz/½ cup parmesan, grated	110g/4oz tomato paste

Method

- Preheat oven to 180°C/350°F/Gas mark 4. Bring the water to the boil in a saucepan, add the polenta, reduce the heat and simmer over a medium heat, stirring frequently, for 10–15 minutes until polenta thickens.

- Add the tuna, eggs, parmesan, cod liver oil, liver and calcium to the polenta. Mix well, then turn into a lightly greased shallow baking dish or pie dish. Bake in the oven for 30–35 minutes.

- While the polenta is cooking, cook the rice according to the packet instructions. Drain and set aside. When the rice is cool, mix in the tomato paste and divide it into two servings. When the polenta is ready, allow to cool to room temperature. Divide into two servings, cut into bite-sized pieces and serve with rice.

Nutritional info per serving: Calories 1075kcal; Protein 73g; Carbohydrates 124g; Fibre 12g; Fat 32g; Calcium 2149mg

Lamb with lentils

Preparation time: 10 minutes • Cooking time: 2 hours • Servings: 1

This recipe is based on using lamb shanks which infuses the whole dish with a wonderful flavour. You can replace the shank with any other cut of lamb or use leftover cooked lamb which will reduce the cooking time.

Ingredients

6 lamb shanks

1 Tbsp corn oil

2 cloves garlic, crushed

2 rashers bacon, cut into bite-sized pieces

795g/1lb 2oz/2 cups lentils

100g/3½oz carrots, sliced

55g/2oz celery, cut into bite-sized pieces

475ml/16½oz/2 cups vegetable stock

475ml/16½oz/2 cups water

¾ tsp calcium

Method

- Put the lamb shanks in a large saucepan. In a frying pan heat the oil and sauté the garlic and bacon pieces for 1–2 minutes. Add to the lamb shanks.

- Add the lentils, carrots and celery. Cover with the vegetable stock and water. Bring to the boil and simmer gently over a very low heat for about 2 hours, adding more liquid as necessary.

- When cooked, remove from heat and allow to cool to room temperature. Remove lamb shanks. Take 85g (3oz) of lamb and place in dog bowl. Pour the rest of the mix over the lamb. Add calcium and stir to mix well.

Nutritional info per serving: Calories 1071kcal; Protein 64g; Carbohydrates 92g; Fibre 35g; Fat 51g; Calcium 2330mg

To Share

Magic meal: Take unconditional love, low blood pressure and no lip and add our love, our time and the best food we can. Mix together and you have the recipe for magic moments. Love is... cooking together. Oh ok, so they won't be much help but they will show their appreciation by licking the bowl clean. So, throw a bit extra in the pot and, hey presto, the whole family can eat together.

Avocado and chicken casserole

Preparation time: 20 minutes • Cooking time: 55 minutes

• Servings: 1 dog, 6 human

Dogs just love avocado and it's great for keeping their coats really glossy. This is a delicious meal which all the family will find yummy.

Ingredients

340g/12oz/8 cups spinach noodles or pasta

1 large avocado, peeled and sliced

2 Tbsp fresh lime juice

3 Tbsp olive oil

35g/1¼oz/¼ cup flour

1 tsp cornflour mixed with a little milk

500ml/19fl oz/2¼ cups skimmed milk

50g/1¾oz/½ cup Cheddar cheese, grated

3 skinless chicken breasts, diced

tabasco sauce, optional

Doggie Version add:
¾ tsp calcium

Method

- Preheat oven to 180°C/350°F/Gas mark 4. Cook the noodles according to package directions, drain and set aside. Drizzle the avocado slices with lime juice and set aside.

- Heat the oil in a saucepan over a low heat. Stir in the flour and cook over a low heat until the mixture bubbles. Add the cornflour and milk, and mix slowly, stirring constantly until the mixture thickens. Add the cheese and stir until it has melted. Reserve ⅓ of this sauce. Mix the remainder with cooked noodles.

- Place the chicken in the bottom of a lightly greased baking dish. Spoon the noodle mixture over the chicken. Place avocado slices on top and pour the reserved sauce over the avocados. Bake, uncovered for 35 minutes. When cooked, divide mixture in two. In one half, add the calcium, mix well, place in dog bowl and serve at room temperature. The other half is all yours.

- Add a dash of tabasco sauce to your version to spice up this dish.

Nutritional info per serving: Calories 1405kcal; Protein 85g; Carbohydrates 153g; Fibre 16g; Fat 53g; Calcium 1755mg

Beef and black bean stew

Preparation time: 5 minutes • Cooking time: 30 minutes

• Servings: 3 dog, 3 human

This is a recipe for your slow cooker or crockpot.

Ingredients

900g/2lb minced beef

2 Tbsp garlic powder

2 x 425-g/15-oz tins
sweetcorn, drained

2 x 425-g/15-oz tins
black beans, undrained and mashed

2 x 170-g/6-oz tins tomato paste

700ml/25fl oz/3 cups water

240ml/8½fl oz/1 cup sour cream

450g/1lb/4¾ cups Cheddar
cheese, grated

16 pieces cornbread

Doggie Version add:
1 tsp calcium

Method

- Brown the beef in a non-stick frying pan. Mix in the garlic powder. Reduce the heat to low, cover and simmer for 10 minutes.

- In a slow cooker, over low heat, combine the sweetcorn, beans, tomato paste and water. Mix well. Add the beef and sour cream. Raise heat to high setting and simmer for 20 minutes.

- When cooked, divide the mixture into two. For the doggie version add the calcium and mix well. Divide each half of the mixture into 3 servings and sprinkle the cheese over each one. For the doggie version break 2 pieces of cornbread into each serving and serve at room temperature. For humans serve warm cornbread on the side.

Note: You could also freeze the servings in bags to use another day.

Nutritional info per serving: Calories 1326kcal; Protein 86g;
Carbohydrates 116g; Fibre 17g; Fat 58g; Calcium 1325mg

Salmon stroganoff

Preparation time: 10 minutes • Cooking time: 35 minutes

• Servings: 3 dog, 4–6 human

A fishy take on stroganoff. This recipe is a little fiddly, but well worth it.

Ingredients

900g/2lb spinach noodles

1 tsp calcium

400g/14oz tinned salmon plus
170g/6oz tinned mushrooms

110g/4oz/1 cup breadcrumbs

6 Weetabix/100g similar cereal

55g/2oz tinned pimentos

2 Tbsp corn oil

350g/12½oz/1½ cups cottage cheese

350g/12½oz/1½ cups sour cream

Human Version add:
120ml/4fl oz/½ cup mayonnaise

1 clove garlic, crushed

3 Tbsp onions, grated

95g/3½oz/1 cup Cheddar cheese,
grated

1½ tsp Worcestershire sauce
plus 1 tsp salt

Method

- Preheat oven to 180°C/350°F/Gas mark 4. In a bowl, combine the noodles, salmon, mushrooms and pimentos. Combine the cottage cheese, sour cream and garlic; add to the noodle mixture and mix well. Divide mixture into two portions and in one, stir in the cheese and calcium. For the human version, omit the calcium and stir in the mayonnaise, onions, Worcestershire sauce and salt.

- Transfer each version to a greased 2L/4 pint/2qt baking dish. Crush Weetabix (omit for humans) into the breadcrumbs, mix and toss this mix with the oil; sprinkle over each stroganoff. Bake, uncovered, for 30–35 minutes. Serve doggie version at room temperature.

Nutritional info per serving: Calories 1498kcal; Protein 77g; Carbohydrates 145g; Fibre 11g; Fat 67g; Calcium 1924mg

Vegetable rice quiche

Preparation time: 15 minutes • Cooking time: 45 minutes

• Servings: 1 dog, 6 human

This is great for veggies. The doggie version has liver to provide vitamin B12 and there are eggs and cheese for protein.

Ingredients

8 eggs

720g/25oz/4 cups cooked rice

675g/1½lb broccoli, chopped

110g/4oz green peppers, chopped

2 cloves garlic, minced

95g/3½oz/1 cup Cheddar cheese, grated

110g/4oz pimento

110g/4oz mushrooms, chopped

240ml/8½fl oz/1 cup skimmed milk

Doggie Version add:
30g/1oz cooked liver, diced

½ tsp calcium

Method

• Pre-heat oven to 190°C/375°F/Gas mark 5. Beat 2 of the eggs and add to the rice. Stir until well blended. Divide mixture in two. Press half of the mixture onto bottom and up sides of a lightly greased 23cm (9in) plate or shallow baking dish. Repeat to line a second plate or dish with the other half of the mixture. Set aside.

• Add the broccoli, pepper and garlic to a non-stick frying pan and cook over a medium heat, stirring occasionally until lightly cooked, about 4 minutes. Set aside to cool slightly. Stir in the cheese, pimentos and mushrooms.

• Divide the mixture in two. For the doggie version, stir in the diced liver and calcium. Spoon each half into the two prepared quiche bases. In a large bowl, beat together the remaining eggs and milk until well blended. Divide in half and pour over the vegetables in each quiche base. Bake until a knife inserted near the centre comes out clean, about 35–45 minutes. Let the doggie version cool to room temperature, scoop into dog bowl and serve. The human version can be eaten hot or cold.

Nutritional info per serving: Calories 1211kcal; Protein 72g; Carbohydrates 133g; Fibre 21g; Fat 46g; Calcium 2294mg

Braised squash with green lentils

Preparation time: 15 minutes • Cooking time: 30 minutes

• Servings: 1 dog, 2 human

A healthy vegetable side dish to go with one of the main meals.

Ingredients

45g/1½oz/½ cup lentils

2 tbs olive oil

2 garlic cloves, crushed

sprig fresh thyme, or
1 tsp dried thyme

2 bay leaves

1kg/2¼lb/5 cups butternut squash
or pumpkin, cut into bite-sized pieces

455g/1lb fresh tomatoes, chopped

juice of 1 lemon

Doggie Version add:
⅛ tsp calcium

Method

• Bring a pan of water to the boil and add the lentils. Reduce the heat and simmer over a low–medium heat until soft, about 30 minutes.

• In a large frying pan heat the oil, then sauté the garlic, thyme and bay leaves for 1–2 minutes. Add the squash, stir together and cook gently for 6–7 minutes. Drain lentils, add to pan and stir in. Add the tomatoes and cook gently for a further 20 minutes, stirring occasionally. The dish shouldn't be too runny, so allow some of the liquid to evaporate.

• Remove bay leaves and thyme (if using fresh). Divide the mixture in two. In one half stir in the calcium and place in dog bowl with a main course. Allow to cool to room temperature and serve. Enjoy the other half with your main course.

Nutritional info per serving: Calories 500kcal; Protein 12g; Carbohydrates 93g; Fibre 29g; Fat 15g; Calcium 439mg

Egg and vegetable casserole

Preparation time: 10 minutes • Cooking time: 30 minutes

• Servings: 1 dog, 6 human

This recipe has everything! Eggs (almost the perfect dog food), pulses,

vegetables and grains. Good for all the family.

Ingredients

455g/1lb broccoli

225g/8oz red peppers

2 medium sweet potatoes

170g/6oz squash

12 eggs

475ml/16½fl oz/2 cups cottage cheese

540g/19oz/3 cups cooked barley

540g/19oz/3 cups cooked lentils

95g/3½oz/1 cup Cheddar cheese, grated

Doggie Version add:

1½ tsp calcium

1½ tsp corn oil

30g/1oz liver, diced

Method

• Preheat oven to 180°C/350°F/Gas mark 4. Lightly grease two 23cm (9in) casserole dishes. Peel and dice the vegetables (or use frozen vegetables). Place the vegetables in a microwave-safe bowl. Cover with plastic wrap and cook on high for 3 minutes. Alternatively, boil or steam the vegetables for 3 minutes. Set aside.

• Mix the eggs and cottage cheese in a large bowl. Add the barley and lentils, and mix well. Divide the mixture in two. Pour half of this mixture into one of the casserole dishes. Top with half of the well-drained vegetables and grated cheese. Pour half the remaining egg mixture over vegetables. For the doggie version add the diced liver, oil and calcium to the egg mixture and mix well. Pour half this mixture into the other casserole dish, top with the remaining vegetables and cheese and pour the remaining egg mixture over vegetables.

• Put both casserole dishes in the oven and bake for about 30 minutes. The eggs should be set and the top lightly brown. Cool dog version to room temperature and serve.

Nutritional info per serving: Calories 1252kcal; Protein 85g; Carbohydrates 134g; Fibre 35g; Fat 45g; Calcium 2041mg

Glazed parsnips and carrots

Preparation time: 10 minutes • Cooking time: 35 minutes

• Servings: 1 dog, 2 human

A yummy vegetable side dish to add to a main course.

Ingredients

310g/11oz parsnips

310g/11oz carrots

2 Tbsp sesame seeds

2 Tbsp olive oil

2 Tbsp maple syrup

zest and juice ½ orange

Doggie Version add:
⅛ tsp calcium

Method

• Preheat oven to 190°C/375°F/Gas mark 5. Peel or scrub the parsnips and carrots and cut into bite-sized pieces. Bring a pan of water to the boil, add the carrots and parnsips and cook for 5 minutes. Drain.

• In a bowl, mix the sesame seeds, olive oil, maple syrup, orange zest and juice. Pour over the parsnips and carrots. Turn into a roasting pan and bake in the oven for 15–20 minutes until just brown.

• Divide the vegetables in two. In one half add the calcium and stir to mix. Place in a dog bowl with a main course and serve at room temperature. The rest is for you to enjoy hot, with your main course.

Nutritional info per serving: Calories 396kcal; Protein 5g; Carbohydrates 54g; Fibre 11g; Fat 20g; Calcium 303mg

Chinese stir-fried vegetables

Preparation time: 15 minutes • Cooking time: 10 minutes

• Servings: 1 dog, 2 human

This quick and easy oriental vegetable dish makes a pawfect

accompaniment to a main course.

Ingredients

3 Tbsp sunflower oil

1 tsp sesame oil

2 garlic cloves, crushed

170g/6oz carrots, diced

170g/6oz broccoli, chopped

1 red pepper, deseeded and chopped

170g/6oz mushrooms, chopped

30g/1oz seaweed (dried seaweed soaked for 10 minutes or dried flakes)

400g/14oz Chinese cabbage, shredded

225g/8oz beansprouts

3 Tbsp soy sauce

Doggie Version add:
⅛ tsp calcium

Method

- Heat oils in large wok. Add garlic and stir-fry for 1–2 minutes. Add the rest of the vegetables and stir-fry until done al dente (just with a little 'bite'); about 8 minutes or so. Pour soy sauce over vegetables.

- Divide in two. In one half, add the calcium and stir to mix. Put in dog bowl with main course and serve at room temperature. The rest is all yours!

Nutritional info per serving: Calories 363kcal; Protein 12g; Carbohydrates 33g; Fibre 13g; Fat 24g; Calcium 499mg

Snacks and Treats

Special treats make a change from the bog-standard dog biscuit. They are the perfect way to fill a rainy afternoon, create the best party, treat your dog or just enjoy a sunny day. This chapter includes a delicious cake that your pet and friends (and you, if they allow) can tuck in to; yummy ice cream for cooling down on a hot day; fortune telling cookies with a difference; and simply the best way for you both to spend a day in the garden.

Molasses spice cake

Preparation time: 10 minutes • Cooking time: 1 hour • Servings: 15

This is the perfect cake for a chop-lickin' treat.

Ingredients

170g/6oz peanut butter

85g/3oz/⅔ cup brown sugar

3 eggs

240ml/8½fl oz/1 cup molasses

240g/10oz/2 cups
wholewheat flour

1 Tbsp lecithin granules

1 tsp ground cinnamon

½ tsp ground ginger

½ tsp ground mixed spice

240ml/8½fl oz/1 cup boiling water

4 tsp baking soda

200g/7oz cream cheese

½ tsp vanilla extract

400g/14oz/2¼ cups icing sugar

1 tsp ground cinnamon

Method

- Preheat oven to 180°C/350°F/Gas mark 4. Lightly grease a 23cm (9in) cake tin. Beat together the peanut butter and sugar until well mixed. Add the eggs one at a time, beating well after each addition. Add the molasses and blend well.

- In another bowl, combine the flour, lecithin, cinnamon, ginger and mixed spice, and slowly add to the creamed peanut mixture, beating slowly to blend in.

- Dissolve the baking soda in boiling water (use a big jug as the soda will really froth up). Slowly add to the cake mix, beating slowly to blend in. The mixture will be very runny. Pour into the prepared cake tin and bake in the centre of the oven for about 1 hour, or until a cocktail stick inserted in the centre of the cake comes out clean. Leave for about 5 minutes and then turn out on wire rack to cool.

- Lightly beat vanilla extract into cream cheese. Sieve icing sugar and cinnamon and gradually add to the cream cheese, mixing well. Cover and refrigerate for a few hours to firm up, then use it to cover the cake.

Nutritional info per serving: Calories 226kcal; Protein 7g; Carbohydrates 33g; Fibre 3g; Fat 8g; Calcium 214mg

Ice-cream

Preparation time: 5 minutes • Cooking time: 30 minutes • Servings: 10

This recipe is for vanilla ice-cream but you can add any flavour that you think your doggie will like. Unusual, but yummy for pooches, is fish. Add 55g (2oz) of cooked, flaked fish to egg mixture before freezing. Another good flavour is liquorice or aniseed. Aniseed is the catnip of the dog world; they love it!

Ingredients

2 eggs

475ml/16½fl oz/2 cups single cream

240ml/8⅓fl oz/1 cup milk

2 tsp vanilla extract

¼ tsp calcium

Method

- Beat the eggs until light in colour and fluffy; about 1–2 minutes. Beat in the cream and milk. Add the vanilla (and any other flavouring) and calcium and mix well.

- If you have an ice-cream maker, freeze according to the directions. Otherwise put into a freezer-safe container and freeze overnight.

- The more you beat the ice-cream and the more air you incorporate the softer the ice-cream will be. Sugarless ice-cream tends to be quite hard so you will need to remove it from the freezer for a few minutes before scooping out a serving.

Nutritional info per serving: Calories 204kcal; Protein 4g;
Carbohydrates 3g; Fibre 0g; Fat 20g; Calcium 139mg

Fido fortune cookies

Preparation time: 5 minutes • Cooking time: 5 minutes • Servings: 3

The perfect cookie for a dog party. Buy or make your own fortunes, place inside the cookies and let your pet and the party guests learn their fate! Nutritional information is based on a serving size of 2 cookies.

Ingredients

1 egg

35g/1¼oz/¼ cup brown sugar

2 Tbsp sunflower oil

⅛ tsp calcium

30g/1oz/¼ cup cornflour

2 Tbsp water

Method

- Beat the egg and sugar together until thick and smooth. Add the oil and calcium to the egg mixture, mix well. Whisk the cornflour into the water and a little of the egg mixture until smooth. Add to the egg mixture and beat well.

- Heat a frying pan to medium heat. Drop a heaped teaspoonful of the batter onto the pan and use a spatula to spread the mixture into a round cookie shape about 8cm (3in) in diameter. Brown the cookie on both sides.

- Remove the cookie from pan and while warm and soft, add fortune paper and fold the cookie in half by pinching the sides together. Place on wire rack to cool and firm up. Use the rest of the mixture up in the same way.

Nutritional info per serving: Calories 191kcal; Protein 2g;
Carbohydrates 22g; Fibre 0.1g; Fat 11g; Calcium 140mg

Cheesy beef bites

Preparation time: 20 minutes • Cooking time: 45 minutes • Servings: 2

The number of cookies you make depends upon how big or small
you cut the dough. The nutritional information is based on
a 55g (2oz) serving. If you have a large dog you can cut the
dough into bigger cookies.

Ingredients

270g/9½oz/3 cups rolled oats

350ml/10fl oz/1½ cups
beef dripping

710ml/25fl oz/3 cups
boiling water

360g/12¾oz/2¼ cups polenta

3 Tbsp brown sugar

350ml/10fl oz/1½ cups
skimmed milk

280g/10oz/3 cups Cheddar
cheese, grated

3 eggs, beaten

1¼kg/2¾lb/9 cups whole
wheat flour

1 Tbsp calcium

Method

• Pre-heat oven to 170°C/325°F/Gas mark 3. In a large bowl combine the oats, dripping and water. Let stand for 10 minutes. Stir in the polenta, sugar, milk, cheese and eggs. Mix well. Add the flour slowly, with the calcium, kneading well after each addition to form a stiff, smooth dough.

• Break off handfuls of dough and roll into long, round strips about 1cm (½in) wide. Cut into 2.5 cm (1 in) pieces and place on a lightly greased baking tray.

• Bake for about 45 minutes, turning the baking tray round half way through the cooking. Turn off the oven and leave to dry out for a few hours or overnight. These will keep in an air-tight tin for a long time because of their low moisture content.

Nutritional info per serving: Calories 130kcal; Protein 8g;
Carbohydrates 20g; Fibre 2.8g; Fat 2.5g; Calcium 184mg

Poochie peanut butter

Preparation time: 0 minutes • Cooking time: 0 minutes • Servings: 1 (2 Tbsp)

This is the best fun you and your pet can have. Take a nice summer's day and sit out in the garden with a jar of peanut butter and your dog.

Ingredients

1 summer's day

1 garden chair

1 much loved dog

1 jar of peanut butter

2 fingers

Method

• Make yourself comfortable in your chair. Have poochie sitting at your feet. Placing two fingers in the jar of peanut butter, take a generous scoop. Offer to your pet and, if possible, slip peanut butter behind the top front teeth.

• Sit back and watch his/her tongue work overtime.

Nutritional info per serving: Calories 188kcal; Protein 8g; Carbohydrates 7g; Fibre 3g; Fat 16g; Calcium 14mg

Index